beyond Terror and Betrayal

D. A. Walters

beyond Terror and Betrayal is a work of fiction. Names, characters, and incidents are the products of the authors' imaginations, or are used fictitiously. Any resemblance to actual events, locales, or persons, living or dead, is entirely coincidental.

Copyright©2015 by Deborah Walters
Library of Congress Control Number TXu001976934
All rights reserved.

Without limiting the rights under copyright reserved above, no part of this publication may be reproduced, stored in, or introduced into a retrieval system, or transmitted, in any form or by any means (electronic, mechanical, photocopy, recording, or otherwise) without the prior written permission of the copyright owner and publisher of this book.

Book Cover Design by Alex Riley

For my children
Brian, James, Jeffrey, Lindsay, and Auriel

beyond Terror and Betrayal

Prologue

The man took his time walking through the facility. He entered through the South entrance. It was quite sterile. All the walls were done in basic ivory linen, the paint used by landlords because it gives an apartment a clean look and an air of spaciousness. He was impressed with the layout, with the individual rooms as well. His interest was piqued at the sight of the command center. It was beyond his expectations. He ran his hands over the equipment and studied the displays.

"Did you make a detailed instruction book for all of this?" asked the man.

"Yes, of course," said Dr. Louis Antwon walking around the room taking each manual from under each machine and placing it on top. The long strands of his graying hair flopped down in front of his face as he bent over. When he put the final manual in place, he pushed his hair up and smoothed it over the large balding area. "There is a manual for every component here. I made them readable and easy to understand."

"Excellent. What about the other side?"

"It's ready," said Irwin Selbring. "However, I think you should experience it the way your guests will."

"If you say so," said the man.

The three men made their way through that side and to the outside. Then Irwin led the way down a well-hidden path to the North side. He turned around several times to make sure they were following him. This next side was his pride and joy. To him, creating this 'oasis of beauty' as he called it, in the middle of a mountain was his crowning achievement.

"Come over here," said Dr. Antwon. "I need to program this so you can have access."

He talked the man through the process, locked the door again, and made the man gain access on his own.

"Will this work on the other side, too?" asked the man.

"That will get you into everything," said Dr. Antwon.

The man walked through the door. The entryway would rival any five-star hotel. He checked out every one of the common rooms as well as the rooms for the individuals.

"Very impressive," said the man. "Very impressive."

Irwin beamed with every compliment the man gave.

"How can we get from one side to the other without going outside?" asked the man.

"Please follow me," said Dr. Antwon.

He led the way. This was his pride and joy. He knew they were going to need to go from one side to the other. He insisted that while they were hewing out the caverns for each of the sides, that they also create a tunnel connecting them. He knew they would need to limit access, so he designed doors and the access codes to make it easier for those who had unlimited access.

The man put in his code and watched the door opened. They walked through the tunnel. He put the code in on the other side, and as that door opened the other door closed.

"I'm impressed," said the man. "What if we need to give other people access? Do you have the steps written down for that?"

"We wrote everything out," said Irwin, "even which light bulbs go where and where to buy them."

"Now I didn't see any signs of venting and air purification," said the man.

"It's all away from here," said Dr. Antwon.

"I'd like to see that," said the man.

"Are you sure you want to go now?" asked Dr. Antwon. "It's quite a walk."

"Let's go gentlemen. Lead the way."

Dr. Antwon led the way around the side of the mountain and stepped through some foliage to a rather obscure path. It wasn't hard to walk on, but other trails had been created so no one could simply go from start to finish directly. With each crossroad or Y in the road, the man could tell how please the two men were. The men stopped and turned to face the man. Irwin gestured towards machines that purified the air and pumped it in and out of the mountain.

There was no doubting the fact that he had chosen well.

"Well, gentlemen, I am very pleased," said the man. "You have proven to be vital to the completion of this project. I do hope you understand that you cannot tell anyone about this place."

The man reached inside his jacket.

"And I hope you understand that I cannot take the risk."

The man raised his gun and shot Dr. Antwon. He fell to the ground. Before Irwin could comprehend what had happened, the man shot him. Then the man walked over to Dr. Antwon, shot him twice in the head, walked around to Irwin and shot him twice more.

"That takes care of everyone. Your silence is greatly appreciated."

Chapter One

    Laura Darmer sat at the kitchen table looking over copies of Newsweek containing the "Where Are They Now" series. She had every issue since the first one that depicted the pictures of Afmad Yamani and Osama Bin Laden on the cover. Two special issues were spawned from the original, the one concerning the kidnapping and release of both Michael Braedon and herself by Yamani and the death of Osama Bin Laden. The worldwide activity caused by these issues made it increasingly difficult for any of those featured on the cover to continue their campaigns. The website offered reward money for information leading to the capture of those whose lives they covered. Between what was offered by the magazine and the money added to the funds by companies and individual citizens, there were millions of reasons to tell all.
    International bounty hunters found even more reasons to expand their searches and governments whose intelligent agencies were conducting covert operations in the usual manner found it in their best interest to step it up a notch. As incredulous as it sounded there were those who believed that Osama Bin Laden sacrificed himself in order that his Al Qaeda organization could continue relatively unhampered. Laura couldn't help imagining how the rhetoric played out among the main players. The organization continued without missing a beat, and the events happening in the world almost had the Al Qaeda stamp of approval.
    Laura put the magazine down. It amazed her that something that was put into place to confine her captor had netted such amazing results.

Yet, just knowing that Yamani was free for the time being and in hiding somewhere, gave her a sense of uneasiness. She often thought about where he might be. She knew with the new passport and new look he could be anywhere. She tried to shake the feeling and picked up another issue. In every one, the main article was written by Hal Milridge. He was a master writer and interviewer and this series changed his life. He found himself following up leads in every corner of the earth.

The man had been in this part of the world many times and once again realized how much he hated this sand and heat. He pulled down the visor, opened the mirror and looked carefully at his face. He knew beyond a doubt this was going to be a long haul. If he could convince these hardcore followers of the Chosen One that he was indeed him, he knew he could convince anyone.

The car made its way over the sand and stone road. The ride could be described as bumpy at best. The *Chosen One* looked carefully in all directions. It had to be here somewhere, but everyone knew the terrain could change almost overnight. He tapped the driver's shoulder.

"There," he said pointing off slightly to the right. "I think that's it."

The driver turned the wheel and headed towards the area. All the other vehicles following him did the same. He stopped the car just before an area of debris. The *Chosen One* got out, walked quickly towards it, stood with his hands on his hips and visually surveyed what was around him. The driver came and stood beside him.

"There's nothing left," said the *Chosen One*. "The ones chosen who survived said the bounty hunters were out to get me and they knew for a fact someone sold me to them. They never thought it would end like this."

"We never know what is in store for us," said the driver. "All I know is that we must continue our work for the Cause."

"And continue we shall."

Looking along the ground he spied a piece of metal glistening in the sunlight. He walked over, squatted, and dusted off the metal. His fingers dug down until he could get under it. Then he ran his hand along it towards the debris. Using his other hand to steady himself he moved along like a crab not letting go of the metal piece. When he got up to the point where the debris started, the metal piece ended. He pulled it out of the ground as far as he could and looked at the end of the piece of pipe. Sticking out were two sets of wires. The *Chosen One* started to laugh.

"Perfect," he said as he stood up and dusted off his hands. "Let's get this cleaned up. We must get this rebuilt. Too much time has passed and been wasted already."

The noise from the floor below could barely be heard behind the massive wooden doors and thick frosted glass of the executive section of Craustof Technologies. This was off limits to everyone who was not part of the upper management of the company. Only those who had a personal invitation were able to enter through the doors into the inner offices.

Farred Mahayin stood facing the workers who had been called. Each one sat quietly in his seat and all were dressed in the usual worker uniform, minus one important detail, the logo patch denoting the company. He turned off the video and addressed the men.

"You have heard what the leader wants," said Farred. "Are there any questions?"

Not one of the men raised a hand or uttered a sound.

"I have each of your envelopes with all the instructions for the project and all the paperwork you'll need. From here you'll go directly down the hall to the second room on the right. There they'll make sure you're outfitted properly."

Farred walked to the door and watched as the men stood, walked out of the room and proceeded down the hall. Years of research and millions of dollars and now the time had arrived.

Although Heinz field wasn't old by any standard, Ray Ellerman took no chances with the safety of the fans, his employees, and players. Every year before the start of football season, he had the entire stadium checked for any type of structural problems. As far as he was concerned, it was his reputation on the line and he wouldn't do anything to damage it.

Early that morning, the inspectors arrived and as they were instructed, proceeded to go over the stadium with a fine tooth comb. They started with all the exit ramps, escalators, and elevators. Ceilings, floors, roofs, railings, stairs and their understructure were all checked. Nothing was left to chance. As several of the inspectors climbed onto the roof to check the quad pods, Pat Victor, the head of security shook his head. There wasn't anything that would make him get up there to check those. He watched the inspectors for a while as they took a brush and removed the loose dirt and grime from the crevices of the quad pods. They sprayed the pods and wiped them. Then they made note of their observations.

Pat always thought Mr. Ellerman was being a bit over cautious in his manner. Everything was brand new. It was solid. He'd bet his life on it and told his friends that very thing on many occasions. He took off his cap, ran his fingers through his red hair and put the cap back on. Then he turned and walked away. The inspectors watched as he walked out of sight. One of them marked each support while the other put adhesive onto a small silver disk. He carefully placed it, opened a can of paint and painted it to match the quad pod. He and his partner packed up everything and moved to the next one.

Chapter Two

Hal Milridge walked out of the coffee shop on Liberty Avenue in Pittsburgh and looked both ways. Although most of the city businesses were closed at this time of night, several along Liberty stayed open for the crowds going to the stadium across the river. The football game was about to start. Traffic was still snarled, but the sidewalks were nearly devoid of people. Hal walked to the right down the sidewalk past bars and restaurants filled with people watching the pre-game show. He crossed Ninth Street and looked ahead for his car. He parked it on the end spot before a driveway, but as he approached he could see it wasn't there. Looking down the street he found his car badly parked, rear end out more than a foot from the sidewalk, and the corner of the passenger bumper poised slightly over the curb. Even if he was drunk, he'd never park that badly. He stopped to get the keys out of his pocket and to choose the right one. As he did, he slyly looked around. Across the street were three men who seemed to be watching every move he made. He took out his cell phone and checked the time.

Scenarios raced through Hal's mind. He walked closer to his car and stepped off the curb to go around to the driver's side and checked his phone again. Two buses traveling in the opposite direction got stuck in traffic directly in front of the three men. Hal stepped back on the curb, ran to the corner, and turned down Seventh Street.

When the buses pulled in front of them, the tall man pulled out his phone, keyed in a number and pressed send. In a split second Hal's car exploded. Metal and glass flew in every direction. The force of the explosion damaged the cars in front and behind Hal's. Windows of the businesses directly alongside blew out, parking meters shattered and pipes severed. Gas spilled from the tanks of the cars and the fumes were ignited by the flames from Hal's car. The car in front exploded propelling metal pieces through the side of the first bus. The third car exploded. Debris pierced the second bus. The bus driver at the corner of Seventh and Liberty screamed into his phone.

"This is David Phlemming, I work for Port Authority. Three cars have exploded on Liberty Avenue between Ninth and Seventh. There are injuries on the buses on Liberty. All hell's breaking loose."

"Try to stay calm Mr. Phlemming. Is your vehicle clear?"

"Yes, ma'am. I can't move out of here. Traffic's snarled."

"Are there people still on the other buses?"

David climbed down the steps of the bus and ran across the street. He watched the drivers getting people off the bus and directing them down his way.

"The drivers are getting the people off and directing them towards me. I can see several people on the buses in the seats where the windows were blown out. Oh God, the second bus is leaking. The passengers need to get out of there before that bus explodes!"

"Mr. Phlemming, stay clear of those buses."

People on David Phlemming's bus got up and walked off to get a better view. Hal watched the three men walk away in the opposite direction, cross the street, and walk into the café. Within a minute the three men came out dragging his contact person. Sirens blared from every direction. The men turned towards the crowds and walked towards the bus on Seventh Avenue. Hal took a small camera from his pocket and took pictures. The four men walked briskly down the sidewalk. There was a loud creak and the second bus exploded. Metal pieces and glass shot across the street striking the men. They fell, bleeding profusely, face forward to the ground.

Hal got out his press ID. No way was this going to get past him. He made a call to his desk and reported the events.

"Bill," said Hal, "look, this is connected to what I was doing here. It was my car they blew up. That started the chain reaction. Then they went after my contact."

"You got pictures?" asked Bill Epson, his boss.

"Yes, and I'm taking more. We need these guys identified."

Bill got up from his chair, opened his door and yelled.

"Justin, get on line one, it's Hal. Take the dictation and get this on the wire stat!"

While Hal dictated the story to Justin, he took pictures of the scene and the men who blew up his car.

Emergency personnel arrived on the scene and cleared as much of the traffic out of the area as possible. It looked like a missile had exploded. The injured were being loaded on stretchers and put inside ambulances away from immediate danger. The dead were covered. All others were escorted to a safe distance from the scene. Officers gathered information from witnesses. Measures were taken to ensure that the spectators from the Steelers' game against the Ravens would be diverted away from the carnage.

The sounds of metal being cut and ripped apart filled the evening. Nothing said in a normal tone of voice could be heard. The bus David Phlemming was driving was taking on passengers. Once it was filled, it drove away across the Smithfield Street Bridge to Station Square where the passengers could safely get onto other buses. Then he returned to do it again.

Hal's phone rang.

"Yes,"

"You got a camera crew on the way," said Bill. "Let's get you on the air."

"I see them."

Hal motioned to the crew.

"Holy shit!" said Jake. "What the hell happened?"

"They tried to eliminate me," said Hal.

"What the fuck? Who?"

"The three right here," said Hal pointing to the men on the sidewalk.

"There's four," said Jake.

"Yah, one was my contact."

"Let's get you on air."

"Get me some real detailed shots of these guys," said Hal to Sam, "close-ups of hands, faces, everything."

"You got it," said Sam.

"You're on in 5, 4, 3, 2, 1," said Jake.

"Good Evening, this is Hal Milridge on Liberty Avenue in Pittsburgh where a car bombing has set off a chain reaction involving several vehicles, two Port Authority buses, and businesses." Hal pointed to where his car was parked. "That used to be my car. It was blown-up just after I walked past it. Within minutes the car in front and behind exploded. Windows shattered in the buses and metal pierced their sides. The windows were shattered on the businesses here. The bus drivers quickly got all the passengers from the bus who were capable of walking. The injured, those unable to walk, remained on the buses. The situation intensified when bus number two exploded. Emergency personnel arrived quickly on the scene and as you can see are working to free the injured. Just across the Allegheny River, the Steelers will be taking on the Ravens and in just a few hours, people will be teeming over the Roberto Clemente and Fort Duquesne Bridges to get to their cars parked on this side. We will bring you updates as they become available."

Jake signaled Hal that he was off the air. Hal walked over to Sam.

"Did you get some good shots?"

"Great ones," said Sam "and some strange things too."

He showed some of them to Hal. Hal pulled out his phone and scrolled down through his contacts.

"Hello."

"Tom, this is Hal."

"Hal!" said Tom. "What's going on?"

"I'm on Liberty Avenue. There's been an incident. You need to get down here somehow."

"Why?"

"Let's just say, it'll remind you of the last time you were in Baghdad."

"Shit!" said Tom. "I'm at the station. Be there in a few."

Tom Richards walked out of his office and into Jim Prescott's without knocking. Jim was the station manager of WXDX. Tom's role as mediator between Afmad Yamani and Laura Darmer made WXDX the number one most listened to station in the tri-state area and Prescott the most envied manager.

"Jim, something's going on in the city, on Liberty Avenue. Hal said it'll remind me of Baghdad the last time I was there."

"Let's get you in there," said Jim picking up the phone. Whatever was happening, just the mention of Baghdad was enough to get Jim's attention.

The camera crew filmed detailed views of the scene. Hal looked down at the men on the sidewalk. He reached in his pocket and touched the disk his contact gave him. He nodded. If he was right, no one should move any of the bodies. Hal took out his phone and made another call.

"Hal, nice piece," said Bill.

"Thanks. Listen I need the Feds in here."

"Why?"

"I think at least one of these four is a human bomb and if they touch them to turn them over, they're going get blown sky high."

"It's never easy with you is it."

"Yah, that's why you like sending me places."

"Hold on."

Hal kept an eye on the bodies and what was going on in the street. He knew that for everyone working the scene, this was about as bad as it could get here. He could tell by the heightened voices, that this was the tensest situation they had every found themselves in. If only they knew what was across the street.

"The cavalry is on the way," said Bill.

"Good."

"Can you see the chief?"

"Yes."

"He should be getting a call."

Hal tapped the cameraman and pointed to the chief. They watched him talk on the phone, look over at the sidewalk, and put the phone away. He motioned for three officers, talked to them, and they walked across the street taking up their positions.

"Thanks Bill."

Tom Richards hurried around the corner coming from Seventh Street. Hal wasn't kidding. It looked much like Baghdad when he was there to bring Laura home. There were nights when he woke up in a cold sweat from dreaming about the missiles being detonated behind them as they made their escape. He spotted Hal and hustled over to him.

"What the hell happened?"

Hal quickly filled him in. Then he called Sam to show Tom the pictures.

"This one was my contact. This is his hand."

Tom took one look, his mouth gaped, and he looked back at Hal.

"Sam, can you get those pictures out of the camera?" said Hal. "I don't want anyone getting those. Then take some general shots of the disaster."

"Will do," said Sam taking the disk out of the camera and replacing it with a blank one. He slipped the disk into the lining of his wallet and then began shooting pictures of the cars, buses and stores.

"I'll be right back," said Tom as he stepped off the curb.

Tom walked up to Chief Graham and carried on a brief conversation with him. The chief gestured to the different areas of Pittsburgh as he talked. Tom continued to talk as he looked around at the devastation that lay before him. The number of people who escaped was miraculous and the number who were dead and injured, horrific.

Roger Gimshaw got out of his car on Seventh Street and walked to Liberty Avenue. He had been with the FBI for over twenty years and had been assigned to Pittsburgh two years after nine eleven. In all the time he had been there, about the only thing he had engaged in was a few drug operations and maybe some gun play. Even the G-20 summit was almost incident free. He always silently resented his friends and colleagues who had been given assignments with excitement and drama. He looked around. The sight of the devastation took him by surprise. He walked across the street to inform Chief Graham that he was on site and got his view of the events. Then he crossed the street and walked up to Hal and flashed a badge.

"Are you Hal Milridge?" he asked.

"Yes, sir," said Hal.

"Roger Gimshaw with the FBI. I was told to see you after I checked in with the chief. What's this about these men being possible human bombs?"

"If you look closely at the man who's in the middle, the one's whose head is closer towards us, you'll see his shirt is torn on the underside of his left arm. If you look carefully you'll see several wires, very thin ones running down the seam of his sleeve. Unless you get really close, you won't see them. I caught a glimpse of a red one when a light just happened to hit it. Then I bent down and could see others. Now, either he's carrying wire for some reason or he's equipped with a bomb."

Roger shot him a look.

"Three of those men were across the street watching this side right before the first car exploded. Then I saw them go into a café and come out dragging that man," said Hal pointing to the man to the left. "They were dragging him down this sidewalk when the bus exploded and they were hit by flying debris."

"Why didn't the bomb explode when they fell?"

"I'm not a bomb expert, but I was thinking it could be that it had a system whereby you pressed it to activate the bomb and released it to explode. If that's the case, if anyone moves him, they're going to blow everything up including themselves."

"Damn," said Gimshaw, "This is Pittsburgh. Nothing like this happens here. Next thing you'll tell me is that this is some terrorist group."

"Who else sends human bombs?" asked Hal.

The dining room table was filled with tent cards, legal pads, piles of small cards, two laptops, and a printer. In front of Gina and Angelique was a large floor plan of the reception hall. They numbered the tables and were placing the guests at them. Raquel and Nicole printed table place cards double checking with Laura and Michael about which guests should be seated together. Gwen and Laura went over the responded list one more time and turned it over to Margo and Monique to double check. Brigit walked in with boxes of favors that had been delivered earlier in the day. They each had to be checked to make sure all were undamaged.

Loud talking was heard from the game room.

"Michael and Mark really get into these games, don't they," said Margo.

"More than you know," said Gwen. "If they were home, they'd be there."

"When the Steelers are away, it's party time," said Laura. "We fix them everything they could possibly need and then leave for a while. It's the best time to shop and get a latte."

"I can't believe they're making your husbands watch this," said Gwen.

"I actually think they enjoy it, too," said Gina.

"Look how cute these are," said Brigit unwrapping the first favor.

"They are cute," said Margo. "Much nicer than they looked in the book."

"When do all these things have to be delivered to the hall?" asked Nicole.

"Thursday," said Laura. "We'll be able to peek in on the set up Friday when we're there for the rehearsal dinner."

"Was working through the night on a Monday into Tuesday on our agenda?" asked Monique.

"Only when there's a Steeler game and a wedding in one week," said Laura.

Michael came bounding up the steps.

"How's it going up here?" he asked.

"Great," said Laura. "How are the Steelers doing?"

"Kick-off is in a few minutes."

"What did you forget?" asked Laura.

"We want some nachos and I forgot to make them."

"You're going to miss kick-off."

"I'll put it on in the kitchen," said Michael. "It won't take me long to make them."

Michael headed into the kitchen, picked up the remote and turned on the television. He turned up the volume and was about to change the channel when he saw Hal.

"Good Evening, this is Hal Milridge on Liberty Avenue in Pittsburgh where a car bombing has set off a chain reaction involving several vehicles, two Port Authority buses, and businesses."

"Laura, Gwen get in here," Michael shouted. "Mark!"

The two women hurried into the kitchen. Michael pointed to the television.

"That used to be my car," Hal continued. "It was blown-up just after I walked past it."

"Where is he?" asked Gwen.

"Liberty Avenue," said Michael.

"Pittsburgh?" asked Gwen.

Michael nodded.

"Within minutes the car in front and behind exploded," said Hal. "Windows were shattered in the buses and metal pierced their sides. The windows were shattered on the businesses here. The bus drivers quickly got all the passengers from the bus who were capable of walking. The injured, those unable to walk, remained on the buses."

Mark hurried in.

"What's going on?" he asked.

"The situation intensified when bus number two exploded," said Hal. "Emergency personnel arrived shortly on the scene and as you can see are working to free the injured. Just across the Allegheny River, the Steelers will be taking on the Ravens and in just a few hours, people will be teeming over the Roberto Clemente and Fort Duquesne Bridges to get to their cars parked on this side. We will bring you updates as they become available."

"That's Pittsburgh?" said Mark.

"Yah, that's Pittsburgh," said Michael.

"Liberty Avenue," said Gwen.

"What the hell happened?" asked Mark.

"A car bombing," said Michael. "Hal's car."

"Why?" asked Gwen.

Laura walked into the dining room, went to the computer and clicked on her radio icon for WXDX. When she was in Paris, she liked to listen to Tom Richard's show in the morning. She figured if Hal was on a street in Pittsburgh, Tom wouldn't be far behind.

Nothing was being reported during the Steeler pre-game show. Those who were watching as well as those in the stadium had no idea about what was happening in the city. The ladies listened as Tom Richards interrupted WXDX's programming to report on what was happening in the city. He interviewed Chief Graham who had called for an investigation into the bombing. The city arson squad was already en route and they were trying to piece together the accounts of eye witnesses.

"What do you think?" asked Gina jiggling her foot. She always did that when she was nervous.

"I don't know?" said Brigit. "Why's Hal in Pittsburgh?"

"Most likely on assignment," said Nicole.

"On a Monday night, on Liberty Avenue, right before a football game," said Laura. "Not exactly the best place for a meeting."

Chapter Three

Sam got close to the body, squatted, and took as close a picture of the man's side as possible. The picture showed thin colored wires running down the man's arm. He took several more trying to get more detail. He stood up and walked over to Agent Gimshaw and showed him the pictures.

"If you upload this to a computer," said Sam, "you should be able to enlarge that section and maybe see a little more."

"Let's do it," said Gimshaw. "Wilson, help Sam get this off to Fitch. I want him to have something concrete to study on his way here."

"Sure," said Agent Marcus Wilson.

Gimshaw took out his phone and made a call. Then he walked over to Hal and Tom.

"Hal," said Gimshaw, "if you're right in your thinking and this is a message from one of those groups, it'll level part of this block if it goes off."

"I agree with you," said Hal. "I've seen it happen."

"Could this have been any worse?" asked Gimshaw shaking his head and looking around.

"He could have gotten into the stadium," said Tom.

The very thought of that made Hal shiver. That stadium was packed. What if that was the plan? Was his contact a set up? Was it all to create a diversion for something bigger?

Gimshaw looked from Tom to Hal.

"One wouldn't do it," he said.

"It would start a panic," said Hal.

"Are you willing to stake your life that only one is a human bomb?" asked Tom.

"No way," said Hal. "Probably at least three are. I'm not sure about the man they took from the café. Sam!"

Sam hustled over.

"Yah."

"Can you get shots of the other men, as close as you can safely get."

"What are you looking for?"

"More wires."

"Shit!"

Sam went to work. He meticulously focused every picture, zooming in on certain areas. He knew the camera could capture things the eye could not readily see. Then the computer could magnify those sections to make them clear and defined.

Buildings sat in the exact places where the other buildings had been before they had been destroyed. Each one was furnished with electricity that Yamani was so conscientious to have brought from the city a great distance away.

The *Chosen One* had never been to the camp. In fact, he wouldn't have had any idea of its existence had it not been for a disgruntled follower. He looked around and smiled. He knew Yamani would be rolling over in his grave if he had any idea of what was going to be happening in his name. One thing he was certain of was that Yamani was certainly burning in hell for every atrocity he had committed during his life on earth. Even though Yamani's demise hadn't come at his hands as he would have loved, it was enough to know that the world was rid of this man once and for all.

The *Chosen One* sat at the desk in the office and took a notebook out of the bottom drawer. He opened it and took out the pictures. He sat them down one next to the other and studied them carefully. He had done this dozens of times, but he always had to look at the real person first before attempting to make the transformation.

He got up and walked to the small closet, unlocked it and took out a case. He placed the case on the desk and unlocked it. He carefully took out the contents and began applying them one at a time in a specifically prescribed order. Magically his countenance changed as did his mannerisms and even in his personality, there was a deliberate transformation that took place.

Every small detail was attended to and when all was finished, he closed and locked the case and returned it to the closet which he locked. He walked to the door of the office, unlocked the door and yelled down the hall.

Four men hurriedly walked into his office and stood before his desk.

"It is imperative that we step up the recruiting," he said.

"Yes, sir," said Kannid. "I think we would be more successful if you used the internet as we had before."

"Yes, I understand that recruiting for the Cause was very successful when we had used the internet," said the *Chosen One*, "but things have changed. After the incident which caused so many unfortunate consequences, I have decided it would be much better to take a step back and do things in a more traditional manner."

"Yes, sir," said Kannid. "What is it that you want us to do?"

"I want you to take these papers into the city and the villages and hand them out to every man of age. Do not answer any questions other than to tell them that all their questions will be answered at the meeting."

"Yes, sir."

The *Chosen One* handed each a stack of papers and the men left.

Trucks pulled up Liberty Avenue and stopped just after Ninth Street. Commander Sutton got out and walked up to Gimshaw.

"Agent Gimshaw?" he said.

"Yes."

"Commander Sutton. What's the situation?"

"Four dead on the sidewalk. One definitely a human bomb, possibly all four."

"This is Pittsburgh, isn't it?"

"Last time I looked, Commander," said Gimshaw. "The scene across the street is somewhat stabilized, but we can't take any chances."

"We need to get that barrier up," said Sutton.

"Without moving them so much as a hair."

Commander Sutton looked at Gimshaw and walked back to his unit. Hal got ready for his update report and positioned himself so the work being done on the sidewalk wouldn't be shown. He knew it was important to focus only on what was going on with the buses and the victims. He walked across the street, found the chief and interviewed him. Chief Graham seemed to be oblivious to anything other than what was on his priority list. For him, the most important part of this was what was happening to the two buses and the passengers.

The men worked on building the containment structure, placing the component parts as gently as possible. Every one of them knew what was at stake, and along with physically jarring the body, any sort of vibration that could cause the body to move could prove deadly.

"They're not thinking of clearing the wreckage, are they?" asked Commander Sutton.

"I don't know," said Gimshaw. "All I want them to do is get the people and bodies out of there. To hell with the wreckage."

"Before your guy gets here, we have to seal off this area," said Sutton. "Every one of these buildings has to be evacuated and should have been already."

"Several in the immediate area have been," said Gimshaw. "I saw the Chief give the order and the buildings empty. He didn't go deep, just along Liberty."

Agent Gimshaw walked over to the Chief Graham and walked him away out of hearing distance of anyone around. He laid out what was at stake.

"Port Authority isn't going to be happy if they have to leave here without their buses in tow," said Graham.

"They'll get over it," said Gimshaw. "How long until the rest of the wounded and dead are out of here?"

"The last ambulance just left."

"Good. You need to start getting everyone out of here, now."

Gimshaw looked down at a map the Chief had on the hood of his cruiser. "All buildings in this area have to be evacuated." He drew a circle on the map with his finger. You also need to seal off every way into the city."

The Chief motioned for Oliver Packer, the Chairman of the Port Authority to join them.

Oliver, this is Agent Gimshaw of the FBI," said Graham. "We need your help."

"What do you need?" asked Packer.

"We're going to be evacuating the buildings in this area," said Gimshaw. "We can't allow the people to go around finding their cars and then leave. We need them out of here immediately."

"I can get buses in here," said Packer looking at the map. "They can pick up here, here, here, and here and shuttle the people over to the Station Square. Then they can return for as many pick-ups as needed."

"Second, you're going to have to leave the damaged buses here until this operation is over," said Gimshaw.

"It won't take us that long to get them out of here," said Packer. "I need to get them back to the garage."

"No deal," said Gimshaw. "We can't chance any further activity in that area."

"Chief Graham, you know we need to do this," said Packer. "I have to get those buses back."

"Mr. Packer, as soon as the situation has been diffused," said Gimshaw, "you'll be able to get them."

With everything for the wedding done, the ladies made a batch of hot chocolate, some fresh baked cookies and retired to the living room to get comfortable. Laura moved the laptop to the table beside her and they listened to every update Tom made and watched Hal's reports.

"Why did Hal change the angle when he's giving his reports?" asked Gwen.

"What are you talking about?" asked Margo.

"When Hal did his first report, he was standing on the sidewalk and you could see his car to his right and bodies behind him and to the left," said Gwen. "As he talked, the camera man showed other things, but he came back to that same place at the end. All the other ones are of him with his back to the buses."

"How do you remember those things?" asked Nicole.

"Oh, I don't know. Maybe it was all those months of looking for a needle in a haystack."

"Probably," said Raquel.

"Let me find the first one again?" asked Laura.

Laura went on the website and searched for the first report. Then she walked into Michael's office and grabbed the projector. When she came back into the living room, she hooked it up to her computer and aimed it at a blank wall. She pressed play and they watched.

"See those bodies?" said Gwen. "The only time you see them is in this one."

"Let me save this," said Laura. "Now I'll pull up the other reports and we can compare them."

"It's been quiet downstairs," said Margo. "I haven't heard any screaming."

"The only time they get quiet is if it's getting close," said Gwen.

"Ten to seven us," said Laura. "That's not good. Okay, let's look at these."

It didn't take long to watch the reports and for them to see that Gwen was right. Only the first one showed the bodies.

"Do you think if we ask Robert to do his thing he'd think we were paranoid?" asked Gina.

"Most likely," said Laura.

The coordinated efforts between the FBI, the city, and Port Authority soon rendered the Golden Triangle little more than a Ghost town. During the time of evacuation, a containment structure had been constructed around the bodies. Military personnel secured the perimeter. Sam continued to snap pictures and Jake filmed every detail. On the corner of Seventh and Liberty, Police Chief Graham stood with Agent Gimshaw and Commander Sutton. They looked down the street towards the North Shore.

"There's seven minutes left to the second quarter," said Graham. "We have two hours, two and a half max, unless we go into overtime."

"We couldn't be that lucky," said Gimshaw.

A car pulled up and Armand Fitch stepped out. Gimshaw walked over to him.

"Fitch, good to see you," said Gimshaw.

"What's the situation?" asked Fitch.

"Four dead men lying prone, touching. You got the photo."

"Yes."

"We took others. They're ready for you over there."

Fitch walked over to the computer. He looked through the pictures and selected several from each group. Something on one of them caught his attention. He worked on the picture continually enlarging one small section.

"See that?" asked Fitch. "That's a digital detonator. Someone somewhere has a control device. If these guys don't detonate when they're supposed to, that person will detonate these bombs."

He shook his head and looked at Gimshaw.

"Have any ideas?" asked Fitch. "Any ideas what they're intending to blow up?"

Gimshaw looked over at Hal and then back to Fitch.

"Heinz Field," said Gimshaw. "It's packed with Steelers' and Ravens' fans."

"Well you better hope these are all of them," said Fitch, "because if there are any more, it's going to be gruesome."

"We can't do anything about it," said Gimshaw. "That game's on national television. If we do, the person with the device will know."

"Look," said Hal. "My guess is he won't detonate until the very end of the game. With everyone preoccupied with what's going on here, it'll catch the city off guard even more. They need to be certain that people are still working on this scene and that can be done."

"Do whatever it takes," said Fitch. "My concern is how much they're packing and what damage it can do."

Gimshaw looked at the barricade. There wasn't enough money in the world to get him to go inside there and try to diffuse bombs that someone else was controlling from somewhere else. If their assessment was right and they were targeting Heinz Field, the number of dead and injured would be in the tens of thousands. He looked at the manpower around him. This would never do. He stood on a fine line. To the one side would be the claim that if he called in reinforcements and nothing happened, he could possibly cause a public panic. To the other side would be the claim that he could have somehow prevented the disaster from getting as bad as it could, if he had just called for help when he first found out. Public panic due to the sight of additional personnel could be quelled. Public panic due to bombs going off in a stadium and not having enough personnel to deal with the situation would be uncontrollable by the time personnel arrived. He took a deep breath and blew it through his lips.

Hal taped the next update. Any shots of him were tight shots showing very little of the scene. The rest of the report was voice over shots that were filmed by Jake of what had transpired earlier. Only when Hal was talking directly to Bill did he update him on the real circumstances.

"What the hell!" said Bill. "You are in Pittsburgh, right?"

"Believe it or not," said Hal. "Listen, I need some numbers."

"Shoot"

"John Blakeworth, Ray Ellerman, Paul Hennerly, and General Anderson."

"Give me two minutes and I'll text them to you."

"Thanks."

"Keep me posted."

Hal looked back towards Gimshaw and Fitch was gone. He knew he was inside the containment. He said a silent prayer for his safety and for the discernment of answers. Hal walked over to Gimshaw.

"I don't know what you decided," said Hal, "but regardless, you need to inform the Commissioner and owners about the situation."

"I know," said Gimshaw.

"Always err on the side of caution," said Hal. "At least that way you can live with yourself."

Hal clicked on the text message and displayed the numbers for all the parties. Gimshaw made the first three calls. Without telling the men exactly what was transpiring, he convinced each that it was imperative to meet. Agents were dispatched to the grounds to transport them to the other side of the river for a meeting.

"Why General Anderson?" Gimshaw asked.

"I know him," said Hal, "and he has the authority to act. Anyone else might run you around until they're certain you know what you're talking about. Anderson knows I wouldn't call him or suggest you call him unless there was cause."

"There are always people who will say we acted in haste," said Gimshaw.

"I don't think we are," said Hal, "and I think Fitch would agree. I can make the call and put you on, if you want."

"Make it."

Fitch knelt down at the head of the man whose device wires were partially exposed. Carefully, he moved the torn sleeve of the man's shirt using what looked like plastic tweezers. On the inside Fitch could feel nervousness rise, but his hands and actions were deliberate. Every action made so as not to disturb anything else. Although there was an unwritten time limit, they needed the information from the device this man was carrying. Every bomb was wired in a particular fashion. The trick was to ascertain if they changed the colors in hopes of fooling the person trying to diffuse it and sending him also to his eternal reward. He visually traced each wire from start to finish, chose a tool and began.

Hal called General Anderson. He had known him since he served under him in the military. Hal had kept contact with him and the general was there whenever Hal needed him.

"Hal," said Anderson when he answered the phone. "To what do I owe the pleasure of this call?"

"Pleasure isn't quite how I'd put it," said Hal. "I take it you haven't seen any of my reports during the past couple of hours."

"No I haven't. Why don't you bring me up to speed?"

Hal quickly told the General everything that was happening from the beginning up to the present moment.

"Gimshaw's a good man. Let me speak to him," said Anderson standing up and picking up his keys from the table.

Hal handed the phone to Gimshaw.

"Good evening, General Anderson," said Gimshaw.

"Listen, we're going to get you help in there. Have you talked to the owners?"

"They're on their way over."

"Anything from Fitch?"

"Not yet, but these things can't be rushed."

"I'll be on sight in less than an hour. Keep me updated."

"Yes, sir."

Gimshaw handed the phone back to Hal.

"Is there anyone you don't know?" he asked.

"In my business you meet a lot of people."

The owners and commissioner were immediately ushered into a trailer along Seventh Street. It had been brought in to serve as a command center. The three men sat down at the table and waited. Gimshaw arrived minutes later.

"Gentlemen, thank you for coming. I'm Agent Gimshaw with the FBI," he said. "We have a situation and need your cooperation."

"What happened out there, Agent Gimshaw?" asked Ray Ellerman, the owner of the Steelers.

"A car was intentionally blown up and it started a chain reaction which ultimately involved several cars and two Port Authority buses."

"Injuries?" asked John Blakeworth, the commissioner of the NFL.

"I don't have the figures yet for the injured, nor do I have the number of dead."

"Dead?" said Ellerman.

"Believe it or not, that's not the problem," said Gimshaw. "Three men, believed to be the perpetrators of the car bombing and a fourth man dragged from a café shortly after the bombing, are what we have come to know as suicide bombers."

"What?" asked Paul Hennerly, the owner of the Ravens. "This isn't the Middle East."

"Our thoughts exactly," said Gimshaw. "However, one of the world's foremost authorities in diffusing suicide bombers is working on trying to diffuse the bombs on those four men as we speak."

"Where do we come in?" asked Blakeworth.

"We had to ask ourselves; what would suicide bombers be doing in Pittsburgh, on a Monday night in September. We came up with your game. Where else could they destroy or maim more than sixty-five thousand people at one time?"

"And you didn't discover this until this incident tonight?" asked Hennerly.

"No, we didn't," said Gimshaw. "It wasn't on any of the intelligence reports."

"So now what?" asked Blakeworth.

"These bombers have a failsafe method," said Gimshaw. "If they don't detonate on time, someone else will detonate them. Hopefully these four are the only ones there are. If not, it could be very gruesome."

"What do we need to do?" asked Ellerman.

Fitch emerged from the containment carrying several pieces of a unique apparatus.

"One down," he said, "and if they didn't change things from one to another, the others can be done a lot easier. I wrote the steps. I need someone to read them."

"I can do that," said Tom. "Just tell me when."

Fitch laid each piece down separately keeping distance between them.

"Totally undetectable," said Fitch. "No security measures would pick this up. Look how thin these are, no noise, and the timer, glass. All contacts so small as to not be felt, and shielded."

"How much damage could that do?" asked Hal.

"One hell of a lot," said Fitch, "but even with the four of them, it's not enough to take down the stadium."

"Get the bombs off and we'll go through their pockets," said Tom.

The alarm rang and Petru Wadimar sat up and put his feet on the floor. His dark hair was unruly from tossing and turning. He walked into the bathroom and closed the door. His wife stirred and sat up in bed. When Petru came out of the bathroom, he sat down on the side of the bed, leaned over and kissed his wife, Sorina. She was a beautiful brunette and the love of his life since school.

"Are you getting up already?" she asked.

"I need to go over some of those figures for the presentation, today," he said. "I want to make sure I didn't miss anything."

"You always do well," she said. "You know it's all right."

"I wish I had your confidence," he said getting up.

"I'm just going to sleep a little more and then I'll get your breakfast."

"You have time, it's early."

He walked out of the room, sat in front of the computer in his office, pulled up the files, and began reading through everything for the umpteenth time. He had worked for this company for nearly ten years and had gone above and beyond all the time. Finally, someone noticed his work and was giving him a chance. If this presentation went well, it would mean another step up the corporate ladder. He had been waiting for another opportunity.

His first promotion came when he devised a unique explosive chemical gel compound that could be used in oil and gas extraction. His second promotion was the result of creating a "skin" that could insulate wires and make them impervious to scans. This was a big step forward in eliminating premature detonation. The third promotion that got him where he was today was an explosive device thin enough and small enough to slip into a crack in a rock or between boulders.

This was his greatest work ever. He worked sometimes late into the night doing research. He was determined to give this his best effort. He was thankful Sorina was totally devoted to him and supported him every step of the way. She magically kept the children quiet during the times that were so pressing.

Page after page he read aloud to get the feel for what it was saying. This way, what his eyes missed, his ears would catch. He looked at the figures and charts in the appendix to make certain they were in the proper order and that he had explained them fully. He paused about halfway through the presentation to find the list he was given. There were email addresses where a copy of the presentation had to be sent and a list of phone numbers to call after the presentation had been emailed to let each of them know the presentation had arrived. He nodded his head multiple times as he went through the instructions. He put down the list and resumed reviewing the project.

    Fitch walked back into the containment and Tom situated himself closely enough to be heard. Although he wasn't inside, the nervousness he felt continued to grow. If Fitch made one wrong move or if the one in charge decided to detonate while Fitch was in there, he wondered whether the containment would actually hold.
    Tom had been a calm, laid-back D.J. up until the time he agreed to help Laura Darmer get her fiancé, Michael Braedon, back. Then he found himself doing things he never would've dreamed of doing. Things he only read about in books had happened in his life and now he was only a few feet away from suicide bombers. Just reading those words in print gave him agita. Yet, here he was.
    Fitch methodically diffused each bomb, bringing the components out one at a time and then going in to do the next one. Once all four were lying outside the barricade, he returned to the bodies. He had drawn a diagram of the four men and had labeled them A, B, C, and D. When each group of components was brought out, he tagged each piece with the appropriate label. He searched each man, going through every pocket.
    Fitch emerged from the containment structure. He handed what he was carrying to Tom. He pulled a piece of cloth from his pocket and wiped his face. Tom took what he was holding and laid it out on the hood of the vehicle. The contents were identical; a small amount of money, less than a hundred dollars, and a ticket to Heinz Field for the game that night.

Chapter Four

At the camp, one new building was added to serve as a meeting and training building. By the size of all the buildings that had been at the camp before, it was evident that Yamani had never had that many of the followers at the camp at any one time. This was different. It was absolutely necessary for there to be such a building. The man entered the room and looked around. There were hundreds of men present. He took his place at the podium.

"I thank you all for answering the call of the Divine One to become part of the ones chosen to fulfill his mission," said the *Chosen One*. "I know that you have all prayed about this decision and have not entered into it lightly. For those of you who have decided that this is your calling, the Divine One will see to it that you are rewarded for your obedience and courage. Your families will also be rewarded monetarily. I will outline what it is that you will be expected to do, and then if there are any questions, you may ask them.

For the next hour the *Chosen One* outlined what would be expected and how the expectations would fall in line with what was expected of them by the Divine One. When he was finished, he permitted questions to be asked and patiently answered all of their concerns. At the end of the session, contracts were distributed to each man in attendance. Every line of the contract was read and explained. They approached the desk one at a time to sign the document and to have the *Chosen One* sign it also. Once they had finished signing it, they were escorted out of the door and taken to another building that would become their home for the duration of their stay.

As the line came to an end, the *Chosen One* looked up to see ten men sitting in their seats.

"Is there something that you need to have clarified?" he asked.

"No sir," said Adarine. "It's just that as I sat here praying for guidance, I felt certain that the Divine One did not want me to commit to this at this time. If I were to leave my family right now, with things so unresolved, there would be great untold suffering. I feel, in my heart, that the Divine One is telling me to get all these things straightened out, first, so I can truly devote myself to the Cause."

"It is wise of you to pray and discern what the Divine One is telling you," said the *Chosen One*. "You must follow what he is telling you to do."

One by one, the others made excuses as to why they were unable to commit to the Cause at the time. The *Chosen One* did not flinch once, nor did he say one malicious word to any of them.

"If you wait a few minutes, I will have someone transport you back to the city."

General Anderson arrived in the field, entourage in tow. His first order of business was to survey the situation and get the update from each individual party. The bomb components were among the newest developed. How the information got into the hands of terrorists was a question to be answered and answered swiftly as soon as this situation was resolved. He knew that another layer had just been removed from the American citizens' safety. He looked at the tickets. On each was a section number and none were the same.

"Do we have a diagram of the stadium?" asked General Anderson.

"Yes, sir," said Agent Gimshaw. "We already indicated the sections."

General Anderson looked at the sections. They formed a sort of wedge.

"Pardon me, General," said Tom, "but we need to find out if these were the only tickets purchased."

"Go on," said Anderson.

"Ticket orders are limited to a specific number per purchase. Mr. Ellerman is trying to find that out right now how many tickets were sold in these orders."

"Could we be that lucky?" asked Anderson. "Any identification on these four?"

"None," said Fitch. "Only money and a ticket."

"The information Mr. Ellerman is getting should have a credit card attached to it and an address," said Hal. "That will give you something."

Ray Ellerman emerged from the trailer along with Paul Hennerly and John Blakeworth. He brought several sheets of paper over to Agent Gimshaw.

"Tom was right," said Ellerman. "Sixteen tickets were sold. Here are the ticket numbers and the information on the buyers."

"Did they get in?" asked Gimshaw.

"They should have," said Fitch.

"We don't have the time to send people to check," said Gimshaw. "We'll waste a lot of time calling for workers, assigning sections and then getting word back."

"Jake," said Hal. "Get us online."

Hal took out his phone and scrolled down through his numbers. In the press box on the fourth level of the stadium, Eric answered.

"Yes," said Eric.

"Eric, this is Hal Milridge, I need a favor."

"Right now?"

"Right now."

"What do you need?"

"I need you to pan these sections right now and televise them immediately. I don't care what happens on the field. It doesn't matter. Pan the sections for five seconds each."

"How many?"

"Twelve."

"Go," said Eric.

Hal dictated numbers of sections in order, eliminating the sections where the four dead men would have been. Ray Ellerman was glued to the computer screen and picked out each seat almost immediately when the section was shown. Tom kept a close eye on what Ray was pointing out. Each of the men was dressed just like the four on the side walk. He looked down at the diagram again and put a circle in other sections. When he was done, he turned to Hal.

"Have him scan these sections," said Tom, handing Hal a new list. "Tell him to go back to the field for a few seconds and then go to the other sections."

Hal relayed Tom's request and within another two minutes, they were finished. Hal had Jake go back to the last sections and pause on each section. In each one, Tom pointed to a man and asked Ray what the seat number was.

"How do you remember all those numbers?" asked Tom.

"I've always had a penchant for numbers," said Ellerman. "I hear a phone number once and I never forget it."

"Now what do we have?" asked General Anderson.

"Our group has a person in each of these seats," said Tom. "They intend to bring down this stadium."

Petru sat at the kitchen table. Sorina had fixed breakfast and the two of them were enjoying the quiet of the morning. They knew one of the children would soon wake and their quiet time would be gone.

"I put out your good suit for today," said Sorina. "Everything's in order."

"Thank you," said Petru. "What're you going to do this morning?"

"After the children have breakfast, we'll finish packing."

"They're getting excited aren't they?" he said.

"Very. Going on vacation to America is something big for them."

"I'm glad the presentation will be over. Then I'll be able to enjoy our trip."

"Unless they need you for something," said Sorina. She knew her husband was always at the beckoned call of his bosses. More than once, he was called away from family gatherings to do something that just couldn't wait until the next work day.

"They promised me they wouldn't call or bother us in any way while we were out of the country."

"Does that mean you're leaving your computer here?"

"Now, Sorina, you know I'll need it for our pictures."

Sorina smiled at him. He got up from the table, put his dishes in the sink, and then gave her a kiss before returning to his work.

He looked at his watch. He still had time left to go over things.

The driver of the truck seemed to be taking every detour possible in going back to the city. The trip was taking a lot longer than any of them had anticipated. Finally, the truck came to a stop. Both doors opened and closed and then the canvass flap was opened. The men looked out and there was nothing around them but sand.

"You have to get out," said Kannid. "The truck has to cool. It is overheating."

The men jumped down from the back of the truck into the sand.

"Where are we?" asked Wusnar. "We should have been back at the city by now. What have you been doing, driving around in circles?"

"Once the truck has cooled," said Kannid, "we will be on our way. Unfortunately for you, the *Chosen One* has decided that your destiny lies with the Divine One."

Kannid moved behind the truck and Raseem opened fire on the men. Adarine dropped to the ground as soon as he heard the first shot. Several started running, but were quickly hit. Kannid watched as the sand was dyed with the blood of the men.

"That is finished," said Kannid. "Let us go."

"Don't you want to check on them?" asked Raseem.

"Not one of them is moving," said Kannid, "and even if they aren't dead yet, they will die of thirst in this heat."

The truck started right up. Raseem turned it around and headed back in the direction it came from.

Adarine listened until the noise from the truck disappeared. He raised his head and looked around.

"They're gone," said Adarine.

No one moved. He got up and walked to each man. He was certain they were dead. The wind started to pick up and Adarine judging from the direction the wind always blew at that time of year, set his course to get to the city. After he had gone on a while, he looked back and saw that even the footsteps he had just made were being wiped away by the wind. He started praying, prayers of thanksgiving because he knew he was being rewarded for following the will of the Divine One.

Karen sat in section five-o-four, seven rows from the front in the fifth and sixth seats, with her husband Arthur. The game was intense and when the Steelers completed a first down, the crowd was on its feet, screaming and stomping. Karen stopped and grabbed the seat in front of her. She could swear she felt the section sway a bit.

"Did you feel that?" she yelled to Arthur.

"Feel what?" he asked.

"Did you feel the section sway?"

"It's built so it'll sway a bit or else it couldn't hold the variance in weight."

"No," she said. "This is different. Something's wrong."

"It's just your imagination," he said and turned his attention to the game.

On the next play, the Steelers brought the ball within three yards of the goal. The crowd was screaming and stomping. Karen could feel the hair on the back of her neck stand up. Once again she felt a shifting in the section. This time she looked down. The liquid in her glass was tilting to the left.

"You had to have felt that," she said.

"It's just the people stomping their feet," said the man sitting next to her.

Let's get out of here," she screamed. "Something's wrong."

Again the section shifted and the liquid in her cup spilled out. The section was noticeably tilting. Karen stood up and so did Arthur.

"Let's go," he said.

Other people from the section hurriedly walked to the aisle and towards the exit.

Arthur grabbed Karen's hand as they ran down the ramp leading out of the stadium. Above the din of the crowd, they heard the unmistakable cracking of concrete and the eerie groan of compromised metal. A mist of concrete dust filtered down past the lights. On the way out, Karen stopped for a moment as they came to a security guard.

"Leaving so soon?" he asked.

"Section five-o-four is moving," she said out of breath. "It's tilting. It's going to fall."

"Nonsense," said the security guard, "it's just vibration from the crowd."

"No it's not," said a man. "It's going to crack off."

The security guard watched people race past him. The Steelers were winning and there should be smiles on their faces, but when he looked at them all he saw was fear and dread.

He shrugged his shoulders and walked down the walkway.

Arthur unlocked the doors to the car as they approached it. He opened the door, Karen quickly got in, and he closed it. He ran around to the other side, got in and started the car. A small procession of cars wove its way off stadium grounds and headed towards the parkway. Arthur thought for a moment and made a turn at the next light.

"Where are you going?" asked Karen.

"I want to get a good look at that," he said. "We should be able to see it from Mount Washington."

Karen took out her phone.

"That security guard didn't believe us," she said. "Do you think if I call 911 they'll believe me?"

"I don't know. Too bad we don't have Mr. Ellerman's number."

Karen pressed numbers on her phone.

"Hey did you call me to ask me to go to dinner?" asked the voice. "I'm starved, but I don't get off for another two hours at least."

"Shut up, Doug and listen to me," said Karen.

"Okay,"

"Section five-o-four at Heinz Field is cracking and falling."

"What!"

"You heard me," she said in an agitated tone.

"How do you know?"

"We were watching the game in that section. We told the security guard, but he said it was just vibration. It's not. The whole damn section is tilting!"

"Karen, hold on. Did you call 911?"

"Do you think they're going to believe me? They'll think I'm crazy or drunk. Douglas, people are going to die over there. The people in that section and anyone caught underneath."

"Karen!"

"If that section goes, they won't be able to get out from there."

"Karen! Where are you now?"

"We're heading for Mount Washington. We want to see what's happening. Doug, I think someone sabotaged the stadium. I think it's going to come crashing down. All those people are going to die!"

The picture of the stadium crashing down went fleeting through Doug's mind. Instantly he thought of Tom's phone call. "It'll remind you of the last time you were in Baghdad," the caller said. He felt a tingling of fear and a prickly sensation up his back.

"Karen, don't hang up. I'm going to make a call and see if we can get some action."

"I'm not hanging up."

Chapter Five

Ray Ellerman was usually a very calm person. Nothing in the business world of the Steelers ever caused him consternation. Today was different. Suicide bombers with tickets to the game were lying dead on Liberty Avenue and now a call from a spectator reporting that a section of the stadium was breaking away. All of this was more than he ever had to deal with in all his years. He tried to wait patiently as his head of security went to assess the situation, but the minutes dragged on.

"Mr. Ellerman," said Pat Victor, head of security at Heinz Field.

"Yes, Mr. Victor."

"The security officer said there were a number of people who left rather early. One woman reported that section five-o-four was tilting. He tried to calm her by telling her it was only vibrations, but another man backed her story and they left."

"Did he check on the report?"

"No, he didn't think it warranted checking."

"And?"

"Well, sir, as unlikely as it seems, section five-o-four is indeed tilting and there are visible cracks. I can't explain it."

"Mr. Victor, if that section goes, we won't be able to get the people out using that ramp. Start with section five-o-five and move the people off that deck and down to the lower level."

"With all due respects, sir, they're not going to want to miss any of the game."

"Commissioner Blakeworth is going to suspend the game until we can get that upper deck emptied. Once that's completed, start getting those under that section moved to the other side. Mr. Victor, don't let anyone use that ramp; even those below."

"Yes, sir."

Michael walked into the living room.

"You girls all done?" he asked.

"Everything we can do is finished," said Monique. "Game over?"

"No," said Michael. "Suspended."

"Suspended?" asked Gwen.

"Something about something with a player," said Michael. "Not a lot of info."

"Car bombing on Liberty Avenue and a suspended game," said Laura. "I wonder what's really going on."

"I don't know," said Mark. "First they stop filming the action on the field to show us people in the stands, twice and now this."

"What are they showing now?" asked Gina.

"Just highlights of the game."

"Did you turn it off?" asked Margo.

"No, I figure they'll have an answer in about fifteen minutes and the game should be back on," said Michael. "They're not going to suspend it indefinitely. They'd have a riot on their hands, especially with these fans."

The announcement was made to those in the stadium concerning an emergency situation with one of the players that would result in a delay in the game. It was the first time such a delay was called and the ambiguity of the message had spectators wondering what was happening. From across the stadium those who were in the upper deck watched as the people in the seats opposite them stood and walked calmly towards the ramp. A rumble and creaking was heard and section five-forty-one cracked. The right part dropped more than a foot dislodging seats and tossing people to the floor. Screams echoed through the stadium and hands reached down to help those who fell. They struggled to keep their footing. Concrete pieces and dust rained down onto the roof below. The vibrations from the people running down the stairs caused the structure to move again, dropping further and creating a gaping hole.

The sudden noise and screaming made Pat Victor look towards the opposite side of the field. He immediately moved his personnel into position to try to keep order as the deck was evacuated. He felt the low vibration under his feet and heard the moans as more cracks manifested and other sections shifted. This was hell coming to life before his eyes.

He hit the green button on his phone. Across the Allegheny River, Ray Ellerman answered putting him on speaker phone so everyone would hear.

"Yes, Pat."

"It's coming apart," he said yelling to be heard over the screams. "The stadium is coming apart. Multiple sections on the upper deck have cracked and there are gaping holes where the concrete has shifted. We're doing our best to get the people off this level, but their mere walking is causing some of the already broken sections to shift more. We can't use the ramp by five-o-four and there are breaks on every level of the exit ramps. If this continues, we're not going to be able to get everyone off this level."

He stopped as the concrete underneath his feet began to vibrate. He stepped quickly towards five-o-four and the place where he was just standing dropped. He heard chunks of concrete fall onto the roof.

"What was that?" asked Ellerman.

"That was the place where I was standing giving way," said Victor. "We need help over here. We have to get these people out of here and away from the stadium. Concrete is falling and I don't know whether the roof is catching it all or if it's smashing the cars."

"Mr. Victor, this is Police Chief Graham. We're going to get you help right away."

A loud rumble was heard followed by a crash and screams. Then Pat Victor's phone was silent.

"Dear God," said Paul Hennerly. "We have to get the players and coaches out of there. There's no way to continue the game."

"Call them," said Blakeworth. "They leave now, as is, in uniform."

"They can crowd on our buses and get the hell out of there," said Hennerly.

"I feel like I'm picking and choosing who should live and who should die," said Ellerman blowing his breath through his lips.

Fifteen minutes passed and the game still had not resumed.

"Something's not right," said Gwen.

"Call him," said Gina looking at Laura.

Laura picked up the phone and dialed the number. She remembered how many times she had made this call when they were planning to get Michael back.

Tom jumped as he felt the vibration of his phone. He took it out, looked at the display and answered.

"Hey, Laura, what's up?" he asked trying to sound normal.

"Why don't you tell me what's up?" she said. "I've seen all of Hal's reports, listened to yours, and now the game has been suspended."

"All I can tell you is that there was a car bombing on Liberty Avenue, four guys died on the sidewalk. It's a shame. They were going to the game. They had come out of a café and were really wired. Someone reported a crack in the concrete on the upper deck, and they were looking in other sections for more. It's really like a puzzle especially the last part if you get my drift. Oh and tell Michael, General Anderson said hello. I have to go. I'll call you later."

Laura put down the phone. She had a strange look on her face.

"So?" asked Gina.

"I don't know," said Laura. "He said all he could tell me was that there was a car bombing on Liberty Avenue."

"We know that," said Gina.

"He said four guys died on the sidewalk. It was a shame because they were going to the game. They had come out of a café and were really wired."

"Okay," said Mark. "How do you get wired in a café? Too much caffeine?"

"He said someone reported a crack in the concrete on the upper deck and they were looking in other sections for more."

"Wow," said Nicole.

"Then he said it was like a puzzle, especially the last part, if we get his drift," said Laura turning to face Michael. "He said to tell you General Anderson said hello."

"General Anderson?" said Michael. "They never bring him anywhere unless there's a threat to national security."

Armand Fitch carefully disassembled one set of the devices trying to get some clue as to who the key person might be. What he was sure of, was that the signal would come from a phone. He picked up the next set and began working.

Hal and Tom walked out of the trailer. The screams, could be heard from across the river.

"Do you think the person's watching the game?" asked Tom.

"Don't know," said Hal holding his phone to his ear, "but I do know we can't let them know anything's wrong."

"Yah."

"Barry, this is Hal. Go to commercial. Play every one of them you have and get the hell out of that place. It's going to come crashing down. Get those press boxes empty, but tell them they can't say anything about it. Tell them to send it back to their stations."

"Okay," said Barry.

"Call me when you're safe on the other side of the river."

"Which one?"

"Pick one."

Fitch had gone through all four of the digital devices by the time Hal and Tom walked over to him.

"Anything?" asked Hal.

"Whoever's going to detonate this is out of the country," said Fitch.

"How do you know?" asked Tom.

"They programmed a country code."

"Can they detonate themselves?"

"Only by trying to remove it," said Fitch, "and I'm not sure they were told that."

"With as much activity as is going on over there," said Hal, "I think one of them would've done it by now if they knew."

"I need to see what's going on," said Tom walking away.

"Where are you going?" asked Hal.

"Down by the bridge."

They ran down Seventh Street across Penn Avenue and onto Fort Duquesne Boulevard. The camera crew followed them. They ran down as far as possible and up the ramps to the bridge getting the best vantage point of the stadium. From their position they saw emergency and military personnel deploy and take up positions. Parts of the upper deck dangled precariously, some swaying and twisting as other sections gave way.

Hal's phone rang.

"Yah," he said.

"We're across the river," said Barry.

"Is it them?" asked Tom.

"Yah," said Hal.

"Where are they?"

"Across the river."

"Which one?"

"Where are you?" asked Hal.

Barry looked around.

"We're at the light by Station Square and ahead of us is a trolley line."

"Bridge by Station Square."

"Give me the phone," said Tom.

Hal handed him the phone and Tom started talking and pacing up and down the ramp. The camera crew hustled to the other side of the bridge.

Jake continued filming everything. Hal motioned to Tom who nodded and hurried over. They had a bird's eye view of the stadium and everything that was happening on the ground. Jake changed position trying to get other shots.

Tom handed the phone back to Hal.

"Where'd you send them?" asked Hal.

"Up to Mount Washington. They'll be able to see everything from up there."

"I wish I was down there?"

"Really?" asked Tom. "After trying to evade missiles in Baghdad, even this is too close."

Hal smiled. He picked up the microphone again to do another update.

Michael walked back into the living room carrying a file case. He put it on the coffee table and began leafing through it.

"Turn on the TV," he said. "I think I know what Tom was talking about. Here it is." He pulled out a piece of paper and looked at it. "Do you remember when Yamani gave me the names of the books and Tom suggested they might be big pieces of a children's puzzle?"

"Yes," said Robert. "I remember."

"The last piece was bombs," said Michael. "Those guys on the sidewalk weren't wired with caffeine. They're wired as in a bomb. They were going to the game."

"Shit!" said Mark. "When they were showing the stands they were looking for more of them."

"Tom said there were cracks in the concrete on the upper deck," said Laura. "Did they show that?"

"No, just the lower levels," said Mark.

"Why are there cracks in the upper deck?" asked Brigit. "Isn't that stadium relatively new?"

"There shouldn't be cracks unless someone sabotaged it," said Michael. "This is why Anderson's there. I'd bet everything I own on it."

Chapter Six

Petru took a quick shower and put on his suit. He looked at the clock in the bedroom. It was almost time. He walked back into his office and picked up the paper with the instructions. They were very specific. Each person had to be emailed individually. Petru surmised that with the sensitivity of the project, it was important that not one of them knew who else was receiving the information.

He created each individual email, personalized each one, attached the presentation and then sent them. When he was finished he checked the time. He looked at the list of phone numbers and programmed them into his phone along with their name. As soon as his alarm rang, he began making his calls. Each one went to voice mail almost immediately and he left the same simple message.

When he finished, he put the papers into his briefcase and left his office.

General Anderson shouted orders to the men outside the stadium. The soldiers were dressed in combat gear. They calmly led the spectators away from the stadium to vehicles that would transport them a safe distance away.

"I need to find my car," said a woman dressed in traditional Steeler garb.

"I'm sorry, ma'am, but I can't let you do that," said a soldier.

"But you don't understand," she said. "I just bought it today."

"I do understand, ma'am, but I still can't let you do that."

He helped her onto the vehicle and several others after her. Then the driver drove away.

Chief Graham came up to General Anderson.

"I positioned the emergency vehicles around the perimeter," he said. "How much longer until they're all out?"

"Don't know. We're down to two exits."

There was a rumble and a large section of the upper deck fell against the roof and went through. The screams were deafening and General Anderson motioned for several of his men. As they hurried over, an explosion rocked the far end of the stadium.

"Jesus Christ!" said General Anderson.

"Holy shit!" said Jake. "It's fuckin' Armageddon."

Tom shook his head. Suddenly he was back in Baghdad outside the Embassy with the passenger door open. He could feel the adrenaline coursing through his body as he waited for Laura to get in. His foot hit the accelerator and he heard the whistle of the missile and then…another explosion rocked the night. Tom looked over at the stadium. Debris was airborne and there was the sound of raining concrete. In front of their eyes, Heinz Field was being reduced to rubble and all who were still inside were frantically trying to escape the holocaust.

Tom looked at the stadium through a pair of binoculars. He watched people pushing and shoving trying to get ahead of the person in front of them. Anyone who did not or could not move quickly enough was mowed down and trampled by the frenzied crowd. He scanned the sections and saw men sitting calmly, unaffected by what was happening around them.

"Can you see those men just sitting there?" he yelled to Sam.

"I see them."

He focused his camera on one and as he took the shot, the man was blown up. Sam kept shooting and the cameraman filmed the crowds.

"Can you get some of the activity outside the stadium, too," asked Hal.

"Already on it," said Jake.

It was wall to wall people moving through the exits that looked like additions to the stadium instead of being part of it. Explosions rang out and the exit closest to section five-o-four blew apart sending fans through the air and to the ground.

Hal began again to describe what was happening. Although he was trying to stay calm when reporting, there was a tone of excitement and horror in his voice. The local stations would be tapping into his feed and he knew the cities of Pittsburgh and Baltimore would be awe-struck at the sight.

To the right, Commissioner Blakeworth, Ray Ellerman, and Paul Hennerly watched. Another explosion rang out and the whole stadium area went dark. The dust and debris hanging in the air clouded any light the moon gave off making it difficult to see anything. Hearing the screams, the stomping of running feet and explosions were worse than being able to see.

Ray Ellerman's mind played out what he'd witnessed over and over again and added new dimensions that his mind created from the sounds. Why hadn't they hurried the evacuation a little more? Perhaps more lives could have been saved. Why hadn't that security guard checked out the woman's story?

Paul Hennerly looked over at his friend.

"There was nothing more you could've done," he said.

Ellerman shook his head.

"You gave your orders based on what you were told," said Hennerly. "I've been with you the whole time and there isn't one thing I would've done differently.

The explosions were closer together now. The metal quad pods burst and ripped from their moorings and were propelled through the air. Helicopters flying in a safe zone aimed large lights onto the scene.

Tom counted each explosion, putting a strike on a page in his notebook. He knew how many bombers there were. He had that figured out from the information they had been able to get. Now it was different. The quad pods and exits were exploding. He surmised that somehow they were able to plant devices that couldn't be detected. It was harder to distinguish between individual explosions.

The first of the explosions had already happened by the time Barry and his crew reached the lookout point on Mount Washington. They stopped the van, got out and ran towards the railing. Karen and Arthur stood spellbound looking across at the seats they once occupied.

"Oh my God!" screamed Karen. "What's happening?"

"I don't know," said Arthur.

From their perch they could see mass bedlam in the stadium as the series of explosions went off one after another. Even from that distance they heard the screams and the crashing of the concrete as the sound bounced off the hills that lined the rivers. Seats flew in the air. Railings impaled people trying to get through. Some were tossed in the air like rag dolls and hit the ground with a thud.

The whole side where Karen and Arthur had been was now nothing more than mangled steel and rubble. Arthur pulled his wife closer to him. He knew they could've been buried somewhere underneath all those tons of concrete. Arthur looked behind him and saw the players standing there shocked at what they were witnessing.

The cameraman panned the group. The looks on their faces told the story. By this time, the news had broken. Hal had been on camera from the first report of a problem with the upper deck.

Armand Fitch listened to the explosions coming from Heinz Field. He watched carefully the four digital devices in front of him. Even though they had been disconnected from their explosive package, he knew they would receive the relay. If he was lucky, his patience would prove invaluable.

He wanted nothing more than to be able to see what was going on. Liberty Avenue was like a morgue compared to the activity when he arrived. The remains of the cars and buses sat unmoved and every building was silent.

He turned his undivided attention back to the devices. A light came on in one and a series of numbers appeared. Never taking his eyes off the device, Fitch wrote the numbers on a piece of paper.

"Three seconds," he said. "It took just three seconds."

Two minutes later a light came on in another one and then another and then the last. Each time a series of numbers flashed. He checked them against the first. They were the same. One person was in charge. One person had the power.

Fitch opened the case, carefully bagged each item and put them away. Then he closed, locked the case, and started down the sidewalk towards Seventh Street, leaving only those guarding the scene.

Chapter Seven

Petru walked into the Craustof Technologies. He stopped briefly and looked through the window on the door that led to the work floor. He remembered the first day he worked there. He was one of about ten chemical engineers employed by Craustof. He worked hard to earn his place upstairs and now he had the chance to enter the executive section.

He walked up the stairs to the second floor and down the hallway past his office to the center area. There you could look over the railing and see what was happening on the main floor below. There was a stairwell that led down to the lab where he conducted his experiments. Straight ahead, on the other side of the open space, was the receptionist's desk. His eyes focused on the two large wooden doors with frosted glass panels of either side. Behind those closed doors were all in upper management, including the CEO and President of the company. Blurred forms of people could be seen when they came close enough to the frosted panels.

Petru smiled, turned around, and walked to his office. All he wanted was a few minutes to collect his thoughts and relax before the presentation began. Helena walked into his office with a cup of coffee.

"Are you ready?" she asked handing the cup to him.

"Yes, I think so," said Petru. "Thank you for the coffee."

"I'm really going to hate to see you go."

"I'll still be on the same floor."

"I know, but every person who has been on this side and walked through those doors on the other side has changed so much that I don't even get so much as a hello anymore."

"I promise I'll come and say hello every morning," said Petru smiling.

"I'm going to hold you to that promise," said Helena walking to the door. "By the way, good luck."

Sirens blared as emergency vehicles from around the area teemed over the bridges and access roads to get to the disaster scene. The explosions had long since ceased and the once impressive Heinz Field was nothing more than rubble.

Hal walked onto the field and looked around surveying the carnage. Everywhere he looked, workers were moving pieces of concrete, systematically clearing sections looking for those who had been buried. Even with the massive explosions, most of the debris was carried away from the field and Hal stood on a clearly defined fifty-yard line. Clearing the rubble and reclaiming the dead would take weeks. This was by no means over.

The country had once again been put on high alert, something many had forgotten as the years from September eleventh put distance between that disaster and the present. General Anderson joined him looking exhausted.

"He's on his way, you know," said the General.

"Knowing him, he'll land right here," said Hal pointing to the field.

"I've been in war zones that didn't look this bad."

"They had a captive audience," said Hal looking around. "They intended for this whole thing to come crashing down and every exit to be blocked." He paused and thought about the four bodies lying on the sidewalk across the river. "It would've worked, you know, had the events on Liberty Avenue not taken place."

The sound of propellers grew louder and the pilot landed the helicopter in a clear area on the field. As soon as they touched down, the door opened and President Bartram exited. General Anderson hurried to the President.

"President Bartram," he said.

"General Anderson, what's the situation?" he asked out of habit. Looking around he knew the situation was as grave as it could be.

"Governor Lakely has been on the scene for about the past hour and was apprised of the situation as soon as we realized the magnitude of the plan. Equipment and personnel are on their way from other parts of the state, West Virginia, Ohio, and Maryland. We're using PNC Park and the hospitals are inundated."

"The situation on the other side?"

"Taken care of."

"Good," said the President. "Any leads on the perpetrators?"

"Yes, sir."

"Really?"

The man walked into Dr. Hempton's office. He hadn't been there since before the facility first opened. Dr. Hempton was completely absorbed by the tasks he was doing and didn't hear the man come in.

"Are we still on schedule?" asked the man.

Dr. Hempton jumped at the sound of his voice. "Don't you believe in knocking?" asked Dr. Hempton.

"Why do I have to knock in my own place," asked the man. "I asked you if we were still on schedule."

"I don't know about *we*," said Dr. Hempton, "but I know *I* am on schedule."

"I don't need your attitude. All I need from you is a yes."

"And you got my answer. Everything is on schedule on this end. You have nothing to worry about here."

"Let's keep it that way. I have a few other things that need to be taken care of. Put those things away and listen to me."

Petru stood in the front of the room. He put down his laser pointer and stepped forward.

"Does anyone have any questions?" he asked.

"Excellent presentation, Petru," said Farred Mahayin. "You very thoroughly explained this project. I have no doubt we'll have great success with this."

"Thank you, sir."

"I had several calls from our other members commending you on the presentation you sent them as well as the congenial voice mail you left. They're not always so complimentary."

"Thank you, sir."

"Now, I think everyone in this room is in agreement as were the others that you are very deserved of the promotion to vice-president in charge of chemical research."

"Thank you, sir," said Petru smiling.

"Your new office will be ready when you get back from your holiday," said Mahayin. "For now, could I impose upon you to take all of your personal items from your office and bring them when you come back to work. We'd like to get the office ready for your replacement."

"Of course," said Petru.

Mahayin walked up to Petru, reached in an inside suit coat pocket and pulled out an envelope.

"As you know, promotions bring with them bonuses. We thought you might need this for your holiday," said Mahayin handing Petru the envelope. "Enjoy your time off. You deserve it."

"Thank you, sir.

"Oh and something to keep the boys occupied on the plane," said Mahayin handing Petru a bag containing two wrapped packages.

The others walked out of the room and Petru turned to pack up his computer and presentation materials. Josep handed him his briefcase and folio.

"I shut down your computer for you," said Josep, "and packed your things. I know you must be in a hurry to leave."

"Thank you. I'm a bit excited."

"Have a great holiday."

"Thank you."

Petru returned to his office and cleaned out his desk drawers and took all his personal items and put them in a mesh carry-all. He walked out of his office, said good-bye to Helena and then left the building.

It was early morning and everyone was still watching the reports coming in from Pittsburgh. Hal looked especially tired, as did all the people on the scene. Everything that could be done was being done and this was going to be a slow and painful process.

With all the planning for the wedding, Michael had forgotten about giving their tickets to someone. Now he thanked God for that slip of the mind.

Laura stood up and stretched.

"I can't watch this anymore right now," she said. "I think I'm going to start breakfast. Anyone going to work today?"

The rest of them looked at her and shook their heads.

"Didn't think so. I'll be around the house somewhere. If anything new happens, yell for me,"

Laura walked into the bedroom and grabbed some new clothes. A nice shower would surely revive her, she thought. She sat for a moment on a chair and woke up her computer. She wanted to see if the disaster made the top news of the day. Sometimes things that happened in Pittsburgh were never given the press they deserved, good or bad. As soon as she looked, however, she knew this was different. There were headlines across the top of pages and pictures. She logged into her email and there were nearly twenty from people she knew asking how she was and whether or not she heard. She quickly answered each one and told them she'd talk to them when they arrived for the wedding. In the right lower corner of her screen an alert popped up. Laura clicked on it.

"Miss Darmer, it is me. I need to talk to Mr. Braedon. It is urgent."

Petru parked his car in the bank's lot, walked in and went directly to a teller.

"Good morning, Petru," said Morana. "How are you today?"

"Very well," he said taking the check from the envelope. He looked at the amount and stared. It was a certified check for more money than he had seen at any one time in his life. If he worked for the next five years at his job, he wouldn't make this much. He turned the check over, signed it had handed to Morana.

"Do you want all of this in cash?" she asked.

"No, no," he said.

Petru turned the envelope over and listed accounts and amounts to be deposited and how much cash he wanted. Then he handed it to her.

"I made out this check when Mr. Mahayin came in," she said. "Congratulations on the promotion."

"Thank you."

She finished the transaction, counted out the cash, and handed him the slips complete with the new balances.

Petru counted out some of the money and put it into his wallet. The rest he handed back to Morana.

"May I have this converted into United States Currency?"

"Certainly, it'll just take a few minutes."

She came back, counted out the money, and handed it to him along with a conversion chart.

"The exchange rate has been pretty stable," she said. "This will give you some idea of what you're spending."

Petru thanked her and walked out of the bank.

Adarine barely made it through the back door of the house before collapsing in the nearest chair. He was hot and sweaty and desperately needed water. His wife took one look at him and hurried to get him a glass from the kitchen.

"What happened?" she asked.

"Rana, we have to leave," said Adarine trying to catch his breath. "We have to leave before they find us."

"What are you talking about?"

"I cannot tell you until we are away."

Adarine walked into the bedroom and took out their travel bags from the closet. He put them on the bed and then began to take clothing out of the draws and off the hangers.

"Adarine, where are we going?" she asked folding the clothes and putting them in the bags.

"I'll decide on the way."

Rana shook her head, but knew her husband well enough to understand that something horrible happened and leaving was the only option. She finished their bags and then went into the children's room and packed everything that would fit. Adarine came into the room and handed her the passports for her and the children.

"I can't be seen leaving here with you. I can't allow anyone to see me. They know I left with the others. I will meet you at the airport in Frankfurt. Thank the Divine One that they do not know my name."

Rana nodded. She watched Adarine sneak out the back then she called for the children. Once they were in the house she had them wash and put on clean clothes. They grabbed their backpacks and walked out the door with their mother.

Rana and the children walked down the street to her friend's house.

"Would you please watch the house for me?"

"Of course," said Kaela.

"Since Adarine has answered the calling, I am going to take the children to visit my family. I can't bear being alone right now."

"I understand. May you have a safe journey."

Rana and the children continued walking out of the neighborhood to a place where they could catch a bus to the city and then to the airport.

Chapter Eight

Laura stared at the computer screen. Not since the day they had received the advanced copies of the magazine with the stories chronicling their ordeal had they heard from him. She assumed he was somewhere deep in hiding. Now, there was an ever so slight feeling of nervousness rising inside.

She picked up her phone and called Michael. She knew he was only in the other room, but she didn't want to alarm the others at the prospect that Yamani would once again be in their lives. She hoped it wouldn't be the case. What could he possibly want?

Michael looked at his phone and answered it.

"Yes," he said.

"Could you please come to the bedroom?" she asked.

"Be there in a sec."

Michael walked into the bedroom and closed the door.

"What's up?" he asked.

Laura pointed to the computer screen.

Michael sat down. He looked up at Laura and she nodded. He clicked on the message and logged into the site that the two of them had used.

"I'm here. What's so urgent?"

"Ah Mr. Braedon, it is good to speak with you again. You have seen what is happening in your city?"

"Yes, we're watching it."

"I want you to know I had nothing to do with it."

"Why would I think you did?"

"There are those who are still trying to link me to terroristic activities. I assure you I have done nothing. All I know is some of those who have been arrested in other happenings have been saying we are taking responsibility for these acts. I take no responsibility for these acts. Nor do I take responsibility for the act that is happening now."

"Why are you telling me this?"

"Mr. Braedon, I know you and Ms. Darmer understand that when I give my word I keep it."

"Yes, we do."

"I believe there are people in high places who are trying to get me; trying to discredit me; trying to make me the scapegoat."

"For what reason?"

"Mr. Braedon, they are not going to say it is some no name person, someone who is building his reputation. They want someone who at one time was visible. Someone they already hate so they can work the citizens into a frenzy." Yamani paused a moment. "There are things in the works, Mr. Braedon, things that will make nine eleven look miniscule. Just look at what happened tonight. I know the death toll will be much greater than that was."

"Can you tell me who's doing this?" asked Michael.

"I do not know. I only have unconfirmed information. I need to find out how much of this is true. It is very difficult for me to seek out this information."

"What do you want from me?"

"Help me find who is trying to frame me and expose them for what they are."

"I need to know what other events they are trying to connect you to."

"That I can send you."

"Then I need to look into it. After that I will make my decision. Is that agreeable?"

"Mr. Braedon, it is agreeable. Thank you. Check your email in a little while."

With that, he was gone, just as he had been so many times before. Michael took a deep breath and blew it out. Laura tapped his shoulder.

"Michael, are you going to do this?"

"What would you do, Laura?"

"I'd do it. I don't know why, but I'd do it."

Petru walked through the door to his home. He put down his briefcase and the box of his personal items. Lucian and Grigore ran up to their father and almost pushed him over.

"Are you all ready to go?" he asked.

"Yes," said Lucian jumping up and down.

"I'm ready," said Grigori.

"Good," said Petru.

"Are we going now?" asked Grigori.

"In a little while."

"You two, how about going to your room and making sure you packed everything," said Sorina walking into the room. "If you forget something, we can't come back for it."

"Okay, Mama," said Lucian and the two boys ran down the hall to their room.

"How did it go?" she asked.

"I got the promotion."

"That's wonderful," she said giving him a kiss. She looked past him and saw the box beside his briefcase. "Why did you bring your things home?"

"My new office won't be ready until I come back," he said. "Mr. Mahayin asked me to take my things so they can get my old office ready for someone else."

"Why don't you put the box in the closet and you can grab it when you go back to work."

Petru picked up the box, opened the closet door, and put the box on the floor in the corner. Then he pulled the envelope from his briefcase and the bag from the box.

"Mr. Mahayin gave me my bonus check before I left and I went to the bank."

"You got a bonus?" asked Sorina. "How much?"

"More than I've ever seen. I put most of it in our accounts."

Petru took the slips from the envelope and handed them to her. As Sorina went through the slips, her mouth gaped more and more.

"Mr. Mahayin thought we might want to use it for vacation, but I can't be that frivolous."

"This is so unexpected. It's wonderful."

"I had some money converted to United States currency so the boys can pay for things."

"They'll love it."

"Is everything packed?" he asked.

"We're all ready. We only need to take a few things to your mother and give her a key."

"We'll still have time to get the boys a surprise gift and something to eat," said Petru. He yelled down the hall. "Are you boys ready?"

"Yes," they yelled running down the hall.

"Let's go."

The boys came running into the living room.

"Mr. Mahayin sent these for you," said Petru handing each of the boys a package.

The boy tore open the wrappings. Their eyes got big and their mouths dropped.

"Can we get games?" asked Grigore.

"If we leave right now," said Petru.

Edgar Reinholdt, the President and CEO of Reinholdt International sat in his usual seat in the conference room. With him were Albert Paxton, his Chief Operations Officer, Ivan Retrovski, and Franz Schmidt. Ivan and Franz were two who had worked on the SecReSAC project and had not been implicated in the espionage incident.

Ever since that incident, things around Reinholdt International were never quite the same. New security measures had been added and monitoring of world events, both seen and behind the scenes became the norm. For a company like Reinholdt International which dealt with issues of national security for most of the world's powers, its own security was of utmost concern. Up until a year ago, the company had never experienced even so much as a minor threat. Then came the embezzlement of intellectual property known as SecReSAC and the world was brought to the brink of complete destruction. Now every time there was an inkling that something was amiss, Edgar insisted it be investigated.

"Have you made any headway on that security breach," asked Edgar.

"We've traced it to Romania," said Ivan.

"Romania?" asked Albert. "Are you sure?"

"Yes," said Ivan. "I traced it myself. And what's more, the company has questionable investors."

"What kind of investors?" asked Edgar.

"My sources say they're linked to some terrorist organization," said Ivan.

Edgar took a deep breath. Terrorism…the very word sent ripples of fear through Edgar's being. He had dealt with a fanatic religious organization that had been behind the embezzlement. Yamani had certainly been a formidable opponent, but aside from those who did his bidding, the organization answered to one man and one man only, him. Terrorists, on the other hand, have a vast network and hierarchy in place.

"Do we know the name of the company?" asked Albert.

"Craustof Technologies," said Ivan.

"Don't they specialize in mining?" asked Albert.

"Yes," said Ivan, "but some are questioning their actual purpose. They think the mining business is just a front for terrorist activities."

"How so?" asked Edgar.

"My contact says the amount of business they do and the amount of money that's in their accounts is inconsistent," said Franz.

"Inconsistent, how?" asked Albert.

"By hundreds of billions of dollars," said Franz.

Edgar removed his glasses and shook his head.

"Has the money been traced?" he asked.

"They've tried," said Franz, "but every attempt ends in a dead end."

"If there's one thing I've learned over the past year," said Edgar, "it's that no one is one hundred percent successful in covering his tracks."

"Well these people seem to have done it," said Franz.

"Get in touch with your contacts and get a list of the dead ends," said Edgar.

"I see where this is leading," said Albert leaning back in his chair.

"Do you have a better idea?" asked Edgar.

"No," said Albert, "it was the first thing that crossed my mind."

"Good," said Edgar. "Then let's get started."

Helena pulled Petru's file and marked the decisions management had made. She knew his file needed to be sent to the executive section before he returned from vacation. She liked to get things done immediately; it was always her way. She took out a large envelope from the bottom drawer of her desk. Mahayin walked in and stood just inside the door.

"Helena," he said smiling, "it was very good news about Petru, wasn't it?"

"Yes, sir," she said. "It couldn't happen to anyone who was more deserving."

"True," he said looking around the office. "I wanted to come by and speak to you personally. We're going to be renovating the offices over the next three to four weeks. I'm asking everyone to pack up their offices and take their things with them. Whatever is left will wind up being hauled away as trash."

"Yes, sir," said Helena. "Is the entire building being done?"

"Just this floor," he said. "Everything downstairs will remain the same. No need to renovate the work floor. Too much machinery down there."

"Yes, sir."

"Oh, and Helena, I don't want this to be a hardship for you, so I have a check to pay you for the time," said Mahayin handing her an envelope.

"Thank you," said Helena. "That's very kind of you."

"Whenever you've finished packing everything, you can leave. I'll be in touch when we'll be resuming operations."

"Alright."

Mahayin smiled, turned and walked out of the office. Helena picked up her purse and put the envelope in it. She walked over to the closet and pulled out a stack of plastic crates. She emptied each file drawer, putting the contents into a crate. As she finished, she grabbed her keys to take the filled crates to the car.

Helena was a creature of habit and always parked her car in the same space every day. When she got to the parking lot, her car was surrounded with tractor trailer trucks. She wove around them and to her car. She put the crates in her trunk and walked back around the trucks.

When Helena returned to her office, she looked at Petru's folder sitting on her desk. Before she forgot, she wanted to make sure it was with everything from the executive side. She picked up the folder and walked to the receptionist area in the center of the floor. The sound of hammering filled the air. Surely they hadn't begun working already.

The receptionist area was empty. The only thing left was the desk and file cabinets. Helena walked a little closer to the opening in the floor. Down below, machinery was being crated. She looked up and over to the executive section. All the lights were off and there was no movement by the door. Helena turned and walked back to her office. She closed the door slightly, bent over and put Petru's file in her bag. She heard footsteps coming closer and stood up. Mahayin walked to the door and took two steps inside. He looked around, slapped the papers he carried in his right hand against his left, turned and continued walking. Helena peered through the crack in the door and then silently came from behind. She watched as Mahayin walked into Petru's office and walked out without the papers. He looked around and then walked to the stairwell.

Helena waited until she heard the door close and Mahayin check to make sure it was locked. Then she walked to the end of the hall and slightly moved the venetian blind. She watched him get in his car and leave. A few seconds later she heard the trucks begin to move out. She walked down to Petru's office, walked in, and looked around. She spied the papers in the trash can and picked them up, folded them and put them in her pocket.

Helena walked back to her office and picked up her bag. Then she walked down the hall back to the open area. The noise of hammering had stopped and as she peered down, she saw that the floor had been emptied and nothing or no one was moving. Across the open space, the door to the executive section was open.

Somehow she knew she was the last one in the building. She was sure Mahayin was making his final check before leaving. The question was why. She walked around the area to the large double doors. Cautiously, she stepped in and began walking down the hall. Every room she walked into was cleaned out. Having gotten to the last room, Helena turned around and headed out of the area. As she passed each room, she couldn't help but look into them. She passed one then stopped suddenly and backed up looking into the room again. On the floor she spied something shiny, so she went into the room and bent down to pick it up. Between the two side desk drawers, she saw a paper sticking out. She opened the drawer until the paper slipped out easily. She bent down and looked towards the back of the drawer and could see other papers tacked against the wall of the desk. She felt alongside the track of the drawer for the release, pressed it and removed the drawer. Carefully, she loosened the papers, pulled them out and put them in her bag. Then she checked behind the other drawer, but found nothing. Whoever cleared this room was not as meticulous as the others, so she decided to search further. Her search turned up other small items and papers in the trash can. She placed everything in her bag and quickly walked down the hall to the other side, down the stairwell, and out of the building.

Chapter Nine

While the first responders were picking up the pieces and searching for anyone trapped under the rubble, Hal continued his coverage of the scene. When his replacement finally arrived, Hal gladly turned over the microphone to him. His body was craving sleep, but he knew there was much more at stake and answers needed to be found. Through all of this, Tom had been reporting everything locally. Now the two of them sat in a private conference room in the hotel with President Bartram, away from the commotion. They were soon joined by Armand Fitch, Roger Gimshaw, and General Anderson.

General Anderson sat down with a cup of coffee. Although there were times when he ran on very little sleep during engagements, the stress of this event weighed very heavily on him.

"Gentlemen," said General Anderson, "I thought it infinitely important to meet before we left the field. I want to know where we stand on all this."

"Well, sir," said Armand Fitch, "the devices used for these bombers were among the most sophisticated in the world and totally undetectable by any type of scan. The power of one of them could have done tremendous damage to this building. In fact, I would estimate that two would have brought this building down."

"Why, then, did they need so many over there?" asked Gimshaw.

"This building is compact and they would have been capable of creating a chain reaction. The stadium, however, is singular in nature, so they had to gauge how much destruction one bomb could do in an open venue situation."

"If they were this successful in this endeavor," said President Bartram, "we are vulnerable. It was only by chance we were able to get as much information as we had and able to evacuate as many people as we could."

"As of yet, no one has come forward to claim responsibility for this," said Gimshaw.

"We need to find out who supplied them with these devices," said Fitch.

"Well, there's only one person I know of who can answer that question," said President Bartram. "I'll need pictures of it."

"They're right here on this computer," said Fitch.

"Here's the email address," said the President writing it on a piece of paper. "Just send it and I'll call him."

"Any luck finding out who the remote detonator was?" asked the General.

"The four devices we were able to intercept gave us a number," said Fitch. "The same number appeared on each device."

"Then we need to trace the number," said General Anderson. "Once we have it, we can have that person picked up immediately."

"It's not that simple," said Fitch. "The country code is Romania."

"Are you telling me someone from Romania triggered this disaster?" asked President Bartram.

"Exactly," said Fitch. "It's not that it can't be done. It's just going to take a little longer."

"Does anyone else, other than those in this room know where these calls originated?" asked President Bartram.

"No," said Fitch. "We're the only ones who know."

"Then it needs to stay that way," said President Bartram, looking around at the others.

Qadir knocked on the back door of Yamani's home. Usually he sent a message first so that Yamani would know to expect him, but today he forgot. This was too important. Maranissa pulled aside the curtain and looked out. She smiled and unlocked the door for Qadir.

"I did not know you were coming," she said.

"I am sorry. I forgot to send a message. May I see him, please? It is urgent."

Maranissa left the room and went to another part of the house. Yamani soon came to the kitchen.

"Qadir, what is it?" said Yamani. "My wife said it is urgent."

"Yes, sir," said Qadir.

He took a paper from his pocket and handed it to Yamani. Yamani unfolded the paper and sat down at the table.

"Where did you get this?" asked Yamani.

"From my cousin Adarine."

"Did he tell you who was recruiting these men?"

"Yes, sir," said Qadir. "He said it was you, sir."

Yamani looked up at Qadir.

"Me?"

"Yes, sir. He said you were recruiting many men. He and other men were picked up in his town and taken by truck, but he couldn't tell exactly where they were taken. When they got there, there were many other men. They went inside a building and you talked to them about how important the Cause was. He said you talked about how they were chosen by the Divine One to answer the call. He said you told them that some would be required to make the ultimate sacrifice, but the Divine One would reward them and their families."

"Were they all chosen?"

"All were given contracts to sign," said Qadir, "but Adarine and nine others told the man that after praying about it, the Divine One told them it was not the right time for them. The man told them they would be taken back to the city and they were put in the back of a truck. He said the truck drove and drove all over the place and then stopped. The driver told them that they had to get out because the truck was overheated. Then the other man who was driving with them began shooting them. Adarine fell to the ground when he heard the first shot. He was the only one not killed."

"Qadir, the Divine One indeed was watching over Adarine and protecting him."

"Yes, sir."

"This is very troublesome news," said Yamani. "We must find out more."

Gina sat at the kitchen table sipping a cup of coffee. The house was quiet. Only she and Laura were awake.

"What kind of explosive device could they have gotten into the stadium," asked Gina. "Don't you have detectors for those things?"

"Detectors, hand held scanners, pat downs, you name it."

"Then how did they get past?"

"Maybe they were undetectable," said Laura. "It wouldn't surprise me. I wonder why the quad pods buckled."

"Some sort of reactive acid?"

Laura raised her eyebrows, got up from the chair and grabbed her laptop from the counter.

"You're not looking that up are you?" asked Gina.

"No, but I'm going to look to see when the last time the structure was checked. I'd hazard to guess they'd do it right before the start of the season."

"You think they put that on the internet?"

"It has to be somewhere."

The phone rang and Laura quickly answered it before it could wake anyone.

"Hello," she said.

"May I speak to Laura or Michael? This is Hal Milridge."

"Hal, this is Laura. How are you?"

"Tired, exhausted, hungry, puzzled. How about you? All ready for the wedding?"

"Everything's finished except for saying I do."

"Would you mind some early company?"

"You know you're always welcome. Will Tom be coming early?"

"I think you can count on that."

"Good. It'll be great to see you. When are you coming?"

"We're on the plane now. Call you when we land."

"Have a good flight. Get some sleep."

Laura put the phone down and looked at Gina.

"Hal and Tom on a plane heading for Paris?" said Laura. "Why?"

"Have no idea, but can probably guess."

Laura shook her head. Just four more days until the wedding. Nothing could possibly interfere with it. Gina could tell what she was thinking.

"Listen, four more days until the wedding," said Gina. "You're going to be walking down that aisle regardless of what's going on. I'll personally see to that."

"Will you also personally see to it that the groom is waiting down front?"

Dr. Hempton walked through the facility. He had always dreamed of being the director of his own medical facility and now that dream had become a reality. He walked down the hall to the emergency room and saw patients in triage and others being wheeled in on stretchers. Putting a trauma center in this neighborhood was sheer genius and he knew if he kept the standards high, this would become one of the most envied places of its kind.

He was extremely pleased with the way everything was being run and the quality of service his people were giving. This made all the difference in the world.

While the trauma center took up the first three floors of the facility, the upper floors were off limits to normal personnel and trauma patients and their families. They had access only to the ground floor, first floor, and second floor.

After he had made his rounds on the three public floors, he headed down a hallway towards a large brown wooden door. Reaching in his pocket, he took out a key and inserted it. The door opened and Dr. Hempton walked in.

The elevator took him up to the fourth floor. This was his real domain. Here he used all his skills to create and make a person as good as new.

The man's visit put him on edge. How dare he even insinuate that things were not on schedule! He prided himself on being able to deliver everything no matter how small or large in perfect condition and on time.

Dr. Hempton opened his folder and began making rounds. This time he intended to take his time, put each subject through their paces and objectively assess where each person was on the timeline. For his own peace of mind, he needed to know this.

Albert Paxton was doodling on the yellow notepad in front of him. He had a lot of things to do and this impromptu meeting was not on his list. Ivan and Franz sat in silence not knowing why the meeting was called either. Edgar Reinholdt walked through the door, closed it and walked to the table.

"What's so important it couldn't wait for our regular meeting?" asked Albert

"This," said Edgar putting a photo on the table.

"Where did you get this?" asked Albert.

"From President Bartram," said Edgar.

"I don't understand," said Ivan. "Why would President Bartram send you a picture of the device we invented? Did you send him a picture of it?"

"No," said Edgar. "This was found on a suicide bomber in Pittsburgh."

"How did they get it?" asked Albert.

"I have no idea, but we need to find out and fast," said Edgar. "I can't begin to fathom how this got into the hands of those people, but they must have had it for some time to be able to produce enough to level that stadium."

"Do you have any other information about how they pulled this off?" asked Albert picking up the picture.

"Nothing other than asking whether or not I knew anything about this device," said Edgar, "and whatever is being broadcast. If they know anything else, they're not saying."

"No one has come forward to take responsibility for this act," said Ivan. "Usually someone does by now."

"Unless they're planning more of these attacks," said Franz. "Then the longer they can stay anonymous the more havoc they can cause."

"Well we better start finding out what's going on right under our noses," said Edgar. "I want to know who's involved, without them knowing we know. We need to find out where this information is going and we need to do it under the radar."

Ray Ellerman stood in the parking lot looking at what used to be Heinz Field. His family had owned this franchise for years and the Ellerman name was synonymous with Steeler football. To the people of Pittsburgh and the fans, they were one and the same. Although his players and coaches were safe, Ray had lost a lot of friends. There was no magic play to call to make it all better. He thought back to the days when the Steelers ended their seasons with some of the worst records in football. He remembered how his father sat up nights worrying about how to get the team moving in the right direction. Back then it seemed cataclysmic. Now it seemed trite.

John Blakeworth walked over to him and put his hand on Ray's shoulder. Ray stood shaking his head.

"I don't even know where to begin," said Ellerman.

"I usually find prayer helps," said Blakeworth, "but that's just me. Business can wait. These people and their families are first priority."

"I know. No matter what we do, it's never going to be enough."

"No one expects it to be enough. All they expect is for someone to care."

"The rest of the family's on the way. They should be here sometime today. I know they told me when, but right now I really can't remember."

"I'm surprised I can remember my own name," said Blakeworth. "My mind's going from one thing to another and not really solving anything."

"What if they're targeting the NFL because of the number of people who are in the stadiums?"

"I thought about that. Do I cancel games, just in case? Do I let the games continue and risk lives? If we cancel, are we giving in to them?"

"I don't have any answers," said Ellerman, "but we've never backed down or cowered before anyone. I can't see us starting now."

"You can believe I'm going to receive a whole lot of unsolicited advice."

The two men stood watching the activity in silence. Scott Ellerman and his father Henry walked over to them. Henry had raised this franchise from infancy and while there had been hard times before, nothing compared to the devastation he saw before him. The entire stadium was in ruin, but that was insignificant to the number of people killed and injured. Stadiums could be replaced, human lives could not.

As soon as the media saw the senior Ellerman arrive, they descended on him to get his reaction. He simply held up his hands and quieted their questions.

"I know you want my reaction to what has happened. My reaction doesn't matter. What matters are the feelings and emotions of all those who had friends and loved ones who came to this stadium to see two great teams play. Right now they're beside themselves because they have no way of knowing if their friend or loved one is counted among those who have died, those who are injured, or those who were fortunate enough to escape. While I know you have a job to report the news, perhaps it'd be to your advantage to do so with a little more compassion at this time."

With that, Henry Ellerman turned his attention to the rescue efforts. He walked over to a group of workers and not one reporter followed. After speaking to them for several minutes, he walked closer to the wreckage, bent down, and started moving some debris. Ray and Scott hurried over to their father.

"Dad," said Scott, "what're you doing?"

Henry turned around. He was holding in his hands the flag that once flew above the stadium.

"I want this flying," said Henry almost choking on his words. "I want those bastards who did this to know we're strong. We'll never be intimidated by the likes of them."

The *Chosen One* stood out on the small porch of his office and residence. In the open area he could see the men being put through their paces by his men. Each one of them wore a number pinned to the back of their uniform. It was the only way the *Chosen One* could identify who was who. He grabbed the clipboard and settled in to watch and make notes.

One thing he looked for was adherence to command. The men had to be able to listen and do exactly as they were told. After they had gone through the entire training multiple times, the *Chosen One* signaled for his men to begin the next phase. This was the most critical.

The men were given the order that they were not to react to anything that was said or done. They had to stay as still as statues regardless of any noise or anything that might startle them. When the instructions were finished, they were allowed several minutes to put themselves into a state of peace before the activity began.

The *Chosen One* watched sometimes shaking his head and other times nodding. With each one, he wrote comments and put symbols. He knew some of the men would progress faster than others and while there was a little leeway as far as time was concerned, all these men, plus more had to be ready within weeks. One thing was for certain, they would either be ready or die trying.

Helena put her bag on the table and started taking all the items she'd collected out of it. She put the papers found in the desk in a pile and started a second one. Next she straightened all those that had been crumpled into balls. In another pile she put the papers she found in Petru's office. All the other items and bits and pieces, she took out of the bag one at a time and placed them on the table. There were bottles of different liquids and gel-like substances with cryptic labels. There were thin pieces of filament, spools of ultra-thin shielded wire, rolls of tape, sheets of thin plastic and other assorted odds and ends.

Each of the objects in itself was curious, especially for mining. None of what was sitting on her table would be durable enough to be used in such an operation. Now she was intrigued about what went on behind those big doors and frosted glass windows. She always thought it was just a way of isolating the upper echelon of the company from the common workers and middle management. Now she wondered what the real purpose was.

Helena put her bag on the floor, picked up the remote for the television and turned it on. Then she sat in the chair, picked up a stack of papers, and began reading. Some of them contained nothing more than random letters and numbers along with gibberish. One by one she put the papers aside. There were papers with long lists of numbers that were obviously organized in a particular order, yet meant nothing to Helena. Whatever it was, she knew it had nothing to do with mining. Anything to do with the mining business, she knew inside and out, even the new research and inventions. This was a new part of Craustof's dealings she knew nothing about.

She stopped for a moment to watch the news reports. The scenes of the destruction of Heinz Field were being replayed. She watched and marveled that it had all been caught on film. She listened as they interviewed Ray Ellerman.

After the interview, the local newscaster gave just the headline about the event and the time it happened compensating for the time change in Romania. Helena continued watching until the end of the broadcast. Then she turned it off.

Helena picked up the stack of papers she found in Petru's office. Each of them caused her to have even more questions. What she was seeing on these pages was not a picture of the company she thought she worked for. She moved the paper to the done pile and found the envelope she was given by Mr. Mahayin. She turned it over, opened it, and took out the check. When she saw the amount on it, her mouth dropped and she stared at it for several seconds. Now she knew beyond a doubt something was wrong…radically wrong.

Chapter Ten

President Bartram met with members of his security council as soon as he returned to the White House. They immediately admonished him for visiting the site without first consulting them. He knew their concern really wasn't because he had done so; it was because they were left out of the loop for so long. Those types of concerns weren't important to him. He felt his presence at the site was infinitely important and chose to act on his own volition. He shook his head and marveled at people's agendas.

Ms. Harlan buzzed him to tell him Prime Minister Fairfield was calling. He picked up the phone.

"Prime Minister Fairfield, how are you?"

"President Bartram, I called to find out how you were. I've been following everything that's happened. Is there anything I can do?"

"Tell me who did it?"

"I wish I knew. Any leads?"

"Loads, just nothing definitive."

"Intelligence didn't pick up any rumblings about this happening?"

"Absolutely nothing. Everything was the usual things we've been dealing with almost every day. There was nothing that even remotely pointed to the fact this might occur," said President Bartram. "That's what has me so concerned. If it was one of the groups we've dealt with in the past or are hunting down, they'd be rubbing it in our faces that we were unable to stop them. There's nothing. Just silence. It has me wondering what's next."

"I thought about that too. I thought for sure someone would come forward," said Prime Minister Fairfield.

"We're following up on everything we have. It's going to take time, and time is something we don't have. We need to find them fast."

"If we find out anything, we'll let you know immediately. I know the other leaders will do the same. As I said before, if there's anything we can do, please let us know. Now is not the time to be insular. If we're going to find and defeat these people, we have to work together."

"I agree, and thank you."

Messages of shock and offers of help came in from around the world. President Bartram took as many calls as he could along with attempting to stay on track with all of the normal activities. He had learned long ago that the main aim of these people was to create fear and disruption. He would tolerate neither and knew he had to set the example.

Alex Fierson, Gloria McConnel, Lisa Tessle, and Levi Brandson, all part of President Bartram's staff walked into the office.

"Sorry for the interruption," said Alex, President Bartram's Chief of Staff.

"Don't be," said the President. "What can I do for you?"

"Mr. President, I've arranged for you to address the nation in an hour," said Gloria. "All of the networks have been informed as has the press corp."

"Good," he said. "I want this to be an address only. No questions. I don't want speculation from the press. And I don't want them explaining to the people what they think I said and spinning it for their own agendas."

Gina walked into the hallway from the garage. She was carrying large bags from the office supply store. She set them down, closed the door behind her, picked them up, walked through the kitchen, and into the dining room.

"What's in the bags?" asked Paul taking several from her.

"Necessities," she said.

She pulled out large presentation tablets, boxes of markers, pens, tape, tabs, reams of paper, colored cardstock, index cards, folders, and memory sticks.

"What's all this for?" asked Paul.

"We're going to need this."

"For what?"

"We have work to do. We have to find out who attacked the stadium?"

"Are you crazy?"

"Not in the least. You know we have to do this."

Paul shook his head. He knew when his wife got an idea stuck in her head, there was no talking her out of it.

"Look, all I want to do is help," she said. "I think we can do things easier and quicker than formal governments can."

"Can't it at least wait until after the wedding?"

"No. We still have four days until the wedding. We can do a lot in four days."

"Sweetheart, we really don't know much. How are we going to find them?"

"Well, when Hal and Tom get here, they'll have information. We can start there."

"Okay, but right now I want to go home, shower and get some clean clothes."

Farred Mahayin leaned back against the big, soft, comfy pillows. It wasn't often he had the time to enjoy some of life's little pleasures. For the past several months his days had been consumed with getting things ready. Everything had to be perfect. It was what was expected and he understood explicitly what anything less than perfect would mean. Right now, though, he needed to put that out of his mind. He needed time to relax and recharge.

Anna Roudalco sat on the bed, leaned over, and gave Farred a kiss. She brushed the hair from his forehead and kissed him again. He closed his eyes and tilted his head back. Anna knew how much he loved his neck kissed and she was more than willing to perform this little pleasure.

She ran her hands down his chest and followed them with kisses. As she got to his navel she stopped and kissed him again on his lips. He knew her tactics oh so well. No matter when or where, Anna loved to tease. It was part of the dance and he loved it.

He gently pushed her up and skillfully untied the sash on her robe. He ran his hands over her breasts and shoulders, slipping the robe off down her arms. His fingers glided over the soft skin of her back down to the top of the crack in her rear and then back up again to her neck.

"Don't toy with me, Farred," she said. "Remember how I make you scream?"

Farred pulled her across him onto the bed and grabbed her wrists pulling her arms above her head.

"Not tonight, my love."

The house was quiet when Michael came back into the living room. Everyone had gone home. He went downstairs and gathered everything that needed to be taken back to the kitchen. It was a minor disaster, but he soon had everything straightened and climbed the steps with an armload of dirty dishes and left over snacks to put away. When he had everything put away and the dishes in the dishwasher, he went into the living room and gathered what had been left in there. By the time Laura finished showering and dressing, Michael had the house straightened.

She came into the dining room and looked at everything on the table.

"Michael," she said. "What's all this on the table?"

"I don't know," he said walking into the room. "It was there when I started straightening this room."

"I guess we'll find out when everyone gets back," she said as she walked to the kitchen,

Laura poured a cup of coffee and sat at the kitchen table.

"What have you decided to do about Yamani?" she asked.

"I don't know," he said sitting down across from her. "The man wanted to take over the world by means of destruction if necessary. He has kidnapped people, tortured them, killed them, destroyed entire villages, psychologically brainwashed his followers. I could go on and on."

"I know."

"I look back at what he did to us and I'm still angry. I still would like my five minutes alone with him." Michael paused and shook his head. "Yet, even with all that, he kept his word. How does a man who's such a monster have such a redeeming quality that many men who're upstanding citizens don't possess."

"I don't know," said Laura. "The fact remains that he said he didn't do this and I believe him."

"Me, too. How do we go about proving it?"

"You and I can't do it ourselves. We need help. We have to tell them about it."

"That should go over really well," said Michael. "Hey guys, you know the guy we worked so hard against last year, well he called and he needs help. So, how about it? Everyone ready to help?"

"Yah, that'll go over really well."

In the short amount of time since Henry Ellerman arrived on the scene, he and his sons, with the help of volunteers, set a pole upright and raised the flag. Henry looked up at the colors waving in the breeze. To him it was more than a symbol of his country. To him it was a clear message to those who had orchestrated this, 'that we had not been defeated, that we were strong, and that we would triumph.'

Roger Gimshaw walked towards the small crowd with Jeffrey Easterly, the head of the FBI. They paused for a moment before speaking.

"Mr. Ellerman," said Gimshaw. "I'd like to introduce you to Jeffrey Easterly. He's the head of our organization."

"Good to meet you," said Ray Ellerman extending his hand.

"Good meeting you, too," said Easterly.

Ray Ellerman introduced both Agent Gimshaw and Director Easterly to his father and brother. The five men walked through a makeshift path onto the field. Not much of the structure remained. Large cranes had been brought in to secure remaining tall pieces of the structure in order to give the workers a safer environment. The site was devastating even for someone like Easterly who had always claimed to have 'seen it all.' One pie shaped section looked relatively untouched. Easterly pointed to it.

"That's where the four who were killed on the sidewalk on Liberty Avenue would've been sitting," said Gimshaw anticipating his question.

"Figures?" asked Easterly.

"Still too early to project," said Gimshaw. "People were taken from here by bus to Station Square on the other side of the Monongahela. We quickly set up to get all their information. Wounded were taken to area hospitals. Information still has to be gathered from them. The dead are there." Gimshaw pointed to PNC Park.

"How many hospitals?" asked Easterly.

"As many as we could utilize. Those with only minor injuries were sent further out. Those who were critical were kept close. As soon as we suspected, all hospitals were put on alert and told to increase staff. Communities were asked to send as many emergency vehicles as possible. General Anderson took charge as soon as he got here and brought in the military to help."

"Excellent work, Roger."

"I only wish we could've found out earlier. So many more lives could've been saved."

"I want to go to PNC Park and have a look around there," said Easterly.

When the two men walked onto the field at PNC Park, Jeff Easterly's mouth dropped. To him it was reminiscent of the scene after the battle of Atlanta in the movie "Gone with the Wind." Never had he seen anything like it. There were groups of two and three workers around the field, moving the coverings and trying to find any sort of identification. All personal effects were bagged, labeled and recorded. A tag was then affixed to the person identifying them. Afterwards, family members would have to be notified, and funeral directors would be able to collect the bodies.

"I want to see Liberty Avenue."

President Bartram walked to the podium to give his address.

"Good afternoon. As most of you are aware, there was an attack last evening on Heinz Field in Pittsburgh, Pennsylvania. This attack was premeditated, preplanned, and meant to take down the entire stadium leaving everyone dead. This was the most clandestine attack of its nature. There was not one inkling that anyone was planning such a horrific deed."

"As we have become accustomed, usually one group or another will claim responsibility for the act within hours. No one has claimed responsibility for this. There are no undercurrents, no conjectures as to who the perpetrator was. All we know is who didn't do it. Those groups have come forward and denied involvement."

"I was made aware of the potential crisis by General Anderson who had been called and was at the scene. I immediately notified my flight crew that I was leaving to go to Pittsburgh. During the time it took to tell my secret service and the helicopter to arrive, the bombs began going off. General Anderson immediately called to tell me and I informed him I'd be there as soon as possible."

"We touched down on the field of Heinz Field over an hour later. The devastation I witnessed was heart-wrenching. General Anderson had command of the field and the number of emergency personnel already on site was nothing short of a miracle. The military secured the site and aided in the evacuation of those who were uninjured onto buses to be taken safely to another destination. A seemingly never ending line of ambulances picked up the wounded and raced off to hospitals around the area. PNC Park, the home of the Pirates baseball team, is now being used as a morgue."

"I have no facts, no figures as to the number of persons who were in the stadium, the number of dead or injured or those who were lucky enough to walk away. Those numbers will come much later and I will not speculate. What I do know is that an investigation is already underway using the information we were able to gather from the scene. I give you my assurance that those who planned and executed this attack will be identified and brought to justice."

"When I got back to Washington, I heard from many of the world leaders. All of them had the following message. They told me that their thoughts and prayers and those of their citizens were with all of us. They offered whatever help we need. And they impressed upon me that this is not a time to be insular. This is a time to work together to find these people and bring them to justice, because an attack on one of us is an attack on all of us."

"Finally, I have a message for those who orchestrated this. I know you will see this message, whether you're watching now or will find it on the internet. You picked on the wrong country. You picked on the wrong city and you picked on the wrong team. We'll find you and it won't take us ten years to do it either. Get out your calendar and start crossing off the days, because your days are numbered."

With that President Bartram turned and walked out of the room.

Chapter Eleven

Farred Mahayin sat across the table from the man at a street café. It had been more than six months since he was in his presence. He had done everything he was asked to do and always stepped it up a notch.

"Did you get everything out of the building?" asked the man.

"Yes. Everything has been moved and is being stored in different locations."

"Did you destroy everything linking yourself to Craustof?"

"Yes, sir, everything,"

"And the other matter?"

"Taken care of as we discussed," said Mahayin.

"Good. I have your new assignment. You'll be overseeing operations at our new northeastern facility. We'll send for the equipment. We have some of your employees already hired. The others you'll hire from that district."

"Yes, sir."

"You're to have no contact with anyone from the other facility except those who will join you. Are we clear on that?"

"Yes, sir."

"You're on a strict time schedule," said the man. "We must take advantage of events that play into our hands."

"Yes, sir."

"Everything worked well. Our patience has been rewarded."

"Yes, sir. There's no reason to change anything in the execution."

"Not unless someone gets too close. You'll find the list in your desk as usual. The final decision will be made shortly."

"What about President Bartram's threat?"

"You let me worry about the President," said the man. "He's not going to get anywhere with his investigation. I can promise you that."

Everything had been put in the oven. Laura figured everyone would be back later to wait for Hal and Tom to arrive and would need something to eat. With dinner done, she took out her planner to look over her lists one more time. The wedding was only days away. It was so close she could almost smell the flowers in the church.

She took a deep breath. Yamani's call was something she never expected. She thought he was gone; thought their lives were free of him forever. Her mind began racing. What if something happened and the wedding didn't take place. Would she and Michael ever be able to get married or would something always come up and stop them.

Michael walked up behind her and put his arms around her waist. She put her head back against his shoulder and looked up at him.

"What's that look for?" he asked.

She shrugged her shoulders.

"Laura, I've known you long enough to know your shrug means something."

"Nothing, really."

"What're you doing with that list out?"

"Just going over it one last time."

"I thought you and the girls did that Monday night."

"We did. I just want to make sure it's all done."

"Sweetheart," he said, "there's nothing going to keep me from marrying you on Saturday."

Laura smiled. She closed the planner and turned around to face him.

"I think things are going to get crazy around here," she said.

"Laura, when aren't things crazy around here? It's just a constant state of life for us."

"You're so right," she said laughing. "Just promise me no matter what we're in the middle of, we'll get married Saturday."

"I promise."

He reached down and gave her a kiss and the doorbell rang. Michael answered it.

Gina and Paul came in and Gina went immediately to the dining room. She started opening the packages and taking all the supplies out.

"So you're the one who brought all this in," said Michael.

"Yes," said Gina.

"May I ask why?"

"We have to find out who blew up that stadium."

"What?"

"You heard me. We have to find out who blew up that stadium."

"Gina, President Bartram already started the investigation."

Gina stopped, put her hands on her hips and looked at him.

"Come on, Michael by the time it gets through all that bureaucracy do you really think they're going to find who did this? I don't. Governments don't exactly have a great track record when it comes to things like this. If it's going to be solved, it's going to have to be done by some other party and I can't think of any other group better suited than us."

"I feel a headache coming on," said Paul.

"You know I'm right," she said. "What government would've been able to do what we did and get both you and Laura back? None of them."

"She has a point," said Paul looking at Michael.

"I know and I'm eternally grateful," said Michael.

"As far as the government is concerned, five months from now they'll still be arguing about who did it and why they didn't know the perpetrators were going to do it."

Laura walked in and looked at the table with everything laid out on it. It reminded her of the day they decided it was up to them to get Michael back. As convicted as Gina was then, Laura knew she couldn't wait to begin working to find those responsible for the bombing. She wondered if Gina would be able to sell the idea to the others. Laura smiled.

"So you think we can do this?" asked Laura.

"Yah," said Gina. "I'm sure of it."

"We don't have much to go on," said Michael.

"That'll all change when Hal and Tom get here," said Gina unfolding several sheets of paper filled with writing. "I have a few questions I want to ask them."

No matter what Helena looked at concerning Craustof, it in no way resembled the company she knew. What she had found were bits and pieces of a puzzle; a puzzle she needed to solve. There were names, codes, phone numbers, directions, commands and maps. She was certain none of this was meant to be found. It was meant to be destroyed before the place was vacated. The only thing that bothered her was why Mahayin purposely threw the papers in the trash in Petru's office.

Helena picked up that set of papers and started reading through them again. Similar coding appeared; words that made no sense in their own context. Some things actually looked as though a preschooler had written them in their own language. Yet there were numbers and words that kept repeating. One by one she put the papers neatly in a pile. She stared at the next page, a chart of sorts with names, numbers, emails, and times. It went on for pages. None of the names were familiar to her nor were the emails or numbers. She looked carefully at the times, they were all minutes apart. She went back to the first page. *Email a copy of the presentation to each of the following. AFTER you have finished emailing ALL of them, call each and leave a message to check their email. Begin each call EXACTLY at the time listed. Make the message short. Do not be late or early for any call.* She read it over twice, trying to absorb what was being conveyed.

Helena put down all the papers, looked at the piles on the table and then at the check from Mahayin. A chill went up her spine and an unexplained sense of fear pervaded her. Suddenly, she didn't feel safe. She got up and checked the locks on the door and every one of the windows. She looked at the clock. She had plenty of time to get to the bank. She collected the papers and took them into the bedroom. She slid open the closet door and took out two suitcases.

It didn't take long for Helena to pack her clothes. She started taking pictures from the dresser, but stopped.

"Helena, stop!" she said aloud. "You can't do this. It has to look like you're going on vacation. You can't take everything with you."

She took a deep breath and then divided the papers between the suitcases. She checked the timers on the lights then picked up the suitcases and moved them into the hall by the door. The refrigerator was next. The last thing she wanted to do was come back to spoiled milk, fuzzy leftovers, and smelly garbage. All that taken care of, she put the check in her purse, took one last look in all the rooms, picked up her suitcases, and walked out.

Edgar Reinholdt sat at his desk, phone in hand. He counted the rings until he heard Michael answer.

"Edgar, how are you?" asked Michael.

"I'm doing well," said Edgar. "How are you?"

"Busy, getting ready for the wedding. You're still coming aren't you?"

"Of course. Gabrielle has been trying to decide what to wear for weeks. This has given her an excuse to shop almost every day."

"That's great," said Michael laughing. "When are you getting here?"

"That's what I wanted to talk to you about. We hadn't planned on getting there until Friday, but something's come up and I need to meet with you."

"Business or pleasure."

"Business."

"When were you thinking of coming?"

"As soon as possible," said Edgar. "Michael, this is urgent."

"Call me when you have your arrival details and we'll get you at the airport. We'll meet with you as soon as you get here."

"Thanks, Michael. Talk to you soon."

Edgar walked down the hall to Albert's office and walked in.

"I got your message," said Edgar taking a seat in front of Albert's desk. "What do you have?"

"This," said Albert handing him a sheet of paper.

Edgar looked at it and read the short paragraph that was contained. He looked up at Albert.

"Have you followed up on this?' he asked.

"Yes. We're trying to find out who's been taking the materials out of the facility."

"Do you have any ideas?"

"I've narrowed it down to two. I'm going to need some more time. I need to be able to go over those recordings and then somehow be able to catch either one or both taking things. We thought it was just the information they were taking. Who would've thought they were building prototypes."

Edgar shook his head.

"This puts a whole new light on things. I'm leaving as soon as possible for Paris to meet with Global. You find anything else, you know how to reach me."

Helena endorsed the back of the check in front of the teller.

"I see you got a bonus from Mr. Mahayin also," said Morana. "How do you want this?"

"Cash," said Helena. "It's also my vacation pay."

"Where are you going?"

"I'm going to the Bahamas to just relax on the beach."

"I've always wanted to do that. Just sit on the beach sipping a drink like you see in the pictures."

"With no one to bother you," said Helena

"What a nice thought. I hope you have a great vacation. I need to go get this for you."

Morana came back and counted out the money for Helena and then gave her the receipt. Helena separated the money putting some in her pockets and the rest at the bottom of her purse.

She got into her car, drove to the shopping area, and pulled into a parking spot. She reached in her pocket and pulled out the money. She took the rest of the money from her purse, counted it, and put it into four piles. She put money back into her purse and then unzipped her computer bag and placed money into the zippered pocked inside. Then she got out of the car and opened the trunk. She hid the other two piles in the suitcases. As she got back into her car she saw a man standing beside a bright red Ferrari. She always dreamed of owning one. She smiled, started the car and pulled out of the lot.

Helena drove to a small town and parked in front of the copy center. She went inside and printed out directions. She looked over the directions on the way back to her car. Down the street a few spaces was a bright red Ferrari. Helena got into her car and put the key in the ignition. She shook her head.

"Two in one day," she said aloud. "Amazing."

President Bartram walked along the walkway outside the White House. He couldn't shake the feeling of betrayal he was experiencing. He couldn't quite explain it, but this latest attack seemed much more than a terroristic attack. It felt personal. There was more to this than a blatant attack against the United States.

He knew whoever was behind this was protected behind layers of concealment each of which would result in a dead end. How to approach this was something that would take a great deal of thought. While he trusted those in his cabinet, some of those in other capacities worried him. He wasn't sure about their loyalty.

He had learned much over the past year, enough to open his eyes on the many different ways of rectifying a situation. During this time, he and other world leaders had become closer, forming a true camaraderie and not just a superficial relationship for the sake of photo opportunities. No one outside of their circle would ever fully understand how close the world came to total obliteration.

Now he was certain this could potentially be one of those times again. Whether total annihilation was their ultimate goal or not, he knew their actions were designed to cripple a country and its citizens. He couldn't allow that to happen. No matter how uneasy he felt, he had to convey to the people that he was capable of taking care of the situation.

Sometimes being the leader was a lonely position. He had learned that much of what he thought needed to stay within himself. There had been presidents and other leaders who had their words come back to haunt them when those who had been seemingly loyal turned those words against them for political and monetary gain.

He knew Prime Minister Fairfield was right. Now was not the time to be insular. This could happen anywhere and the more people involved in trying to find these perpetrators, the better. He also knew this wouldn't be a favorable stance to take no matter who the leader was or the country. There were those who felt that their country was doing little more than intruding in another country's affairs and had no business doing so.

Outwardly, he knew he had to follow all the proper channels, but his gut instinct was to take the nonconventional route that achieved results in a short span of time. The inroads he had made during that crisis might once again be utilized. He knew beyond a doubt that those who had been privy to what was happening then, were just as loyal now as they had been.

He replayed in his mind the conversation he had with Edgar Reinholdt that day when Yamani was launching missiles. He smiled when he thought about cool, calm Edgar letting loose and telling him exactly what he thought. Every word came back as though he was hearing it for the first time.

"I know from a political standpoint how difficult this is for you to handle, but that, Mr. President, is your job. Please understand that this situation is impacting not only on your political arena, but the business of two corporations and the personal lives of many individuals. I know you and the others feel you have a lot riding on this, namely your re-elections. Well for some of us it's our entire existence. When you think about that, Mr. President, you'll understand that I won't jeopardize anything I'm involved in."

President Bartram shook his head and smiled. As much as he hated to admit it, what Edgar said was true. There was so much work to be done and one term never seemed like enough time.

Today was not much different than a year ago. There were still problems to solve domestically and the American people may be distracted by this attack, but they wouldn't forget what needed to be done. They would expect the problems at home to be solved and the terrorists responsible for the attacks brought to justice.

He needed those working on domestic problems to stay focused and deliver solutions. He knew whoever was responsible for the attack on the stadium wanted the entire government to switch gears and become preoccupied with finding them. That wasn't going to happen and he intended to make it clear to all those in Washington. It was going to be business as usual and he was going to also expect that from the rest of the nation.

Pittsburgh was going to need special attention. He was going to make sure it got it. It was time that Washington showed it was able to do things without getting bogged down in committee.

As he continued walking he made mental notes of who he wanted to meet with and what the reason was. When he got back to his office he immediately made his to-do list. It wasn't long before Lisa Tessle his Personal Assistant and Alex Fierson his Chief of Staff came into the office carrying the remainder of the agenda.

"I'll be with you in one minute," said President Bartram. "I just need to finish this."

Lisa and Alex sat in chairs in front of the desk. President Bartram looked up as soon as he finished.

"Now, where are we in regards to the agenda?" he asked.

"Pretty much, it's a wash today," said Lisa. "I called and rescheduled most of the meetings. Whatever wasn't pressing, I asked for some time and have placed reminders in my memos to get back to them late next week."

"Good. Alex, I want you to find the Pennsylvania delegation and I want a meeting with them immediately."

"Yes, sir. What time do you want this meeting?"

"Within the hour, if possible."

Alex got up out of his chair and walked out.

"I want to meet with all committee heads in two hours and the Security Council in three."

"Are you sure you want to cut things that tight?" asked Lisa.

"These aren't meetings where anything will be up for discussion. This is going to be a meeting where they listen and then go and do what I want. I don't have time for discussions right now."

"Yes, sir. Anything else?"

"I want to meet with the NFL Commissioner and the Owners tomorrow at one o'clock in Pittsburgh."

"Yes, sir."

Helena's mind wandered onto all sorts of topics. She ran scenarios about being chased and how she'd hide from her would be attackers. Somehow, she tried to tell herself she was letting her mind run away with her. After all, she worked for Mahayin and Craustof for the past ten years and never had any doubts about the company…until now.

She exited the road. She always stopped at this point every time she made the Bucharest to Frankfurt run. About five years ago, it became her job to be a courier of sorts. She'd come to Frankfurt, meet with a man named Masun at the same hotel every time, stay the night, and return to Bucharest.

Here she'd get gas and something to eat before continuing. She sat at the table in the corner and took out the notebook she kept in her purse. She looked over the notes she had made the night before. There were a lot of questions that needed answered and she knew she wasn't thinking clearly enough to come up with those answers. She took a few more bites of her sandwich and wrapped the rest. She refilled her coffee and went back to her car. She couldn't seem to shake the ominous feeling.

The wind blew as she opened the door and she turned her head to get the hair out of her face. She pushed it back with her left hand and as she did she spied a red Ferrari parked at the end of the row. Helena hurried, unlocked her door and quickly got in the car. She started it and looked to her right. There was another way out of the parking lot around the back of the building where the truckers parked. She backed the car out of its space and cautiously went back until she could make the turn to get on that road. She turned right at the end of the road and then went up several blocks before she turned left to weave her way back to the highway.

Now, she was sure someone was watching her and the sooner she could get to her destination, the better. She didn't even want to make a call to her friend from her phone because she didn't want them to know where she was going.

"You know you're letting your imagination get the better of you," she said to herself.

But even hearing those words from her own mouth didn't make her feel any less apprehensive. She knew whoever was following her would be only a few miles behind her. Her original plan was to stop at that same hotel in Frankfurt, but now she was having second thoughts. The more she thought about it, the more certain she was that it wasn't a good idea. Instead, she thought she should go straight through Frankfurt and then find a nice hotel somewhere on the second stretch.

Morana looked at her message again and then turned down the street that led to the park. She reduced her speed when she entered the park. Children were playing in the playgrounds and on the fields. She remembered coming here as a child and how much fun it was to play with all sorts of new friends. Morana read the signs on the groves looking for the one that signaled the next turn. As she got further away from the main road, the number of people dwindled. Two more turns and she pulled her car into the parking lot.

Mahayin sat on a picnic table and motioned to Morana. She smiled and walked towards him. He got down from the table and stood waiting until she joined him.

"Good to see you, Morana," he said. "It's a great time for a walk, isn't it?"

"It is," said Morana. "I saw a lot of people walking along the main road and path."

"I prefer places that aren't so crowded. Shall we?"

He gestured to a path that led along the tree line. Morana joined him and they walked a while just talking about trees, flowers, and things they did as children.

"Did you bring the information I asked for?" asked Mahayin.

"I did," said Morana. "Josep cashed his check and deposited it. He's staying home. He said this was unexpected and he already promised his friend he would help him with some outdoor work. Helena cashed her check and took it all in cash. She said she's going on a vacation. She's going to the Bahamas. Petru cashed his check and put it in three different accounts and also took some in cash. He had me exchange some for U.S. currency."

Morana reached in her pocket and took out a piece of paper and handed it to Mahayin.

"These are their account numbers and card numbers that are attached to each account. I included Helena's even though she took it all in cash. She may change her mind and deposit it."

"Excellent," said Mahayin. "You have done an outstanding job."

"Thank you," said Morana.

She looked at her watch.

"Do you need anything else? I have to meet some people soon and I want to get home and freshen up first."

"No, you've given me everything I need. By all means, you can go. I just want to put this info into my phone in case I lose the paper. I'll see you next time I come into the bank."

Morana turned and walked back up the path. Mahayin waited a moment and walked through the trees. He walked briskly until he had successfully overtaken her. As he watched her approach closer on the path, he screwed the silencer on the gun. He waited for the most opportune moment and fired.

Chapter Twelve

Edgar greeted everyone in the conference room. They had become close during the time when Michael and Laura had been held hostage by Yamani and his followers.

"I don't know exactly where to begin," he said taking his seat. "Once again we've discovered that information is being taken from us somehow. This time it isn't that we caught them doing it, rather we found evidence of our inventions and proprietary work being used in other industries far removed from our general purpose."

"When we get so far along in our research and we're certain it's going to result in something new and different, we apply for the patent. This keeps any of our competitors from trying to steal what we have and begin the process themselves. The plans for several of those research projects have been stolen and have made their way into Romania to a company called Craustof Technologies. From what we were able to find out, they deal in technology used in mining."

"It took us weeks to trace it. We ran into one dead end after another and had to find new starting places. It's happening right under our noses, but this time it's even more invasive. Before I left, Albert Paxton showed me this," said Edgar.

Edgar handed a small drive to Robert and waited until the first picture was projected. Then he walked up to the wall and began talking and pointed to areas.

"This is the prototype being built for the project," he said indicating the one in the foreground. "Over here, another one is being built step by step along with the first. If you look closely you can barely make out numbers on tiny stickers. On the table is a piece of paper with writing. I'd bet everything I own it has the instructions for constructing the prototype."

"Once Albert found this one, he immediately had an inventory done of components. That second document shows what he found. As you can see, this number shows the number of parts before we made the prototype. This column shows how many were used to make the device. The next shows how many there actually are left and the last column shows how many have been stolen."

"How did they get their hands on these parts?" asked Paul.

"I don't know," said Edgar shaking his head. "Albert, Franz, and Ivan are trying to track everything, but the closer we seem to get, the further away we are."

"Is this everything?" asked Henri.

"No," said Edgar, "I wish it was. I received an email from President Bartram with this picture. He wanted to know if I knew who had developed this next component. We developed it. We have a patent pending for it. It's not even on the market. Yet…" he paused and took a deep breath, "it was used in the attack on Heinz Field."

Hal walked into the dining room and looked at the assortment of office supplies on the table. It was a striking contrast to the way the house looked the last time he was there. He looked around and envisioned all of the stacks of papers, the charts on the walls and the pictures of Yamani displayed one after the other on the sideboard. Laura walked into the room and stood by the table.

"I bet you're wondering what this is all about," she said.

"Yes," said Hal, "I'm a little curious."

"Well, Gina seems to think, and I agree, that we need to find who's behind these attacks. We can't afford to wait around for another ten years while we rely on intelligence reports."

Hal looked down, shook his head, and smiled.

"Well intelligence certainly didn't give us a clue that anyone was considering blowing up Heinz Field," said Hal. "There wasn't even a rumble."

"If we wait for intelligence, half the world could lay in ruin."

"How does she intend to do this?"

"She's hoping you may be able to answer some of her questions and shed some light on what happened," said Laura. "This isn't just some isolated event. I think they're going to strike again and they're going to strike again quickly."

"I hope to God you're wrong," said Hal, but deep down he had to admit he was thinking the same thing.

Tom walked into the room, took a look at the items on the table and pointed to them.

"Gina?" he asked.

Laura laughed.

"She intends to find them, doesn't she?"

"Yes," said Laura. "That's exactly what she intends to do. She should be back soon. They had to meet with Edgar."

"I figured that was who Bartram was referring to," said Tom.

Laura looked from one to the other.

"The devices used to detonate the bombs were state of the art," said Hal. "Bartram suggested pictures of the components be emailed to an expert. That expert had to have been Edgar."

"Michael received a frantic call from Edgar asking for an emergency meeting," said Laura. She took a deep breath and looked at both men. "Well, I don't think there's any escaping this. As Gina said, 'we have to do it.'"

True to his word, President Bartram kept each meeting to under an hour. At the beginning of each one, he prefaced it by telling all present that it was going to be a one-sided meeting. He was going to talk and they were going to do as they were told. Now was not the time to put anything up for discussion. He knew those types of discussions would only result in wasted time.

The first two groups, the Pennsylvania delegation and the committee heads were by far the most cooperative. When it came to the Security Council, however, that was another story. More than once he had to stop and put his hand up to silence one of them. He told them he felt as though this was only the beginning and they had better brace themselves for the barrage that was most likely forthcoming.

Once those meetings were completed, President Bartram went to the Oval office. Everything that could be done by those in Washington was being done. The FBI Director, Jeff Easterly was on site in Pittsburgh now and the CIA Director, John Hanke was out of the country at the present time.

"Ms. Harlan, see if you can track down Edgar Reinholdt. I'd like to speak with him at his earliest convenience."

"Yes, sir."

President Bartram took a piece of paper and began making notes. Ideally, he'd like to meet with all those who worked to get Michael Braedon and Laura Darmer back from Yamani. He knew the reason why they had so much success was they were free to move without government approval. Even as clandestine as the FBI and CIA were, they still had to move within the confines of the government. He knew what the group had been able to accomplish in several months would've taken years with the red tape. He wrote his wish list on the paper. Edgar would have to be the liaison between them, if he'd consent to do it.

Ms. Harlan walked in.

"Mr. Reinholdt's on the phone for you."

"Thank you," said President Bartram picking up the phone. "Mr. Reinholdt, how are you doing?"

"I'm fine, Mr. President. How are you?"

"I was wondering if you had received that information."

"Yes, I have."

"Are you able to shed some light on it?"

"As a matter of fact, I can."

"Mr. Reinholdt, I know you're incredibly busy, but it's of the utmost urgency that I meet with you. I was wondering how soon that might happen."

"Mr. President, tell me where and when and I'll be there."

"Tomorrow I'm meeting with the Commissioner and the owners of the NFL at one o'clock in Pittsburgh."

"Do you have to leave immediately after?"

"No."

"What if we meet afterwards.

"I'll send you the details. Oh and Mr. Reinholdt, if you have the chance to speak to Mr. Braedon, tell him I look forward to talking to him again about our project in greater depth."

"I'll make certain I tell him. I'll see you tomorrow afternoon, Mr. President."

Edgar put down the phone and returned to the dining room. All of the supplies had been transferred from the table to the sideboards and platters for dinner were placed in the center. Edgar sat down next to Gabrielle.

"I'm sorry," he said. "It was President Bartram. He wants to meet with me tomorrow in Pittsburgh."

"He's going back to Pittsburgh?" asked Hal. "Why?"

"He's meeting with the Commissioner and the team owners," said Edgar.

"Why does he want to meet with you?" asked Michael.

"He wants to discuss the components and what I know," said Edgar. "Michael, the President said that he's looking forward to talking to you again about your project in greater depth."

"What project?" asked Michael.

"I don't know. That's all he said. I assumed you were working on a consult with him."

"No. I haven't spoken to President Bartram since right after he addressed the joint session."

"I think he wants to talk to you about this," said Gina. "I think he wants us to find these people."

Paul shook his head and smiled. He knew once his wife got an idea, she would somehow make everything, no matter how minor, refer back to it. It was her ability to seemingly be so illogically logical that made him love her so.

"Where are you getting this?" asked Pierre.

"Okay, hear me out. How long did it take them to find Bin Laden, ten years? He doesn't have ten years to waste trying to find these people. In ten years they could obliterate a hell of a lot of people and landmarks. Think about it. If he goes the conventional route, which he will because it'll be visible to the people of the U.S. and the world that he's doing something, it'll get bogged down in all the government red tape. If he asks us to do it, we can move without those confines and use methods that would take months and years to get approved through committee. Look at the magazine spread. How long do you think it would've taken to get that moving if it was tied up with government forces? I'll tell you. We'd still be waiting. Michael, I'm no mind reader, but I think President Bartram expects to meet with you tomorrow along with Edgar."

Laura looked at Michael and nodded her head.

"I think she's right," said Laura. "You need to go. Just make sure you're back by Saturday."

Afmad Yamani sat at the kitchen table. There were papers in neat piles all over the table top. He made notes in his tattered notebook. It was his constant companion now. When he had been in Iraq, he had hidden it well amid other books that no one ever touched. It had been over a year since everything came tumbling down. He considered himself blest to have avoided capture. He was safe, for the time being, and he was able to run everything from the comfort of his home. He was grateful for the program his followers had obtained from Edgar Reinholdt that allowed him to still keep in contact with his people without being traced.

His core group of faithful; those he trusted without question, were his eyes and ears throughout the world. He relied on them to keep him updated on everything that was happening, everything that was said, and any rumors related to him and the Cause.

In front of him was a map of the world. On it he had drawn small red circles indicating all the places that had been rumored to be on the "list." He went through all the messages he had received and checked to make sure he hadn't missed any locations. Although he had all this information, he still didn't have dates and times. Those were not part of the knowledge they were able to intercept.

Maranissa walked back into the kitchen. She smiled at her husband. She knew how much disappointment he had suffered at the end of their time in Iraq, but she was glad to finally have some sense of normalcy to their lives. They had blended well into the community and she had made new friends, something she had not had before. She had kept track of what was happening with Laura through what was reported in the newspapers and magazines.

"The wedding is this Saturday," she said.

"Yes, I know," said Yamani. "You would like to go, would you not?"

"Yes," said Maranissa smiling. "I would like to see them get married."

"Perhaps I can arrange for you to be there."

"What about you?'

"With the amount of media that will be there, it would not be good for me. Let me see what I can do."

"How is your work coming?"

"I have so much information, but not everything I need. There are so few I can trust absolutely, that the process is slow."

"Do not fret, my love," she said touching his hand. "You will have all you need. The Divine One will see to it."

Yamani smiled.

Helena walked up to the desk at the hotel.

"Ms. Rudarsnyan, how nice to have you back again," said the clerk. "I don't remember seeing a reservation for you."

"This was a spur of the moment decision," said Helena. "Is it possible for me to get a room?"

"Of course," he said. "The one you always stay in is available."

"Great," she said.

"How long will you be with us?"

"Just until morning. I'd like to just pay for everything now."

"Very good," he said and he gave her a receipt. "Just leave the key on the dresser as you always do. Hope you have a nice stay."

"Thank you."

Helena went up to the fourth floor and opened the door. She put the key on the dresser and then walked out of the room and closed the door. She exited the building, got in her car and started to drive. She looked around and saw no sign of the red Ferrari. She drove through several streets and made her way back to the main highway. As she was making her approach, she spotted the red Ferrari exiting to go into Frankfurt. She knew he didn't see her and she was grateful.

She continued driving until she had gone quite a distance, then exited the highway and looked for a hotel for the night.

Helena opened the door to the office and walked up to the front desk. The clerk looked up.

"Good evening," said the clerk.

"Good evening," said Helena. "I'd like to get a room for the night."

"Certainly," said the clerk. "Could you please fill this out?"

Helena filled out only the parts required and signed it. She paid in cash and asked for a six o'clock call. She planned on getting on the road early.

Once in her room, she made sure the door was locked, opened a suitcase, and took out clothes. She decided to take a shower now, so she wouldn't be delayed in the morning.

After she finished her shower, she went through her suitcases and made sure the money and papers were well secured. She moved the money in her computer case to a different compartment. As soon as she had everything done, she crawled into bed and was asleep in no time.

Petru, Sorina, Lucian, and Grigore stood in line to get a picture with Mickey Mouse. Lucian and Grigore leaned over to the right to see Mickey. The people in front of them moved forward, and then it was their turn. They ran up to Mickey, hugged him, turned around, and had their picture taken. When they were done, they jumped and skipped back to their parents.

They walked over and sat at a table in a food court. They could see the monorail train above them, going through the building.

"Sit here," said Sorina, "and I'm going to get us something to eat."

"Are we going to the park?" asked Grigore.

"Tomorrow," said Petru. "Tonight, we're going to get a good night's sleep so we can have enough energy to be at the park all day."

"Yay!" the boys screamed and jumped up and down.

Sorina smiled and shook her head.

Petru pulled out a book showing the rides from the park.

"What do you want to ride?"

"I want to ride this," said Lucian pointing to the Mad Hatter Ride.

"Can we go on this?" asked Grigore pointing to Peter Pan.

"Whatever you want," said Petru.

He and the boys went through the book and as they picked out rides, he found them on the map and starred them. By the time they finished, Sorina was back. She handed a tray to Petru and a cast member handed another tray to her.

"Thank you," said Sorina.

"You're welcome," said the girl.

Sorina spread napkins out before the two boys and placed their food on it.

"Can we stay and watch the fireworks?" asked Grigore.

"Of course we can," said Sorina.

"We decided which rides we're going on tomorrow," said Lucian.

"All of them," said Petru pointing at the map.

Once dinner was finished, Hal and Tom began to tell the story of what really happened in Pittsburgh Monday night. Gina started making notes while they talked. Some of the questions she had for the two of them now had multiple parts. Once they were finished, Hal took out his wallet and took out a small card Sam had given him. He got up and walked over to Robert.

"Sam, the photographer, took some shots for me. I asked him not to show them to anyone. He gave me the card that night."

Robert got up and picked up Laura's laptop. He put the card in and pulled off the pictures. What he saw made his jaw drop.

"You have to be kidding me!" said Robert looking at Hal.

"It's no joke," said Hal. "When I saw it, I was as surprised as you are."

"What are you talking about?" asked Gwen.

Michael put the projector on the table and handed the cable to Robert.

"May as well get this set up," said Michael.

As Robert projected the pictures, Hal described what they were seeing. As Robert changed the picture there was a collective gasp from the group.

"He was my contact," said Hal. "I didn't notice the tattoo until Sam had taken this picture. It definitely sent a chill up my spine."

"If he's connected with this," said Jean, "things are going to get critical quickly."

"He's not," said Michael.

"What?" asked Jean.

"I said he's not."

"How do you know that?"

"He told me."

"He told you!" said Jean. "How? When?"

"The morning after the attack on Heinz Field," said Michael. "He sent a message asking to speak to me. He said it was urgent. He told me there were those who'd been in his organization who were determined to see to it that he'd be blamed for this attack and all the ones that'll be happening. He asked for help."

"You're not serious about helping him, are you?" asked Jacques.

"After what he did to you and Laura!" said Angelique.

"How do you know he's even telling the truth?" asked Margo.

"Everything you're saying, I've thought about," said Michael, "and so has Laura. The fact remains he always kept his word. He never lied to us."

"That's true," said Pierre, "but it doesn't erase all the horrible things he did."

"No, it doesn't," said Michael, "and it never will."

"So are we going to help him?" asked Gina.

"Gina!" said Paul.

"Listen, I'd rather have that man with us than against us," she said, "or have you forgotten how formidable he can be."

"No I haven't forgotten," said Paul. "I don't know." He paused for a moment. "Michael, whatever you decide to do, I'm with you."

As he looked around the others were nodding their heads.

"That went better than I thought," said Laura.

Chapter Thirteen

The new building was designed to be identical to the one in Romania. It felt like home. Farred Mahayin sat at his desk organizing everything just the way he liked it. Soon the quiet would give way to the loud noises of set up. It had been ten years since the facility in Romania had opened. This opening would go much smoother this time.

He looked over copies of the floor plans and made notes and changes. He wanted everything the way he was used to having it. This was going to be an extremely hectic and crucial time and the last thing he wanted to have to do was fumble around trying to find who or what he needed.

In this business, timing was everything and the man would tolerate no excuse for not being ready. Time and again Mahayin had proven himself reliable. That was how he was able to move up in the ranks to run everything from this end.

On the calendar on his desk, multicolored highlighted dates brought quick attention to the operation to be carried out. The map on the wall showed locations with color coordinated markings. Mahayin opened the bottom desk drawer and took out a binder. He leafed through the pictures and the details of each site. The undertaking was unlike anything ever before tried in the history of the world.

This was his time to make his mark on history. Right now, no one could know it was his genius that was orchestrating it all. He was sure the man thought he was in charge, but Mahayin knew differently. Time would show who the mastermind was. In due time, the world would hear the name Farred Mahayin and cower in fear.

When the phone rang, Helena answered it. She'd been up for about fifteen minutes and was dressed and ready to go. She walked out to the desk and handed over her key.

"I hope you slept well," said the clerk.

"Very well," said Helena.

"Please help yourself to breakfast. It's set up in the room there," said the clerk gesturing to his right.

"That's very nice," said Helena, "but I have to get going."

"At least take something with you."

"Thank you."

Helena walked into the room. She poured a cup of coffee and added cream and sugar. She fixed a bagel and wrapped it. Then she wrapped a pastry and took an apple. She opened her purse, put everything in it except the coffee, and went out to her car.

She could barely press the button on her automatic opener to release the trunk lock. As soon as it raised, she lifted both suitcases into the trunk and closed it. She unlocked the car doors, put the computer case on the floor in the back, and got in. After locking the doors, she took the bagel, pastry, and apple out of her purse, and then started the car.

The first thing she needed to do was get gas. If she followed the same plan as yesterday and only stopped when she needed gas, she'd arrive by early evening.

The island breeze and the sound of the ocean was a relaxing change to the events that had transpired only days prior. John Hanke, the head of the CIA, took his seat at a table.

"Gentlemen and ladies," he said, "I'm glad you could join me."

The group smiled and laughed. Each of them was well aware that this was not an invitation one could decline. They'd been called away from whatever business they found pressing to attend.

"The incidents that happened in Pittsburgh have the entire nation on edge," said Hanke. "The major question being asked is why intelligence didn't pick up on this. The President knows if there had been any rumblings they would've been contained in the daily briefing. I cannot impress upon you the importance of finding as much as possible about the perpetrators. Whatever you find, you're to report directly to me, no one else. Is that understood?"

There were mumblings of the automatic 'yes, sir' and heads nodded in agreement.

"What do we know about the incident that happened in Pittsburgh?" asked Clayton Pearse.

"Not a whole lot," said Hanke, "other than they were trying to bring down the whole stadium. It's possible it's a diversion to make us change what we're doing and go on a wild goose chase. Anything's possible."

"I got the idea that the feeling is this organization might strike again," said Harrison.

"There's nothing to indicate other attacks are planned," said Hanke.

"How do you know?" asked Whitler. "We don't even know who did this."

"I've been around long enough to recognize a group that's just trying to make a name for itself with a big splash," said Hanke.

"So you think this group was utilizing all its resources on this one hit?" asked Whitler.

"I'd say yes," said Hanke.

"Then I don't understand why they're not taking credit for what they did," said Harrison.

"People who take down stadiums aren't in their right minds," said Hanke, "and we can't possibly figure out how that type of mind works. Well, enough of that. Let's get on with this meeting."

The room selected for the Presidential meetings was larger than the previous one because of the number of attendees. President Bartram arrived well before his scheduled first appointment and sat at the table enjoying a cup of coffee and some peace and solitude. These moments were few and far between. He had a full day planned and he hoped to be closer to his goal by the end of the meetings. What began as just one meeting between him and the commissioner and owners of the NFL teams, turned into four meetings, all of which were extremely important in their own right.

General Anderson arrived early for the meeting. He entered the room with the commanding presence as he did wherever he went.

"General Anderson, so good of you to meet me this morning," said President Bartram getting up to greet him.

"My pleasure, Mr. President."

"There's coffee if you'd like any," said the President gesturing to the sideboard.

General Anderson poured a cup of coffee and then sat down at the table.

"What can I do for you?" asked General Anderson.

"I need to ask you a few things and run some things by you."

General Anderson took a sip of coffee and nodded towards the President.

"Something's bothered me from the moment I heard about the attack," said President Bartram. "For the life of me, I can't fathom how there couldn't have been some indication an attack of that nature would be coming."

"I agree. I would've expected something to have been reported."

"There was nothing in the intelligence briefings from Mr. Hanke's agency. That has me concerned."

"And well it should."

"General Anderson, I don't trust that man. I never have. I have no concrete reason for this feeling of distrust, just a feeling in my gut."

"There are times when I find my gut is all I need to use to make a decision. You're a good judge of character."

"If I put all my faith in him and the agency, I can almost be certain this'll blow up in my face."

"Then you have to go with that feeling. My question is how're you going to bypass him?"

"Oh I intend to use the agency. I just don't intend to put my faith in it. That's the other reason I asked you to come here. I have the utmost faith in Jeff Easterly and I know he can handle things here."

"Easterly's a good guy. I've known him for a long time. If he can find out who did this, he will."

"Unfortunately, much of this is not within his jurisdiction," said President Bartram. "If I was working with him, I wouldn't hesitate to let things run their course. We can't afford to allow these people to do this again."

"I understand, but I don't think this is going to be solved in a short amount of time, especially if it has to go through all the government red tape."

"I was thinking the same thing. How well do you know Michael Braedon?"

"Michael and I've been friends for years. Why?"

"Then I assume you know everything that happened with the situation involving him and Ms. Darmer."

"Most of it. What he was at liberty to divulge."

"The truth is when we found out about the situation from Mr. Reinholdt, there was nothing we could do to deal with it conventionally. Anything would've signaled Yamani that we knew what was going on. So we kept everyone in the dark and trusted that Mr. Reinholdt could keep him in check and Mr. Braedon and his group would be able to resolve the situation. That took a great deal of trust from the leaders and to this day, no one but those who were directly connected have any idea how close the world came to being destroyed."

"Are you proposing you might want to ask Michael and his group to look into this for you?'

"That's exactly what I'm thinking," said President Bartram leaning forward and placing his hands on the table.

Sorina finished packing her purse for the day. Somehow she was able to fit everything they could possibly need for their outing to the park. The boys were running and jumping around in anticipation of visiting the Magic Kingdom and all things Mickey. Petru started the computer and then connected the camera to the dock. As soon as the icons appeared, Petru clicked on the folder with his presentation. It was empty. He clicked out and went in again. Empty. He went through the long way loading the program and then opening the file. It was gone. Everything pertaining to Craustof was gone. Petru opened other folders and documents and they loaded. The only ones missing were those related to his work.

"Are you almost finished?" asked Sorina.

Petru looked up at her.

"It's gone," he said. "It's all gone."

"What's gone?" asked Sorina.

"Everything that had to do with Craustof."

"Are you sure you put it on the computer, too?"

"Yes, I backed it up, but I accessed it from the computer for the presentation."

He put his fingers to the screen and read each icon. He bypassed a folder and came back to it.

"Sorina, did you put a folder on my computer?"

"No, I haven't touched it. Why?"

"You didn't put this folder named Pawn on it?"

"No, honestly. Open it."

Petru opened the folder and clicked on the document. As soon as it opened he read: *You are being set up! Be careful! Josep.*

Sorina looked at Petru.

"What does he mean? How're you being set up? For what?"

"I don't know," said Petru reading the words again. "He put my computer away. He must have erased everything then."

"Why?"

"I don't know."

Petru downloaded the pictures from the camera into a new folder. Then he closed the computer and put it away.

President Bartram opened his book and turned to the page reserved for his meeting with Jeff Easterly and Roger Gimshaw. There were cryptic letters and numbers in various sections of the page. The President looked at them carefully, nodding his head as he read down to the bottom of the page. There was something gnawing at him, a feeling things weren't right. With his office there was always the tendency to pick and choose those you relied on with care and he knew he could trust those in his immediate circle. Now, however, he was almost certain he was being betrayed. Although that bothered him, it was more that the country was being betrayed. He vowed he'd make it right.

Gimshaw and Easterly arrived together and exactly on time. They entered the room and greeted the President.

"Gentlemen, thank you for coming," said President Bartram. "Please take a seat."

The three men sat and then the President started.

"I know you're extremely busy," he said. "How're things going?"

"Slowly," said Gimshaw. "We don't want to make mistakes, especially in identifications."

"Understood," said the President. "Do you have enough help?"

"Right now, yes," said Gimshaw. "General Anderson has everything under control. We're fortunate to have him here."

"He's the best there is," said President Bartram. "The reason I wanted to meet with you is because I'm concerned. I'm concerned we knew nothing about this attack. Nothing at all. There was nothing on any of the intelligence reports. How could that be?"

Easterly looked down and cocked his head. He wanted to say exactly what he thought, but he didn't know how the President would react.

"Jeff, it seems to me you might have something to say," said the President. "If you're worried about what I might think, don't. I want your honest opinion."

"Okay, then here goes," said Easterly. "I don't trust Hanke. There's something about him that isn't right and I'm not just talking about a feeling here. There've been times when our operatives have stumbled upon some things his agency should've caught and he's dismissed them as having no basis. Then an incident occurs and he claims there wasn't even a rumble. Sir, too many people have died because of his agency dropping the ball."

"And another thing, the incident with the Seals in Afghanistan," said Easterly, "I believe with my whole being they were set up and I wonder who pointed the finger at them. It makes me angry, sir, very angry."

"Well then what I have to say may not be so out in left field as I thought," said the President. "For some time, I've wondered about Mr. Hanke. He's given me every possible excuse as to why we were left in the dark on more than just a few occasions. What I need from you, Jeff, and your agency is total cooperation apart from any dealings with the CIA. From this point on, whatever you find is not to be reported to them. If what I've surmised and what you've just voiced are true, then it's quite possible Mr. Hanke no longer has the United States' best interest at heart. I have no concrete proof, but I know it'll be forthcoming. Everyone makes mistakes, especially when they believe they can't be found out."

"Excuse me, sir," said Gimshaw. "What about the areas of this mission that're within their jurisdiction."

"From this point on, nothing you deal with will be within their jurisdiction," said the President. "I'll be meeting with Mr. Hanke when he returns and at that time, I'll charge him with finding out who's behind all this. I intend, for the sake of protocol, to make it look as though it's business as usual. However, I don't intend to only go that route. Your agency is very vital to finding out who is behind these attacks. I know it'll be stretching your scope and I also realize you can't broadcast it because I don't want Mr. Hanke or any of his agents to find out."

"Yes sir," said Easterly.

"I'm going to do my best to keep Congress busy so they stay out of your affairs. I think it's important for the country to keep running and I don't want them to deviate from the important matters that concern the well-being of all our citizens."

"General Anderson will be acting as a liaison between your agency and the White House. That doesn't mean that if there's something you need to talk with me about, you can't do so. I'll always be available. Gentlemen, I want this solved ASAP and I intend to do what has to be done."

Farred Mahayin looked at his watch. One thing he valued was punctuality. It said a lot about the character of a person. The door to his office opened and Anna Roudalco walked in. Her dark hair was pulled smoothly back behind her shoulders. She wore a black fitted suit with a white satin blouse and open-toed pumps. She smiled as he greeted her with a hug.

"Welcome to my new office," said Mahayin.

"Very nice," said Anna.

"We have much to do," said Mahayin. "He expects everything to be ready by the end of this week."

"I know," said Anna. "I saw the timetable before we left Romania." She looked around the space.

"I see you've made yourself comfortable," she said running her hands over the leather on his chair.

"I need the familiar," he said. "I don't want to be searching for things. With time this tight, every second counts. I still don't understand why there's such need for haste."

"We can't allow them time, even time to breathe," she said sternly. "Once everyone begins arriving, things are going to be very hectic. Have you done something to insure mistakes are not made?"

"Everything is itemized, color and number coordinated with a failsafe system," said Mahayin. "Once we begin, we'll follow this plan exactly. There'll be no room for deviation. There are times when I don't think he trusts those of us with all the details."

"You're absolutely right. He doesn't."

Chapter Fourteen

One thing Yamani had learned in his life was if you wanted to be truly successful, you had to oversee everything of importance yourself. Even though he wasn't out in front, he ordered every move and ran things from the comfort of his home. Over the past several months, he had received many emails and messages concerning the activities that had commenced. He was unsure of who this new group was and what they were trying to do.

Before him on his work table, lay printed emails and messages. He meticulously logged each one and put them in an order of sorts within his notes. On the map he marked areas and compared them to other reports. He put the pen down and rubbed his eyes.

"Something is not right," he said aloud. "How could they not have known? It is all here. Right here."

He pulled a sheet of paper from underneath a pile of books. He had listed all those who could've had any active role in the incident. Some had already been crossed out because in Yamani's mind there wasn't enough motive for them to be involved with the planning and execution of such an event.

He had his favorites, if they could be called that, but he wondered whether it was that they could possibly be involved on another level or whether it was because he just loathed them purely and simply. He took a deep breath and cleared his mind. After a few minutes, he returned to the list and further eliminated several more. Then he added to the list several individuals who had not as yet appeared to have anything to do with the event or its aftermath. For Yamani it was interesting. The FBI director was heavily involved with the investigation as was his department, especially the Pittsburgh office. However, not one mention had been made of the CIA director.

Yamani printed Hanke's name in all capital letters on the paper and circled it. He and Hanke went way back to when Yamani was in exile in Africa. It was Hanke who would leak Yamani's whereabouts. It was because of him that life in exile was anything but normal.

Maranissa knocked on the wall, a quiet rhythmic pattern. Yamani put everything away in the cabinet and locked it. He walked to the far end of the room, turned out the lights, and keyed in a code on the panel. The door moved towards Yamani and then slid to the right. He walked through, turned and keyed another code. The door slid again and then moved into place. He walked through a narrow padded hallway about halfway down its length and turned facing the right. This time with a wave of his hand, a portion of the wall moved and he slipped through. He waved his hand again and it went back into place.

Yamani walked into the kitchen and Maranissa walked out of the room. He motioned for the other man to be seated. Yamani poured two cups of tea and sat down.

"What do you have?" asked Yamani.

"Two things," said Khali. "Rumor has it they are going to strike again. They have moved the operations."

"Do you know where they are going to strike?"

"No, only that it will happen within the next ten days."

"Do you know who they are?"

"Not yet. We are trying to follow back to the original facility and forward to the new one. It is not easy."

"What else?" asked Yamani sipping his tea.

"We are almost positive the man is coming to meet with others involved. The meeting is to take place out in the open at a café. I will find out which one before then."

The *Chosen One* looked out over the men who were going through the training he had devised for the mission. He needed to make certain they would follow every command to the letter. He looked at the diagram on the clipboard he held. Each circle represented a man who was identified by a letter and number combination. These combinations could then, in turn, be checked against another list which listed the man's complete name and where he was from.

He looked at the clock on the wall and did some quick calculations to ascertain the time difference between the camp and the destination of the men.

He turned his attention back to the men and watched with earnest as they were put through their paces. As he did so, he put a colored mark on the men he knew were ready. He flipped several pages to check the number that had to be sent. As with any resource, he liked to send just a bit extra in case something unforeseen happened. There was no sense in holding up a project just because a human resource was not available.

With this project, the *Chosen One* knew that everything revolved around time. It was imperative that each component worked in tandem with another. The timing was crucial. Minutes too late or too early could spell disaster for a project.

"My dear followers," he said in a loud voice, "when I call your name, I want you to go back to your rooms and wait for further instructions."

He began calling the names of all those who were not checked off on his list. Through his observations, he determined these men needed more training before they would be ready to follow through on a mission.

"My dear followers," said the *Chosen One* after all the men who were called had left, "you have done well. You are now ready to continue your mission in another place. You will now get into the backs of the trucks to be transported to your new place. I know you will do well."

With that, each of the men moved and took their places in one of the trucks near the training field.

"Kannid," said the *Chosen One*.

"Yes, sir."

"Here is all the documentation you will need to get you through the checkpoints. Make sure you are the lead truck and also make certain you tell them how many trucks are covered by these documents."

"Yes, sir."

"May the Divine One be with you."

President Bartram took his seat at the table and motioned for everyone to be seated. Around him were the owners of the NFL teams and Commissioner Blakeworth. He knew most of these men had been through this before during the attack of nine eleven, however, now it was much more personal.

"Gentlemen, thank you for taking time from your busy schedules to meet with me," said President Bartram. "I've been wrestling with what to do about the games and I'd like to hear what you're thinking."

"Sir, I'm not sure how I feel about it," said Fred Sutherton, owner of the Browns. "Part of me says cancel the games, because we can't take the chance they'll strike again. Then another part says the probability of them striking another football venue is like lightning striking the same place twice. I don't know."

"I've been thinking the same thing," said Harold Delton, owner of the 49ers. "Then I get mad and think I don't want to run scared and give them that satisfaction."

"I understand that," said President Bartram. "We have public safety issues to consider, but also the idea of being held hostage by fear isn't something I want to condone either."

"I really feel, we need to cancel this week," said Sam Glendich, owner of the Cowboys, "out of respect for all those who lost their lives. I think if we didn't, we'd come across as being calloused and uncaring."

"I agree," said Ray Ellerman. "I'm also not sure our guys would be ready to play this weekend."

"Disrupting the season by a week is one thing," said Commissioner Blakeworth. "Totally throwing in the towel on the season is something else. Canceling the games out of respect is perfectly acceptable and I feel it should be done. As for the rest of the season, we need to see what's going to transpire. I hate to put this on a week to week basis, but that's where we are."

"We can't afford to lose the season," said Bill Komner, owner of the Miami Dolphins. "It'll cripple us."

"Gentlemen, I understand," said President Bartram, "and I'm in agreement with your plan. Whatever I can do to make your decisions from this point on easier, I'll do so. You're going to have to be even more diligent as far as security is concerned from this point on, even after this is solved."

Helena had been on the road since early morning. She crossed over the border into France. It wouldn't be long now.

She came to a gas station and decided to fill up. Once she was finished, she pulled her car closer to the store. She went in to use the restroom and get something to drink and a snack. As she was paying she noticed the sign for mobile phones.

"How much are your phones?" asked Helena.

"They are different prices," said the young woman behind the counter. She brought several out for Helena to look at.

It didn't take long for Helena to make her decision. After it was activated, she returned to the car and started driving. She pulled into a parking spot in a shopping area, took out the phone and placed a call.

Brigit had just walked in the door when her phone rang. She looked at the display and even though she didn't recognize the number, she answered it.

"Hello," said Brigit.

"May I speak to Brigit?" asked Helena.

"This is Brigit."

"Brigit, this is Helena."

"Helena! Oh my, it's been such a long time. How are you?"

"I'm alright. I need your help."

"What's wrong?"

"May I come to see you?"

"Of course, of course," said Brigit. "Where are you?"

"I just got into France."

"Call me when you get near Paris and I'll give you directions."

President Bartram greeted Michael and Edgar and the three men sat in the sitting room.

"Gentlemen, thank you for meeting with me," he said. "I don't exactly know where to begin. This incident is causing me great concern, not only in the fact it occurred, but also in the fact we knew nothing about it. I'm having a hard time believing something of this magnitude could transpire without there being any forewarning."

"I agree," said Michael. "There had to be some sort of indication something big was in the works. Do you think someone just ignored a warning or thought it was preposterous?"

"I think, someone may not have our best interest at heart," said President Bartram. "I've been having my doubts for a while now. There've been other instances where we would've been totally in the dark had it not been for some other informants. I hate to think someone on my staff can't be trusted, but I'm beginning to think it's true."

"If you really feel that strongly, then you need to bypass that person," said Edgar.

"That's exactly what I intend to do, but not blatantly. I have to use that department."

"Who are we talking about?" asked Michael.

"Hanke, CIA."

Michael let out a whistle. Edgar sat back in his chair.

"I have to give him this job, because it's his territory so to speak. I just don't think anything will come of it. I need to find out who did this."

"What do you need?" asked Michael.

"I need your help," said President Bartram. "I need someone who can move around without having to go through channels. What you did last year was incredible. I ran it by General Anderson and he said to ask you."

"The answer is yes," said Michael.

Helena pulled her car into a parking space. All she wanted was five minutes to relax before calling Brigit. She looked around to see if there was any sign of the red Ferrari. She was certain she had lost him at the hotel.

Helena walked into Starbucks and ordered a coffee. She sat in a comfy chair, closed her eyes and took a sip. It was hard for her to grasp all that had happened over the last few days. She wondered what it was all about. Why was the red Ferrari following her? She never did anything. She always did her job well, and was never in trouble of any kind. It just didn't make sense. For a brief moment she tried to tell herself it was just coincidence, but she knew better.

Dr. Hempton's personal office was like one you always saw in the movies or on television. It had the rich dark wood furniture and the overstuffed leather seats. This was definitely the executive treatment. He ran his fingers over the detail work on the front of the desk and then opened the drawer and pulled out several folders. Even the folders were high end...none of those cardboard manila-looking folders here.

His work was extremely important and he knew that he had to be meticulous in what he did. There couldn't be any shortcuts and details could not be overlooked. He was certain that it was why the man had chosen him. He knew from his reputation that he was a stickler for details. More than once, that attribute had gotten him ridiculed by his peers, but now he knew beyond a doubt that it paid off. His bank account could attest to the fact.

He opened a folder and separated the pictures in it. There were multiple views of the face and head. Somehow, the photographer managed to get photographs of the top of the head. Dr. Hempton marveled at the patience some of these views must have required. He carefully studied each picture and made notes concerning little oddities.

Once he finished with those, he moved on to the hands. Some people never looked at hands, but for Dr. Hempton, hands fascinated him. The wrinkles and creases, the shape of the fingers and the pudginess of the palm went into distinguishing one person's hand from another's.

Each of the study sessions took hours, but he wouldn't dare even attempt surgery without thoroughly studying the pictures. He knew how much time, effort, and attention to detail had gone into this project up to this point. Now it was his turn to dazzle everyone with his brilliance and abilities.

Chapter Fifteen

Brigit poured a cup of coffee and put it on the table in front of Helena. Then she sat in the chair across from her.

"What's going on?" asked Brigit.

"I think I might be in danger," said Helena.

"What do you mean?" asked Brigit.

"The place where I work; something isn't right about it."

"Go on."

"The day before yesterday, a friend was promoted and he was asked to take all his things with him. Then I was asked to pack up my office and take everything with me because they were going to remodel that floor. I specifically asked if they were doing the whole building, but Mr. Mahayin said no. It'd be too much trouble with all the machinery."

"That makes sense," said Brigit.

"Brigit, they packed and moved all the machinery out of the building. Everything was gone. Even the top executive office area was cleaned out. That's not all. I took all my things down and came back to make one last check to make sure I didn't forget anything. I was behind my door when Mr. Mahayin walked into my office and checked to see if it was empty. He left, went to Petru's office and put some papers in his trash."

"How do you know?"

"I saw him walk into Petru's office with the papers and walk out without them. When I heard him close the door and check the lock, I peeked out the window and watched him leave. Then I started walking around and looking in all the rooms. Brigit, I found things and I took them all. I have all sorts of things."

Helena took a drink of her coffee and put the cup down.

"The papers in Petru's office had his name on them. Nothing else I found had any identification. I made mental notes of where I found what and wrote it down."

"When are you supposed to go back to work?"

"Mr. Mahayin said he'd call, but I don't think I'll be going back."

"Why not?"

"Before he left, Mr. Mahayin gave me a check. It was for more money than I would make in years."

Henri walked into the kitchen.

"Hello, Helena," he said, "It's nice to see you again."

"It's great seeing you, too."

"I'm sorry to interrupt, but Michael and Edgar are back and we need to get updated."

"Henri, Helena believes she's in danger. She believes something's going on where she worked."

She quickly reiterated to Henri what Helena had said.

"Helena," said Henri, "what company did you work for?"

"Craustof Technologies," she said.

The cup slipped out of Brigit's hand and hit the table. The coffee splashed her and she grabbed the cup before it could fall to the floor.

"Helena, do you have a phone?" asked Henri.

"Yes, but I turned it off before I left the city."

"What about your car?"

"It's outside. I couldn't risk flying." She paused. "I know it sounds like I'm paranoid."

"We need to move it," said Henri.

"Helena, the money from the check," said Brigit, "did you deposit it into your account."

"No, I got cash."

"You're carrying all that cash?" asked Brigit.

"Yes, and it makes me nervous. That's why I brought everything in with me."

Henri took out his phone.

"Jean, on your way to Michael's, can you and Angelique stop here? I need you to help me with something."

"Is he coming?" asked Brigit.

"They'll be here in a few minutes."

"Helena, I need your permission to hide your car and remove its box."

"Why?"

"Helena, we don't think you're paranoid," said Brigit. "We believe Craustof Technologies is a front for a terrorist organization."

"What!"

"We're just now beginning to uncover things about them," said Brigit.

"Like what? Who?"

"Let's do this," said Brigit. "We need to make sure you're safe. Jean and Henri will take care of the car. Robert will deal with your phone and computer. Henri will put your things in the guest room. Tomorrow we'll take care of getting your money into a new account, preferably numerous ones."

"Okay," said Helena.

"Now, you said you took things from Craustof that was left. Where is that?"

"I have everything with me."

"Let's get everything together to take with us to Michael's. If you want, we can put your money in the safe."

"That'd make me feel much better."

The doorbell rang and Henri answered it.

"What can I help you do?" asked Jean.

Henri closed the door and led them into the living room.

"Helena, this is Jean and Angelique. This is Helena. She worked for Craustof Technologies."

"Holy shit!" said Jean.

"Exactly," said Henri. "We need to hide her car and get rid of its box."

"Immediately," said Jean.

Helena handed the keys to Henri. She pulled money from its hiding place in each suitcase and handed it to Brigit. Then she opened the computer case, unzipped the compartments and removed the money from there.

"Only one more place," she said as she reached to the bottom of her purse. "There, that's it, aside from what I have in my wallet."

Henri handed the keys to Jean, took the money from Brigit and Helena and walked out of the room.

Helena pulled papers out of their hiding places, along with plastic bags containing odds and ends.

"Before you take the car, there are crates in the trunk with files from Craustof."

Farred Mahayin stood in the garden amidst beautiful spring blooms. The sound of the fountain was soothing and he was enjoying the late afternoon sun and warmth. His phone vibrated and he answered without looking.

"Yes."

"How are things going?"

"As well as can be expected."

"What's that supposed to mean? I want that facility online by Friday."

"It will be as soon as the workers arrive," said Mahayin.

"They're scheduled to arrive tomorrow. Supplies?"

"They're here. What about the other thing?"

"You let me worry about that. That's none of your concern. You just do what I tell you."

Jean and Henri pulled into the garage and Benjamin closed the door.

"What's going on?" he asked.

"We need to hide this car and get the box out," said Henri.

Benjamin lifted the hood of the car and looked in.

"No, you don't," said Benjamin pointing to a device mounted up under the upper curve of the wall. "What you want to do is get this car away from here. Even if you take the box out, whoever wants to can track the car with this."

"What's that?" asked Jean.

"A sophisticated tracking device. It measures how long the car is at rest, the turns, everything. Even how many times the doors have been opened."

"Are you telling me they'll know every place this car stopped?" asked Henri.

"That's exactly what I'm telling you and they'll start looking here. So you want to get it far away from here."

"Like where?" asked Jean.

"Where's she supposed to be?" asked Benjamin.

"First of all, how do you know it's a she?" asked Jean.

"Look at the car. Of course it's a she. So where's she supposed to be?

"I don't know," said Henri taking out is phone.

"Brigit, ask her where she was supposed to be going."

"Okay," said Brigit. "Where are you supposed to be going?"

"I told the girl at the bank I was going to the Bahamas," said Helena.

"She's supposed to go to the Bahamas."

Lucian and Grigore jumped up and down as they exited *It's a Small World*. Petru's arms jerked up and down as his sons began running with excitement towards *Peter Pan*. The line was long and the wait time was over an hour. Thank goodness for the FastPass. Petru looked at the clock.

"Let's get in line," he said. "It's almost time for us to get on."

"Yay!" yelled the boys.

Petru looked up at Sorina who was smiling. He looked around at all the people passing by. Across from him he spied a man watching them intently. Petru looked away and paid attention to the boys.

The ship carried them through London and into Neverland. The boys were mesmerized by everything they saw.

"We'll have to get the movie and watch it," said Sorina when they exited the ride. "Anyone hungry?"

"Me!" said Lucian. "I'm starving."

"Let's get something to eat while we're in this area," said Petru. "Then we can head to Tomorrowland and the race cars."

Sorina stood in line for the food and Petru and the boys found a table. He took out the map and marked off the rides they had ridden since the last time they stopped for a break.

"Soon we will have gone on everything we wanted to ride," said Petru to the boys.

"Can we go on some again?" asked Grigore?

"As long as we have time," said Petru.

He looked up to see how far Sorina had made it in the line and he spied the same man watching him. The words from the file went through his mind. He took out his camera.

"Smile for me, boys," he said as he snapped a picture.

He looked up and saw Sorina coming. He aimed the camera and took her picture and then snapped one of the man.

Helena booked the flight to the Bahamas, printed out the confirmation, and then walked out of the office supply store. She got into the car and handed the confirmation to Henri.

"So they're taking my car to Madrid?"

"Yes," said Jean. "We have to get it away from here. They're tracking you, Helena and by now they know you've stopped in Paris."

"What if they come looking for me now?"

If they're tracking you, they'll check to see if you've made reservations to the Bahamas. If they want you as badly as it appears, they'll check every possible flight that leaves from the continent until they find the one you're on. That's why we chose Madrid. It gives us a reason to get the car away from here. They won't do anything until the car gets to Madrid."

"What about getting on the flight?"

"You'll be checked in and you'll appear on the passenger list."

"Helena, your money is traveling," said Angelique. "You won't have access for a while."

"That's fine."

"The crates are back in the car," said Jean. "If that's what they're after, then they'll be satisfied that nothing's been touched."

"I thought you needed the information in the files."

"We do. They've been copied," said Jean.

Ms. Harlan stood to the side of President Bartram as he signed the stack of papers. With each one, she explained briefly what document it was and indicated where each was to be initialed and signed.

"What time's Mr. Hanke supposed to arrive?" asked President Bartram.

"Momentarily," said Ms. Harlan looking at her watch.

"Is this everything?"

"Yes, sir."

"Good. When he gets here, send him in immediately."

"Yes, sir."

Ms. Harlan opened to door to her office and turned around.

"Mr. Hanke's here now, sir."

"Send him in."

"Mr. Hanke, the President will see you now."

John Hanke walked into the President's office. President Bartram walked from behind his desk and greeted Hanke.

"John, good to see you," said President Bartram. "Thank you for coming back so soon to meet with me."

"It's good to see you, too, sir."

"Have a seat."

President Bartram waited a moment before speaking. What he wanted to say was not what should be said at this time.

"John, I'm greatly concerned by the fact there was nothing in any of the intelligence reports concerning this attack. I would think something of this caliber would've been noticed."

"It has me concerned, too, Mr. President. I can assure you if there'd been anything concerning this, we would've checked it out no matter how thin the lead."

"I know that, John. In light of what's happened, I want you to step up your operations. We need information. We can't afford to be blindsided again."

"Yes, sir, I understand completely. I've already met with many of our operatives and have given them further orders concerning this."

"Some of what you need to know, Jeff Easterly's department has. I've authorized him to make certain information available to you. I want you to contact him so he can give you that information. Perhaps your department can more effectively get answers to some of our questions."

"Yes, sir," said Hanke making notes. "Why don't I just take over this investigation and that'll free up Jeff's department for other things."

"Jeff's department is turning over to you everything that comes under your jurisdiction and keeping in their department only what falls under theirs," said the President. "John, I want these perpetrators found and I want them found quickly. I'm not about to wait ten years. I also expect to be kept apprised of what's happening. If something else happens, John, and I find out you or any of your agents knew ahead of time, it won't go well for your department."

"Yes, sir," said Hanke putting his notebook into the inside pocket of his suit jacket.

The two men got up and President Bartram walked John to the door, and watched him as he left the office.

The convoy pulled up to a group of buildings in Volgograd near the building that housed Craustof Technologies. Mahayin stood in the parking lot checking the time on his phone.

Kannid got out of the truck and walked over to him.

"What took you so long?" asked Mahayin. "I expected you here hours ago."

"We made excellent time considering the number of detours we had to take so no one knows exactly where we are from," said Kannid. "I am certain that we have arrived with ample time left. The *Chosen One* would never jeopardize such an important mission."

"Whatever," said Mahayin. "Get them settled. We have a schedule to keep."

"Okay," said Gina. "Let's see what we have."

She walked over to a large sheet of paper taped to the wall. On it were major details of the bombing in Pittsburgh. She had been working, putting every piece of information they had in some sort of order.

"Now where do we go from here?" she asked.

"The components used in the bombing were devised and embezzled from my firm," said Edgar. "We're in the process of tracing them, but as I've told you before, the trail has been leading us to dead ends. Rumor has it they were going to Romania, to a company called Craustof Technologies."

Helena gasped.

Brigit interjected. "Helena worked for Craustof."

"What do you mean worked?" asked Tom.

"Up until the day before yesterday, I worked there. Then I was asked to pack my office and take everything with me because they were going to remodel the upper floor. By the time I had cleaned out my office, everything had been removed from the building, machinery included."

"So now we may never know whether or not Craustof was the intended destination of what was taken," said Edgar.

"All the pictures from Hal and Tom and all that information has already been gone through," said Jacques. "We have the pictures and the information from Edgar. Can we go through what Helena has?"

"Sure," said Helena still stunned by what Edgar had said.

She opened her computer case and started pulling out papers and plastic bags. She stopped and looked around the table.

"Before we start looking through these, I want to tell you a little about Craustof. From what I knew, we supposedly worked in the field of mining technology. Some things that were developed didn't seem to go along with the mining aspect, but I never questioned anything. The configuration of the building was also interesting. The bottom floor held the work area where things were constructed and in some instances actually manufactured. It also held the research labs. The upper floor was divided into two parts. The part where I worked was accessible to all workers. In the center of that floor was an open area with stairs that led to the work floor. There was a large opening in the floor so you could see down to the work area. Across the open area was the executive section. There were huge heavy doors and frosted glass, so all you could see were shadowy figures."

"The files stacked there are from my office and these papers are from my friend Petru's office. He had just been promoted. He was told the same thing I was; that they were remodeling and he needed to take everything with him. Mr. Mahayin put these in Petru's trash can after Petru had left and he thought I was gone also."

She handed the papers to Henri and he put them on the table in front of him.

"Excuse me," said Edgar. "I know that Petru is quite a common name, but I had a brilliant engineer who worked for me a number of years ago. His name was Petru Wadimar."

"He's my friend," said Helena.

"Now this just gets stranger and stranger," said Gina.

"Do you think he could've been the contact?" asked Robert.

"Never," said Edgar. "I've always known Petru to be an honest man."

"Petru would never do anything criminal or underhanded," said Helena. "Edgar, where's your company located?"

"It's located just outside of Frankfurt," said Edgar.

Once again Helena sat stunned. She put her hand on her forehead and began shaking her head.

"This can't be happening," she said.

"Helena, what can't be happening?" asked Brigit.

"Edgar, do you have someone who works for you named Masun?"

"Why yes," said Edgar. "He is one of my most devoted workers. He works on very high security projects. Why do you ask?"

"About five years ago, Mr. Mahayin asked me to be a courier. It came with a really nice increase in pay, plus the company paid all expenses. I'd drive to Frankfurt, meet with Masun and get whatever had to go back to Craustof, stay overnight and return the next day. I had no idea what I was receiving; only that it was business related."

"This's more than even I can handle," said Gina.

"What else do you have, Helena?" asked Jacques.

"All of this, I found in the executive section. I labeled everything so I could remember where I found it."

She placed an assortment of papers, bottles, wires, plastics, tape, and other assorted items on the table. Hal picked up a plastic bag containing wire pieces.

"Do these look familiar?" he asked showing them to Tom.

"Shit!" said Tom.

The sounds of sirens penetrated the silence and Josep looked towards the sound. Off in the distance he could see the flashing lights speed across the intersection. He took his key out of his pocket and then felt something rub against his leg. A soft meow caught his attention and he reached down and picked up the gray and white kitten.

"What are you doing here?" he asked. "You hungry?"

He stroked the soft fur and lifted the kitten in the air.

A shot rang out and Josep fell to the ground. The kitten wriggled out of his grasp and ran into the yard. A man walked up close to the stoop and unloaded three more rounds in Josep's body.

Chapter Sixteen

Traffic leading to Madrid-Barajas Airport was snarled. Andre looked at his watch. He still had time. He had made great time driving from Paris. This was the first traffic he'd encountered. He checked his wallet and made sure he had money. He intended to enjoy himself while he was here.

Once Andre turned into the long term parking lot, traffic thinned out. He drove until he found a parking place and pulled in. He unbuckled his seat belt, turned off the car, and reached into the back to grab the bag off the seat.

He opened the door, closed it, and locked it. He took two steps towards the terminal when an explosion rocked the area throwing him into the air. He landed face down on the roof of a car with such force the roof caved down.

Flames leapt high in the air dancing over the adjacent vehicles. Glass burst and shattered. A second explosion sent metal and glass flying, hitting other vehicles and raining down on Andre. Passengers waiting for the shuttle to take them to the terminal began running as quickly as they could away from the exploding cars.

The leaves of the trees moved as the gentle breeze blew along the bank of the river. Farred Mahayin sat at a café table sipping espresso. A Middle Eastern gentleman quietly walked up and sat in the other chair at the table. Mahayin looked at his watch.

"You're late," he said without even glancing the man's way. "I don't tolerate tardiness."

"There were circumstances," said Ammar. "Things you would not understand."

"Do they deal with this project?" asked Mahayin.

"No, they do not."

"Then they're of no concern to me," said Mahayin looking at him. "You asked for this meeting. What do you want?"

"Your superior needs what I have," said Ammar.

"Really?"

"Trust me, I know what I am talking about."

Mahayin looked Ammar in the eyes.

"Well where is it? I don't have time to waste."

The ambulance pulled up to the emergency entrance of the clinic. Two attendants jumped out of the front seat, hurried around the back of the ambulance, and opened the doors. They pulled out the gurney and wheeled it quickly inside.

Not wasting any time, the staff started to work on Andre. With all protocol followed to the letter as Dr. Hempton directed, the best possible care was given to the patient.

Dr. Hempton came into the emergency room to help the doctor.

"Was this the only person injured?" he asked.

"Yes," said the ambulance driver. "It was crazy. So many vehicles damaged and only one person hurt."

"Well, we can certainly be thankful for that," said Dr. Hempton. "Was there anyone with him?"

"People said they saw a woman running towards the terminal. They assumed she was with him, but she didn't come back to see if he was alright."

"She must have been in a hurry to catch a flight."

Dr. Hempton looked at the other doctor.

"Notify the operating room that we're going to be bringing this man in for surgery."

"Alright."

Dr. Hempton washed his hands and walked out of the emergency room. He waited until he got into the hallway to take out his phone.

"He's here. We're taking him to surgery. Yes, I know what to do. They said a woman went running into the terminal to catch a flight."

He put the phone in his pocket, turned, and walked back to the emergency room.

Michael sat at the kitchen table watching the news. Helena poured a cup of coffee and sat down.

"Where's that?" she asked.

"Parking lot at Madrid Airport," said Michael.

"That's my car, isn't it?"

"It looks like it."

"Look, the crates are melted and the files are nothing but ash. They want me dead, don't they?"

"It's beginning to look that way. We need to keep you safe."

"How?" asked Helena.

"They have no idea where she is, right?" asked Gina.

"Right," said Michael.

"Her car never came here. It went to Brigit's and then the garage," said Gina. "So those are the only two places they'll look."

"Robert did you put her on the list?" asked Michael.

"She's winging her way to the Bahamas as we speak," said Robert.

The hum of machinery could be heard all throughout the facility. Within days the factory had come together much sooner than anticipated. Farred Mahayin sat in the chair at his desk. The project was running ahead of schedule but only one key position was missing.

"How's the new facility?" asked the man.

"Everything's on line and ahead of schedule," said Mahayin.

"Good. Perhaps we can move things up a day or two."

"Not a problem."

"Can everything be ready in forty-eight hours?"

"Definitely. We would've been ready sooner if we hadn't had that problem in the lab," said Mahayin. "I told you we shouldn't have used Petru. We should've used an employee who wasn't valuable."

"Did you solve it?"

"Yes, but what if something goes wrong we can't solve?"

"Don't worry. I know where Petru is if you need him. You just take care of what I tell you to do."

Dr. Hempton prepared for surgery. He almost never assisted with surgery on emergency patients. It had to be an extreme emergency and this was one of those times.

Andre had been prepped and was waiting in the room when Dr. Hempton and the other surgeons walked through the doors.

Soft music was playing through the speakers, the choice of the primary surgeon. Dr. Hempton listened a moment and then nodded his head in approval. He fussed a moment with his one glove, checking to be certain that the small device he had hidden hadn't slipped.

As the surgery continued, Dr. Hempton tried to find a time to slip the device into the incision. With the number of people working on Andre, it was virtually impossible for all eyes to be diverted at one time. He decided it was too risky to attempt the implant. There would have to be another solution. He was certain he could figure out a good one and the man would never have to know.

Yamani and Maranissa sat close together at an outdoor café in Italy. They spoke in quiet tones. Behind them, tables had been joined together to accommodate the group of men who had assembled to have lunch. Not much in the line of conversation happened during the course of the meal. What small pleasantries were exchanged showcased the many different accents of those in attendance. Once the meal was completed and the table was cleared, Yamani signaled to Maranissa to listen. She opened her purse and took out a pen and a small piece of paper, placed them on the table, and slid them over to her husband.

"Congratulations seem to be in order," said a man with a British accent.

"Yes, this first one seems to have gone off without problems," said another whose accent gave him away as being Australian.

"I must admit I had my reservation of hitting something that large," said the Spanish man, "but your people have proven it can be done and done effectively."

"This couldn't have been done without you and your ability to keep the reports squelched," said a man whose voice could be heard over a speaker phone.

When this man spoke, Yamani drew nothing more than a circle as one would do when circling an answer on a paper.

"Viktor, I must thank you, personally," said the voice, "for all your efforts in securing the necessary permits for our new facility."

A Russian accent replied, "No one will bother your people in this facility. I've made certain of it."

"Are you still on schedule even with the move?" asked the Italian.

"Even as we speak, production has begun and we'll be ready on schedule. Don't worry about that. My people know what's at stake. Whatever you can do to keep your people out of the way of my people would be appreciated. We all have a lot to gain if this plan succeeds and a whole lot to lose if it fails."

"Are we going to fail?" asked the Italian.

"Not where I'm involved," said the voice.

There was so little time to have any personal conversations and Michael and Laura would steal away to their bedroom whenever they could just to catch a few minutes. Sitting on the loveseat with her shoes off was one of the most relaxing things she could think of doing.

"Michael, we need to rethink our honeymoon," said Laura. "I really don't think we can take the time right now to go away like we planned."

"I know," said Michael. "As much as I really want to get away for a while, we promised, rather I promised President Bartram we would do this."

"I think we're going to need to go and find Helena's friend," said Laura. "If they're this hell bent on trying to kill Helena, I think they're going to try to kill him too."

"Well we know they're at Disney World. I'll cancel our other reservations and book new ones," said Michael.

"We can take our honeymoon when this is all over."

Everything Clayton Pearse uncovered led him to believe the group responsible for the attack on Heinz Field was not a one-hit-wonder. The information his connections were providing, though not the plan in its entirety, was enough for him to ascertain that at least six additional attacks were being planned if not more. While some of the details were sketchy he felt there was enough information to pass along.

Clayton stood at the edge of the fountain tossing coins into it. He remembered throwing coins as a young boy and trying to get them to land in the smaller pools. Even today, it wasn't as easy as he thought it might be. His phone rang.

"What do you have?" asked Hanke.

"I thought we were meeting," said Clayton.

"Unfortunately, I have more pressing matters."

"My contacts say the group is going to strike again."

"I've heard nothing. What makes you so sure?"

"They've named a target…West Edmonton Mall in Alberta, Canada."

"Do you have a date?" asked Hanke.

"No, only that it'll be soon."

"How soon?"

"Within the week."

"I highly doubt they'll be ready that soon. There isn't an organization out there aside from regular military that could respond that quickly."

"Perhaps," said Clayton, "but I think it warrants a warning to the Canadian government."

"Well, this is what I'm going to do. Let me see if I can corroborate this through any other agents. Then I'll decide. Anything else?"

"Not at this time."

"Contact me when you have something concrete."

Clayton looked at his phone and put it in his pocket.

Qadir stood by the fountain watching his two children toss coins. He had listened intently to everything that was said. He walked over to Clayton and stood next to him.

"Tell me," said Qadir, "do you trust that man you were talking to?"

"He's my boss," said Clayton.

"Yes, but do you trust him?"

"Let's say, I'm wavering on that."

"He will do nothing, you know, just like the last time."

"What do you mean?"

"The stadium, you warned him," said Qadir. "He did nothing."

Clayton tossed a coin in the fountain.

"Your boss' acquaintances, I am sure, would be frowned upon."

Qadir turned towards his daughter.

"Tallia, come get some coins."

Tallia ran over to her father and put out her hands. Qadir put coins into them.

"Share with your brother."

Tallia walked towards her brother carefully carrying the coins.

"What acquaintances?" asked Clayton.

"Leaders…ISI."

Clayton took a moment to process the letters and then nodded slightly.

Qadir looked at Clayton and then to his children.

"Tallia, as soon as you are done, bring your brother. We will go get ice cream."

The children ran to their father. He bent down and scooped up his son. As he did, he passed a card to Clayton.

"You need to see this man, now. Show him that."

Qadir took his daughter's hand and walked away.

There were piles of paper all around Tom and in front of him was a colorful chart. He picked up a diagram of Heinz Field and began entering times for each of the sections. When it came to that pie shaped section that remained relatively unscathed, he needed to find the notes from Fitch.

Suddenly something clicked. He went back to the chart and looked again at the times. Each one was exactly two minutes apart. He took a pencil and began connecting the dots. He had no idea why, but to him it made sense. Then he stopped. His jaw dropped.

"What's that look for?" asked Nicole.

"The papers," said Tom.

"What papers?" asked Nicole.

"The papers Helena brought. The ones she found in Petru's office. Where are they?"

"They're here somewhere," said Nicole.

"We have to find them."

Nicole looked around at the piles stacked all over the dining room. She walked out of the room.

"Hey, aren't you going to help?" Tom called after her.

"Be back in a sec."

Tom started going through the piles that were close to him. As he looked at the topics written on post it notes and knew immediately Gina had organized everything.

"Gina," he yelled.

Gina walked into the room followed by Nicole and Helena.

"I'm right here," she said. "We'll find them."

"Why do you want Petru's papers?" asked Helena.

"Do you remember what was on them?"

"Names, emails, phone numbers, and times," said Helena.

"We have to find them."

Gina walked over to a stack on the sideboard. She removed the top half of the stack, took off some papers, and gave them to Tom.

"Why do you need these?" asked Gina.

"I think I might be on to something. I don't suppose you know where everything is that Hal and I brought. I need the reports from Fitch."

Gina walked up to another pile, leafed through the pages, and then put papers in front of Tom.

"Anyone know what the time difference is between Bucharest and Pittsburgh?" he asked.

"Seven hours," said Helena. "Pittsburgh is in the same time zone as Disney World, isn't it?"

"Yes," said Tom.

"Petru and his family are in Disney World," said Helena. "We talked a lot about his vacation."

"Can you take Petru's list and adjust the times for Pittsburgh?"

"Sure"

Tom took Fitch's report and added the four times to his list.

"Let me know when you're finished."

"Done," said Helena.

"Read them off, please," said Tom.

"11:00, 11:02, 11:04, 11:06," said Helena.

He picked up a paper and turned it to face Helena.

"Do you recognize this number?"

"That's Petru's number. It's his house number. Why is it on here?"

Tom looked at Gina and Nicole.

"We know who detonated those devices," he said.

"Who?" asked Nicole

"Petru," said Tom.

"Petru would never do anything like that," said Helena.

"I don't think he knew," said Nicole. "According to this, he was to email a presentation to each of them and then call."

"Oh my God," said Helena shaking her head.

"They fuckin' set him up!" said Gina. "Those bastards!"

"Helena, do they know where he is?" asked Nicole.

"Yes, Mr. Mahayin knew he was going to Disney World," said Helena. "They wouldn't…" She stopped. "Who am I kidding? Of course they would."

Chapter Seventeen

Anna Roudalco slipped out from under the covers and grabbed her robe and put it on.

"Where are you going?" asked John Hanke.

"Just getting something to drink," she said.

"After all that, all you can think about is something to drink? Seriously, Anna?"

She reached down and kissed him.

"Want something?" she asked.

"Whatever you bring me."

"I'll put the coffee on and we can sit on the balcony. It's supposed to be a beautiful morning."

She walked into the kitchen and turned on the coffee maker. She poured two glasses of juice and walked back into the bedroom and placed them on the table across the room from the bed. Anna reached behind the edge of the curtain and pulled the draw cord. Hanke squinted his eyes as the sun brightened up the room. Anna opened the doors and the morning noise replaced the peace and quiet.

He put on a robe and slippers and joined Anna on the balcony. It was hard for him to believe at one time that they had once been on opposite sides. She had been a most formidable adversary. But there had come a time when bridges had to be built and an air of respect cultivated. Ever since Hanke had joined the CIA, he viewed it as nothing more than a stepping stone to get what he truly wanted. The more he worked on the "side of justice," the more he knew it could be manipulated for his personal gain. He also was aware that if Anna was not on his side, she'd make it her main project to take him down. Therein began the courting of Anna as he liked to call it. And it hadn't been easy.

The animosity between the two was something that had to be conquered one step at a time. It took months for him to even get her to say one single sentence to him. There were times when he felt giving up on her would just be the easiest course, however, he knew the price he'd ultimately pay without her on his side.

The day he finally felt he had accomplished his Anna objective, he decided to share with her his idea for Craustof and its face to the public and its real purpose. He watched as her eyes lit up at the very thought of such an enterprise. To be able to affect such chaos, such fury, and change in people's lives was thrilling beyond words. Incapacitating nations, ruining economies, crushing cities, over-throwing governments was now within reach. The thought of ultimate power was now conceivable.

Anna would soon become his eyes and ears at Craustof. This was his company and he hired Mahayin to manage it. Although Mayahin never gave any cause for concern, no one was trusted one a hundred percent. Anna became his watchdog, making sure everything was done to specification.

Hanke knew how to keep her happy. The house on the island was their getaway; unknown to anyone but them. His time with Anna was the highlight of his frequent overseas trips. The need to check in with his agents was third only to Anna and Craustof.

Even though Anna was the closest person to him, his confidant of sorts, he still never confided everything he knew to her. Because of this, only he knew how much of a success the actual incident in Pittsburgh was. No one else knew how much he had learned.

Mahayin was right about Petru, but he'd never let him know it. Petru was a mistake. He could lead everything back to Craustof. That was something that just couldn't happen. Hanke sat staring through Anna instead of at her. His mind was formulating a solution. He got up walked over to Anna, and kissed her on the top of her head.

"I'll be back in a couple minutes. I need to take care of something."

Anna knew that look and that tone. She also knew not to ask.

Despite the bombing in the parking lot, Delta Flight 167 bound for Miami via New York left Madrid's International Airport on time. They had made good time across the Atlantic.

"At the rate we're going, we should arrive in New York almost thirty minutes early," said Noah Bingham, the pilot.

"Who knows, maybe everyone will board early and we can get to Miami at a decent hour," said Scott Delton.

He and Noah had flown this route for the past five years. Arriving that early in New York was unprecedented. Scott was looking forward to arriving in Miami. As soon as they were finished, the crew would be off for five days.

Heather was making her rounds through first class.

"Do you have any idea if we're on time?" asked Aaron Phillips. He was on his way to New York for a friend's wedding.

"As a matter of fact, we're running a little ahead of schedule," said Heather. "As long as we don't get tied up in traffic, we should arrive early."

No sooner had she finished her sentence than the fasten seat belt sign came on and the captain made the announcement. When his announcement was finished, he contacted the tower.

"This is Delta Airlines Flight 167 requesting permission to land," said Noah.

"Delta Flight 167, you are clear to land on runway one-three-R," said the tower.

"Roger tower, we are starting our approach."

Brady watched his instruments as the Delta Flight approached. He looked from screen to window and back until he could see the plane clearly.

"Delta Flight 167, I have a visual on you," said Brady.

"Roger," said Noah.

There was a low rumble. Brady looked up from the instruments.

"Jesus Christ!" screamed Brady. "We have an emergency! Delta Airlines Flight 167 just exploded!"

Hanke returned to the balcony and gave Anna a kiss before sitting down.

"Everything alright?" she asked.

"It will be soon," he said. "Sometimes what we think are the best ideas have a habit of coming back to bite us in the ass."

Anna smiled at him. She loved when he used those phrases that to her were so funny when taken literally. Hanke smiled.

"We should've never used Petru for the project," he said. "He was too important for that type of task."

Anna was never one to say 'I told you so,' but in this case she had to clamp her lips together to keep from uttering those words. Petru had proven to be a faithful and critically important employee. Now, his time with the company was done. Whether or not he had figured out that he had actually made the phone calls that detonated the bombs remained to be determined.

"So what're you going to do now?" she asked.

"I've taken steps to rectify the situation. As much as it pains me to do so, I can't afford to do nothing."

Anna nodded.

"Now as for Farred, he's a different story. I don't trust him. He'd sell his own mother, if it'd get him ahead."

"I think he already has," said Anna taking a sip of coffee.

Angelique grabbed a brownie off the plate in the kitchen and took a bite. Suddenly she was back at the time when Michael was Yamani's guest and they were trying to find a way to get him back. Laura spent a great deal of time cooking and baking. It was one way for her to get rid of the nervous energy. Now here they were again, but this time, the stakes seemed even higher. She poured a cup of coffee, turned on the television, and sat down at the table.

"We interrupt our program to bring you this special report. Delta Airlines Flight 167 en route from Madrid to New York City exploded in mid-air after getting the clearance to land. Air traffic controllers watched in horror as the plane carrying 327 passengers and crew exploded. We'll bring you details as they become available. To repeat,

Delta Airlines Flight 167 en route from Madrid to New York City has exploded in mid-air."

"Oh my God," said Angelique, quickly getting up and hurrying into the other room. "Listen, Delta Airlines Flight 167 from Madrid to New York exploded in mid-air right before landing. That's the flight Helena was supposed to be on."

Helena put her hand over her mouth and shook her head.

"Whoever's doing this obviously wants to make sure you didn't somehow escape," said Paul looking at Helena.

Gina shot her husband a wide-eyed look.

"We need to keep you hidden," said Jean looking at Helena, "totally hidden, until we can solve this."

"Then let's step things up, people," said Gina. "This thing isn't going to solve itself."

General Anderson was never a man to mince words. He told you what he thought and when he met with President Bartram earlier that morning he had no trouble telling the President exactly what he thought of John Hanke and his handling of the situation.

When President Bartram reiterated the conversation he had with Hanke concerning the explosion of Delta Flight 167 and the car bombing in Madrid, he told General Anderson that Hanke ran a check of the passenger list and turned up no connection. The general's first response was "bull shit!" followed by "Hanke's nothing but a damned liar." The President was quick to point out that he didn't believe Hanke's report one bit.

General Anderson turned on the light in his living room and put his keys and phone on the lamp table. Once again there was a major incident with no prior notice and no connection with anything else. The idea didn't set well, especially with a man who had as much experience as he had dealing with intelligence during many of the wars and police actions the United States found itself involved in.

Now he wanted to know what the truth was, He knew there was only one group of people outside of the perpetrators themselves that might have the answer.

"Hello," said Michael.

"Michael, this is General Anderson."

"General, what can I do for you?"

"The car bombing in Madrid and the explosion of Delta Flight 167 above New York City. John Hanke says they're not connected."

"Of course they're connected. I know the connection personally."

Under normal circumstances, Albert Paxton would never think of bothering his boss when he was away on for a holiday, but he felt the situation warranted it. In front of him, on the desk was more evidence than he would've believed he'd find. Albert rubbed his temple as he waited for Edgar to answer.

"Hello," said Edgar.

"Edgar, this is Albert. I found our problem."

"Go on."

"I have evidence Masun has been the one requisitioning parts. He's made a second prototype of every project he's worked on."

"Can you see it on the security feeds?"

"Yes, and I also have his signature on two sets of papers for every project."

"Have you confronted him?"

"No."

"We need to catch him delivering it. How soon will this prototype be finished."

"Within a week."

"Call me, when you're on final phase."

"Listen, I don't need to tell you this situation could get a whole lot worse" said Albert. "If they decide to use any of these new things, they'll take terrorism to a whole new level."

With things as they were and the necessity of keeping everything of importance well hidden, sometimes the cost was calculated in time. Things could not go through direct channels. They had to be diverted and every track had to be well covered so as not to give away precious information. He knew his men did the absolute best they could at getting him everything as quickly as possible and the delivery of the envelope was no different.

The *Chosen One* opened the envelope and took out a DVD. He shook his head. People actually still used these. He put it in the computer and waited. Yamani's face appeared and one of the speeches he had given was playing.

The *Chosen One* sat back, watched, and kept stopping it; moving back to grab phrases and words. He found it amazing the man gave the speech in English instead of Arabic. He started practicing phrases and made a conscious note of word choices. If he was going to convince people he was the real thing, the real Yamani, he was going to have to address the masses.

He knew the disguise was working. No one, not one person ever questioned who he was. Those he interacted with every day would overlook any mistake in speech he would make. They just said it the right way and he agreed with them.

Giving a speech would be the final test. It needed to be done. He was running out of men to recruit in the area and he needed so many more. He turned his attention back to the speech that Yamani was giving. He grabbed a pen and started making notes.

Chapter Eighteen

Helena's car made three stops in Paris before it made its way to Madrid. Starbucks, Brigit's house, and the garage were certain to be searched. It was just a matter of time. Who was going to do it and when were the questions.

Aside from pictures and references to family, everything in Brigit and Henri's house was taken down and away from the premises. They knew they couldn't prevent whomever from searching their house, but they could control what was found. Each time they left, they set the alarms and hoped it would be a deterrent.

For the past couple days, Monique did all of her work from the Starbucks where Helena had stopped before going to Brigit's house. Today was no different. She pulled the computer from her bag and placed it on the table at the café. She knew she was lucky to be able to find such a good seat. Lately, she had to sit at one table and then jockey for position until she was able to get the seat of her choice. She took out her notes and put them on the table beside her computer. Then she made sure her phone was in its proper place.

Monique held the mug with two hands as she took a sip of her coffee. She knew it was highly unlikely anything would happen while she was there, but if they were right, then it could be another piece to the puzzle. From her place she could see anyone who entered the café and anyone who parked on the street for that matter.

Several hours passed and Monique was absorbed by what she was doing. Out of the corner of her eye she thought she saw a splash of red. Looking up from what she was doing, she saw a red Ferrari pull up to the curb and park. Without hesitating, Monique picked up her phone and snapped pictures of the car and its passenger. She continued typing, watching the man as he entered.

He looked around the café and then headed for the far end. Starting there, he stopped at every table where a woman sat. He paused just long enough to make the woman look up at him. When he came to Monique, she looked up.

"Did you want something?" she asked.

"I thought you were someone else," he said.

"Who are you looking for?"

"A woman who said she'd meet me here."

"Oh, did you meet her online?" asked Monique.

"Ah, yes," he said.

"Did she send you her picture?"

"Yes."

"Can I see it? Maybe I'd recognize her if she comes in here."

He took a picture from his pocket and showed it to Monique. She shook her head.

"Sorry," she said, "I haven't seen her in here and I'm here a lot. Can I ask your name in case she comes in while I'm still here?"

"Serghei," he said and he walked to the door.

Monique waited until after the car was out of sight before picking up her phone.

Nicole put down the phone and looked out of the restaurant window at the garage across the way. It wouldn't take him long to get there. She waited patiently, but he didn't show. She picked up the phone and called Laura.

"He's not here," said Nicole.

"He's not?" said Laura.

"We must've missed something."

"The house," said Helena. "After the café, I went to Brigit's."

"Just stay there," said Laura. "We're going to check out Brigit's house."

Serghei parked the car in another block. He walked up to the front door and opened it with ease. He went in and closed the door behind him. From the tracker he knew the car stopped here, right outside this house. Chances are she went in. Most likely she knew someone here. He looked again at the log. She wasn't here all that long and then the car was on the move again. Still he couldn't take any chances. He knew he was looking for anything concerning Craustof.

The house was pristine. Not one thing was out of place. He quickly pulled the cushions off the couch and chairs, opened the drawers in the end tables, upset lamps, pulled pictures out of their frames, and took down artwork from the walls before he pulled up the area rug.

Everything came crashing out of the china closet and he went through the chest containing the flatware. Chairs were kicked to the side and the table moved so the rug could be rolled up. The sideboard was emptied and not one thing was where it belonged when he finished.

He moved into the kitchen ripping out drawers and dumping their contents. Not one cupboard was left untouched and even the oven, microwave, dishwasher and refrigerator were ransacked.

He hurried into the study. Again, nothing was out of place. There was no sign that Helena had stopped here. He took a picture off the wall and revealed a wall safe. He took a tube from his pocket and squeezed a gel substance on the door of the safe. Within seconds, he opened it. He took out money, all Euros and some jewelry. He felt along all the walls for anything that might be hidden and nothing.

Henri opened the door to the house.

"What the hell!" he said.

Jacques put his fingers to his lips and quietly moved into the living room.

Serghei stopped and listened. He could hear the sounds of the outside clearer. Someone was in the house and he had to get out of there. He reached in his pocket and pulled out a vial and unstopped it. Cautiously, he peeked around the door frame from the study. There was the definite smell of outside. He had to make a run for it. He couldn't get caught. The man would never understand.

Serghei ran down the hallway and into the living room. Jacques stepped in front of him to block his path. Serghei tossed the liquid from the vial at Jacques. Jacques put his arms up and turned his face to protect it. Serghei pushed Jacques over and ran as fast as he could out the door. Henri ran through the doorway after him.

Jacques ran outside.

"Get it off!" he screamed. "Get it off!"

Henri stopped and turned. Jacques was desperately trying to take off his shirt. His skin was on fire. Henri looked around and ran to his friend.

"Oh my God!" said Henri. "He got you with acid! Someone call an ambulance!"

Henri's neighbor came running, dragging a garden hose. He unscrewed the nozzle and started getting water on Jacques trying to flush off the acid. Another neighbor ran over and grabbed the hose that was neatly wrapped on the side of Henri's house. He took off the nozzle, turned the valve and ran over to Jacques.

"We have to get this shirt off," said Henri. "I'll be right back."

"Just make it stop!" screamed Jacques.

Henri ran into the house and looked on the floor in the kitchen. He grabbed a pair of rubber gloves and scissors and ran back outside. He put on the gloves and then took the scissors and cut up the back of the shirt. Then he got between the two neighbors who were dousing Jacques with water and cut up the front of the shirt. Henri dropped the scissors and took hold of the collar of the shirt with both hands. He gently pulled the shirt down the arm. It was sticking to Jacques skin. As Henri tugged, Jacques screamed and Henri stopped.

Nicole kept her eyes on the garage. She had no idea how long it would be, but she couldn't risk missing him. The red Ferrari stopped against the curb directly across from the restaurant. The driver got out and walked to the garage entrance. He tried the door. It was locked. He looked around and then reached in his pocket and took out a small tube. After he took off the cap, he applied it to the lock on the door and waited.

The lock fell to the ground and he kicked it aside. He pulled on the door, opening it just enough to squeeze in.

Nicole slid down off her chair. She tapped the person sitting next to her.

"Could you watch my things for a few minutes? I need some air."

"Sure. Take your time."

Nicole walked out the door, looked both ways, and hurried across the street. As she got closer, she heard metal clanging on the concrete floor. Nicole peered into a window. Serghei cleared counters and rummaged through boxes of papers. He stopped, slammed his fists on the counter and turned around. Nicole moved quickly from the window. She stood perfectly still trying not to make a sound.

Serghei took out the tube again and applied the liquid to the lock on the file cabinet. It opened with ease and he went through file after file discarding them on the floor. When they were emptied, he spied a corkboard. He walked over and looked at the papers pinned to it. He pulled a piece of paper off the board and walked to the door.

Nicole took her card case out of her purse. She walked closer to the door. Serghei opened the door and hit Nicole. She dropped the case.

"Sorry," said Serghei. He bent over and picked up the case and handed it to Nicole. She glanced at the paper in his hand.

"Thank you," she said and put the case in her purse.

She walked down the street to the corner and waited for the traffic to ease so she could cross the street. The red Ferrari passed her, and she watched him drive out of sight.

"He's coming your way," she said and put her phone in her pocket.

Sirens rang louder with every second that passed. Police cars and an ambulance pulled in front of the house. Doors opened and the officers quickly got out and hurried over. Medical personnel dropped to their knees beside Jacques. The two neighbors kept the water running over Jacques until they were told to stop.

Officers took Henri aside.

"What happened?" asked Officer Alleman.

"I came home and when I walked into the house, it had been trashed, ransacked. I said something and Jacques cautioned me to be quiet. He walked into the living room. I guess the person heard us and he came running through the hall and into the living room. Jacques tried to block his way. The man threw a liquid on him and fled out the door. I started to chasing the man until I heard Jacques scream."

"Can we see the house?"

"Yes, of course."

Henri led the officers into the house. The officers walked carefully through the rooms.

"How did he get in?" asked Officer Alleman.

"I don't know," said Henri. "I used my key as usual to open the front door."

Another officer examined the front door.

"It wouldn't have mattered if you used a key or not," he said. "The catch is burned away."

Laura looked at the clock. She hadn't heard from any of them for well over an hour. She kept going back and forth between her planner and the project she was working on. The door to the garage opened. Nicole, Monique and George walked in.

"All done?" asked Laura.

"All done," said George.

"So what happened?" asked Gina.

"He came into the café first and checked out every woman there," said Monique. "When he came to me, I asked who he was looking for and if he had a picture. The picture was of you Helena. I complimented his car and asked his name. He said it was Serghei."

"Serghei?" said Helena shaking her head. "I don't know anyone by the name of Serghei."

"When he stopped at the garage, he ransacked the place," said Nicole. "He found a paper on the bulletin board and took it with him. When he came out the door, he bumped me and my card case fell. He picked it up. I got a look at the paper. They put down that she had new brakes done."

Nicole took the card case out of her purse.

"Here," she said. "His greasy fingerprints are on here."

"Nice," said Hal. "Very nice."

"I followed him until he was out of the city," said George. "He's on the main road heading East. He got what he needed here. My guess is he's going back to Romania."

Michael looked at his phone and answered it.

"Yes, Henri," he said and he listened for several minutes. "Alright, we'll be right there."

Michael shook his head and looked at his friends.

"There's been an incident at Henri and Brigit's house. Serghei was there when Henri and Jacques got there. The house was ransacked. They startled him. Jacques tried to stop him, but he threw a liquid on Jacques. Henri says it was an acid. He's on his way to the hospital. Henri can't leave the house. The police are there."

Nicole shook her head and put her hands over her face. Monique put her arm around Nicole.

"Let's get going," said Robert. "Laura, Michael, we can't risk you being connected with any of this because of Helena. We'll call you."

Serghei checked in the mirror to see if anyone was following him. He knew the only ones he had to worry about were the two men who showed up at the house, but he was certain he had taken care of them. Neither got a good look at him and they would be too preoccupied with the welfare of the one to even give him a second thought. To them he would just be a simple, small time burglar.

The phone rang and Serghei answered it.

"Are you finished?" asked the man.

"Yes, I'm on my way back to Romania," said Serghei.

"How did it go?"

"She wasn't at the coffee shop. There was no trace of her at the house either."

"What about the garage?"

"I found her bill. She had brakes put on the car."

"Did anyone catch you?"

"What do you take me for? An amateur?" asked Serghei. "I know what I'm doing."

"Then how do you explain losing her in the first place."

There was a definite click and Serghei put down the phone.

By the time Nicole arrived at the hospital, the doctors had already been tending to Jacques for some time. She paced back and forth waiting for some word about her husband's condition.

"Mrs. Fradard, I'm Dr. Aspen. I'm handling your husband's treatment."

"How is he?"

"Right now, he's resting. A lot of damage has been done to his arms and upper torso. If it hadn't been for the quick thinking of those men using the garden hoses, it could have been much worse."

"When can I see him?" asked Nicole.

"I can let you see him for five minutes, that's all. We have a lot to do. We're going to keep him sedated through this process, so he most likely won't know you're there."

Nicole nodded her head.

"After you've seen him, then we'll talk about what the treatment will be."

Dr. Aspen led her into the room. A nurse pulled a chair next to the bed. Nicole shook her head and started to cry. How could this have happened? What sort of monster were they dealing with?

"My sweetheart," she whispered. "I love you."

She brushed his forehead with her fingers. She looked around at all the machines.

"We'll find him," she whispered, "and he'll pay….dearly."

Nicole reached down and kissed Jacques on the forehead.

The neighbors were putting back the hoses and righting the furniture outside that had be knocked. The police had taken statements and their team responsible for gathering evidence was systematically going through the house. As they finished, their neighbor next door took as may pictures as possible of everything. When she was finished, other neighbors began putting the room back together.

When Brigit arrived, two of her neighbors were working on changing the lock on the front door.

"Brigit, it's going to be alright," said Claude. "It's a horrid mess, but we're here to help."

"Thank you," said Brigit.

She took a deep breath and walked in the house. Furniture was being righted by some, while others were picking up pictures and glass from the floor. Everything that could be saved or repaired was placed in one area, while those things beyond help were placed elsewhere.

As Brigit walked past, her neighbors greeted her and she tried to smile. The most heartbreaking sight was where the contents of her china closet were strewn. It was in there that she kept all the precious mementoes from their children. Many now lay unrecognizable, shattered on the floor.

Brigit wiped a tear away and continued through the house. The man had left a trail of destruction that ended in the study.

Henri turned as Brigit came into the room.

"Are you alright?" she asked him.

"I'm fine," he said.

"It's a mess, but things can be fixed and replaced…well most of them. And Jacques?"

"I don't know," said Henri. "He was in so much pain and I couldn't help him."

Chapter Nineteen

Keith Schieb walked up the short flight of stairs to the back door of Helena's apartment. The flowers on the small porch were withering in the heat. He reached in his backpack, took out a bottle of water, unscrewed the lid, and gave each plant a small drink.

"Sorry, guys, I wish I had more," said Keith screwing the cap back on and putting the bottle back in the bag.

He looked around the porch, walked to the window, and cupped his hands around his eyes as he peered in. All the drawers were pulled out and the contents strewn on the floor. He looked straight through the rooms and could see the front door was opened.

He hurried down the stairs and around to the front of the building. No one was on the street at all, and he opened the front door of the building carefully. He started taking pictures. He climbed the stairs and walked down the hallway to apartment 104. The door was open more than what it looked like from the other side. He pushed the door with his sleeve and shook his head. Trashed was not really the word for what had been done to this place. It had been destroyed.

Keith quickly took as many pictures as possible. Just being in the apartment made the hair on his neck stand on end. What could they possibly have been looking for? He walked carefully trying not to step on anything. The door to the bedroom was open. The mattress and boxed springs were upset and rested against the window sill. The night stands were upended and not one drawer remained in the dresser. Keith looked up at the mirror. He could see a man tearing apart the closet. He took multiple pictures.

A dire sense of urgency pervaded him and he hurriedly walked out of the door of the apartment, down the hallway, and ran down the stairs. His mind raced as he hit the pavement. Thank goodness he had presence of mind to park far enough away so no one would know his car. One more block and then down the next street.

He got in the car, closed and locked the doors, reached behind him for a shirt. He took off the one he was wearing and put on the other. He shoved the old shirt under the seat, took out a pair of sunglasses, and put them on.

"Let's see who you are," said Keith as he pulled away from the curb. He drove to the next intersection, turned right and drove down the street until had a clear view of the apartment building. He parked between two cars and waited. Within minutes a man emerged through the doorway. He stopped, put a cigarette in his mouth and lit it. Then he walked down the steps, turned right and walked towards the back of the building. He stopped briefly to glance towards the second floor and then continued.

Keith sat patiently watching where he went. The man ducked into an alley. Soon a red Ferrari whisked its way out of the alley and drove off in the opposite direction. Keith kept shooting until he was out of sight. He pulled his car out of its place and took the directions from the seat.

"Okay, let's find this place," he said.

The directions took him around the outskirts of the city until he was on the road where Craustof Technologies once had their headquarters. He slowed as he got close.

"7238, 7250," he said as he passed each building.

There was a fence and a large parking lot. He kept driving.

"7450?"

He drove a little more and then turned around. He made the pass again. Nothing. Once more, he turned around. When he got to the fence with the parking lot, he slowed down and put down the window. Ever so faintly an area of dirt could be seen. He stopped the car and took several shots. Then he drove off. He took his phone out and called Hal.

"What was the address of that building again?"

"7352. Why?" asked Hal.

"It doesn't exist anymore."

Yamani finished putting everything together. This was all the information he had been able to gather up to this point. He took the time to make notes and include those. It was imperative that the information make it to Michael.

He had already summoned Mr. Wassum, because he knew he was the only one he could spare at the moment to complete such an important task. Qadir would pick up the package at the house and deliver it to Mr. Wassum at the airport. It was something they had done many times before.

"Ah, Qadir," said Yamani, "I am glad you are early. I will feel better when I know that Mr. Wassum has the package and is on his way."

"Yes, sir. Does Mr. Braedon know he is coming?"

"I will contact him and tell him. I am sure he will find all this information useful. Please tell Mr. Wassum that there may also be a package coming back to me in return. If that is so, then I will have to once again impose upon you to meet Mr. Wassum to get it for me."

"I will gladly do that for you."

"Here, Qadir, it is ready. Please tell Mr. Wassum I wish him a safe journey."

"Yes, sir."

Gina leafed through the paperwork in front of her. She pulled sheets and copied information to a notebook. Paul looked up from his work and looked at his wife.

"What's going on," he asked.

"You know all that machinery?"

"Yes."

"Well it has to be somewhere. We need to find it and that's not going to happen with us sitting here," said Gina putting down her pen. "We have to get out of this house. We're not going to solve this by sitting at this table."

"Where do you want us to go?"

"I don't know where you need to go, but I need to go to Russia and follow up on these invoices."

Gina pulled the laptop in front of her and started looking for flights.

"Is that where you tracked the machinery?" asked Paul. "To Russia?"

"To Volgograd," she said.

The group sat watching with intent the speech delivered by Afmad Yamani. It had been over a year since they first heard the man address his followers in such a manner. Today, after that long hiatus, he once again commanded the attention of everyone who was using any television, radio, or internet accessible device.

His words were to the point as they had been in the past. He took responsibility for the actions that had occurred; the devastation at Heinz Field and the explosion of Delta Airlines Flight 167. He promised this was only the beginning; that those who had turned against him before would be made to suffer and suffer greatly.

In true Yamani fashion, as quickly as he appeared, he disappeared.

"That wasn't him," said Laura shaking her head. "I don't know who that is, but it wasn't him."

"How do you know?" asked Henri.

"His eyes," she said, "those were not his eyes."

Monique could clearly see the pictures of Yamani laid out one after another in order on the sideboard. She remembered Nicole remarking how even though Yamani had aged, there was no mistaking those eyes.

"If that's not him, who is it?" asked Monique. "I believe you, Laura. Who would go to such extremes to make themselves look like him?"

"I don't know," said Laura.

"Well, I didn't think it was him either," said George, "but for an entirely different reason." He got up and started pacing. "I heard his voice so often I could hear it in my head even when he wasn't on that screen. Whoever this is, he's doing a pretty good job of mimicking him, but there were certain places where he breaks character and sounds nothing like him. When he addresses his followers, he's pretty damn close, but when he talks about Heinz Field and the Delta Flight, he loses his accent."

"Give me a minute and I'll start it again," said Robert

Robert began the speech again and they listened intently to try to hear what George heard.

"Amazing," said Pierre. "I didn't pay any attention to any of that before, but you're absolutely right."

"It's definitely not him," said Margo. "He never used contraction, ever. I remember thinking about how his language always sounded so formal. This man used a lot of contractions."

"Some of the rhetoric is perfectly Yamani," said George. "He had to have studied his speeches and took what he liked or what he needed. It's the only way he could have gotten even remotely close to mimicking him."

"I was going to say that I had been at that place with him right before I left," said Laura. "Then again, if he studied the speeches, he could have recreated that backdrop anywhere."

"Makes you wonder what else this man's done," said Gina.

Yamani sat looking at the screen, watching with fascination as a speech was given to his followers. His eyes scrutinized the video while his ears picked up the flawed pieces of audio. He was amazed at how much the man looked like him. But the way he sounded, how he said some of the words, Yamani could tell the man had studied his speeches. Then again, there were phrases and words that were totally out of character with his manner of speaking.

There was no way he could counter such a thing publically. He couldn't afford to expose himself at this time. After all, the world was convinced he was dead. When it was finished, he got up from his seat and made his way to the desk in his office. Sitting down, he opened the bottom drawer and rifled through to find his old notebook. He removed it and placed it on the desk. Carefully, he turned to the section where he had written all the names of those who had been with him in Iraq. Beside each name was a notation that identified the current condition and possible whereabouts of each. There were very few question marks…three…only three. Those were the three he needed to find and find quickly.

Out of the three, one stood out. Yamani always gave those he knew the benefit of the doubt. Sometimes it was warranted and other times it turned out to be an error in judgment. This time, he feared it was an error. The one, Ammar, had at one time been friends with Ahmed, the one who had betrayed him at the end of his time in Iraq. It was because of Ahmed that he made the decision to obliterate his camp and those he personally selected to be there at the time. Ammar, he spared. He believed Ammar had been away from Ahmed long enough that he was actually working for the Cause and not against it. This turn of events, led Yamani to believe otherwise. He needed to find Ammar now more than ever before.

Hal picked up the jacket he had been wearing when he was in Pittsburgh. He reached in the pocket and pulled out a small disk. With everything that happened, he totally forgot about the disk that his contact had given him. He held it up.

"Can we take a look at what's on here?" asked Hal.

"What's that?" asked Robert.

"When I met with my contact in Pittsburgh, he told me there were things I needed to see because things were going to happen that would make nine eleven look like nothing. He slid the disk under his napkin and then went to the men's room. I cleaned off the table and pocketed the disk. Then all hell broke loose."

Robert took the disk and inserted it into the computer.

"Whoa! Wait 'til you see this!" said Robert changing from the monitor to the wall.

He went rather quickly through the pictures. They showed an mixture of rooms, tables with items laid out in neat rows, men all dressed alike sitting in folding chairs, lines of men going from one station to another, and pictures of close-ups of seemingly random men and women.

"Maybe we can go through those again," said Hal, "a little slower this time."

Robert laughed.

"I wanted you to see how important these were," he said. "I think your guy just showed us the whole process of getting ready to go to Pittsburgh."

President Bartram walked through the rose garden. Inside he was seething. He had been lied to by Hanke. He listened as Hanke told lie after lie and he watched his face when they met right after the attack on Pittsburgh. If he hadn't known of the deception, he would've believed every word that man uttered.

Once again the country was at the hands of terrorists. This time, was different. This time the terrorists had insider information. They knew where the vulnerability was and how to take advantage of it.

While there may be some truth to the adage that lightning never strikes twice in the same place, President Bartram knew beyond a shadow of a doubt that the United States was definitely still a place where terrorists might strike again.

President Bartram felt as if his hands were tied. There was nothing he could do through the chain of command without Hanke finding out about it. He wondered just how many other agents were involved or was Hanke actually acting alone. There were too many unanswered questions.

And now, there was the speech given by Yamani. Whoever was in charge of these terroristic activities was working hard to place the blame on Yamani. But why? What did they have to gain by placing the blame on a dead man?

He stopped for a moment. Then he picked up the pace and headed for the door.

True to her style, Gina knew the only way to get anything done was to take a strong stance. She remembered how they walked around almost like zombies when Michael had been taken. It wasn't until she stood in front of everyone and took a stand, challenging their ability to do the job that things began to get done. This time, she knew she was going to have to get them moving once again. This time, they'd have to leave the house and go where the answers could be found.

"Wedding is first and foremost," she said to herself as she wrote down everyone's name on a piece of paper. "Remember Gina, you promised Laura the wedding would go on as planned."

"Talking to yourself again?" asked Robert.

"Sometimes, it's what I do best," said Gina.

"I hear you're going to Russia."

"As soon as the wedding's over, I'm going. I know I'm going to find that machinery."

"Gina, not all of us can leave here at once, if that's what you're thinking."

"I know," said Gina. "It's just that this is different from the last time. We're not going to be able to solve this unless we follow up on leads. That means having to go wherever."

"Well I thought you might find this interesting," he said putting some papers in front of her.

"What are these?"

"I did some checking. You know, the Pittsburgh attack was a really big endeavor. Whoever was responsible had to do a great deal of planning. They had to purchase materials, get tickets for flights, hotels, food, and a lot of other things. So why is it no one knew anything?"

"I don't have that answer," said Gina.

"You know that wire is a special order. Up until two days ago, only two places ever ordered it. One was Reinholdt International because they developed it and now use it in some of their other research projects. The other was Craustof."

"You said up until two days ago," said Gina.

"Exactly," said Robert. "Two days ago, they shipped a large order of that wire to an address in Volgograd. Gina, I think you'll find your machinery at that address."

"How much wire are we talking?"

"Ten times what they ordered before. Oh and it gets better. It seems the only reason they were able to supply this company with the wire was because they had Edgar's permission."

"Edgar would never do that."

"Now the other two components are also proprietary. Once again, they were only shipped to Craustof and Reinholdt until two days ago. Those shipments also were only allowed with Edgar's permission. Those new shipments are also going to that address in Volgograd."

Gina looked at the paperwork.

"Robert, they plan on doing a hell of a lot of damage."

"Yes they do. Now, it seems the internet was very active concerning undercurrents of terrorist threats against Pittsburgh. I checked back to see just what was out there. Although the time wasn't exactly there, it wouldn't have been difficult to assume when the attack was going to happen. So why didn't intelligence agencies pick up on this?"

"Maybe they're part of it," said Gina raising an eyebrow.

Chapter Twenty

Nolan Shugg continued reading carefully through all the information that had come to him from his operatives while he waited on the phone. There it was...a report that Canada was next on the terrorist list. Reading further, he found the agent went so far as to corroborate it with other sources. Someone was being careless.

"Yes," said the man on the other end.

"What's going on?" asked Shugg. "I have agents who have evidence that Canada's next. I thought this was a secret operation. I thought you said no one would find out."

"Has anyone found out? Have you told anyone?"

"No."

"Did you do what I told you and tell them they report only to you?"

"Of course, what do you take me for. The point is, you were supposed to make sure no information about this would be leaked. What happened?"

"You can't stop people from talking."

"So this could all blow up in our faces. You said it was foolproof."

"Listen. That information stops with you. The only way this is going to blow up in our faces is if one of you doesn't do your job. I spent a lot of time putting this together. I'm not stopping now."

For Helena, most of her time was spent in the dining room. It was one of the rooms she was able to be in since it had no windows or doors.

Her days consisted of trying to help find out any details of Craustof; what it was and what it had become. She knew the names of all those in the executive section. After all, they had all once been on her side of that reception area. She made a list of all their names and also entered any details she remembered about them. Some she could remember addresses or phone numbers. What good that would be, she didn't know. Every day, she read the news from home, trying to see if anything was mentioned about Craustof.

Helena scrolled down the page, looking at the headlines. She stopped on *"Man murdered in front of house."* She clicked the link and began reading. It was a short article that started by saying that authorities weren't certain who killed the man or why he was killed. She read down and saw the name Josep Oldin. Helena gasped.

"Josep," she said. "Laura."

"What?" asked Laura wiping her hands on a towel.

"They killed Josep."

"Who's Josep?"

"He worked at Craustof. He's a friend of Petru's."

"How do you know they killed him?"

"I just read it. He was killed outside his house," said Helena. "They're going to go after Petru, I know it. We have to warn him."

Nicole sat next to Jacques' bed. It was still hard for her to grasp that someone would actually do this to her husband. He opened his eyes and looked at her.

"How are you feeling?" she asked mostly out of habit.

"Right now, alright," said Jacques. "Those pain meds are wonderful."

"I bet they are."

"We have to find him," said Jacques. "We have to find him before he does anything else. How are Henri and Brigit?"

"They're fine. The police finished and the insurance company responded immediately."

"It was a real mess," said Jacques, "and I can't even help."

"All we want you to do is get better and stronger. You need to rest."

Jacques closed his eyes.

Michael unfolded the paper from the box Yamani sent, and when he was finished there was an enlarged map of the world with colored symbols. They crowded around looking at it with great concentration.

Tom ran his finger over a symbol in the United States.

"Pittsburgh," he said moving his finger to another spot. "Edmonton." He looked up. "Could this be a map of the places that are going to be hit?"

"What else is there?" asked Laura.

Michael drew out a homemade envelope made of parchment paper used for baking. He opened it, reached in and drew out the contents. There was a stack of pictures of people. Michael put them down one at a time until they were all spread out on the table.

Hal picked one up and looked closely at it.

"Hanke," he said. "Head of the CIA."

Laura picked up another one and looked at the men on it. She turned the picture over. On the back, Yamani had taken the time to identify everyone.

"Look here," she said. "He put the names on the back."

"He's very thorough, isn't he?" said Tom.

"Always has been," said Laura.

"Okay, we know their names," said Hal. "Now we need to know who they are."

Robert grabbed the stack of pictures he printed from the disk Hal had been given. He separated the pictures of the individuals from the rest, then he matched them up with the pictures from Yamani.

"Well, now, this is getting interesting," he said.

Before the box from Yamani had arrived, he contacted Michael to tell him it was going to be forthcoming. Michael asked if there was a way to send things back to him and Yamani told him that the courier had been instructed that there might be something to be carried back in return. It was also, at this time Yamani told Michael there might also be a man who would seek him out. Yamani believed the man had pertinent information and therefore had made certain the man was given a card to give to Michael as a form of identification. Yamani also told him what had transpired between Pearse and Qadir.

When Michael received a phone call from a man asking to speak to him, he sent Henri and Jean to bring the man to the house.

Michael looked up and extended his hand to Clayton.

"Mr. Pearse, I'm Michael. I was told you might be coming."

Clayton handed Michael a card.

"I was told to give you this."

The sign of Yamani was on it along with the initial Q. Michael passed the card to Laura.

"Qadir," she said quietly.

"How did you get this card?" asked Michael.

"I had a phone meeting with my boss," said Clayton, "and after it, a man talked to me. He said I needed to come see you and to give you that card so you knew he sent me. You see, I gave information concerning Pittsburgh to my boss, and he did nothing, absolutely nothing."

"Let me guess, your boss is John Hanke," said Hal.

"Yes," said Clayton.

"Go on," said Michael.

"The day I met the man who gave me the card, I told my boss about West Edmonton Mall. He said he'll try to see if the other agents can corroborate my information. I asked him to warn the Canadian government, but he insists the information must be checked out first. Look, I'd stake my reputation my information is right. This group is not going to stop at Pittsburgh. They're going to hit West Edmonton and then they're going to hit again and again and again. If something isn't done, there are going to be millions of people dead and I mean millions. Look, I knew about Pittsburgh for a month. I passed that information along as soon as I had it. I knew it was going to be Heinz Field 48 hours ahead of the attack. Again, I passed on the information. So the fact that I know West Edmonton Mall, means this is going to happen very soon."

Gwen spread the pictures out on the table in front of Clayton. Clayton looked at the pictures and started pointing to each one.

"That's Logan Wilson, head of Australian intelligence."

Gwen turned the picture over and read the name on the back. Clayton continued, pointing to each one.

"Enzo Jacarusa, Italy, Nolan Shugg, Canada, Remigio Vargas, Spain, Anton Morel, France, Ethan Shelford, UK, Katsu Tanaka, Japan, Viktor Arsenyev, Russia."

One by one Gwen turned over the pictures and checked the names on the back.

"Amazing," she said.

Clayton looked at the other pictures.

"Where did you get these?"

"From our contact," said Michael.

"These men are never seen together," said Clayton. "They'd never work together."

Gwen put several pictures that showed the men sitting at tables together.

"These pictures were taken the day you talked to your boss," said Gwen. "It wasn't very far from where you were."

"Fucking bastards!" said Clayton.

Things at Craustof were bustling. This time, however, they had learned much from their success at Pittsburgh. Diagrams hung on the walls with detailed instructions outlining each step of the process. Things were a little more complicated now that they were in Russia. While it was true no one would bother them here, it was more difficult to reach their targets.

This time, however, there would be no mistakes. Only those who were expendable would take part and only those high enough in the organization would know all. As the men were fitted, they were given a number for identification and logistic purposes. They moved from one room to another through a maze of checkpoints acquiring everything they needed, one item at a time.

Farred Mahayin looked at the floor plans again. He ran his finger around the outer perimeter of the mall, pausing at each door. Then he moved through each floor and re-calculated distances. From what he could tell, everything was perfect. He picked up a clipboard from his desk and went through the list from beginning to end. As he looked from the paper to the diagrams, he nodded his head. Indeed, this was good. He was very pleased.

He walked to the last station and handed the clipboard to his secretary.

"Make sure you record the correct number to the man. We can't afford any mistakes.

John Hanke looked over all the information collected by the agents under him. With each topic he made notes and corrections. True to his word, Clayton Pearse passed along the information concerning West Edmonton Mall. Hanke quickly cut it and put it in another file. Nothing that had anything to do with Craustof would find itself in any document bound for the President's office. Instead, he set to work inventing a story; one that would put all thoughts far away from Canada.

As soon as he was finished, he sent the report to be printed and delivered. As long as he was in this position, he'd be able to keep the smoke screen up.

What he really needed to know was how much Jeff Easterly's department knew about the incident in Pittsburgh. He didn't like the fact that the FBI was still on the case. It should've been his and his alone.

"Easterly here."

"Jeff, this is Hanke."

"John, how are you doing?"

"Doing well. I haven't seen anything regarding any of the evidence found in Pittsburgh."

"I was going to call you this afternoon. As it stands, we've been trying to trace back the phone number, but everything leads to a dead end."

"What about the people who got into the stadium?"

"Again a dead end. Everything was paid for with pre-paid cards and the addresses were nothing more than P.O. Boxes. Whoever's in charge of this has really done their homework. There's nothing traceable so far. What about your end?"

"I'm afraid it's pretty much the same here. Nothing, not even a rumble, concerning what happened in Pittsburgh."

"It's exasperating. I have to say a lot of time in Pittsburgh, right now, is spent trying to identify the dead. Some will never be identified."

Chapter Twenty-One

Laura stood in the foyer. Her heart was beating fast and she felt nervous. She had waited so long for this day and there were times she thought it'd never happen. Even now, even though it was only moments away, she was still wary something would interfere.

The music started. Laura grabbed Gwen's arm.

"Is he down there?" she asked.

"What?" asked Gwen.

"Is he down there?" asked Laura.

Gwen walked in front of the doorway and looked down the aisle.

"Yes, he's down there. Are you ready?"

"Ready."

There weren't many quiet moments with the kids as excited as they were on this vacation. Today they had been swimming in the warm sunshine and were so tired they fell asleep for a nap. Petru took the time to get caught up on the news from home. He went through the articles and read what was of interest. Just as his mother did, he checked the obituaries. He did it every day. Once in a while there was a name he recognized from the old neighborhood, one of the older ladies who lived on his street. This time, however, was different.

He quietly read Josep's obituary. It had all the usual things an obituary had except the cause of death. Usually one would be able to tell by something that was in it, but there was nothing.

Petru put Josep's name into a search engine and pulled up an article. As he read the details of Josep's death, he shook his head. It was Josep who warned him that he was being set up. Be careful he said.

All Petru could think about was the note, Josep's death, and the man in the crowd.

West Edmonton Mall was a bustling place. As a matter of fact, it was the place to be on a Saturday. People hurried through the walkways with children in tow. Madeline sat down at a café table and sipped her coffee. She put her purse on the table in front of her and opened it. Reaching in, she took out a mirror, took off her glasses, and looked closely at her features. She smiled and ran her tongue over her teeth. She smiled again and lifted her top lip up as far as she could and moved her face from left to right and back again. Disgustedly, she put the mirror back in her purse. She took another sip of coffee and looked over at the woman sitting at the table next to her.

"Do my teeth look alright?" asked Madeline smiling at Clara.

"Excuse me?" asked Clara. She wasn't sure she'd heard correctly.

"Years ago, I had an accident. My face hit the steering wheel and I cracked my teeth," said Madeline. "They fixed them, but they're a little different. It took me years to get over it and then I put it out of my mind for the last twenty years. But now I lost my job and all I can think about are my teeth. I have panic attacks because of them. So, do you think they look alright?"

Madeline gave a big toothy smile at Clara.

"Yes," said Clara. "I think they look fine."

"It must just be me."

"You know, we're always the most critical of our own features," said Clara.

"You're so right."

Clara began reading her book secretly hoping that Madeline wouldn't ask her any more questions. A man sat down at a table directly behind Madeline. She took off her glasses again and ran her tongue over her teeth. She stood up, picked up her purse and walked to the next table where the man was seated.

"Mind if I join you?" asked Madeline pulling a chair from another table over so she'd have somewhere to sit.

"Please, join me," said Derrick.

"Do my teeth look alright?" asked Madeline smiling at him.

"Why do you ask?" asked Derrick.

"Years ago, I had an accident and I hit my face on the steering wheel and I cracked my teeth," said Madeline. "They fixed them, but they're a little different. It took me years to get over it and then I put it out of my mind for the last twenty years. But now I lost my job and all I can think about are my teeth. I have panic attacks because of them. So, do you think they look alright?"

Madeline gave a big toothy smile at Derrick.

"They look fine from the front," said Derrick. "Let me see your profile."

Madeline turned her face to the left.

"Your profile looks fine."

"What about the other side?" asked Madeline turning her head to the right.

"They look fine that way, too."

"I guess I'm being just too critical," said Madeline, "but it's just that I remember what my teeth used to look like, and I think my teeth look totally different now."

"Well, I never knew you before your accident, so I can't tell you whether your teeth look different," said Derrick. "I only know that your teeth look perfectly fine as they are."

Madeline stood up, picked up her purse, and put her chair back where she found it. She looked around the area and saw a young couple sitting and studying. She sat down at the table beside them. Neither of them looked up. Wendy was making notes on a chart, using colored pens to separate ideas. Mike picked up different cards, read them, turned them over and put them down again. Madeline took out her mirror, smiled and ran her tongue over her teeth. Then she put the mirror back in her purse. She tapped Mike on his arm and he looked over at her.

"Do my teeth look alright?" she asked smiling at him.

"Do your teeth look alright?" asked Mike.

"Yes," said Madeline.

Wendy looked at Mike without raising her head.

"Why do you ask?" asked Mike.

"Years ago, I had an accident and hit my face on the steering wheel and cracked my teeth," said Madeline. "They fixed them, but they're a little different. It took me years to get over it and then I put it out of my mind for the last twenty years. But now I lost my job and all I can think about are my teeth. I have panic attacks because of them. So, do you think they look alright?"

"Your teeth look very nice," said Mike. "They complement the rest of your face very nicely."

"Do you really think so?" asked Madeline.

"Yes I do."

"What about my profile?" asked Madeline turning her head first to the right and then to the left. "Does my profile look okay?"

"Yes, your profile looks very nice, also."

"I'm just trying to find out if they look okay. They don't look anything like my teeth used to look before the accident and they make me look totally different also," said Madeline. "Sometimes, I look in the mirror and smile, but I just don't look like me at all."

Mike looked away and picked up another card to read. Madeline stood up, took her purse, and walked out of the area. She started walking towards the Ice Palace. A blonde woman in her forties walked towards her.

"Excuse me," said Madeline.

"Yes," said the woman.

"Do my teeth look alright?" asked Madeline smiling at her.

The woman looked at Madeline, shook her head and briskly walked away. The voices around Madeline began to distort. She looked at the people passing her. They were pointing and laughing. Some had that smirking look of disapproval as they stared at her teeth. She started walking faster. Her legs began feeling like gelatin. She was breathing faster.

Madeline walked as quickly as she could. She held onto the wall when her legs felt like giving out. She could see the door. She had to get out of there. It was getting hotter, but her hands were frozen. She ran the fingers of her right hand through her hair and pulled on it. Sometimes, if she felt pain, it'd bring her back to reality. She could hear her heart beating and she was sure it was skipping beats. She just knew she was dying. Her legs felt stronger now and she walked briskly towards the door. It was coming in waves now and the door seemed so far away. She pushed past people knocking some aside. She walked up to a man dressed all in tan, standing with his arms crossed. She grabbed his shirt.

"I'm having a panic attack and you will talk to me!" she screamed.

The man didn't move.

"Do you hear me! You will talk to me!"

Madeline grabbed the man's shoulder with her other hand and shook him. He did nothing but stared straight ahead with his arms still crossed. Madeline pulled at his arm violently and ripped the sleeve from the shoulder. There adhered to his arm was a clear device with wires running into the sleeve of the shirt. Madeline put her hand over her mouth and backed up. She let out a scream.

"No," she said shaking her head, "no, not here."

She looked both ways, down the passages. She could see other men, identical to the one in front of her.

"Terrorists," she said almost inaudibly. "Terrorists."

"Excuse me?" said a man walking up to her. "Did you say terrorists?"

Madeline nodded her head and pointed to the man whose sleeve she ripped.

"He has a bomb," she said to the man, "and there's another one and another.

Madeline pointed at the other two.

"They're going to kill us all!" she screamed. "Run! Get out of here! Everyone's going to die!"

The other man started yelling. He grabbed his wife's hand and headed swiftly towards the door. Madeline let out a scream and ran towards the door.

Michael and Laura walked up the aisle. As they neared the back, Laura spied Maranissa smiling at her and dabbing her eyes. Laura smiled back and tapped Michael.

"Maranissa," she whispered.

Michael looked over at Maranissa, smiled and nodded. He looked around to see if Yamani was anywhere in sight. Maranissa, as though reading his mind, shook her head slightly.

For over the better part of an hour, Michael and Laura greeted their guests. When the last guest passed, Michael walked back inside. Maranissa was waiting for everyone to leave before exiting. Michael motioned for Laura to join him.

Laura walked in and went over to Maranissa.

"Maranissa, it's so good to see you," said Laura. "You look beautiful."

"Thank you. You look gorgeous. I am so glad I was able to be here."

"I'm glad you came. How have you been?"

"I have been doing very well."

"I wish I had more time to spend talking to you," said Laura.

"Me, too, but I promised I would start back as soon as the ceremony was over."

"I understand. Please give him our best and thank him for making it possible for you to come and share our day."

"I will tell him."

"Perhaps at another time he will allow you to come back."

"Perhaps."

Melinda yelled into her cell phone as she quickly made her way to the nearest exit.

"Get out of the mall, now," she yelled. "There're terrorists. I don't care if you found the perfect sweater. What good is it if you get blown up? Get out of the mall. Run! Keep running until you're off the property. I'll call you back and pick you up once I get the car. Do you understand me?"

There was a pause as she listened.

"Just start screaming and yelling terrorist as you're running out of here."

Melinda put her phone in her pocket and hurried faster.

Mike and Wendy made their way down the corridor towards the exit. As he looked to his left, he saw a fire alarm. He grabbed Wendy by the hand and yanked her towards the direction of the alarm. He pulled down the lever and immediately an ear piercing alarm sounded.

"Let's go!" he yelled.

People stopped, listened and then started running for the exits. Parents picked up young children and carried them. Some even paused a moment to put an older child in a stroller with a younger child sitting on the older child's lap. Slower people were shoved aside to allow those who were faster to get by.

Mike and Wendy pushed open the door and ran to the car. Mike started the car and headed to the outer road. He turned and brought himself parallel to the mall.

"What're you doing?" asked Wendy.

"I want to see if the people are getting out."

"Mike, we have to get out of here!"

"We will," said Mike. "I just need to see people leaving for myself."

As they headed to the other doors, they could see that there was only normal traffic going in and out. Mike drove close to the door and put the car in park.

"Get in the driver's seat and wait for me," he said as he got out of the car. "It'll take me less than a minute."

As Mike ran towards the door, Wendy got into the driver's seat. Mike ran to the door, ran inside and past a man dressed all in tan.

"Terrorists!" he screamed as he looked on both sides of the wall.

He saw another fire alarm, ran to it and pulled the lever down. Then he turned and ran outside and to the car.

"Now where?" she asked.

Mike pointed to the far end of the mall.

"They're there, Wendy. I saw one standing by that entrance."

"How long do you think we have until they start exploding? Jesus, I can't believe I'm even saying that." said Wendy.

"I don't know. I hope enough time for the mall to empty. Head for that door."

Wendy pulled the car to the curb and Mike got out leaving the door open. Wendy watched Mike as he went through the door.

"Come on, come on, come on," said Wendy jiggling her left leg. She looked in the rear view mirror and watched people pouring out of the mall and into the parking lot. She looked back at the door and people came running out. She searched the crowd for Mike.

"Where are you!"

Wendy stared at the door. She saw Mike push the door open. A loud explosion rang out. Glass and concrete propelled through the air. People were airborne and others were struck down in mid step by the force of the explosion, pinned by the falling glass and concrete.

"Mike!"

It was a time of trust for Yamani. Being unable to freely move about and take care of things himself had made him dependent upon those he trusted most in his life. He relied on them to do what had to be done. His job was to think things through carefully and then devise the plan. This situation was proving to be most intricate.

Spread out on his desk, were pictures of all the men who had met at the cafe. He made notes concerning each in a notebook. He was absolutely certain they were the reason no one knew the event in Pittsburgh happened. He also knew as long as they remained involved, this group was going to be able to operate without hindrance.

Stopping this was going to take coordination and timing. These men weren't about to announce to the world where they were going to be. One thing was for certain, wherever they weren't at the moment was in danger.

He gathered the pictures, put them inside the notebook and returned them to the bottom drawer of his desk. Then he went out to the kitchen. There was a rap at the door and Yamani looked out the window first and then answered it.

"Gehran, come in," said Yamani. "What brings you here?"

"I have something you might find interesting," said Gehran handing Yamani an envelope.

"Come, sit."

Yamani sat opposite Gehran and opened the envelope. He took out the contents and looked through the pictures.

"Where did you get these?" asked Yamani.

"Khali," said Gehran. "He saw Ammar and followed him. He thought maybe he could find out something. When he sat at the table, Khali thought he was going to have some lunch. Then the man at the next table seemed to turn to talk to him. Kahli said he just started taking pictures, because it looked suspicious."

"Tell Khali he has done well," said Yamani. "Now, Gehran, we must deal with Ammar."

The explosions happened one after the other, not like in Pittsburgh where there was about a two-minute interval. There was no time to breathe, no place to run. Doors were only so wide and only so many people could fit through an opening at a time. People shoved, pushed, anything to get out of the building. A young man fell to the ground having his legs knocked from under him. Hands reached down and grabbed him by the arms lifting and dragging him as they ran.

With each explosion, those who made it out were pelted with raining concrete and debris. Emergency personnel arrived on the scene and looked in absolute horror at the chaos and destruction that lay before them. There was a sense of disbelief, a sense of 'where do we begin?' Hearing about it, watching it on television and on the internet didn't do it justice.

Nothing could be done until the explosions stopped. No matter what, the mall was being torn apart and the only thing they could do was help those who could get outside and try to keep them as calm as possible.

Glendon Harrison spoke into his phone.

"We need help," he said. "Get it from wherever you can. This is Pittsburgh all over again."

Laura sat with her stocking feet up on a chair. She leaned her head against the wall.

"You look exhausted," said Monique.

"I think I passed exhausted hours ago," said Laura.

"You have to admit this was fun," said Monique.

"Definitely a lot of fun," said Laura. "I hope people had a good time."

"I'm sure they did."

Hal walked quickly into the room and stopped.

"I hate to break this up, but they hit West Edmonton Mall. I gotta leave," said Hal.

"Time to get out of here," said Gina.

"Keep us posted," said Michael.

Laura picked up her shoes and grabbed her purse.

"Are you going to put those on?" asked Michael.

"My brain says I should, but my feet say 'absolutely not!'"

Chapter Twenty-Two

It was a hot day at the Magic Kingdom and with the sun beating down, Petru decided the Pirates of the Caribbean would be a great ride because of the air conditioning.

"Looks like a lot of people had the same idea," said Sorina.

"At least we'll get cooled off," said Petru.

Grigore and Lucian played with the velvet ropes that separated the lines. It seemed as though children were naturally drawn to them. Even though it was crowded, the line moved along smoothly.

Quintin Dantz followed Petru and his family as closely as possible without being spotted. When they got in line for the ride, he lost sight of Petru. Quintin strained his neck, trying to catch a glimpse of where they might be. He pushed and shoved people as he tried to get closer. He had to get to Petru before they started walking down the walkway.

"Hey, stop that!" yelled one man.

"Sorry, I need to get up with my family," said Quintin.

He ducked under the rope. He could see them. They were getting closer to that point. He cut through two lines and got directly behind Petru, grabbed the camera bag, cut the straps and vanished into the crowd.

"Someone took my bag," said Petru.

He looked around, but couldn't see anyone. Grigore pulled on his hand as they headed down the walkway.

Visiting Volgograd had never been a priority on Gina's list until now. She had dug and dug until she was able to follow the trail of the machinery from the Craustof plant in Romania. Every one that she traced led her here and all to the same address.

It was indeed a beautiful city and there were places she wanted to visit when she had more time. For now, she had to keep her mind on business. This was definitely a matter of life and death. She hoped what she found would be able to be used to put an end to this reign of terror.

The beautiful buildings of the city gave way to the factories and warehouses of the industrial district. Gina looked again at the directions and the address. She cautiously made her way checking out the signs before she came to the streets. She turned up a street and parked in a lot near the building.

Gina grabbed her phone and camera and got out of the car. She started taking pictures of buildings and other things in the area. She wanted to appear to be just another tourist. It seemed the industrial section of Volgograd was as much a tourist site as the main part of the city itself. She watched as people walked close to the buildings and took pictures through the windows. Gina followed suit and took pictures through windows, too. She mentally kept notes as to which pictures were important and which weren't. When she finished, she moved across the street and started shooting other things.

The door to what she believed to be the Craustof warehouse opened and a man walked out. It was evident he was angry. He headed directly towards a man who was standing at a window. Gina took the opportunity to take as many pictures of the man as she could. He grabbed a camera from a tourist and smashed it against the ground.

"No one takes pictures through these windows," he said looking around. "No one!"

Several men dressed in light tan colored uniforms appeared in the doorway. The man turned towards them and addressed them.

"I want all the windows covered. Now!"

The beautiful tropical island would have to wait. For Michael and Laura, the change in honeymoon plans meant going to Florida to intercept Petru. It had been years since Laura and Michael had been to the Magic Kingdom at Walt Disney World and this wasn't exactly what either of them had in mind when it came to celebrating their honeymoon. However, they needed to find Petru before anyone from Craustof did.

They walked past the Pirates of the Caribbean ride. Laura stopped.

"I love this ride," she said.

"Maybe we can ride it later," said Michael. "We need to find them."

"This is like trying to find a needle in a haystack," said Laura.

Michael and Laura scanned the crowd and the lines. They looked down every passageway hoping to find them. Michael stopped suddenly. He pulled Laura's hand and she stopped and walked back a few steps.

"What?" she asked.

Michael pointed to a man rummaging through a bag with a cut strap. Quintin slammed down the bag in disgust, took out his phone and paced back and forth.

"Nothing in the bag," he said. "Nothing on the computer. Nothing work related. All the folders are empty. Are you sure this Petru is here?"

He paused to listen.

"Look, there's hundreds of Petrus in the world. Alright, alright! I'll check the room again."

The man put the phone in his pocket, left the bag on the ground, and walked away.

Laura waited until the man was totally gone from view.

"Obviously, they're here," said Laura.

"Obviously," said Michael. "How the hell did he know where they were?"

He walked over and picked up the bag.

"Are they being tracked?"

"They have to be on this ride," said Michael.

"They'll exit through the gift shop."

Gina sat in the car. She looked through the pictures. There were some amazing shots. There was no doubt the machinery had found its way here. Who that man was, she didn't know. What she did know was the answers she needed were inside that building. She knew she promised Paul she would be in and out, but they needed the information from inside that building.

She watched a steady stream of men file out of the building. Every one of them was dressed in a light tan uniform, the same one she had seen in the pictures from Pittsburgh. She watched as the man who had smashed the camera came out. He closed the door behind him and checked the lock. Then he walked to the parking lot, got in his car and sped away.

There was no one on the street. The industrial section of town had an earlier quit time than the rest of the businesses.

Gina put her camera in one pocket and her keys in the other. She had no idea how she was going to get in there, but she was determined to do it. The door flung open and a worker dressed in tan came bounding out and down the stairs. The door banged against the building and stayed. The man continued running down the street and then turned onto another street where the rest had gone. She patted her pockets making sure she had the camera, keys, and phone. Then she walked quickly across the street, up the steps and grabbed the door closing it behind her.

Gina stopped and held her breath, listening for any sounds of movement. It was so quiet. Even the machinery had been shut down for the day. To her right was a set of stairs going to the second floor. She surmised that what she really needed could be found there. However, she didn't want to miss out on anything. She quickly walked the length of the first floor, snapping pictures of everything she could. She had no idea what was important and what was not. She always felt that too much information was better than missing something critical. She came back to the center of the first floor and looked up.

She climbed the steps and to her left she saw the big heavy doors with the frosted glass panes. One door was ajar. Someone was being careless, she thought. She ventured into what Helena called the executive section. She stopped at the first room, went in and took shots of whatever there was. Then she walked into the second room. There were papers on a corkboard. She carefully removed papers so she could get clean shots of each sheet. She was nowhere near being done. This was taking longer than she thought and she was beginning to feel uneasy. She put the camera back in her pocket and hurried out. When she reached the top of the stairs in the center section, she heard voices coming from the first floor. She quickly slipped into one of the offices on the other side. It was devoid of everything. There wasn't even a desk. She moved behind the door and peered through the crack.

Hal walked around the perimeter of what was once West Edmonton Mall. No matter where he looked, there were emergency personnel working diligently to find those buried under the rubble. The scene in front of him and the memory of Pittsburgh were fusing together and it was difficult for him to separate what was happening from the past.

"You're on in two," said Jake.

"Let's do it from over there," said Hal pointing at what once had been an entrance to the Mall.

Hal positioned himself in the midst of the rubble and Jake counted down to on air time. Hal looked around at the chunks of concrete that lay immediately at his feet. There were holes between huge pieces where one could certainly get his foot caught. Hal's eyes darted from one hole to another as his mind seemed to be hell bent on absorbing everything about the scene. He panned again back from the left to center then quickly turned his attention back toward the left and stopped. Hal moved slowly and carefully over the glass and concrete being careful not to step into a hole.

"Hal, we're on in ten," said Jake.

Hal stopped and got down on his knees. He reached down and grabbed fingers. He squeezed them and they moved.

"Over here!" yelled Hal. "Help me move these rocks! We have someone."

Hal handed over the mic to Justin. Several volunteers rushed over and started moving debris. Hal kept hold of the fingers.

"Can you hear me?" he yelled.

The fingers moved. Hal reached down through the hole and followed the path from fingers to hand to wrist and as far along the arm as he could reach. He bought out his hand and pointed to a taller stack of debris.

"We need to get that cleared," he said.

Three men moved and began tossing rocks and other debris to a clear area. Hal continued squeezing the fingers and talking to the person.

Prime Minister Marshall touched down as close as possible to the devastation. She quickly disembarked, and stood spellbound by the sight of the once great mall. She watched the volunteers and emergency personnel going about and the covered stretchers being moved into waiting vehicles to be taken to Rexall Place. She remembered the words President Bartram spoke to her about bracing herself for what she was about to see. Nothing, however, could've prepared her for what lay before her.

Prime Minister Marshall made her way to an area that seemed to have more activity than the others. She saw camera crews with their attention trained on a specific area and a seemingly small space.

"What's going on?" she asked a reporter.

"They've found someone alive under the rubble," said a reporter.

Prime Minister Marshall walked quickly to the site. She immediately began helping to clear the area next to Hal.

"Mr. Milridge," said Prime Minister Marshall, "when did you find him?"

"About two hours ago. It's good to see you."

Marshall systematically moved rock by rock, clearing layer by layer. As she reached down to move the next rock, she felt skin. It was a large chunk of debris and the last thing she wanted to do was to chance it slipping and smashing the person underneath.

"I need someone right now," she yelled.

Four men hurried over.

"We need to get this off him. I can feel him right underneath this. One of you take this side. One of you lift under that side, one under the other, and one on the other end. We'll lift on three."

The four men positioned themselves and put their hands under the chunk making sure to get a good grip.

"Ready?"

They nodded.

"One, two, three," said Marshall.

The four men lifted the huge chunk and placed it off to the side. For the first time, Hal could see the person whose fingers he had held the whole time. Marshall and the four men cleared more rocks and the man was able to turn his head. His face was scraped and covered with blood.

"Just a little longer," said Hal. "We almost have you all clear."

With a more pinpointed area, they were able to clear the debris and prepare to extricate the young man from the rubble.

Prime Minister Marshall, Hal, and the others watched as medical personnel brought the young man out of the hole.

Hal took his hand again.

"What's your name?" he asked.

"Mike," the man whispered.

It was a slow moving day. Monique and Robert had done nothing all day except relax. The phone rang and Robert reached to answer it.

"Hello."

"How the hell are they tracking him?"

"His computer," said Robert sitting up. "Disable the Wi-Fi card. Use another computer."

"He doesn't have a computer with him now."

"His phone? A camera," said Robert.

"This man knew exactly where to find him."

"Where are you?"

"Outside the Pirates of the Caribbean ride."

"I don't suppose you got a picture of this man."

"Of course I did," said Michael. "I'll send them your way. He's on his way back to their room again."

"I'll take care of that. Be careful. He may not be alone."

The sound of the footsteps and the man's voice got louder and Gina stood motionless. She felt her phone vibrate against her leg and she was certain they could hear it. The man was definitely coming her way.

"Where are you going?" asked Dragos. "There's nothing down that way. No one works over there."

"What if someone got in and is hiding over here," asked Marku.

"You're crazy! No one got in and no one's hiding anywhere."
Marku turned around and walked the other way.
"Come on," said Dragos. "I want to see what's in here."
"You're going to get us fired," said Marku.
"Who's going to tell on us? No one's here."
Marku walked around the hole in the center of the floor and through the door to the executive section.

Gina waited until the sound of the voices got fainter then she cautiously looked around the door. There was no one around and the voices she heard were muffled. She came out from behind the door and ran quickly and quietly to the far end of the hall, down the stairs, and out the door.

Laura watched the exit. She looked once again at the photo Helena had given her. Two little boys came bounding into the gift shop wide eyed. Following them were Petru and Sorina. Laura tapped Michael and point to them.

Laura walked up to Petru and Sorina.

"Excuse me," she said. "I'm Laura Braedon. I'm a friend of Helena Rudarsnyan."

She handed him an envelope.

"You are Petru, correct?"

"Yes," said Petru.

Petru looked at the outside of the envelope and then turned it over and opened it. He took out the letter. As he read it, he nodded his head and smiled. Then he handed it to Sorina to read.

"Petru, this is my husband, Michael."

"A pleasure meeting you, Petru," said Michael. "Is this your bag?"

"Yes, thank you." said Petru. "Someone ripped it away from me when we were in line."

"He's on his way back to your hotel room."

Petru and Sorina stared at Michael.

Two officers hurried quietly up the hall. The door to the room was ajar. The officers positioned themselves on either side of the door. One officer used his arm to open the door slowly. The room was in disarray.

Quintin cleared the top shelf of the bookcase with his arm knocking everything to the floor.

"Freeze!" shouted the officer.

Quintin stopped for a brief second and then ran towards the glass sliding doors. He put his arms up shielding his face as he hit the glass and broke through. He tripped, caught his balance, ran to the wall and jumped over it.

The officers stopped and looked over the wall. Quintin lay spread flat, face down on the ground.

Robert walked into the dining room and put a stack of pictures in front of Helena.

"What are these?" asked Helena.

"Pictures from Gina," said Robert. "She's hoping you might be able to tell her who and what are on them."

Helena picked up a picture. She looked at it intently.

"This is some of the machinery from Craustof," she said. "Every machine had a number to make it easy to identify if it needed repaired."

She pointed to an area on the picture where you could see part of the number. As she went through the pictures, she separated them into two piles.

"Can I fold these?"

"Sure," said Robert.

Helena folded several pictures, butted them together, and taped them. She picked up the file box with all of her things from Craustof. She rifled through until she was found what she needed. She opened the sheet showing the diagram of the work floor. She looked back and forth from the pictures to the diagram.

"He's set up everything exactly the same way it was in Romania," said Helena.

Robert sat beside her and looked at the numbers on the machines and the numbers on the diagram.

"Creature of habit?" asked Robert.

"Most definitely," said Helena.

Helena put the diagram on top of the pictures and moved them out of the way.

After going through additional pictures of machinery, she came to the pictures of the men.

"This is Farred Mahayin," she said, pointing to him.

Robert took the picture and put it by itself. The next picture showed several men who had come out of the building. They were dressed all identically in light tan. Mahayin's back was turned and he seemed to be addressing them.

Robert reached across the table and picked up a folder. He leafed through until he found the picture of the men on the sidewalk in Pittsburgh. He showed the picture to Helena.

"We have a connection," he said.

Sorina walked out of the bedroom closing the door part way. She walked into the dining room and sat next to Petru.

"They're so tired, they fell right asleep," she said.

"The parks have that effect on kids," said Laura. "We're sorry to have to interrupt your vacation, but you're in danger. We have reason to believe Farred Mahayin wants you dead, Petru. He has made several attempts on Helena's life."

"Is she alright?" asked Petru.

"Yes, she's fine," said Michael. "Petru, they're tracking you somehow. We believe it has to be your phone or your computer. Something they'd be able to access at work to put the tracker in or on."

"The phone I use for work, I left at home," said Petru, "and I never take my personal phone to work. They don't even know I have one. I did bring my computer.

Petru took the computer from the bag and put it on the table.

"I don't think they could've done anything, because I never leave this out of my sight," said Petru. "The only person who touched this at work was Josep. He put a message in a folder for me telling me I was being set up. Sorina, it must've been Josep who erased that file."

"Which file?" asked Laura.

"The main presentation file."

"Alright, so it can't be the computer," said Michael. He sat back in the chair.

"The games," said Sorina grabbing her bag. "Mr. Mahayin gave the boys handheld games. They go everywhere with us because the boys love playing them."

She handed them to Michael. He pulled out his phone and made a call.

"That main presentation file," said Laura, "do you have a backup?"

"Yes," said Petru showing her a small drive. "This is always with me."

"He sleeps with it under his pillow," said Sorina laughing.

"Alright, we can't take any chances," said Michael. "Even though that man is gone, they didn't get what they wanted. We need to protect you. They killed your friend, Josep. As far as they're concerned, Helena is dead. They're eliminating everyone connected with them. So we're going to have to act quickly."

Petru grabbed Sorina's hand.

President Bartram decided another meeting with John Hanke was in order. The attack on West Edmonton Mall came without any prior warning and that was not setting well with him. He was certain Hanke knew more than he was admitting, so he wanted to talk to him again.

The President looked at the clock. He had two minutes. He looked over his notes and knew exactly what he wanted to get from this meeting. Ms. Harlan walked into the office.

"President Bartram," she said, "Mr. Hanke is on the phone for you."

"Thank you," said President Bartram reaching for his phone. "John, I expected you in my office for this meeting."

"I know, Mr. President," said Hanke, "but things here are preventing me from leaving."

"Where's here?" asked President Bartram.

"Now, Mr. President, you know I can't divulge my whereabouts over the phone."

"Well, John, let me cut to the chase here. I'm really becoming concerned about the lack of information concerning these attacks. I find it hard to believe there was nothing on the radar. Even the best governments with the best security measures can't seem to keep things under wrap. Someone somewhere always knows what's going on."

"Believe me, sir, I find it hard to believe myself. I know our guys are doing the best they can. They're everywhere and they've been exhausting every avenue with regards to these attacks. That's why I couldn't spare the time to come back for this meeting."

"My question to you is this; how do you get your information?"

"I'm not sure I understand what you mean."

"When an agent discovers some sort of anomaly, does he or she report it to someone else or does it come directly to you?"

"I don't believe in the telephone game," said Hanke. "I insist on direct report."

"Good."

"Why?"

"Well, I was just thinking. Since we've been in the dark on at least two occasions, it might be someone down the line who was conveniently leaving out information and only passing on selective intelligence."

"That wouldn't happen in my organization," said Hanke. "I trust my agents implicitly."

"Well then, I guess we're back to square one on this," said Bartram. "I don't see where any progress has been made."

"On the contrary," said Hanke, "I believe we're making progress."

"Really? Then perhaps you can explain how they were able to blow up West Edmonton Mall without any sort of intelligence leak."

"There are rumblings, but they point nowhere," said Hanke. "We can't issue intelligence reports without corroboration. We can't continue to put the nation on high alert because we overheard some shepherd talking to his flock."

"And we can't continue to operate blindly."

"Believe me, sir, I understand. If I had the information, I'd pass it along immediately and not wait for the morning briefing. I'll charge the agents with digging deeper to find the answers we need."

"I want to know everything, every little rumble. I don't care where the information comes from. I don't care if you've had a chance to corroborate it or not," said Bartram. "Let me put it this way, John, I want to know if someone combs their hair the wrong way. Is that clear enough for you?"

The underlying threat from President Bartram did nothing but anger Hanke. As far as Hanke was concerned, no one was in charge of intelligence but him. From his vantage point he had control over the entire situation and no one would dare to go against him. He controlled the flow of intelligence to every agency throughout the world. They knew whatever he wanted them to know which included nothing of the attacks that were planned.

Aside from the President sticking his nose into what Hanke considered his business, there were two others who needed to be dealt with and dealt with immediately.

Ever since the President assigned Jeff Easterly to investigate the attacks on Pittsburgh, Hanke knew he needed to control the amount of information Easterly had access to. The other was Clayton Pearse. He was getting way too close to the source for comfort. Hanke knew it was only a matter of time before Pearse would tell the wrong person. The time to do damage control was before it was needed.

"I need you back in the States," said Hanke, "immediately."

Chapter Twenty-Three

The news about the attack on the West Edmonton Mall had made it to the front page of every known newspaper and to the top story spot on every service. Edgar Reinholdt put down the paper and folded his hands in front of him on the desk. It was inconceivable this was happening again. There was nothing he could do to stop these terrorists from using what his company had designed. Never did he think it would be used for such death and destruction.

Albert Paxton knocked on the door and then walked in.

"I hope I'm not disturbing you," he said.

"Not at all," said Edgar.

"Just thought you might want to know Masun has put in a request for a few hours off tomorrow. He said he has an appointment he couldn't make after work."

"What did you tell him?"

"I told him it wouldn't be a problem," said Albert. "He assured me he'd return just as soon as he could."

"What do you think?"

"I think he's meeting someone."

Edgar nodded his head.

"This could be a great opportunity to find out if we're right," said Albert.

"Yes, but none of us can do this," said Edgar. "There's too much at stake should he detect us."

"True."

"Let me see what I can do," said Edgar. "We have to end this somehow."

Jacques sat up slightly in bed. For some reason this angle helped with the pain, but then again so did the pain medication they gave him. When it got close to the time for the next dose, he didn't even have to look at the clock, the pain would begin again. He slept as much as possible because they said that sleep would help the body to heal. Most of the time, there was someone with him, so if he needed anything, they were there to help.

Henri opened his eyes. He took the time to take a nap when Jacques did. He knew Jacques didn't even hear Raquel leave and him take her place. He looked at his friend and smiled.

"How are you feeling?" asked Henri.

"Right now, not bad," said Jacques, "but when the meds wear off, that's a whole different story. How's the house?"

"A disaster," said Henri. "We tried our best to go through everything, to see if anything was missing, but as far as we can tell, he took nothing."

"I didn't think he took anything either," said Jacques. "I'm pretty sure we startled him."

"There was money in the safe, and it was just sitting there on the floor. He didn't even pocket that."

"He had to have been looking for something. Maybe they thought Helena left something there, something from Craustof."

"That's possible, but all they can prove is the amount of time the car was parked outside the house. They might know she opened doors on the car, but they have no way of knowing if she left the car for any time."

"All the time I have to do nothing," said Jacques, "sometimes I can't even put a coherent thought together. All I know is someone has to end this soon."

"That's a definite," said Henri. "There are just so many questions that don't lead to any answers right now."

"Listen, if you can bring me something to do, anything at all, I'd appreciate it. It'll make me feel a little less useless."

In and out. That's what Gina told Paul her trip to Volgograd was going to be. She kept true to her word, well almost. She got what she went to find. She found the connection. Now she had to find someone to get into that building to retrieve the information they needed.

Gina went through everything with Helena and Robert. It felt good to know that her hunch had really paid off. She took the picture of Farred Mahayin and taped it to the wall.

"We need to get someone into that building," said Gina. "The answers are there. There was a lot I couldn't get to."

"Let's say we can find someone to get into the building. How's he supposed to know where to find the information?"

Helena opened a diagram of the facility in Romania. She was certain Mahayin had everything exactly the way it had been there. She had seen him when things deviated in the least. A trash can set on the opposite side of a desk would set him into fits of rage.

"See this," she said pointing to the picture. That's an opening from the bottom floor to the top. That's exactly how the facility was designed in Romania."

"This is the opening that you can see on the pictures. There's a set of stairs that leads from the work floor to the offices," said Helena. "The offices on this side are accessible to anyone. On the other side of this opening are a receptionist's desk and huge frosted glass and wooden doors. Those doors lead to what we all thought was the executive section."

"There's nothing on this side at all," said Gina pointing to the offices where Helena and Petru would have had their offices. "They're all empty. So, the information we're looking for is in that section," said Gina. "I couldn't get much when I was in there. I felt uneasy so I left that area and went to this other section. Good thing I did because those two men came up on the floor right after."

"How did you get inside?" asked Helena. "No one gains access to that section without permission."

"The door was opened a bit and I went in," said Gina. "I only got into a few rooms. Were you ever in that section?"

"Not until that day after everyone left. If you give me some time, I'll find my notes and see if I can at least give you something to go on."

"Robert, we need to use that special site. I want to talk to Yamani. He can get this done."

Farred Mahayin crossed off West Edmonton Mall from his to-do list. He smiled at how well it had gone. Everything they learned from Pittsburgh, they implemented this time. Every single bomb had detonated. Not one person had been intercepted. He looked at the computer screen mounted on the wall. The two figures displayed gave the death tolls from Pittsburgh and West Edmonton Mall. He had it set to update every fifteen minutes. Those figures showed how successful they'd been. They were now over one hundred thousand, a figure that dwarfed the statistics of nine-eleven.

Everything this time had been perfect, especially the logistics. Now he needed to keep that perfection while shortening the time between attacks. Surely it could be done. After all, they were able to do all of this and relocate an entire facility. This time, all they had to do was concentrate on the event.

He looked at the clock on the wall and thought he would've heard from the man by now. It would be nice to have some sort of reassurance he had done a good job. But then again, he couldn't wallow in that sort of disappointment. He had a job to do.

Mahayin opened a drawer on the filing cabinet, took out a folder, and opened it as he walked to his desk.

Dr. Hempton came off the elevator onto the fifth floor. It was quite a stark change from the floors below. The configuration of the floor was mainly a large open space. There were televisions and computers all along the perimeter of the room. Patients sat with headphones listening attentively. From time to time, patients would stand and gesture, bow, extend a hand, and imitate what they heard.

Around the room were large meeting tables and beautiful executive desks. There were areas with chairs set up as if there was an audience and a podium to give a speech.

Dr. Hempton made his rounds stopping at each patient to get an idea of what was being done. He took a seat at one of the tables and listened with interest as a group practiced their skills by role-playing a high stakes meeting. He made some notes in his book. Some things he noticed that he liked and other things that needed improved upon.

"Mr. Renovet," said Dr. Hempton. "I'd like to see you for a minute or two."

The man looked around, then looked at Dr. Hempton and pointed to himself.

"Yes, you," said Dr. Hempton. "Would you please join me over here?"

They moved two tables away from the group and sat down.

"Mr. Renovet, you need to remember who you are. You need to answer and react when someone calls your name."

"Yes, sir."

"I know it sounds a bit different to you, but you're going to have to make the effort."

"Yes, sir."

"Mr. Renovet, I think you're doing quite a splendid job. I can tell you're studying and spending a lot of time in practice. I promise you all this work will be worth it."

"Thank you, sir. When will I be leaving here?"

"Well, you still have a bit of healing to do and some more studying to do if you want to get your speech perfect," said Dr. Hempton. "I promise you, it won't be all that long now."

Mr. Renovet nodded.

"Why don't you rejoin your group. I'll check on you later."

Yamani made notes in his book. The information that Craustof had been found in Russia and had been corroborated was good news. He looked over the list of his people trying to find the perfect person for the job. This was going to take someone who could follow directions, but still follow his heart. As he went down the list he came to one name, paused, and nodded. He continued through the list to the end, and then came back to the same name. His decision had been made.

Yamani looked up at the clock on the stove. He knew it was time for Qadir to come. He now had two more assignments for him. There was a knock on the door precisely at the hour. Yamani answered the door.

"Come in, Qadir. It is nice to see you this morning."

"It is good to see you," said Qadir.

"I have two more assignments for you in addition to what I gave you the other day."

"Yes, sir. I will do whatever you need."

"Mr. Braedon's group has found Craustof and has been able to get some pictures to prove that it is indeed the same company. What they need is someone to get into the building to get information from there. I decided that Zaid would be the person to send. I need you to go to Zaid, give him an envelope. It will only take me a few minutes to get things together for him."

"Yes, sir. I can do that."

Qadir sat quietly as Yamani composed the letter and left to get money to put into the envelope for Zaid. One of the things that made Yamani successful was his insistence that something was done immediately if possible and never put aside. When he came back, he assembled the envelope and handed it to Qadir.

"The second thing I want you to do is go and get Adarine and his family," said Yamani. "I do not want him in some foreign country all alone. He is part of our family and we need to make sure he is safe."

"Yes, sir," said Qadir with a smile on his face.

Yamani handed Qadir another envelop.

"This is for travel expenses. Once he has arrived, we will plan a day when I can meet with him."

When you put an ad out for recruits, there was no telling what caliber of people would answer. The *Chosen One* never thought this would be a problem. After all, all the person had to do was whatever he was told and keep his mouth shut. It seemed simple enough. Yet there were those among the recruits who couldn't figure out their right from their left. Some couldn't follow simple verbal directions to get from one place to another. Still others had no concept in how to read directions. With this type of mission, all of these were extremely important. They were crucial.

He did his best as did his followers to train these men into being productive recruits. He needed them to be able to go forward wherever they were sent and complete the task at hand. Some of them he was able to salvage. These would just take a little more time and he knew they would become true followers.

The ones who irritated him the most were those who couldn't keep their mouths shut. He believed out of everything they were asked to do, keeping quiet was the simplest, yet he had a few who he was certain would never be able to do it.

He couldn't send them on a mission. He couldn't trust that they wouldn't tell all they knew to some poor stranger who just so happened to stand beside one of them. He needed to eliminate that possibility.

The man looked at his watch, the wind was beginning to kick up the way it did on many days. He motioned for Kannid.

"Yes, sir," said Kannid.

"Some of them are never going to get this, no matter how hard everyone tries to help them. We cannot chance sending them on a mission. Their time here must end today to make room for others."

"Yes, sir."

"You know what to do."

"Yes, sir."

The man stood on the platform and addressed the men.

"All of you are doing everything the Divine One has expected of you. We have a special mission for some of you, while another group will be called very soon to complete a mission for the Divine One. When I call you, please make your way to the truck. You will be taken to your destination."

The last thing that Petru wanted to do was upset the boys by cutting their holiday short. They had saved a long time to bring them to Disney World and he wanted them to enjoy every minute. With Michael's help they were able to find another place on Disney property to stay and the boys' games were replaced so Mahayin had no way of tracking where they were.

Lucian and Grigore were even more excited about this place because outside their window they could see zebras and giraffes.

"This is the best place, dad," said Lucian. "I wish I could have a zebra."

"This is a great place," said Petru. "Who wants to go see what the pool is like?"

The boys started jumping up and down. Sorina gathered what they needed and they headed off to the pool. It was a great way to spend the afternoon and then later they would go to Animal Kingdom for a while.

The boys played in the shallow end of the pool while Petru and Sorina sat close by. It felt good to relax.

"What do you think?" asked Sorina. "Do you think we'll be alright here?"

"I don't know," said Petru. "I hope there won't be any other incidents. I know one thing for certain, the next time I think someone is watching us, I will tell someone."

"Why do they want to hurt you?"

"I'm not sure. I've never done anything mean to anyone or anything against the company. I've always done very good things for it."

He sat up straight and turned sideways facing Sorina.

"Whatever it is, it has to do with the company," he said, being careful not to mention Craustof. "For them to have killed Josep and their mission to kill Helena and me, it would be too coincidental not to be. It's what we all have in common."

Petru thought some more. The words of the file from Josep stating he was being set up kept playing in his mind. How was he being set up? What did Josep know?

"Whatever it is or was has to do with something I did…or something they had me do," said Petru.

"What would that have been?" asked Sorina.

"Whatever it was just happened. It wasn't something I did weeks ago. It was something right before we left."

"You gave your presentation and you were promoted."

"I think it has to do with the presentation, but I'm not sure what."

"Let me get some snacks and then we can go through things?"

Petru reached in the beach bag and pulled out the tablet. This was one of the purchases he made with the bonus money. News of West Edmonton Mall was the first thing that came up on the News services. He read the story and went back over the part concerning the timing of the explosions. *"The difference between the attack on Heinz Field in Pittsburgh and the attack on West Edmonton Mall was that there wasn't two minutes between each explosion. The explosions at West Edmonton Mall went one after another. Once again they were detonated from a phone. The bombers, themselves, did not detonate the devices."*

Petru stopped reading. He remembered that morning and the paper with the instructions. After he emailed the presentation to each person, he had to call them. He could see the wording as if he was looking at it. *"Begin each call EXACTLY at the time listed. Make the message short. Do not be late or early for any call."* Each of the calls were two minutes apart.

Sorina put down two plates of snacks on the table, walked over to the pool and got Grigore and Lucian.

"Do we have to eat?" asked Grigore.

"Just have a couple bites," said Sorina. "Then you can go back in the pool."

A cast member came to the table.

"We're going to be doing an art project in five minutes," she said. "If you want to join us, we will be using those tables over there."

"Can we do it, mom?" asked Lucian.

"Please," said Grigore.

"Yes, you can do it," said Sorina.

Lucian shoved the last bite in his mouth and started to get up.

"Wait a minute," said Sorina. "Finish chewing that and wipe your hands."

The boys did as they were told and then were off to make art.

Petru sat shaking his head.

"Why are you shaking your head?"

"I think I know what it was," said Petru.

He leaned over and got very close to Sorina and whispered.

"I think the phone calls I made to all those important people before the presentation detonated the bombs that exploded in Heinz Field."

Sorina gasped and her jaw dropped.

Chapter Twenty-Four

Margo pulled up and parked her car back away from the entrance to Reinholdt International. There were other cars parked along the roadway, the overflow from other facilities along that stretch of road. She could see the entrance clearly and knew from Edgar the car Masun would be driving.

Margo saw the car come up to the crest of the hill and nose out just enough to see both ways. Masun turned and headed towards the city. Margo waited a moment and then pulled out to follow. She followed his every move and was careful not to lose sight of him. Once they got into the city, Masun turned right at the third light. He drove three blocks and pulled into a parking spot. Margo slid her car into a spot.

Masun got out of the car and looked both ways and ran across the street. Sergei walked up to him and handed him an envelope. Masun handed over a small plastic object. Sergei took the object and put it in his pocket and then walked up the street, and around the corner.

Masun looked inside the envelope and smiled. He put it in his pocket and headed up the street. It was a nice day and he wasn't due back to work for at least two hours. He had enough time to go to the bank and get something good to eat before returning. He headed back in the direction of his car and stopped at the corner waiting for the light to change.

Margo started the car. She wanted to be ready when Masun got into his car. She knew he and the man had exchanged an envelope for an object, but from her vantage point, it was difficult to tell what it was. She watched him stop at the corner.

Sergei opened the window.

"Come here," said Sergei.

Mason walked over to the car and bent down.

"Listen, make sure you let him know when you're ready with the next part," said Sergei.

"Definitely," said Masun.

The cars behind the Ferrari started blowing their horns. Mason turned his head towards the traffic and held up a finger. Sergei lifted a gun in his right hand and shot Masun three times in the head. He threw the gun to the floor and took off down the street weaving around cars.

Masun fell backwards on the sidewalk. The blaring horns were replaced by screaming and shouting.

Margo pulled out of her parking place and drove up the street. She looked over and saw Masun on the sidewalk. She turned and followed the Ferrari. Its bright red color made it easy and the amount of traffic made it difficult for him to get any major distance ahead.

"Pearse, are you back in the States?" asked Hanke.

"Yes," said Pearse looking around as he talked.

"I need your help," said Hanke. "I don't have any proof of this, but I think we're being left out of the loop on what they're uncovering in Pittsburgh. I believe information they have would've been vital in stopping the attack on Edmonton. I need you to find out what they have. I don't care how you do it."

"I'll see what I can do," said Pearse.

"Oh, I know you'll do this. I've reassigned your territory until this is over."

Pearse shook his head, put his phone in his pocket, and got in his car.

Margo heard the sounds of emergency vehicles. She knew Masun was dead and she wasn't about to let the Ferrari out of her sight.

"Call Pierre," said Margo.

"Calling Pierre," said the voice.

Margo heard the phone ringing.

"Hello," said Pierre.

"I'm following the red Ferrari," said Margo. "The bastard killed Masun…shot him…right on the corner in the city."

"Margo, where are you now?" asked Pierre.

"Heading out of Frankfurt. He's not getting away this time."

"Don't do anything crazy."

"You might want to tell Edgar."

Margo gunned the car to get on the highway. The Ferrari weaved in and out of lanes passing as many cars and trucks as possible. He passed a truck and pulled back in front of it. Margo pulled into the other lane where she could see him.

Sergei started passing the next truck. It swerved into the lane to avoid obliterating the small car that was traveling far below the speed limit. Sergei moved the Ferrari into the grass median. The second truck swerved into the next lane to avoid the slow moving car. Sergei pushed on the brake trying to control his speed. The second truck plowed the Ferrari pushing it under the side of the trailer of the first truck. All three vehicles came to rest.

Margo stopped the car and got out. She hurried down to the accident followed by several other motorists. One was on the phone frantically trying to explain exactly where the accident was. Two ran ahead to the cab of the first truck, while others ran to the second. Margo and another woman ran to see what had happened to the Ferrari.

The Ferrari was pushed up under the trailer of the first truck. The second truck ripped into the trailer of the first before coming to rest. Twisted and severed red metal jutted out from both trucks. Two men helped the driver of the first truck get clear of the wreckage.

The women caught a whiff of the smell of gasoline.

"Get away from here!" the woman yelled. "Get away now!"

They moved away from the wreckage as quickly as they could. Two men dragged the driver of the second truck out of the cab and carried him a safe distance away. There was a low rumble followed by an explosion and a fireball shot up. Within seconds, the vehicles were engulfed in flames.

The doors of the facility shut and the last of the workers walked out of the door. Zaid looked at the pictures he was given. One by one he put the pictures in his pocket. When the last worker was gone, he knew the building was empty. He waited for about fifteen minutes to make sure no one returned because they had forgotten anything.

Zaid crossed the street. He put his hand on the door handle and heard the click. He opened the door and walked in, then up the stairs and down the main hall. When he came to the center area, there was the opening in the floor. Beyond the opening were the frosted doors. Zaid walked around the opening, opened the door and walked into the section. He walked down the corridor and then around the corner. He saw the room he needed to get to directly in front of him. He walked with determined steps into the office and stop just inside the door. The walls were filled with charts, papers, and maps. Zaid knew there was too much to filter through. He needed to get in, get what he needed, and get out. He started on his left and took pictures of everything that was on the walls. When there were multiple pages, he lifted each page, being careful not to crease or disturb anything. It was essential that nothing looked disturbed. He took picture after picture.

Zaid put everything back exactly as he had found it. He walked out of the office and walked down the hall looking in every room. He walked into one room and on top of a long table were lined up hundreds of wired devices. Zaid took pictures of everything in that room. Once he was finished he exited the building and walked across the street.

Not every day could be a day to be up early. Today Petru and Sorina decided to sleep in and so did the boys. This was going to be the "do nothing" day. Sorina felt that the boys needed some time to just play with the things they had purchased. She got them some breakfast and as soon as they were finished they went back into their room to play.

There was a knock on the door and Petru answered it. Laura and Michael came in carrying a drink holder with coffee and a box with some baked goods. They sat at the table and Sorina got plates, silverware, and napkins.

"Ever since the incident happened, I can't stop thinking about it," said Petru. "I know that whatever it was, happened right before I left for holiday. I also surmise that it had to do with the company I work for because of what has happened to Josep and Helena. Am I right so far?"

"Yes," said Michael.

"When we were at the pool yesterday, I went through some news accounts and from what I have deduced, it was the calls I made from my phone at home that caused the bombs to be detonated at Heinz Field."

"Wow," said Laura.

"Did you know?" asked Sorina.

"Yes," said Michael, "but we were hoping that the less you knew the better it would be for you. That's why we didn't say anything."

"I appreciate that," said Petru, "but you have to know that I knew nothing about this."

"We know that," said Michael. "Your friend has told us how surprised she was that this company had anything to do with things."

"Things are just beginning to make sense now," said Petru. "Josep put a folder on my computer that he named pawn. When I opened it, he was warning me that I was being set up. Unfortunately, by that time, I had already done what they intended me to do."

"It seems that the company, namely the president had involved many people without their knowledge. Your friend had been involved doing things she would've never done if she had known. It wasn't until she came to my house and was introduced to Edgar Reinholdt that she realized what was going on."

"I worked for Mr. Reinholdt," said Petru.

"I know and I believe that when you were courted by this company, they knew exactly what you could do for them," said Laura. "They used a lot of people."

"It makes me sick to think about it," said Petru.

There were five stacks of papers on the table in front of Yamani. Across from him sat Maranissa. All the time he was in Iraq, he never used Maranissa for anything that was related to the organization and spread of the Cause. Most of those intricate details were kept secret from her, for her sake. He never wanted to worry her needlessly. Now he didn't have the luxury. He didn't have as many of his followers around him as he had there. Still, Maranissa didn't seem to mind. She loved her husband and would do anything for him.

"There is so much information," said Yamani. "It is hard to separate what is truth and what is not."

He took a stack of pictures and placed them one at a time on the table.

"All of these men are involved," he said. "Each one is keeping information about these attacks quiet."

He picked up the picture of John Hanke.

"He said nothing about the attack on Pittsburgh, even though he knew about it."

He picked up the picture of Nolan Shugg.

"He allowed the attack on West Edmonton Mall to happen, even though many told him it was going to take place."

He took the map and unfolded it and placed it on the table. He took the pictures and put the pictures beside the circled dots he had on the map. When he was finished, there was a picture connected with each dot.

"See, Maranissa, it is as though these men are in this together somehow. But, what are they gaining by allowing these attacks on their countries?"

"Whatever has been promised them," said Maranissa.

Yamani nodded. There was truth to that thought.

"As long as these men are free, they can keep information from getting to the proper authorities. So we must get rid of these men somehow. Unless there is a reason for them being out in the open, we will never find them."

"Maybe it would be wise to invite them somewhere," said Maranissa.

Yamani smiled and nodded.

"Now, my love, who do these men answer to?" asked Maranissa.

"Whoever the man is pretending to be me," said Yamani. "I believe that's who is in charge."

The news of Masun's murder spread through Reinholdt International. Those who had known him and had worked closely with him couldn't fathom why anyone would want to kill such a wonderful man. Even though Edgar, Albert, Ivan, and Franz knew the truth, none of them said anything to besmirch his memory.

Edgar and Albert sat in the office. Edgar's face showed signs of aging overnight.

"How are you Edgar?' asked Albert.

"You know how people always answer that question by saying, numb? I wish I was numb."

"Edgar, there wasn't anything you could have done to prevent this," said Albert. "You took appropriate action each and every time something came to your attention."

"I know, Albert, but I still feel responsible, and I can't seem to shake that."

"Edgar, you didn't invent these things for the purposes they are being used for. You invented them for the betterment of mankind. You have never done anything to harm anyone."

All was quiet for a few minutes.

"Enough of this sulking," said Edgar. "We have things to do."

"Let's start here," said Albert. "The suppliers we're using have been delivering proprietary parts to another company. We think it's the company that's at the bottom of all this."

"How were they able to order?" asked Edgar.

"They had a purchase order with your signature."

Edgar shook his head.

"Let's put an end to this right now."

Gehran ran through the gray cobblestone street weaving in and around the merchants who were wheeling their carts into place. It reminded him of a giant obstacle course. He was leery of causing an accident, but he dared not take his eyes off the man running away from him. It had taken him some time to find him and now that he had, he wasn't about to lose him.

Gehran watched as the man moved off the street onto a dirt path. He could see that the path was winding and had a slight uphill grade to it. His only hope was that the man would lose momentum before he did and he would be able to catch up to him.

The man looked back and stumbled. He scrambled to regain his footing and continued his assent. It was getting harder to keep up the pace. All he had to do was make it to the top. Going down the other side would be easy and the more space between him and the man chasing him, the farther ahead he would be on the return down. If he went really fast, he could turn into one of the side streets before the man cleared the top.

Gehran tried to keep up the pace. He was thankful for the effort he had given thus far. He said a prayer to the Divine One for help, endurance, and a quick end to what was ensuing.

The man reached the top of the path and stepped up on the old platform that jutted out past solid ground. When the town had a reputation of being the perfect place to rest and relax, people would hike up the hills to get to one of the overlooks and just sped time watching the waves lap at the shore and cliffs all around. He needed just two minutes to catch his breath. He could feel the cool breeze coming up from the water below and it felt good against his sweating skin.

"Ammar," said Gehran as he reached the top. "Please stop. I just want to talk to you."

"I know why you are here," said Ammar. "You came to kill me."

"Why would I come to kill you? I just saw you and wanted to talk to you."

"Then why did you follow me?"

"I do not know."

Ammar backed up. The wood beneath his feet felt soft. He moved to the side and felt a board give way. Gehran stepped onto the platform.

"Give me your hand," said Gehran.

"Why? So you can push me?"

"I am not going to push you. Come on Ammar, we used to be friends."

"We are not friends anymore."

"Give me your hand. Let me help you off the platform and I will let you go."

"No! I know what you will do. You will let me go and then run after me and kill me," said Ammar. "I am not going to let you kill me. I am not going to give you the credit for doing it."

Ammar stomped his feet.

"Ammar, no!" said Gehran.

Ammar put his full weight on the railing and jumped up. As he came down, the railing gave way under his weight and he fell screaming.

Gehran walked as close to the edge as he dared. He looked over and saw Ammar's body sprawled against the rocks. The waves of the sea lapped at the shore and Ammar.

Being with family made Adarine and his wife feel much better about their situation. The moment they saw Qadir at the airport when they landed, Adarine could feel the stress lift from his neck and shoulders. Qadir and his wife opened their home to them and when they got there the children started playing as though they had been playing with one another their whole lives.

From there, Qadir was instructed to bring Adarine to see Yamani. Yamani was certain that Adarine could possibly have information that might be useful. As usual, Qadir came around the back door and knocked. Maranissa opened the door and invited them in. She poured each of them a drink and put a plate of food to share on the table. Then she disappeared into the other room.

"Ah Qadir, it is good to see you again," said Yamani.

"It is good to see you, too," said Qadir. "I would like you to meet my cousin, Adarine."

"Adarine, it is a pleasure to meet you."

"It is a pleasure meeting you, also," said Adarine.

"I understand that some terrible things have happened to you over the past weeks. I would like to hear about them, if you would."

Adarine told his story to Yamani and as he did, Yamani listened attentively and made a couple notes regarding things he needed clarified. When Adarine was finished, Yamani shook his head.

"That was an awful ordeal, but you have shown me something about your character," said Yamani. "The fact that you prayed for guidance before committing to this mission gave the Divine One an opportunity to counsel you. And the fact that you listened to the Divine One shows your love and commitment to him. I know that he brought you safely through all this."

"I felt that he was telling me there was something more he needed me to do with my life," said Adarine. "How could I say no to him."

Yamani smiled and nodded.

"Indeed," he said. "Adarine, do you have any idea where you were taken?"

"No, sir. The truck made many turns and at times I thought we were going around in circles. All I know is that the place we were taken was in the middle of nowhere. It seemed strange to me that anyone would want to be located so far from any city. I could look in every direction and see nothing."

"What were you told when you were there?"

"We were told that we were being chosen for a very important mission, that by answering the flyer, the Divine One had chosen us. We were told that we would be trained so that we would be able to be successful in completing our mission and once we were chosen for a particular mission, our families would be taken care of monetarily."

"I see," said Yamani.

"It was then that I began praying and the man's words began to sound like words coming from a serpent. I felt that he was not sent from the Divine One. I had a pervading feeling of evil."

"The Divine One never masks himself as a serpent nor does he ever exude evil."

"Yes, sir," said Adarine. "When it came time to sign the contract, I couldn't do it."

"A contract?"

"Yes, sir, a contract," said Adarine reaching in his pocket and drawing out a folded paper.

He unfolded it and handed it to Yamani. Yamani took it and read it carefully.

"A contract to be a follower?" said Yamani. "This man is not a chosen one. This man is nothing more than a fraud. The Divine One does not ask or expect his followers to sign contracts. This is an abomination!"

"I agree, sir," said Adarine. "He promised that we were going to be taken back to the city. He lied about that and had every intention of killing us, killing anyone who disagreed with him and would not join him. I had so much fear when I finally reached my home that I didn't even give my wife or family a chance to adjust to leaving. I felt we had to leave immediately."

"Does he know your name?" asked Yamani.

"No, sir."

"Did anyone see you leave with your wife and children?"

"No, sir. She took the children and told her friends she was going to go visit family since I was going to be gone. I went another way. I met her in Frankfurt."

"Qadir, the Divine One has been working in your cousin. He is indeed a faithful follower."

"Yes, sir," said Qadir nodding.

"Pardon me for interrupting, sir," said Adarine, "but I get the idea that whatever this man is asking all these men to do is totally evil. I believe that none of them will make it through their mission alive. I don't know how it can be done, but this man must be stopped."

"Indeed, Adarine," said Yamani, "he must be stopped."

Chapter Twenty-Five

"We have accomplished much this week," said Yamani. "Ammar will no longer be a problem. Although I would have like to have found out information from him, he made the decision otherwise."

"That is a big worry out of the way," said Zaid.

"Now, what do you have for me?" asked Yamani.

Zaid handed him several folders, each containing photos.

"The top one is from his office. I took pictures of everything," said Zaid. "I did not want to skip anything because I did not know what you would deem important."

"Very good," said Yamani taking a pen and marking the folder.

"The second one is from a room I found that had all sorts of clothing, papers, tickets and money lined up on tables. The third folder is from another room. There were devices and wires all laid out."

Yamani looked up at Zaid. He knew by what Zaid had said that another attack was imminent. Hopefully, the pictures would give him the information they needed. Zaid laid an envelope on the table.

"What is in there?" asked Yamani.

"Another set of everything. I thought you may need them."

"Let us see what we have."

Yamani opened the first folder and looked at each picture intently. What he was seeing was a lot of information. It would take more than his eyes to catch everything and more than his mind to grasp the entire picture. He opened the second folder and looked at the first picture. Indeed, there were tickets, but there were two types. As he opened the third folder and looked at the first picture, his eyes shot a glance at Zaid.

"I knew it was important," said Zaid. "I was going to just take the pictures in his office, but something made me stop in both of those rooms. It was a force I could not resist."

Yamani smiled. He knew who sent Zaid to those rooms. His faith taught him that many years ago and he knew never to resist such a force. He was glad to see that Zaid was heeding it too.

"Qadir," Yamani said.

Qadir walked into the room.

"Yes, sir," said Qadir.

Yamani picked up the envelope and looked once more at Zaid.

"Is every picture in this envelope?" asked Yamani.

"Every one of them," said Zaid.

"Qadir, you must get this to Mr. Braedon and the others," said Yamani.

"Yes, sir," said Qadir.

"You must go immediately. Set your travel plans and let me know," said Yamani. "I will have someone meet you."

"Yes, sir."

Nolan Shugg walked away from the meeting with a smile on his face. As the head of the Canadian Secret Intelligence Agency, he had successfully kept his government in the dark as to anything concerning West Edmonton Mall. Now he knew how pleased the man was. He hailed a taxi.

"To the airport, please," he said to the driver.

The driver smiled, and started the meter. The ride was silent, Shugg preferred it that way. He looked at his watch. He needed to make this flight.

"Listen, I'll double the fare if you drive faster.

The driver nodded and stepped on the gas. He weaved in and out of traffic with sharp turns. Shugg was bounced back and forth. He reached to hold on something. The driver made a quick left turn and started down a narrow cobblestone street. He sped up even faster. Shugg hit his head multiple times on the roof of the car. The driver glanced back quickly. Up ahead the road turned to dirt as it entered a wooded area.

"Slow down," Shugg screamed.

The driver kept up the pace.

"Stop! Stop now!"

The driver slammed on the brakes and turned the wheel hard to the left. The taxi swerved and rammed into a tree. The driver opened the door and quickly got out of the car. He checked on the passenger. Shugg was not moving. His head was against the tree. The driver grabbed Shugg's briefcase, ran down the path, pulled out his cell phone and entered a number. He pressed send and ran for cover.

The opening acts at Festhalle never played to a capacity crowd. The show was sold out, but everyone knew the band they came to see wasn't scheduled to perform until last. Even though the concert officially started at seven o'clock, people were still filing in after that time. Everyone was in a great mood. The opening acts, for once, didn't disappoint and the concert goers were generous with their applause.

But even so, those in attendance were anxiously awaiting the arrival of the headliners. They were known for their special effects. They had a reputation of never putting on the same show twice and so many who came through the doors were actually fans who followed them from one city to another. They wanted to be able to say they had experienced everything this band had to offer.

Raina, sat at a strange angle in her seat. She was dressed in a pair of tight jeans that accentuated her muffin top. Her turquoise knitted jersey shirt hugged her many curves and came to rest just at the top of the waistband. Out of habit, she pulled at plunging neckline trying to position it correctly.

"They weren't bad," said Raina, "Not bad at all, as opening acts go, and believe me, I've seen tons of opening acts."

Heather nodded and sipped her drink.

"I remember when Fall Out Boy was the first opening act," said Raina. "You know the opening acts hardly ever really get paid. They do it for the exposure."

Heather nodded some more.

"It was their first time on a big stage and I was in the back. Did I ever tell you about this? Well, anyway, I had to calm those boys down and boost their egos and tell them how good they were going to do. I did such a good job that the venue asked me to be backstage for every concert to make sure the openers were pumped up and were able to go onstage and perform and not disappoint the audience. I met so many people. And when I moved away the venue wanted to fly me back for every concert. That's how invaluable I was."

Heather nodded and Raina continued.

"You know I was asked to be backstage for this concert, but I wanted to sit with you," said Raina.

Raina looked over at Heather who was simply dressed in jeans and the headliner's t-shirt. Heather purposely bought the t-shirt larger so it wouldn't cling and accentuate body areas she wasn't exactly proud of.

"The performers come to expect a certain caliber of visitor backstage and there was no way they were going to allow someone who is as large as you are and dressed in just jeans and a t-shirt back there," said Raina. "Now mind you, I would've loved to have been back there, but our friendship means more."

Heather smiled at Raina, then turned her head and rolled her eyes.

"I've seen this group every single time they've performed. I can't wait to see what they do tonight."

The master of ceremonies took the stage and welcomed everyone again. He thanked the act that had just left the stage and the crowd once again erupted in applause showing their appreciation. He then announced the headlining band and the people were on their feet applauding and screaming. The band took the stage and spots began swirling the hall. A loud explosion rang out near the stage, and another and another. The crowd continued screaming and clapping.

Men dressed all in light tan stood as still as statues along the walls and in the aisles, while others were dispersed among the audience. Explosions rang out in waves. Wood from the stage floor splintered, flew, and impaled people. The curtains were ablaze and the band instruments were unrecognizable. Slowly, the audience realized the explosions weren't part of the show. There was no quick, easy way to get out of Festhalle. Concert goers stood on seats and walked over them.

They pushed and shoved people to the floor and trampled over them trying to get away. Others sat paralyzed in their seats.

The explosions came from everywhere. There was no way of telling which way would lead to safety. Seats blew apart and metal and wood soared through the air. Chunks of ceiling and walls rained down on the people burying them under tons of debris.

"We're being killed in here!" Raina screamed into her mobile phone. "They're blowing us up! You have to save me!"

Mark waited until he reached the dining room before opening the envelope he received from Qadir. He pulled out the stack of pictures and started looking through them.

"Wow!" he said. "Wait 'til you see these."

"What are you looking at?" asked Nicole.

"Yamani sent pictures," said Mark. "He said his man took pictures of everything, because he didn't know what was important. When he said everything, he meant it. We have charts, graphs, maps, tables, diagrams, just everything."

"I knew he could get in there some way," said Gina. "There was no way for me to do it."

Everything that had been on the table was stacked in alternating piles and put on the floor beside the sideboard. Mark passed each picture around as soon as he looked at it.

"This is from a wall chart," said Helena. "There are more parts to this. We need to try and put them together to see exactly what it is."

"Copy them first," said Nicole. "We don't want to cut the originals."

Mark moved a blank piece of paper that separated the next group of photos. They showed items on a table. He placed them side by side.

"Those are tickets," he said.

Brigit looked over at the photos.

"Those are airline tickets. Volgograd to Moscow," she said. "But there's another part underneath."

"What about the other tickets?" asked Gwen.

"Looking now," said Brigit.

Mark took off the next empty sheet.

"Holy shit!" he said. "There are rows and rows of bombs."

He held up the first picture for them to see.

"Festhalle," said Brigit.

"Where's Festhalle?" asked Gina.

"Frankfurt."

"When?" asked Gwen.

Brigit looked up at the clock.

"Now," she said.

Aside from the boys' gaming systems, Michael replaced everything of Petru's that could possibly contain a traceable signal of any kind. The family had relocated to the Animal Kingdom Resort and all new tickets and magic bands were purchased. A brand new account was set up to make sure that their purchases could not be traced. Michael took numerous other precautions so the family could continue their vacation without disappointing the boys.

Lights were on everywhere in the house when Laura and Michael arrived home. No one expected them so soon. In fact, they were so busy studying all of the new information they didn't even hear them come in.

"Goodness, what has your attention so much you didn't even hear us come in?" asked Laura.

"When did you get home?" asked Mark.

"Just now," said Michael.

"That was a short honeymoon," said Gwen.

"We decided to table it for a while," said Laura. "What's going on?"

"Yamani was able to arrange to get information from Mahayin's office complex," said Gina. "They're attacking Festhalle."

"When?" asked Michael.

"Now," said Gina.

Clayton Pearse knew beyond a shadow of a doubt why he'd been reassigned to a position within the borders of the United States. He knew

Hanke wanted to know whatever had been found in Pittsburgh so he could somehow use that information for his own gain. Pearse was bound and determined not to be a party to it. After all, he'd given Hanke information on both Pittsburgh and Edmonton and Hanke did nothing. He was used to having his findings acted upon quickly and to have them summarily disregarded sent him a clear message.

Pearse showed his ID to get onto the scene on the North Side. Although much had been done, the devastation was still there because the investigation was ongoing. Jeff Easterly came over to him.

"Pearse?' he asked. "Jeff Easterly."

"Jeff, nice to meet you," said Pearse extending his hand.

"Rumors have it you've been reassigned."

"The rumors are correct," said Pearse. "Did the rumors also say that I'm supposed to find out everything you know and report back to my boss?"

"Aha, well, that's interesting," said Easterly. "No, the rumors didn't say that. They alluded to the fact that you weren't being as productive as your boss would've liked."

"I see," said Pearse smiling and shaking his head. "I think the rumors have that a bit twisted. I'm positive my boss wanted me out of the way because I knew about this and West Edmonton Mall before they happened."

"Let me guess, you told him and he did nothing."

"Well, just looking around here, I'd have to say, yes."

"Bastard," said Easterly.

"Yah, that's certainly one name I'd give him," said Pearse.

"So, what is it he hopes you'll find out from me?"

"I believe he wants to know just how close you are to solving who's doing this. I think he wants to know if he's still safe."

"What do you mean by that," asked Easterly.

"Well you tell me why this place looks like World War Three happened here when he definitely knew forty-eight hours prior to the attack that it was going to happen. Imagine my shock when I heard about the bombings. I spent a lot of time and effort, not to mention putting myself in some dangerous situations to get this information only to have it totally disregarded and not have anything passed on. He holds that power. Now why is it that he said nothing?"

Easterly shook his head.

"The only thing that makes sense is that somehow, someway, he's part of this mess."

Easterly's jaw dropped.

The explosions rang out for the better part of an hour. Unlike Pittsburgh and West Edmonton Mall, no one came out of the building. The terrorists had a captive audience. The over one hundred-year-old arena was a landmark of historical importance, but in such a short time, the city had lost a treasure.

Emergency personnel waited several minutes after the last explosions before approaching what was left of Festhalle. Every one of them knew their first priority was to find survivors. Once he was notified, President Mason made an appeal for additional emergency personnel and volunteers to aid in the search and rescue.

There was no quick or easy way to clear the debris to get to the bodies. Men and women worked moving pieces of glass, concrete and brick away from where the building once stood. When something was found, they'd call out and appropriate personnel would appear. Soon emergency vehicles were whisking away, yet the line of them was seemingly unending.

Edgar Reinholdt got as close as he could to the scene. Even though he didn't know anyone who had been at Festhalle, it was personal. The emotional pain he felt was excruciating. It was his research, his inventions that caused this catastrophe. There was nothing he could do to take it back, to make things right.

Margo stood next to him.

"I know what you're thinking," she said. "but this isn't your fault."

"Then why does it feel that way?" asked Edgar.

"Well, because you're a person of integrity and you'd never allow anything like this to be done with something you invented. Unfortunately, once those ideas are conceived and come to fruition, we have no way of stopping others from using them for whatever purpose they choose."

"I can't help but thinking, why is it always me?"

"I know how it could seem that way."

Margo thought back to the innocent invention that Reinholdt International had created and through a simple mistake became one of the deadliest inventions ever devised on planet Earth. There were many sleepless nights and many shouting matches as tempers flared from sheer exhaustion and frustration.

"Maybe if we lend a hand for a little while," said Margo.

Edgar nodded.

Afmad Yamani was a stickler when it came to details. He could find things others couldn't find and put together pieces that seemed not to have anything to do with one another and make them fit together like a puzzle.

He went through every piece of paper, reading it from beginning to end. He studied the tables, graphs, and diagrams and made notes. Most of the pages had multiple levels of details. Trying to decipher the codes could take time. Yamani, however, had plenty of time. He turned a page and written lightly in pencil in the margin was 'two for one.' A chill ran up his spine. Could these people actually be brazen enough to try to attack two places at one time?

He thought about the envelope he had sent to Michael and needed to make certain they had seen that same faint note.

Michael walked into the dining room. He paused and looked around the room. For an instant he was back to the time when Laura was being held captive and they were scrambling to try to get her back. The room looked almost the same. There were piles of papers everywhere. Sheets of paper were taped to the walls and easels were set up to hold lists and charts they were working on.

"Yamani wanted to know if we found the penciled note from Mahayin," said Michael.

"A penciled note?" asked Helena.

"He said it's in the margin and very lightly written."

Those around the table began looking carefully at the pictures of all the pages that had been delivered.

"There's a really light note on this one that says 'two for one,'" said Brigit. "Could that be what he's referring to?"

"That's it," said Michael. "He said he is certain it means something."

"Are they really going to try to do two at one time?" asked Gwen.

"That's what this seems to say," said Michael. "I think Yamani's under the impression that is also a possibility."

"Now the questions are which two, when and where," said Paul.

When Hal came back to the house, he looked like a man who had been emotional beaten. What he had seen in Pittsburgh, Edmonton, and now Festhalle had visibly had an effect on him. The human spirit, whether it wants to or not, must handle death. However, death, in that magnitude serves only to severely wound the spirit.

"You need some rest, my friend," said Pierre.

"I need this rampage to end," said Hal.

"I agree," said Pierre, "and we're working on it."

Pierre put his arm around Hal's shoulder and ushered him down the hallway to a guest room.

"Get some sleep. I promise we'll get you when we find anything."

"You know, this makes nine eleven look like it was nothing," said Hal.

Pierre nodded and closed Hal's door.

TWO FOR ONE was printed in large letters on paper on the easel. The names of the cities found in the documents were listed under it. Even though they had the initial listing of cities and the order in which they were to be attacked, this piece of information could definitely change things.

Among all of the information they retrieved were lists of venues that were being considered. Each one had a number beside it, a number that indicated the maximum number of people the venue could hold if sold out. After each number was a slash, followed by another number.

"I know the first number is the occupancy number," said George. "What's the second one?"

"Don't know," said Paul.

"I think I got it," said Helena.

"Got what?" asked Jean.

"I think I know the two cities," she said. "London and Tokyo."

"London and Tokyo?" said Gwen. "How do you figure that?"

"They're eight hours apart," said Helena. "What if he's planning to attack London during morning rush hour and Tokyo during afternoon rush hour?"

Gina started leafing through the pictures until she found the document that dealt with Tokyo. She looked it over again.

"The only thing that's on the docket for Tokyo is the Metro," said Gina. "It says millions beside it."

"What about London?" asked Paul.

"There are a number of things here from venues to the Underground," said Nicole.

"If he wants to make a mark, do something never done before, this'd be it," said Gwen. "He'd have the most people congregated in one place at one time."

"How long do you think we have?" asked Michael.

"Days," said Helena, "if we're lucky."

Mahayin looked over all the details for the upcoming attacks. He needed more men, needed to have them at his disposal. This having to wait until they were delivered to him after each attack, was slowing down the process.

"What do you want?" asked Hanke. "Why are you calling me?"

"I need more men," said Mahayin.

"Why? I know you were sent enough. I have all the figures here, too."

"It's taking too long to get the men to me after each attack," said Mahayin. "It takes days for them to get to me, days for the trucks to get back to wherever, and still more days to get back here. I need to have the resources at my disposal. We can't let them breathe. We have to attack and attack quickly."

"Farred, calm down," said Hanke. "I'll get more men sent, but remember this. You can't go using extra men on a project just because you think you might need them. We already know exactly how many it will take and you have to stick to that number. Do you understand?"

"I'm not an idiot," said Mahayin. "Of course I know that. I'm not going to use extra men on an attack. I want to be able to move up the timetable so that we can attack one right after another."

"Alright, Farred, I'll have the next set of men sent, as many as can be spared," said Hanke.

Mahayin put down the phone and smiled. He was going to be able to finally do something he wanted to do.

Over the course of his life, Yamani had learned the value of patience. Every time he tried to hurry something along, he always wound up having to back track and correct something that just wasn't quite right. This time wasn't any different. He gave people things to do and waited for them to complete them and return. He was thankful that the people he was surrounded by were indeed faithful and always went that extra measure to make certain his instructions were followed to the letter.

He had heard from Sadik that Nolan Shugg had taken his place with his ancestors and he now waited for him to return to get all of the details. Maranissa told him that Sadik had returned and he went directly to the kitchen.

"Sadik, it is good to have you back," said Yamani.

"It is good to be back, sir," said Sadik.

"I take it the job went well,"

"Yes, sir, very well. Since I was destroying his car, I decided to bring his briefcase. I thought maybe there might be something useful in it."

Sadik placed the briefcase on the table and slid it towards Yamani. Yamani opened it and began to look through its contents. There were three folders and a large envelope along with several pens.

Yamani opened the first folder. There was correspondence between Shugg and some other people. The senders and receivers were blacked out so their identities could not be read. Yamani read them and then passed them to Sadik.

"Read them, Sadik," said Yamani. "Mr. Shugg knew all about the bombing of West Edmonton Mall, yet he chose not to do anything."

Once he and Sadik were done with the first folder, he opened the second one. This one also contained correspondence concerning West Edmonton Mall and the fear that someone was going to tell the authorities about it.

"Who is this person that Mr. Shugg is messaging?" asked Sadik.

"That we do not know," said Yamani. "He seems to be the key to all this."

"Mr. Shugg was careful not to identify him anywhere."

"As you know, Sadik, no one can stay hidden forever. We will find him."

Yamani opened the third folder and all that was contained was a summons from the Canadian Security Agency notifying Mr. Shugg in writing that he had to appear before them. Yamani closed that folder and picked up the envelope. On the outside of the envelope were the words 'My Piece.' Yamani opened the envelope and took out the paper. He unfolded it and laid it on the table.

Sadik looked at it.

"What is that?" he asked.

"That, my dear Sadik is a map with the section of the world that Mr. Shugg was going to have as his very own once this is finished."

Sadik looked at Yamani.

"Are they serious?"

"Now we know what is in it for each of them," said Yamani. "This makes it all the more important to deal with these people now. Listen carefully, Sadik. We have work to do and we must do it quickly."

Chapter Twenty-Six

Jacques was now awake a little longer than he was asleep. He picked up the folder Nicole left for him. She knew he meant it when he said he wanted to help. While they couldn't bring everything to him, they could give him enough information to stimulate his thought process and give him a renewed sense of purpose.

He read through the notes and double checked their conclusions. He was absolutely in agreement that Tokyo and London were the choices for the two for one. However, when he looked at the list for London, only the Underground made sense. He took an unusually fat pen, one that was easy to grasp in his current condition, and made a list of places that would be heavily traveled during morning rush hour. He agreed with the Underground. Certainly, a lot of people used it to go back and forth to work. Somehow, it didn't seem like the right answer. This group really wasn't targeting any one sort of venue. They were all over the place.

From his list he chose two. Out of the two, one stuck out more than the other. Jacques circled Heathrow and then crossed it out. The more he thought about it, the Underground would make the most logical choice. He circled it and then rested his head against his pillow.

Helena's idea that the two cities could possibly be London and Tokyo made absolute sense to Yamani. He decided to try to even the odds or tip them ever so slightly in their favor. To do this, he had to make sure that those who were in a position to squelch intelligence reports would no longer be an issue. The old adage of sending an engraved invitation was put to the test by him and true to form his guests came ready for their accolades. Their inflated egos put them in line for their reward, their eternal reward.

Yamani opened a folder and looked at the list. He took out his pen and crossed out four names; Nolan Shugg, Canadian Secret Intelligence Agency, Anton Morel, French General Directorate for External Security, Katsu Tanaka, Japanese Public Security Intelligence Agency, and Ethan Shelford, UK Secret Intelligence Service. The work was far from done, taking care of those who stood in the way moved them one step closer.

Sadik knocked on the door and Qadir opened it. He took one of the cases from Sadik and they put all three on the table. Yamani opened them one at a time and took out everything that was pertinent to the attacks that were going to happen. While they made mention of London and Tokyo along with Paris, the dates and definite decision on the targets were missing. Common to each case was the large envelope with the words 'My Piece' on each of them. Yamani identified each envelope and put the person's name on it and then took out the map.

"How can you just divide up the world for your own purpose?" asked Qadir.

"It is payment for keeping things quiet," said Yamani.

Yamani paused a moment to think. He tapped his finger on the table.

"Qadir," said Yamani. "I need to speak to Mr. Wassum, immediately."

"Yes, sir," said Qadir and he went off.

Everything that had to do with Tokyo and London had been taken out of the packet. He kept going over and over every piece of information trying to find some clue as to date and time. He believed, as did the others, that Mahayin would try to pull off two attacks next. Yamani went through everything concerning the attacks on Pittsburgh, West Edmonton Mall, and Festhalle. There were many similarities and not just in the devices used. It was more than that. The similarities went all the way back to the deployment of the bombers.

Yamani nodded his head and made notes. He might not be able to totally stop these events from happening, but he hoped to deliver a devastating blow that would cripple their efforts.

Pierre knew how important it was to be organized, to have everything in order, now that they possessed the information to hopefully stop the attacks. What they needed was a direct line to the world leaders. It was necessary to be able to take over certain networks if and when the time came.

"Edgar, how are you doing?" asked Pierre.

"Much better today," said Edgar.

"I'm glad to hear that."

"How are things going? I hope you were able to make some progress."

"As a matter of fact, we have. We need you to contact the leaders," said Pierre. "We're going to need their help."

"I can contact them," said Edgar. "What're you going to need?"

"We know they're using phones to detonate. We're going to need permission to take down the network."

"Pierre, I don't know if they'll agree to give you that much power."

"I want them to give that power to you," said Pierre. "They trust you."

"When?"

"We don't know exactly. Unfortunately, they're going to have to be accessible to you."

"I'll do my best," said Edgar.

"Do whatever it takes."

Nothing frustrated John Hanke more than not being able to get in touch with his operatives. This time, he had more to consider. He had the intelligence leaders of virtually every country answerable to him. He needed those lines of communication open at all times. Lately it had been more and more difficult to reach some of them. Even after leaving an ultimatum to get in touch or else, he still hadn't heard a thing.

Even Mahayin was being more elusive than usual and that was enough to make Hanke more than a bit nervous. He needed a 'yes man' in this role. He didn't need anyone thinking beyond what they had been told to do. Somehow he believed Mahayin was beginning to get ideas of his own.

He took another sip of his drink. At least with Mahayin he could send Anna. It was at least comforting to know that she would always answer her phone and he could find out what was going on through her. He had the phone set for speaker so he could do other things while it rang.

"Damn it!" he yelled. "Doesn't anyone answer their damn phone anymore?"

"Who are you yelling at?" asked Anna. "I'm right here."

"Well, what's he doing?"

"Calm yourself. I just got here, my love. Give me some time."

"Don't tell me to calm myself! This is important! And I don't have time to waste, Anna!"

"Such the drama queen, aren't we! I'll call you later, maybe."

"I'll give you maybe," he yelled, but Anna had hung up. "You are such a bitch!"

Farred Mahayin shuffled papers from one pile to another. On his desk sat three clocks, each showing a different time. He looked at his watch and then went back to the stacks of papers. He made notes on the pad in front of him.

A knock on the door seemed to startle him. He wasn't expecting anyone. He had cleared his calendar so he wouldn't be disturbed. Reluctantly, he put down the papers, glanced once more at the clocks and then opened the door.

"Anna," he said, "to what do I owe this visit?"

He knew exactly why she was there. He knew Hanke didn't trust that he could deliver the project on time.

"Can't a girl surprise her boyfriend?" she asked brushing his cheek with a kiss.

Anna walked past him and stopped in the center of the room.

"What're you doing?" asked Anna.

"Just seeing to the details of the project," said Mayahin.

"Everything on schedule?' she asked.

"After this, we'll be ahead of schedule."

"How can that be?"

"He said he wanted the pace picked up and that's exactly what I'm doing."

"What did you do?" asked Anna. "Farred, tell me what you did!"

"Soon, two of them will be crossed off the list," said Mahayin giving Anna a sly grin.

"Farred, you know what he said; one at a time."

"I know what he said, Anna. I also know what can be done."

"He's not going to be pleased," said Anna.

"So what!"

"So what! So what! You answer to him," said Anna raising her voice. "You just can't take it upon yourself to do what you want!"

"Why, Anna? Give me one reason why I can't do two."

"Because he strictly forbade it.

"What's he going to do, Anna? Replace me?" asked Mahayin. "He can't. He knows no one else can pull this off, but me."

"You're wrong, Farred. No one's indispensable."

"I am, Anna, and after this is done, he'll know who's in charge."

The *Chosen One* looked at the number of men who were left in the camp. By all figures, he most likely would have enough men to handle the next series of events, however, it would be very tight. Not one man could afford to be lost. He didn't like the odds and knew he had to reinforce his numbers.

He pulled the flyer from out of his drawer and looked at it. He knew it couldn't go out the same way it had before, so he worked at changing some of the wording. He didn't want it to sound desperate; instead he wanted to play on their sense of duty. He wanted to use that ever present sense of guilt on them.

For a solid hour he worked on perfecting the flyer and copying it. When he was finished he called for some of his most faithful followers. They came immediately and stood in front of his desk.

"I need for you to take flyers into the villages and cities," he said. "It is necessary for us to increase our ranks."

"Yes, sir," they said in unison.

He handed the flyers to them along with a list of places and they left to do his bidding.

Flights in and out of Volgograd International Airport were limited to those that came from and went to Moscow or St. Petersburg. From those cities one could reach almost everywhere in the world. Like any other airport, Volgograd experienced its share of delayed flights and today was one of those days. Throughout the waiting areas, passengers dozed in chairs, some snoring loudly.

Mr. Wassum walked through the airport as he had done countless times over the past three days. He looked to his right and left, scanning the passengers. He glanced at the gate list he carried and then put the card back into his pocket. A man dressed all in tan brushed his arm as he hurried by, but he made no attempt to apologize. Mr. Wassum picked up his pace slightly keeping the man in sight. Once the man turned into a waiting area, Mr. Wassum stopped. From his vantage point he could count how many were waiting. Taking out his phone, he keyed a set of numbers and pressed send. He kept his eyes on the screen waiting for the reply and then put the phone into his pocket. He took out a tag and put it on. Mr. Wassum then began quietly talking to passengers, asking them to move to other waiting areas. As soon as he'd successfully moved all those not with the terrorist group, he positioned himself in the corridor to head off any new arrivals.

A man in airline uniform walked past and relieved the person at the desk. Mr. Wassum looked out the window and watched as the plane moved into position at the gate. Within minutes, the man at the desk made an announcement that the plane was now ready for boarding. The men got up and walked single file through the passageway and onto the waiting plane. As soon as they sat down, they put on their seat belts.

The fasten seat belt sign flashed and the pilot made the pre-flight announcements. None of the men moved, but only sat facing forward. The pilot began moving the plane towards the runway. He slipped a mask over his face and flipped a switch. He maneuvered the plane to the end of the runway and headed it in the direction of the empty field at the end of airport property. Enough fencing had been removed to allow the plane to be driven through and then into the tree lined field past the end of the airport property. The pilot, kept the engine on. He flipped one more switch, disembarked, and quickly moved away from the craft taking care not to be seen. He stuffed the mask into his pocket and hurried towards the road.

Mr. Wassum nodded his head to Khali. Khali nodded back and walked outside of the terminal. Mr. Wassum followed a safe distance behind. Once outside, they got into the car. Sadik followed the signage to get back on the highway. He drove down the outer edge of the airport property, pulled over and Gehran got in.

"Everything go well?" asked Mr. Wassum.

"Everything is taken care of," said Gehran. "I flooded their compartment with the gas."

"Good."

They continued driving a short distance and Mr. Wassum signaled Sadik to stop. He pulled the car over. Mr. Wassum keyed in numbers on his phone. The four men watched as the plane seemed to be crushed under an immense weight. Then he placed another call.

"It has been taken care of."

"And the flight plan?"

"St. Petersburg then Tokyo."

"The other passengers?"

"Safely on the real plane."

"Excellent."

With the news from Mr. Wassum, Yamani knew he had to contact Michael. There was no way he could take care of this himself. They needed to work together to bring this to a halt. Yamani went into his study where he wouldn't be disturbed or overheard. He sent a message to Michael.

"Mr. Braedon," said Yamani, "We have been fortunate to have made another breakthrough."

"What is that," asked Michael.

"We were able to intercept a plane filled with terrorists leaving from Volgograd heading for Moscow. We took care of them and they will no longer be of concern. As far as anyone knows, the plane left on time with its passengers aboard."

"Do you know where the plane was going after Moscow?"

"It was going to Tokyo," said Yamani. "If what you have deduced is true, then the other logical destination would be London."

"We're positive of where in Tokyo, but we have to get clarity on London. Do you know how many men were on that plane?"

"As soon as I have the chance to talk to my man, I will let you know."

"Thank you."

As was done in past efforts of recruiting, the men dropped off the flyers and then returned the following day to collect the recruits. Raseem pulled the truck up to the village from which Adarine and the first group had been recruited. He stopped it and got out. He looked at his watch and then looked around. He was right on time, not early and not late, but exactly on time. Where were the recruits? He saw no men.

Up the street came a group of women. He couldn't understand why they would be coming directly for him. Surely they had not misinterpreted the flyer to think that women were now being recruited. The *Chosen One* would never stand for women fulfilling the duties of men.

"Where are our husbands?" one woman yelled. "They were taken away in one of your trucks and we haven't seen them for months."

"They are very busy doing the work of the Divine One," said Raseem.

"The Chosen One never kept our husbands away from us," said the woman. "He always allowed them to return home every night. Does he no longer feel that family is important?"

"Of course he feels family is important," said Raseem backing up.

The women crowded around him. Raseem was not prepared for this type of confrontation. He was told to go pick up recruits. That was all. The *Chosen One* never said anything about the women being angry.

A woman behind him poked him in the back multiple times with her finger. He turned around to face her.

"They say that he's killing our husbands," she said. "Is that true? Is he killing our husbands? Does he think the little bit of money we receive in return for our husbands working for him is ultimate payment for their lives?"

"I do not know what you are talking about?" said Raseem. "Who has told you this?"

"Never mind who it was that told us. Answer the question."

"The *Chosen One* would never do that," said Raseem. "He values all life just as the Divine One does."

"Well, if that is true, then we want to see our husbands. Do not return without them. And, if by chance you decide not to do anything about this, we will find you."

"Go!" said another woman. "Go quickly! Make sure you tell him exactly what we said."

The women opened a path to the door of the truck and Raseem quickly walked to the truck and got in.

From the time Anna stepped foot into Mahayin's office, he kept her occupied.

"I'll put this down here," said Mahayin putting Anna's purse in the bottom drawer of his desk. "This way I can lock it and we'll know it'll be safe."

"What if I need something?" asked Anna.

"What could you possibly need while you're here?" asked Anna.

Mahayin, knew that Anna was looking for the opportunity to steal away to call Hanke. He couldn't allow that to happen. He couldn't allow

Hanke somehow messing up his plan. This was his time to prove he was capable of handling anything.

"Come, Anna, we have things to check on," said Mahayin. "You've come on a momentous day. Now you will be able to see the master in action."

Anna rolled her eyes and followed Mahayin out of the office.

As he made his way back into the dining room, Michael wondered how they could possibly hope to control hitting two cities that were half a world away from each other. It seemed like an impossible task. He shook his head. Why was he worried about how they would accomplish that? What he should be thinking about was how they were going to stop this from happening.

"Hey, can you stop for a few minutes?" he asked. "I just heard from Yamani. His men were able to intercept a plane with terrorists bound for Moscow and then Tokyo. According to him, they were taken care of and would no longer be of concern. So we know for certain that Tokyo is one of the cities. And he also agrees with us that the other city is definitely London."

"Now what?" asked Gina.

"As much as I hate to say this," said Michael, "we have to get someone to those cities."

"I'll go," said Mark. "I'll take Tokyo."

"I'll take London," said Angelique.

"Get the reservations made," said Michael.

Chapter Twenty-Seven

Nothing pleased Farred Mahayin as much as being able to show off in front of Anna. This was the beginning of his time of triumph. Everything had been put into motion and there was nothing anyone or anything could do to stop it. He unlocked his desk, opened the drawer and brought out Anna's purse.

"There you are," said Mahayin as he put her purse on the desk. "You can have it back."

"What was the purpose of locking it away in the first place?" asked Anna.

"Come now, Anna, I know he sent you. I know he doesn't believe I can do this one at a time, let alone two at once, but I assure you, I can. I'm going to prove it to you and to him. So, you see, my love, I couldn't take the risk of you getting on your phone and telling him what was going on. There was no way anyone was or is going to stop me. So, if you want to let him know what's going on, go right ahead."

Anna shook her head and picked up her purse from his desk.

"I hope, for your sake, Farred, this is a success," she said, "because if it isn't, if anything goes wrong, there won't be a place on this earth or even in this universe where you will be able to hide."

Anna turned and walked out of the office without so much as a goodbye.

Mark hurried out of the terminal. Everything they uncovered led him to believe Tokyo would be one of the next targets. When and exactly where were the two mysteries yet to be solved. As soon as he reached the curb, a limo pulled up and the driver got out.

"Mr. Braedon, it's nice to see you again," he said.

"Nice to see you too, Takato," said Mark.

Takato held the door while Mark got in and then put the bag in the trunk. Once he got behind the wheel, he carefully pulled away from the curb.

"How's everything?" asked Mark.

"Everything seems to be normal. I've not seen nor heard anything out of the ordinary."

"That's how it always is," said Mark. "Nothing seems different until the attack comes."

"What makes you think Tokyo's a target?" asked Takato.

"We were able to intercept a plane on the tarmac in Volgograd. The flight plan filed was for Moscow and then Tokyo."

"What happened to the plane?"

"Crushed."

"Won't they know?"

"The real plane left a few minutes late, and without incident."

Takato shook his head and smiled.

"Now what?" asked Takato.

"Not sure," said Mark.

Takato signaled to go around a bus that was going slower than he wanted to drive. As they began passing, Mark looked up at the passengers. All were seated and staring straight ahead. Every one that he could see was wearing tan.

"Damn!" he yelled. "They're here. Get in front of this bus. Where're they going?"

"That's an airport bus," said Takato. "They're most likely heading for the city."

"What's going on in the city tonight?"

"Nothing except rush hour," said Takato. He took his hand off the wheel and started shaking his finger. "Millions of people use the Metro."

Mark took out his phone.

"They couldn't take out all million," said Takato trying to rationalize what he just said, "but the destruction would be incomprehensible. Depending upon where they detonate, parts of the city could cave."

"Edgar, Mark."

"Mark, what is it?"

"I need all cell phone service into and out of Tokyo and the full extent of the Metro line severed. They're here, Edgar."

"I need permission."

"He'll take your call," said Mark. "That's why I called you."

Anna Roudalco was seething when she left Craustof. No one talked to her that way and no one held her captive for any reason. What he did to her was unforgivable. What he was doing was going to somehow blow up in his face. She knew that. It was only a matter of time. She got into the car and headed towards the airport. There was just one place she wanted to be and it had nothing to do with Mahayin or Hanke. No, where she wanted to be and what she wanted to do would put both of them into a compromising position.

She reached and patted her purse. Through the leather she could feel the outline of the book. That was her ticket to freedom, her way of paying them back and exacting her revenge. She longed for the day when she could tell them to their face just what she had gathered about them.

It was sad, but true that Mahayin was nothing more than a "yes" man. All he was expected to do was follow orders and get the job done. He was not getting paid to do anything else. He was definitely not getting paid to think.

As far as Hanke was concerned, she placated him from the very beginning. One had to do that when one needed information. A smile came to her face when she thought about how susceptible he was when he was sleeping. He would talk in his sleep. Sometimes he would just mutter and she would quietly ask him questions. More often than not, he would answer them. It was those answers, the answers she was given that came when there was no filter from the conscious mind, that she wrote in her book. Along with those notes was every piece of information he confided in her as well as other bits and pieces she was able to find out for herself.

Although Hanke always gave the idea that she was the one he trusted with everything he knew, she knew differently. Hanke trusted no one. But that was alright. She didn't trust him either. From the beginning she knew his objective and she graciously participated and gave him no cause to think otherwise.

She checked in at the airport and found that her flight to Moscow was on time. Once she got there, she would cash in her ticket and purchase one bound for the United States.

The *Chosen One* found the news from Raseem to be extremely disconcerting. He didn't have time for something as petty as a bunch of whining women inquiring about where their husbands were. This was not something that he remotely thought he would have to deal with. He always thought the women would be honored to have their men rally for the Cause, and if they happened to die for it, well, then they would be doubly blessed.

He knew he couldn't ignore it, because if Raseem's account of what happened yesterday was any indication of the conviction of these women, he knew somehow they would find the camp and one day he would open his eyes and they would be staring down at his face.

The only way to solve this problem was to deal with it. These women were nothing more than a cancer trying to attack his plan. He reasoned that just like a cancer had to be eradicated, so too did these women. He knew what had to be done and also who to send to do it.

"Kannid," he yelled.

Kannid came immediately into the office.

"Please close the door. There's something I need you to do for me."

It was almost as though a school bell rang or an old fashioned factory whistle blew and then the buildings in the city of Tokyo emptied in a matter of minutes. Some headed for the buses, others to garages to get their cars or bicycles, but the majority of people streamed underground to the metro.

Katie grabbed her friend's arm as they were running down the stairs.

"What?" asked Lydia.

"We have to go back," said Katie. "I forgot my wallet. It's in my desk drawer."

"You left it again!" said Lydia.

"I'm sorry. I forgot I put it in there after lunch. You coming with me?"

"Yes," said Lydia.

The two women reached the bottom of the stairs, turned, and headed back up the other side.

"If we hurry," said Katie, "We'll still be able to catch the metro we usually get."

"It's so crowded," said Lydia turning around and watching the crowd press together. She estimated that they were already eight to ten deep. As she turned to face forward, she bumped into a man standing on the landing.

"Excuse me," said Lydia.

The man said nothing. He stood still and silent.

"Odd," said Lydia.

Katie emerged from the metro station. Everyone was coming towards them. She waited a moment for Lydia and then they started walking back to the office.

"That was strange," said Lydia.

"What was?" asked Katie.

"Did you see that man I bumped into on the landing?"

"No. What about him?"

"I said excuse me, but he didn't say anything. He didn't even move. He just stood there."

"Maybe he didn't hear you," said Katie. "It's awfully noisy in there."

"I was within inches of him."

A man dressed exactly like the man on the landing brushed past Lydia on his way to the Metro.

"Didn't I? Weren't you?" asked Lydia. "Did you see him? Katie!"
Katie turned around and looked back at Lydia.
"See who?" asked Katie.
"That man dressed all in tan. He looked exactly like the man on the landing."
Katie looked at Lydia.
"There are a lot of people dressed in tan," said Katie. "Look around."
She pointed to men dressed in tan heading for the Metro from different directions.
"That's strange," said Lydia. "Don't you think that's strange?"
"Come on," said Katie. "We have to hurry or we won't get home until really late."
"Okay, I'm coming, but I still think it's strange."

Elliott Manstrom looked at the time on his phone as they neared the terminal at Heathrow Airport. It was already seven twenty-five and they needed to get through security as quickly as possible in order to catch their flight. His wife, Cheryl, walked faster trying to keep up with him. Their daughter, Susan, ran towards the doors wheeling her suitcase behind her. She ran up the ramp and stopped in front of the doors.
"I beat you," Susan said smiling back at her parents.
"Wait for us," Cheryl yelled to her.
"I am," said Susan.
"Ready?" asked Elliott once all three were at the door.
"Let's go," said Cheryl.
They walked inside the terminal and Susan's eyes widened as she took in all of the sights. Hundreds of people were walking by in various directions heading towards their destinations. Susan slowed her pace and looked around. There were people from every country and some were dressed uniquely in their native dress. With all the color around, Susan's eyes were drawn to a man standing by the entrance with his arms crossed. He was dressed simply in a light tan colored shirt with pants that matched and his face had no expression. Susan turned around

slowly, looking everywhere. Down the corridor, she saw another one of those men, ahead of her another, and still another to her right.

She sat in the third seat of the second row. Bradley Newhowser sat next to her in the third row. Mrs. Franklin was in front of the room writing on the board. She finished writing several questions and then turned around.

"Who can answer the first question?" she asked.

Bradley raised his hand.

"Bradley," said Mrs. Franklin.

"Mrs. Franklin," said Bradley, "you know those terrorists who blew up Heinz Field were all dressed the same."

"Yes, Bradley," said Mrs. Franklin. "I'd like you to answer the question on the board, please."

"But, Mrs. Franklin, do you know why they were dressed alike?"

"No, Bradley, I don't," said Mrs. Franklin. "You need to answer the question."

"They dressed alike so the terrorist leader could see where they were," said Bradley persisting with his subject. "And do you know what they were wearing?"

"No Bradley, I don't," said Mrs. Franklin walking back to her desk and sitting down.

"They were all wearing light tanny colored pants and shirts that matched and they sat there with their arms folded."

Susan looked at the men again. Bradley's words played over in her mind, "light tanny colored pants and shirts that all matched with their arms folded."

"Terrorists," she whispered to herself.

Susan's heart started beating faster and she was afraid.

"Daddy," she whispered dropping the handle of her suitcase.

Elliott kept walking. He hadn't noticed Susan had begun to dawdle. Cheryl looked around and Susan was out of her sight.

"Elliott," she said loudly. "Where's Susan?"

Elliott stopped and turned to face his wife. Then he looked around and couldn't see her immediately.

"Daddy!" Susan screamed. "Daddy!"

Elliott pushed through the crowd, following the sound of Susan's voice. Cheryl followed trying to keep up with him.

"Susan," Elliott yelled. "Susan!"

"Daddy, hurry! Daddy!"

Elliott stopped as a group walked in front of him. Cheryl grabbed his arm.

"Where is she?" asked Cheryl. "Susan!"

"Mommy, hurry!"

The group passed and Elliott took his wife's hand and ran towards Susan. Two members from airport security ran towards her.

Elliott hugged his daughter.

"Susan, why didn't you follow us?"

"Daddy, we have to leave," she said. She was trembling.

"I know, we have to get to our plane," he said.

"No, daddy. We have to leave. There are terrorists here."

"Susan," said Elliott, "why would you say that?"

"Look," said Susan and she pointed to each man dressed in the same way with the same blank expression on their faces. "Those are terrorists." Her voice became louder. "We have to leave. Terrorists blow things up. They're going to blow this place up. I want to leave!"

"Afraid of flying, is she?" asked a security officer.

"No," said Cheryl. "She loves to fly."

"Alright, Susan, we'll leave," said Elliott. "We can make arrangements for later."

"What about the rest of these people?" said Susan. "They're going to die!"

Susan looked at the people passing.

"Run! Get out of here!" she yelled, "There are terrorists! They're going to blow this place up!"

Elliott picked up his daughter's suitcase and took Susan by the hand. He walked hurriedly towards the door. Other people began heeding the cry of the young girl and soon there were swarms of people heading for the doors.

"Where?" yelled a man looking at Susan.

Susan pointed to the men at the doors and in the corridors.

"Terrorists!" the man screamed, adding his voice of warning.

Like a wave, the word terrorist rang throughout the terminal. People with baggage dropped what they had and ran towards the exits pushing and shoving those slower than them. An elderly woman was pushed to the ground and two young men scooped her up under her arms and ran with her.

The second security officer took out his walkie-talkie.

"Go ahead," said a voice.

"I need a check of suspicious characters," he said, "all dressed in matching light tan shirts and pants, arms crossed and blank expressions. Check entrances and exits, corridors etc."

"Reason for check?"

"As a young girl just said. I think they're terrorists."

"Which terminal?"

"All of them," he yelled trying to be heard above the people. "All of them."

"What makes you think there are terrorists?"

"I don't have time for this," he yelled. "Just do it!"

He took out his phone and called his friend in terminal three. Feeling the vibration, Cecil took out his phone and looked at the screen.

"Hey Barry, I thought you were working," said Cecil.

"I am. Listen, check your area. Do you see any men dressed all in light tan standing with their arms crossed and blank expressions on their faces?"

Cecil looked around and walk to the end of a dividing wall. He started counting.

"Yes, I count six in my sight. What's this about?"

"I think we're going to get hit. I think they're terrorists."

"What's all that noise?"

"People getting the hell out of here. Get people moving."

"We could get let go for that?"

"The other choice is death."

Just being out of arm's reach of the two of them made Anna relax a little. It was never her intention to get involved in such a manner that she became a go between. She was worth more than that…way more than that.

A car pulled up to the curb. Anna opened the door and got in.

"Hello beautiful," said Pearse giving her a kiss.

"Ahhh," sighed Anna. "It feels so good to be here, even if it's only for a few hours."

"Why just a few hours?" asked Pearse.

"I was sent to see what was going on somewhere else and he's going to expect me back with a report."

"So he's still trying to hide."

"I hardly ever see him," said Anna. "It's like he drops off the face of the earth."

"So to what do I owe this visit?"

"They're going to attack London and Tokyo.

"Which one's first?"

"They're doing both at the same time."

"Who's doing it?"

"I don't know," said Anna. "I don't know who's in charge."

"How do you know?"

"Mahayin was setting things up for it."

"Who's detonating?"

"I don't know. It's always someone different and they never live to see the light of day afterwards."

"Do you know when?"

"No, only where," said Anna. "I saw the Metro circled under Tokyo and the Underground circled under London."

"That's at least something."

"There's no way to stop it. He's been deploying the men already."

Pearse was quiet while he thought about what Anna said. He pulled around and headed for the hotel nearest the airport.

The plane landed at Heathrow. They had already decided that Angelique would take a minicab from the Heathrow to London. Her goal was to hopefully assess the situation and be able to do something before it happened. Pierre had already talked to Edgar about taking the networks down and it was their hopes that being able to do so would in some way enable them to stop the attacks before they began.

If what they found out was correct, it seemed logical that they would somehow use the center of London as their point of dispersion. She needed to get there.

Once they were permitted to disembark, they went through the jet bridge to get into the terminal. Although the sound was muffled there was no denying there was yelling and screaming in the terminal. The passengers began hurrying more, trying to get through the bridge into the terminal to see what was happening.

Angelique stepped into the terminal and watched as hundreds of people ran towards the doors. In the wake there was abandoned luggage and backpacks. Angelique looked around not quite knowing what to make of the mass hysteria. As she surveyed the activity, she noticed men standing still as statues. They were all dressed alike with arms folded. This was exactly what had been reported at the other venues.

"Dear God," she said, "it's not the Underground. It's Heathrow."

Chapter Twenty-Eight

Traffic was rather light as they made their way to the city. The whole time, Mark kept wondering what could be done if Edgar couldn't persuade the Prime Minister to block the phones. He cautioned Takato to keep the bus in sight, but to stay as far away as possible. Even if they were to somehow get control of it, the amount of explosives contained in that small space could cause massive damage.

Mark jumped as his phone rang.

"Yes," he said after looking at the display.

"How're you doing?" asked Michael.

"Well, I've been better and worse," said Mark. "What do you have?"

"Our military will be providing some support, but that'll take at least an hour," said Michael. "That bus has to be stopped before it gets to the city."

"How do you propose we do that?"

"I don't know," said Michael. "Be creative."

Mark put the phone in his pocket.

"Be creative," he murmured. "How far away is Tokyo?"

"At least an hour," said Takato.

"Will the bus follow this road?"

"Yes, it'll follow along this route, but there're multiple toll exits to get onto the different parts of the road. Essentially it'll follow this prescribed route until it comes to one of the downtown exits. Why?"

"We need to get way in front of him."

Takato increased his speed.

"What're you trying to do?" asked Takato.
"We need to stop that bus before it gets into Tokyo."

Kannid drove the truck into the village, stopped and got out. The women must have seen the truck coming from a distance and were waiting with their children near the place where Raseem had parked.

"I bring you greetings from the *Chosen One*. He sends his apologies for not permitting your husbands to come back home to see their families. They have been so busy with everything that has been going on, that he could not possibly spare them for the amount of time it would take to come home, spend time, and then come back. If it would have been at all possible, he would have done it. The *Chosen One* is not without compassion for the families of those who have chosen to follow the Divine One. He has decided that any of you who would want to come with me, may do so. I will drive you to see your husbands. You will be able to spend time with them today and then I will bring you back late this evening. If there is anything you need to get, I will wait, but we must leave here no later than half an hour from now."

The women disbursed quickly and came back as quickly as possible. As soon as they got to the truck, they were helped onto the truck and as soon as all had returned, Kannid started driving.

As usual, he drove making many turns as he headed out to the desert and far away from the camp. No matter what twists and turns he made, his main objective was to head due west and far into the desert. It was the will of the *Chosen One* that these women never be a problem again. Kannid knew exactly what the *Chosen One* meant, but when it came to women and children, he had to follow the will of the Divine One. He knew he would be questioned about where he had taken them and also what had happened. He knew that there were things that could be checked and things that could not.

When he had driven as far as he thought he safely could and still get back, he stopped the truck. He walked around the back and opened the canvas flap.

"You have to get out," he said. "You have get out now and take everything with you."

The women and children gathered all of their belongings and exited the truck. They looked around and there was nothing, no sight of any sort of camp. When they were all out, Kannid lifted his gun. The women pulled their children close to them. Kannid aimed the gun, lowered it and emptied the round into the sand.

"I'm sorry," he said. "This is the best I can do."

He got back into the truck and drove away.

When Anna said a few hours, that's exactly what she meant. There was hardly enough time to make the time at the hotel qualify as anything really intimate, but they did their best. Anna always said that a few stolen moments were worth a scheduled two weeks.

Clayton closed the door to Gimshaw's office and sat down.

"They're going to attack Tokyo and London, together."

"What the hell!" said Gimshaw. "How did you find out?"

"One of my contacts doesn't want to deal with anyone but me. She overheard a conversation and then saw a paper as she walked past some men. She said they were talking about how they wondered why they were sending things to London and Tokyo. They had no idea they were doing mining on those islands. She said one of them questioned why you would put explosives into cracks in Tokyo when they already had earthquakes. He said he was glad he didn't live there because he was afraid of earthquakes."

"How reliable is she?" asked Gimshaw.

"She's the one who told me about Pittsburgh and West Edmonton."

"Did she know when?"

"No, only the cities."

"Do you really think they would try to do two cities half a world apart?"

"We don't have time to question it," said Pearse. "We have to be on alert at both places, no matter whether they're going to try two or only do one, because we would have no idea which one."

Gimshaw picked up the phone.

"Better to err on the side of caution," said Gimshaw. "I remember those words from Pittsburgh."

Angelique heard the cry 'terrorist' being shouted by people trying to alert everyone. Security had not yet moved into evacuation mode and so it was up to the people themselves to actually organize the evacuation efforts.

Several people bumped her as she stood watching. She moved off to the side to clear the way for the passengers still coming behind her.

She took out her phone.

"Hey sweetheart," said Jean, "did you get there safely?"

"Yes," she said.

"What's all that noise? I can hardly hear you."

"We were wrong. It's Heathrow.

"What!"

"It's Heathrow!" she yelled into the phone. "It's not the Underground."

"How do you know it's Heathrow?"

"They're here, Jean. They're all over this terminal. People are evacuating, but security isn't doing anything yet."

"What are they waiting for?"

"I don't know!"

Angelique heard an explosion happen in a distance.

"Jean, it's started!" she yelled. "Call Edgar. He has to shut it down."

She hung up the phone, put it in her pocket, took a piece of paper from her other pocket, and headed for the doors. She looked around and yelled at people as they passed her going towards the runway. One after another after another the explosions went off.

"Come on, Edgar," she said, "shut it down. We can't wait. Shut it down!"

The explosions were getting closer. It seemed like they had configured it to go off with a domino effect. She looked to her right and could see the far end of the terminal explode. She picked up the pace, heading towards the closest door. She tried to block out the fact that the explosions were getting closer. There was a cloud of dust wafting in front of her making it more difficult to see. She tripped over an abandoned piece of luggage and tried to keep her footing, but she fell to her knees. Chunks of debris rained down and Angelique put her arms over her head to protect herself. She felt her phone vibrate in her pocket, but couldn't reach to get it. She couldn't move at all. Her legs were pinned.

"Edgar," she whispered, "you have to stop this."

From the observation deck of the control tower, Frank watched as the terminal was ripped apart. Several men walked out onto the runways and stood as still as statues with their arms crossed.

"What the hell's going on?" he yelled to his co-workers.

"I don't know!" shouted Katrina.

One by one, with a few seconds in between, the men exploded creating in their wake damaged and useless runways.

"Did you see that?" asked Frank. "They just blew up, one right after the other."

"Time to get out of here," said Herman as soon as he reached the top of the stairs. "Take the stairs, not the elevators. Get out of here as fast as you can."

The door opened and three men walked in. They walked to three different points and stood arms crossed. Their faces were set as stone and they interacted with no one. As the air traffic controllers moved towards the door, not one of the men made a move to stop them.

"Move! Move! Move!" said Herman heading for the door.

Once through the door, the sounds of footsteps racing down the short flights were almost deafening. Some took every other step while others ran as quickly as possible. Thunderous explosions rang out and vibrations rocked the tower. Concrete cracked, metal twisted and rivets popped. Suddenly the staircases were not as stable as they had been. Gaping holes appeared where steps had once been. Railings came detached from their moorings. Frank swung around on the landing and grabbed the railing. It broke under his weight and he lost his balance. Katrina and Herman reached and grabbed at him, pulling him back onto the step. He let go of the railing and it fell end over end towards the bottom.

"Thanks," he said.

The door to the outside banged shut as each person exited the tower. Herman looked back up from where they came and then down to the bottom. They were making progress; going faster than he thought possible. Just a few minutes more, that's all we need to get out of here, he thought.

A loud low moan increased in intensity. No one on the stairs stopped. The metal structural tubing shifted on end as the ground heaved up under it. The stairs pulled away from the anchors and tilted precariously. A rip in the concrete left a trough between the stairs and the outside door.

A man and woman screamed as they teetered and fell into the trough. Several men who had begun to run for safety turned back towards the tower. One flung open the door and it dislodged from its hinges. He moved quickly to the right and dropped the door to the ground. The other two dropped to their knees and reached into the trough. The man in the trough reached up and the two men grabbed onto his arms and pulled him up. The third man helped him stand up and move outside. The other two men reached back down inside the trough. They couldn't reach the woman. The third man took off his belt and tie. He handed them over to the men on the ground.

"Wrap this around your wrist," one man yelled to the woman. "We're going to get you out of there."

She wrapped the tie around her wrist and held on to it and to the belt. The two men slowly pulled her up until they could finally grasp her by the arm. The third man grabbed her as soon as she cleared the edge and hurried her outside.

By this time, Herman, Katrina, and Frank were nearing the bottom of the stairs. The trough was too wide to jump over.

"The door," said the one man getting up from the ground, "we have to put the door over the trough."

Two of the men grabbed the door and brought it back inside. It was impossible to drop the door at the bottom of the stairs. It was just too risky. There was no way to do this gently. They positioned the door on their side and then gave it a push at the top. It landed on the other side and bounced twice before settling.

"One at a time," one man yelled over to them. "Quickly!"

"Katrina, go!" said Herman.

Katrina inched along the edge of the trough and stepped as far onto the door as she could. Then she quickly walked to the other side. As soon as she was off the door, Frank stepped onto the door. He hurried across and Herman followed. The six of them ran through the doorway and onto the tarmac. There was a huge rumble and they looked up. More explosions shattered the morning. Equipment and furnishings were propelled through the glass windows.

"Jesus Christ!" screamed Herman. "It's going to go!"

The bus carrying the terrorists continued along the toll road. With every passing minute it got closer to Tokyo. Mark sat behind the wheel of the limo. Takato stood outside the car on the shoulder of the road. He watched as the bus got closer. Mark watched in the passenger side mirror trying to judge speed and time. He watched as two vehicles passed by. The road was clear. Just the bus was visible. Takato hit the back of the limo two times and Mark pulled out. He spun the car facing the wrong way on the highway and drove diagonally towards the bus.

"What the hell!" yelled the driver as the limo headed toward the bus.

The driver moved into the far right lane and Mark steered the limo to mirror his move. Mark pressed on the accelerator. The limo shot towards the bus. The driver jerked the wheel of the bus and sent the bus off the side of the road. Mark followed, not letting up. The limo forced the bus through the guide rails and down into the ditch. Mark stopped the limo and righted it on the side of the road.

Takato ran across the lanes of the road ahead of the cars now coming into view. Mark shut the door to the limo and ran towards the guide rail. He cautiously went through the space made by the bus and made his way down into the ditch.

"What are you doing?" asked Takato.

"We need to get the driver," said Mark.

Takato looked down at the bus. How the driver was able to keep it upright was beyond him. He looked at the men in the windows. They were still sitting faced forward as though the accident was of no consequence.

Mark pounded on the door of the bus. The driver looked over and opened it.

"Are you alright?" asked Mark.

"Yes," said the driver nodding his head. "I need to call this in, but the wires ripped out."

"I have a phone in my car," said Mark. "You're welcome to use it."

"I'll be right back," said the driver looking at his passengers.

He descended the steps and followed Mark up the hill.

"It was you!" said the driver.

"Yes, it was me," said Mark. "I had to. The men on your bus are terrorists. Each one's a human bomb."

The driver stopped and stared at Mark.

"We have to get out of here. Please get in the car."

Takato opened the door for the driver and Mark and then got behind the wheel. He pulled out and started driving towards the city.

"Sir, I apologize for forcing you off the road," said Mark. "I had to stop you before you got into the city."

"I didn't know," said the driver. "I was hired to take these tourists into the city. They paid well, and in advance."

"How did they pay?" asked Mark.

"Money transfer," said the driver.

Mark took a deep breath and blew it out. He knew the driver was in far more danger than just being on the bus.

"Do you know how many of them were on the bus?"

"Yes," said the driver. "There were forty-eight."

There was the sound of an explosion and Takato looked in the mirror.

"That came from the bus," he said.

Mark pressed Edgar's contact on his phone.

"Yes," said Edgar.

"Shut it down, Edgar! Shut it down!"

"I'm waiting for Honomito to call."

"The first one just went off! Shut it down!"

United Flight 928 en route from Chicago's O'Hare Airport had entered Heathrow airspace. Captain Loagan looked at his instruments and out the window at the approaching city of London. No matter how many times he flew this route, he never tired of the sight. Every time he flew over, he tried to identify something new, something different.

Further past the city smoke began to billow above the tops of buildings. A thunderous sound was heard rumbling up from the smoke. The aircraft began to shimmy as shock waves emanated from the center.

Loagan felt a ping of panic. Surely it couldn't be Heathrow he was seeing. He turned on the "fasten seat belt" light.

"Curtis, contact Heathrow."

Melanie walked into the cockpit.

"Why's the fasten seat belt sign on?" she asked.

Loagan knew he had to divert from Heathrow to another airport and do so quickly.

"Anything?" asked Loagan.

"Nothing," said Curtis.

The aircraft wavered. Melanie grabbed the counter.

"What was that?" asked Melanie.

The thundering sounds were getting louder and the aircraft rose and moved sideways as another wave hit.

"Heathrow's not answering," said Curtis.

The airport was in plain sight. They could see smoke rising from the terminal.

"Get the passengers belted in," said Loagan. "We're diverting to Gatwick or Luton, whichever gives us permission to land."

They watched the tower in the center of the field sway and crash to the ground.

Chapter Twenty-Nine

Anna Roudalco shook her head as she waited at the house. She knew this would not set well with the man. As far as he was concerned only one person was in charge, and it was him. For Mahayin to even jest about being in charge would bear horrible consequences.

She knew Mahayin was not even near the top. To get there he would have to go through at least 8 or 9 others and that was just to get to the man. Then again, she doubted he was even privy to that.

To even think it was possible to handle two tasks at one time was ludicrous. She shuddered when she thought of their conversation.

"Just where are you carrying out these two parts of the project?"

"London and Tokyo," said Mahayin.

"Jesus Christ, Farred! How do you expect to take care of things when they're on opposite ends of the world?"

"Anna, it's all under control. I know what I'm doing. It's foolproof."

"When is this happening?"

"Just as soon as I press this button," said Mayahin pressing the button, "And say you may begin. Then it will all be set in motion."

For the first time in her life, she wished she'd never asked a question. How could he possibly think this was okay? How was she going to explain it?

Hanke walked through the door.

"So, what's going on?" he asked. "What took you so long to get back?"

Jean paced the floor with the phone to his ear.

"Edgar, shut down Heathrow."

"Heathrow? I thought it was the Underground."

"So did we," said Jean, but when Angelique got to Heathrow, she saw them. They're already there, Edgar."

"I have to contact Prime Minister Fairfield."

"There's not time for that. Just shut it down," said Jean. "Prime Minister Fairfield will understand."

The sounds of the explosions stopped. Angelique lifted her head. As she looked down to the right there was nothing but twisted metal, pieces of concrete and piles of glass. She carefully turned to look in the other direction. For the most part it was intact. She could see men standing in position still as statues. People who could move were running out, anticipating more explosions.

Angelique knew for certain that Jean had gotten to Edgar and was able to convince him to shut down service to the area. She put her head down and closed her eyes for a few minutes.

As soon as she heard sirens she opened her eyes. She saw emergency personnel entering the area. Angelique raised her head again. She tried to move her arm to touch the security officer walking by, but she couldn't.

Her mouth was so dry and it felt like there was so much grit in it.

"Please," she said as loudly as she could, "please, listen."

The security officer stopped and looked down at her. He got down on his knees.

"We'll get you out soon," he said.

"Please, listen," she said.

"What is it?" he asked.

"You have to get those men; the ones dressed in tan."

He looked around and saw men still standing, doing nothing.

"They're the ones with the bombs," said Angelique. "They have to be diffused before the network is restored."

"How?" he asked.

"There's a paper in my right hand."

The officer lifted her hand and pried her fingers. Then he removed the folded paper.

"I promise, we'll get you out of here," he said.

"Take care of that first."

The atmosphere at the Braedon house was extremely tense. They now had two of their own in harm's way; Angelique in London and Mark in Tokyo. The last phone call from each of them announced the first explosion and was a call for Edgar to take them off line.

Jean paced and kept looking at his phone. The clock seemed to have permanently stopped. Robert kept checking his favorite sites hoping to find out something, anything. Helena flipped through page after page not looking for anything in particular. Each of them was trying to cope in any way possible.

"I'm sure everything's fine," said Gina. "Edgar, worked quickly."

"I don't know," said Jean. "I just have a feeling…"

Paul looked at the figures from Yamani and estimated the number of terrorists that would have been on the bus. He looked at the chart for the Metro.

"With what Yamani and Mark were able to accomplish so far, there are not enough terrorists to take down the Metro in Japan," said Paul. "That in itself is an accomplishment."

"But London still has a full contingency," said Jean. "I wonder how many of those bombs went off before he shut it down."

It was something none of them really wanted to think about.

The city of Tokyo was unfazed by the positioning of the terrorists among them. No one seemed the least bit concerned until police officers and soldiers began to appear. As they were approached, each of the men put his hand to his mouth and then assumed the folded arm position again.

An officer approached one of the terrorists. He grabbed the man's hand, but the terrorist did not resist. As the officer moved the terrorist's arm behind him to put on the handcuffs, the man slumped to the floor.

Police officers also did their best to usher the crowds onto the subway and away from the scenes. They knew that with the network down, people could safely be transported.

It was evident that Mahayin had done his research. He had men positioned in every station and on the trains. No matter where the terrorists were found, they had to be taken above ground. From there they were taken to a designated area in order for the bombs to be diffused.

Mark walked through the area where the terrorists were placed. It was hard to believe that even though they had stopped two waves of them, there were still so many more. He was well aware that the bomb each of these men carried had to be diffused before the network could be put back up.

Mark reached in his pocket and pulled out a piece of paper. On it were the instructions Armand Fitch had written out that night in Pittsburgh. He knew with their success thus far, Mahayin wouldn't have changed anything. He handed the paper to the officer in charge.

"What's this?" asked the officer.

"The directions for diffusing them."

Mark took the figure he was given by Yamani of the number of terrorists that were killed in Volgograd and added it to the number of passengers the bus driver said was on the bus. Then he looked at the chart from Mahayin's office with the total number of men to be sent. Mark subtracted the two totals. Then he compared his answer with the number of terrorists that were lying in the cordoned off area. The numbers were the same. They had them all.

Once the networks had been restored, Hanke watched the reports on Tokyo. Fiasco was the only word that came to mind. How could anyone take something so simple, something that was planned out to the minutest degree and make a shambles of it. He knew how it happened. Mahayin got an idea and instead of following the plan, deviated from it.

What didn't add up was the number of men the Tokyo police were able to intercept. There should have been more. Where were they? There was no way Tokyo could have been taken with the number of men who were apprehended.

Hanke pulled out the list and counted the number of men who were supposed to be there. Less than half! There were less than half of the men in Tokyo than were supposed to be there. Where were the rest?

The more Hanke watched the reports, the more questions he had. More importantly than where were the men, was how did they know? How did the police know the attack was happening and how were they able the thwart it?

Only two people might have that answer and one would never admit it.

The news concerning what should've been the simultaneous attacks went viral. Pictures of Heathrow and the devastation dominated the news. Because of the nature of the facility, there was no way to accurately determine what the number of casualties might be.

There was a sense of relief when they heard from Mark and he was able to tell them that there was not one other explosion after the one on the bus. He assured them he was fine and everything was under control. He was going to be taking the next flight home.

The antithesis of that news was the news concerning Angelique. Because of the sheer number of terrorists as well as the change of target, Angelique did not have the time to escape the attack and its aftermath. She was buried for hours under debris as they worked to free her and others who were trapped.

The moment Jean was notified he was hell bent on making whatever arrangements were necessary to get to London. He was also determined that once Angelique could travel, he wanted to bring her back to Paris.

Helena sat at the dining room table. She crossed out London and Tokyo. She closed her eyes and shook her head. It was just by chance that she had guessed which two her ex-boss might try to do. She credited Tom with planting the seeds of time difference. Right now she could tell you what time it was at any of the cities on the list. She had been practicing at night when she couldn't sleep. It was much better than thinking about what could happen.

"It could've been a lot worse," said Laura. "If you hadn't figured out the cities, it could have been much, much more disastrous."

"I know," said Helena. "I wish I had the answer for which city is next and where. I've been trying to figure it out."

"I wish I could've been in that man's office when he saw the news," said Gina. "He was spitting mad when some tourist tried to take pictures through the window of his factory. I can't imagine what he's doing now."

"I'd like to know what his boss is thinking," said Laura. "I don't know Mr. Mahayin, but it's a given that he doesn't have the connections to pull this off by himself. Someone else is in charge and now Mahayin is going to be doing some sweating."

Anna sat in the gold and cream brocade armchair in the living room. Hanke paced back and forth. Anna watched his every step, every movement, every facial expression. Over the years she had learned to read him well and knew the less she said, the better it would be.

"What the hell was he thinking?" he yelled. "He was given explicit directions. They were written down. They were color coded. Everything was done except for holding his hand and he still fucked it up. Who told him to do two! He was specifically told to do one at a time."

He stopped for a moment and looked at Anna. She could see the anger in his eyes and wanted no part of what he was capable of doing.

"He's a liability, Anna. He's no longer a team player. I don't care what he wants. I can't allow his ego to bring this crashing down. We've worked too hard for this."

He walked over to the bar, took a glass and poured a drink. He gulped it down and continued.

"He can no longer be trusted and he certainly can't be fired. As vindictive as he is, he would go to the authorities and make a deal. He'd sell us all out!"

Hanke walked over to Anna.

"I have an idea, Anna, and it's something you're really going to like."

Chapter Thirty

Anna and Mahayin finished dinner and sat talking over an after dinner drink.

"You know, he was impressed you took the initiative to try to do two at one time," said Anna.

"And I thought you were concerned that he was going to be angry," said Mahayin looking at her smugly.

"Every once in a while he does surprise us."

"I know that the rest will go smoothly. I have everything so organized. You'd be very proud of me, Anna."

"I am proud of you," she said smiling at him.

Anna motioned for the waiter to bring another drink for Farred. Farred excused himself to use the rest room. Anna looked around and emptied a vile into Farred's drink.

Benjamin put down his bottle of water. It was good to hear Andre's voice. When he saw the explosion that landed Andre in the hospital, he didn't hold much hope that anything could be done to save him and now here he was calling to tell Benjamin he was ready to be released. There was only one catch. The doctor refused to let him leave until someone actually came to check him out.

Benjamin told Andre he would take care of it and called Henri immediately. He knew Henri would be able to figure out someone to go and get Andre. It was impossible for Benjamin to go because of his workload.

"Well, we certainly have a little good news," said Henri. "Andre is being released from the hospital."

"That is good news," said Helena.

She had constantly worried about him. She blamed herself for his accident even though she wasn't the one who planned it.

"Benjamin said that someone has to go and check him out of the hospital," said Henri. "The doctor refuses to allow him to leave on his own."

"Can you blame him," said Gwen, "after all he's been through?"

"Not in the least," said Henri. "The problem is that Benjamin can't possibly leave to do it because he has such a heavy workload and he's promised these people their cars would be done."

"I'll go get him," said George.

"It's probably better if one of us goes to get him anyway," said Gina. "They're probably going to try to track him."

"Why would they do that?" asked Paul.

"They're going to want to see if he can lead them back to Helena."

"That's the craziest thing I ever heard," said Paul.

"Crazier than blowing up a plane just in case they didn't blow her up in the car?" asked Gina. "Mark my words. They're going to try to track him."

The *Chosen One* slammed the papers down on the desk. Was there anything that wasn't going to blow up in his face? How long does it take to get news? The way he was receiving it, one would think he was back in the fourteenth century instead of the age of instantaneous news. How could Serghei screw up a simple information exchange? It had gone on for years without a hitch. Change one player and all hell breaks loose.

And then there was Petru. Now he was a liability they never thought to consider. How could he have not seen the ramifications of allowing him to place those calls? At this the man shook his head. But still, he took steps to rectify that situation. That should have been simple too.

How does the man sent to find information from a man with his family at Disney World wind up dead?

He knew the answer to that and all the screw-ups. He was surrounded by idiots; idiots that make stupid, idiotic decisions. Idiots who refuse to listen and follow orders.

No one knew how much was involved with this project. No one knew the risks he was taking. Any day, this could all come crashing down around him. However, as long as he had breath in his body, he would counter anything, including anyone who tried to get in his way or whose action jeopardized the project.

As for him, he thrived on the risk. The more risk the better. This was his idea; his and his alone. He answered to no one. Everyone else ultimately answered to him.

Right now, he had to solve the Petru problem. His unconventional method obviously didn't work. It was time to make the call and have the professionals handle it.

The morning sun shone through the windows as Farred Mahayin opened his eyes. He looked around from side to side. He had no recollection of leaving the restaurant or getting into the car. The driver's side was empty and he tried to reach over to the seat. He leaned forward slightly, but couldn't move far. He tried to reach the steering wheel, but his hands were strapped at his sides. Next, he tried moving his feet but to no avail. In front of him, on the dashboard was a clock. Eight fifty-nine it said. He moved his eyes up and saw writing on the windshield.

"Time to pay for the suffering. Call you at nine."

Farred looked down at his chest. He could see the wires coming out of his shirt. He took a deep breath and closed his eyes.

Anna looked at the display on her cell phone…nine o'clock on the dot. Anna pressed send. The sound of the explosion broke the silence. Pieces of metal flew into the air. Trees surrounding the car splintered and the debris rained down striking close to where Anna was standing. Anna smiled. He was right. She loved this more than anything.

"I lied, Farred. He was really pissed at you."

Jean took a deep breath and put a smile on his face before he opened the door to Angelique's hospital room. He knew nothing more than she had been rescued and the hospital she had been taken to. He walked into the room and over to her bed. She turned her head slightly towards him and mustered a smile.

"Hi," she said quietly.

"Hi. How are you doing?"

"Better now. They didn't detonate them all. More people were saved this time."

It was always like Angelique to think more about others than about herself. It was something that Jean absolutely loved about her.

"I was trying to make sure people knew to keep going," said Angelique. "It was getting harder to see because of all the particles in the air. People were just leaving their bags and running for the doors. I didn't see a bag and I tripped over it. Then one of them detonated near me and I got buried. I was lucky because I could move my head."

"Has the doctor been in to see you?"

"He should be in shortly. He's been here quite a bit and the nurses have been wonderful. I'm afraid I'm not much help to them. I can't do much right now."

The door opened and Dr. Park walked in.

"Hello Mrs. Beaumont. How are you feeling?"

"A little less groggy," said Angelique. "Dr. Park, this is my husband, Jean."

"Very nice to meet you," said Dr. Park. "You have a very brave wife. She insisted they take care of all the bombers before she left the airport."

"Yes, sir," said Jean.

"I know you have questions for me, but if you would like, I can go through everything and if you have questions, you can stop me and I'll be happy to answer."

"I'd prefer it that way," said Jean. "I have no idea where to begin."

Dr. Park began reciting what sounded like a litany of all the injuries Angelique sustained. The more he said, the more thankful Jean was to be able to even talk to his wife. Angelique was going to have to spend an incredible amount of time in the hospital before she would be able to be released. Moving her now was not an option. Whenever that time came, there would have to be coordination on the parts of many intermediaries to make certain she was transported to a facility in France in the safest possible manner.

It was one of those days when the phone just wouldn't stop ringing. All Hanke wanted to do was throw it against the wall, but he refrained. It seemed that every single one of his agents needed something, wanted something, or had some trivial piece of information about the current state of affairs to share. Right now, if he could, he would send the lot of them back to the states to babysit something useless.

When the phone rang again, he answered it without even looking at the screen.

"Yes."

"It's Pearse."

"What the hell are you calling me for!"

"Do you want to know what's going on or not?"

"Of course I want to know what's going on," said Hanke. "That's why I brought you back to the States, because I knew you would get answers. So what do you have?"

"First of all, the phone number that was responsible for detonating the devices came from a number that belongs to a dead person, a Cezar Anestin. It seems that Mr. Anestin had a bank account and had his bills paid automatically from the account. When he died no one notified the bank so they have been paying whatever bills are due."

"Now that's just ridiculous," said Hanke. "What else you got?"

"Some of the names of the people who were killed in the attack are being kept quiet because of who they are and who they were with," said Pearse. "I can send you that information."

"What about who did it?"

"There's not a whole lot to go on, because there wasn't anything left of the bombers or the devices. Several names are being tossed around along with the obvious one, Yamani. I mean since he already came out and said he did it."

"Was there anything else about the phone number?"

"Only that it was disconnected last week because the bill wasn't paid."

"Why wasn't the bill paid?"

"The bank said that the account ran out of money."

As soon as Hanke got off the phone, he did a search to find out who Cezar Anestin was. With connections like he had, it didn't take long to find out that Cezar Anestin was Petru's grandfather on his mother's side.

"Well, well," said Hanke, "so the number doesn't lead to Petru after all."

George walked through the front door of the clinic. There was no one at the receptionist's desk, so he continued down the hall. He glanced into the rooms where the doors were opened trying to find someone who might know where Andre was. He continued walking looking for the nurse's station. As he got closer to the end of the hall he saw David Renovet, a member of the Senate from his district back in Paris. David closed the stairwell door and looked around. Then he walked to a door, opened it and went outside.

George continued to the end of the hall, curious as to whether or not he really had just seen David Renovet. When he got to the end of the hall he noticed a large mirror, nearly the size of a window on the wall beside the door that Renovet had just gone through. George looked through the mirror and could see tables and benches in a garden. David Renovet stood talking to some other people. None of them looked as though they belonged in a hospital. George took one more look and then turned around and started back up the hall.

He stopped for a moment trying to process what he'd just seen. Many of the people in the garden looked familiar, but he couldn't place where he had seen them before. He continued up the hall thinking that maybe if he just focused on something else, he'd remember the names.

The news about London and Tokyo were encouraging, but Yamani knew there was still much to do. They still didn't have all the pieces to the puzzle. Yes, they had a list, but the list didn't have the dates and times of the pending attacks.

He brought together all those he knew he could trust for a meeting of sorts with a family social being the reason for the get together. He felt it important for the families to get together. It was necessary that the children enjoy the company of other children from their old neighborhood. Maranissa thrived on these days. It gave her some much needed time to spend with the other women.

Adarine and his family were excited to have been invited to join the festivities. Once everyone had arrived, the children went to play in the yard while the women worked in the kitchen. It was at these times that Yamani invited his loyal followers into his study where they could discuss the important subjects.

"We were very successful when it came to Tokyo," said Yamani, "and all of you who took part in it deserve our thanks. I wish we would have been able to do something for London, but that was not to be."

Yamani put a paper on the wall that listed the names of the places that were on the list but had not as yet been hit.

"We were very lucky to have received the information for Festhalle and the clue for Tokyo and London," said Yamani, "however, we need to stop them somehow. Even though we have been able to get to four of the intelligence heads, we still have others to find and deal with. While they are walking around loose, the governments will remain blind."

"If I may," said Zaid, "I would not be opposed to going back to Volgograd to find out what they have decided. They have no idea I was there, and so I could go back again."

"I think that would be a good idea, Zaid," said Yamani. "What you brought back was very important."

"We are not going to be able to find the other intelligence people," said Kahli. "I think we are going to have to bring them to us."

"I agree," said Yamani. "The question is how to do it."

For the next hour the men thought about the problem and offered ideas of what they thought might be viable solutions. The final decision belonged to Yamani, but he took into consideration all the input the group had given.

"The final thing is to find who is behind this. No matter what we do, the only way to truly stop this is to find the man who heads it all."

George moved swiftly down a connecting corridor at the hospital. He stopped at the nurse's station.

"Hi, is Dr. Hempton here?" asked George.

"Yes, he is," said the clerk at the desk. "Let me get him for you."

"Thank you," said George.

He looked around as he waited. The facility was quiet, even though it was right in the middle of visiting hours. Dr. Hempton walked up to George.

"How can I help you?" asked Dr. Hempton.

"Dr. Hempton, I'm George Cardonne. We spoke on the phone."

"Ah, yes, Mr. Cardonne. Let's go back to the office so we can talk."

George followed him back to the office and Dr. Hempton closed the door.

"I understand you're here to take one of my patients home."

"Yes, Andre Allard," said George.

"Mr. Allard's quite a lucky man," said Dr. Hempton. "From what I understand, someone had placed a bomb in his car."

"I'm afraid I know nothing about that. I only know that when Andre called his friend at the garage to tell him he was going to be released and he needed someone to come to check him out of the facility, his friend called me because he was unable to come himself," said George. "After listening to him I told him I would come and get Andre. I agreed that after such a trauma, Andre shouldn't be leaving the hospital alone and driving back by himself. I had a client to meet, so I told him I'd be only too glad to get Andre from the hospital and bring him back with me."

"What happened to the person who was supposed to be in the car?" asked Dr. Hempton. "Hopefully she's well and being kept safe from whomever is causing all of this destruction."

"From what the garage attendant told me, unfortunately," said George, not pausing or changing his facial expression, "she was killed when Delta Flight 167 blew up above New York."

"I see," said Dr. Hempton getting up from his chair. "Well then, if you have no further questions, I think we should go to see Mr. Allard."

They walked down the corridor towards Andre's room.

"Just how is it that you knew Helena Rudarsnyan?" asked Dr. Hempton.

"Who?" asked George.

Dr. Hempton opened the door to Andre's room and they walked in.

"Good morning, Andre," said Dr. Hempton. "How are you this morning?"

"Well."

"Glad to hear that. Are you ready to go home?"

"Yes," said Andre smiling.

"Let me get your paperwork in order. It'll only take a few minutes."

Dr. Hempton turned and left the room. Andre smiled and opened his mouth to speak. George put his fingers to his lips and Andre closed his mouth.

"I brought you a new set of clothes," said George handing a bag to Andre. "We figured your old ones were most likely useless."

"Thanks," said Andre getting up from the bed and walking into the bathroom.

It didn't take long for Andre to change. He came out of the bathroom the same time Dr. Hempton came back into the room.

"All ready to go, I see," said Dr. Hempton.

He went over all the papers with Andre making certain he understood. Then he folded the papers and slid them inside a packet.

"Make sure you don't lose these," said Dr. Hempton. "Your doctor may want to see them."

After Pearse called Hanke with the information concerning the phone number, Hanke did nothing but hound Clayton Pearse for additional information. The truth was that the aftermath of Pittsburgh was nothing more than a lot of paperwork and following up on tiny details that most often led to a dead end. Hanke made sure Pearse was not privy to anything he asked the other agents to do. Pearse knew way too much in Hanke's estimation and couldn't be trusted with any other pertinent knowledge.

Pearse was once again in the FBI office on the South Side. He and Gimshaw were finishing reports on the last wave of identified bodies. This was a job that neither of them ever wanted to do.

Pearse took a piece of paper out of his pocket. He took a pen and crossed out Tokyo and London. Gimshaw watched him.

"What's that?" he asked.

"The tentative list of cities that were to be attacked," said Pearse. "So far, it's exact and now that more have been eliminated, the odds are getting even better that it'll happen at one of these."

Pearse felt his phone vibrate and he pulled it out of his pocket. He looked at the display and answered it.

"Yes."

"What do you know about a Petru Wadimar?"

"Why?"

"Hanke's putting out an all call hit on him. He claims he received word from Gimshaw's office that the phone number that detonated those devices in Pittsburgh was traced to this Petru. He is listed as armed and extremely dangerous. Orders are to eliminate him, his wife, and his kids."

"When did this order go out?"

"It didn't yet. I saw it come down and I diverted it for the time being, but I can't stop it altogether. If you know him, someone needs to get to him now."

"Thanks."

Pearse put the phone in his pocket.

"Did you or anyone from this office tell my boss that the phone number that detonated the devices was traced to Petru Wadimar?"

"Absolutely not," said Gimshaw. "Why?"

"He put a hit out on Petru, his wife and kids, saying he's the one who blew up the stadium and that he's armed and dangerous."

"Fucking Bastard."

After the aide took Andre as far as she needed to, he got out of the wheelchair. They walked out of the main entrance and off the grounds. George hailed a cab. The two men got in.

"To the airport, please," said George.

"Yes, sir," said the cabbie.

"May I see that packet of papers?" asked George.

"Sure," said Andre handing it to him.

George pulled everything out. He leafed through the pages one at a time looking at the front and back of each sheet. Then he handed them to Andre. He opened the plastic envelope again and turned it from one side to the other. Each time, he heard something switch sides. He looked in and saw a small device and smiled. He emptied it into his hand and showed Andre. Then he opened the window and tossed it.

Chapter Thirty-One

Enzo Jacarusa of Italy's Security Agency trudged through the thick snow along what appeared to be a path. Ahead of him was a cabin surrounded by trees. He felt as if he had been walking for hours. He walked up on the porch and stomped his feet to remove the excess snow. All he wanted was for there to be a nice warm fire and a hot drink waiting for him. He opened the door and walked in.

"Have a nice walk?" asked Remigio Vargas of Spain's CNI.

"What do you think?" asked Jacarusa.

"I loathe snow," said Logan Wilson of Australia's ASIS.

"Leave it to him to pick someplace as isolated as this," said Vargas. "Whatever it is must be really important."

"After what just happened, do you blame him?" asked Vargas.

"He probably just wants to make sure we're doing our jobs," said Jacarusa. "Seems someone couldn't keep their mouth shut."

"Where is he anyway?" asked Victor Arsenyev of Russia's GRU. "I was here first, and he was nowhere around."

"Maybe he's running a little late?" said Wilson.

"Thanks Victor for doing all this," said Vargas.

"I didn't do anything," said Arsenyev. "It was like this when I got here."

Jacarusa's eyes darted around the room.

"Let's get out of here," he said.

Kahli stayed close to the cabin only long enough to make sure all four agents had arrived. Then he quickly moved as far away as possible, still keeping the cabin door in his sight. He took the device out of his pocket and keyed in the numbers and pressed the button.

He turned towards the door. Six devices detonated and the cabin was blown apart. Kahli cowered close to the ground keeping his head down. The debris from the cabin rained down around the area. When it stopped, all he could hear was the crackle of flames. He walked back to where the cabin once stood. He saw what remained of the four men and knew not one of them survived. He made his way back to the road where Zaid waited.

The walkway outside of the White House was where President Bartram did most of his best thinking. He usually could come up with a definite plan of action. However, this situation was truly trying his patience.

He picked up the pace when he saw his Chief of Staff approaching.

"What brings you out of your office, Alex?" asked President Bartram.

"We have a situation," said Alex.

"What kind of situation?"

"Some hikers were walking through some rather obscure paths quite a distance from the main Appalachian Trail and they discovered bodies."

"How many?"

"Possibly a hundred, maybe more," said Alex, "in various stages of decomposition."

"Did you call Jeff Easterly?"

"He's the one who called me. He's on his way."

"How close can the chopper get me?"

"I don't know. It depends what the pilot thinks."

"Let's go."

If it wasn't news, or didn't have something to do with some world situation, it wasn't to be seen on any screen at Michael's house. No

matter what was broadcast, someone watched and scrutinized every word and image; all in the context of the situation they were working on.

George stopped to watch the coverage of the festival being held in the city. The reporter was interviewing David Renovet.

"Mr. Renovet, I was wondering if I could have a few minutes of your time."

"Of course," said David.

"You have been very involved in this festival. In fact, you are one of a number of senators who have been here for the past three days helping to put up booths."

"This is something the people really love," said David, "and I was involved with it before I was elected and I don't intend to stop."

"Impossible," said George. "That's impossible."

"What's impossible?" asked Michael.

"He couldn't have been helping on the festival for the past three days. I just saw him in Madrid when I picked up Andre."

"Are you sure it was him?" asked Pierre.

"Positive," said George. "I've known him for years and I was really close to him. I could see exactly who he was."

George picked up his keys.

"Where are you going?" asked Pierre.

"To the festival to talk to David. Anyone want to come and get some good food?"

"You don't have to ask me twice," said Raquel.

"Can you bring me something?" asked Helena.

The area was so secluded that there was no need for caution tape. By the time Easterly and his men arrived, the hikers had already identified how far the bodies were strewn. They used sticks and had ripped a bright colored shirt into strips and tied a strip to each stick.

Jeff Easterly walked up to the hikers and showed his badge.

"Jeff Easterly, FBI," he said.

"I'm Cal, and this is Frank, Phil, Jim, and Tony."

"Nice meeting you all. How did you find this?"

"We were trying to find a spot where we could sit have some lunch and we started smelling this dead flesh smell. Then we found this and man, we've never seen anything like it."

"Who called it in?" asked Easterly.

"I did," said Phil. "I'm Agent Hensen's son. It doesn't look like a normal grave site. There are wallets and passports and a lot of other personal things strewn about. I don't know how you're going to sort it out."

Jeff looked around and saw the sticks and cloth.

"What're those?" he asked pointing to the sticks.

"We walked around and marked the boundaries of the area," said Jim. "We didn't want to make a wrong step."

"It doesn't look like anyone except the people who knew about this have been here," said Easterly. "It looks like some of these have been here a long, long time and some have been recently added."

"It's strange, that's for sure," said Tony.

"What brings you guys up the trail?"

"We're riding to raise money and awareness for ALS," said Cal. "A friend of ours has it and it's horrible."

"Good cause," said Easterly. "I'm sorry you've been detained, but we're going to have to ask you some questions."

"Whatever you need," said Phil.

Agents walked the perimeter and searched past it to see if any remains had been overlooked. Everything was photographed and the pictures numbered. Descriptions were entered into a log. When it was finished, those who were trained to handle remains began the arduous task of separating and cataloging.

The workers separated the two bodies that looked like they were dumped last, from the rest.

"Jeff, can you come here?" asked Agent Sparks.

"Excuse me a minute," said Easterly and he walked over to Sparks. "What's up?"

"Whoever did this was no amateur. He or she knew exactly how to kill them."

Jeff looked at the bodies and the precise hit. Each fatal shot was identical and two others had been added.

"Seems he wanted to make sure they were dead or make it look a little less professional," said Easterly.

"They were dumped here," said Sparks. "We just have no idea from where."

"See if there's any identification on these two since we know they're intact."

Agent Sparks squatted down and patted the pockets. When he felt something, he reached in and pulled out the object. He got up and walked back to Easterly and handed him two wallets. Easterly opened the first wallet.

"Irwin Selbring," said Easterly handing the license to Sparks. "He's from the U.K."

Then he opened the other wallet and took out the license.

"Dr. Louis Antwon, France. What the hell. It couldn't be John Smith from down the street."

The man stood in the middle of a garbage dump. He flipped the small object up in the air and caught it many times. He paused and looked at his watch. One thing he hated was waiting. What he hated more was when people were late.

Dr. Hempton walked as quickly as possible across the piles of garbage to where the man was waiting.

"What's the idea of meeting here?" he asked him.

"Suppose you tell me," said the man.

"I don't know what you're talking about," said Dr. Hempton.

"Did you make sure you put that tracking device on your patient?"

"Of course I did. Do you take me for a fool?"

"No, Doctor, not at all," said the man.

"You should be able to easily track him, then," said Dr. Hempton.

"Oh, I was able to pick up the signal alright, but you'll never guess where it led me."

"I have no idea."

"Take a guess, Doctor," said the man once again tossing the object into the air and catching it.

The blank expression on Dr. Hempton's face told the man he had no idea what he was talking about.

"Let's take a walk this way," said the man pointing to a place down the other side of the garbage mound. "I think I see something interesting. We can talk on the way."

Dr. Hempton started walking and passed the man. He slowly and carefully walked down the hill watching each step he took. The man took the gun from its holster and screwed on the silencer. He lowered the weapon to his side.

"Dr. Hempton, that's far enough," said the man. "I must've been mistaken. It wasn't what I thought it was and you didn't do what you were supposed to do, did you, Doctor."

"I don't know what you're talking about."

"You were supposed to make sure that Mr. Allard was a walking tracking device," said the man.

"I made sure he had the device," said Dr. Hempton.

"No, Doctor, you didn't."

The man held up the device.

"Recognize this?" he asked. "I tracked it here. So, you see, Doctor, you didn't do what you were supposed to do."

"There were too many people watching. I couldn't do it," said Dr. Hempton, "and I couldn't take him back up to do it. I did everything you asked and more. I made sure he had it when he left. It wasn't that important."

The man raised his hand and pulled the trigger.

"You're right Doctor, you have done everything I've asked," said the man. "To you he wasn't important, just as you are no longer important to me."

It wasn't easy to find parking in the city. With the number of people attending the festival, parking places were at a premium. George didn't think twice. He drove to Global and parked in their private lot.

They walked a couple blocks to the festival. Raquel sauntered and stopped to look at the different booths. Everything looked amazing.

"Why don't you go and find David," said Raquel. "Call me when you're done and I'll tell you where I am."

George walked through the crowds looking for David. He stopped to talk to neighbors and some clients who were there enjoying the lovely day.

It wasn't easy. But George finally located David.

"David," said George. "How are you?"

"George, it's good to see you. What do you think of the festival?"

"It's wonderful," said George. "I hear you've been working quite a bit on this."

"I've been here so much this past week that my wife threatened to send a bed down here for me to sleep in."

George laughed and shook his head.

"What I have to say is going to probably sound crazy," said George.

"What?"

"I went to a clinic in Madrid, yesterday to visit a friend of mine. When I was there I saw you."

"Me?"

"Yes," said George. "I was going to say something to you, but you went through another door and out to a garden where you were talking to a number of other people."

"George, I've never even been to Madrid and I can assure you that I've been here working all the time."

"I believe you," said George. "Now, I just have a whole lot of questions that need answers."

"If I can help you, you know I will," said David. "This person looked exactly like me."

"Yes, exactly."

President Bartram's helicopter touched down not far from the site. The lack of overhead wires and some barren areas made for the near perfect landing spot. As the President came into view on the other side of the grave site, Jeff Easterly made his way around to greet him.

"Mr. President, it's good to see you," said Easterly.

"Jeff, what in the Sam-hill is all of this?"

"Sir, from what we can deduce just being here a relatively short time is that this is a place someone was or is using to dump the bodies of the people he's killed."

"That's a lot of people, Jeff. I don't think there've been this many alerts concerning missing people. It's puzzling."

"Well, sir, the last two who were dumped here had ID on them. One was from the U.K. and the other from France. So if there are reports about them being missing, we wouldn't know. There are a lot of personal items in that field and it's going to take a long time to clear this."

"Who found them?"

"The group of men over there. They were hiking and looking for a place to stop for lunch and discovered this."

President Bartram and Jeff Easterly walked around the site to the other side.

"Gentlemen," said President Bartram, "I want to thank you for calling this in. Not everyone would take the time to do it.

"Mr. President, it's an honor to meet you," said Cal. "Sir, how could we just do nothing? This is not normal. Civilized people bury their dead. They don't dump them."

"Indeed," said President Bartram. "How did Mr. Easterly find out so quickly?"

"I called my dad," said Phil. "He's Agent Hensen. Just looking at it, this is not something for the local police. The media would have been here and everyone would have known about this and speculated about how it happened. I'm thinking this is part of something bigger."

"I think you may be right in your assessment. Where's your dad, now?"

"He's helping in Pittsburgh," said Phil, "and maybe that's why I thought to call him, too."

"Well, for whatever reason, it was the right call to make."

Jeff Easterly came back over to the group. He and several others had discussed the need to get everything cleaned up in a timely fashion. Because of the time that had obviously passed since the first bodies were dumped, separation was not going to be successfully accomplished on site. It was going to take a lab and sophisticated equipment.

"Mr. President, may I see you a moment," asked Easterly.

"Excuse me, gentlemen."

"There's no way to separate all these bodies here. So, we're going to have to transport. I called additional personnel. What we really need to do is get this cleaned up so no one else happens upon it."

"Agreed. I want someone working on those personal effects," said President Bartram. "Let's see what we can ascertain from those. This goes no further than your agency regardless of where these people were from. No one is to even know it was discovered."

"Yes, sir."

"Something tells me, this is part of a bigger event, either one that's happened or one to come. When you have something, anything, I want to know."

George and Raquel brought back bags filled with delicious food from the festival. She had made George stop on the way back to get some paper plates and plastic ware. She insisted you couldn't eat festival food on fine china, it would spoil the experience. They filled their plates and enjoyed the different tastes and textures. For just a brief time, the tragedies and questions were put aside and they enjoyed each other's company.

After dinner, George sat at the table in a very pensive mood. He picked up a pencil and tapped the eraser against the table.

"This is really bothering you, isn't it?" asked Monique.

"It really is," said George. "I know what I saw and I saw David Renovet at that clinic when I went to get Andre."

"The problem is, there are all sorts of people who were with him here when he was working on booths for the festival at the exact same time," said Monique.

"I know. I also know it would be impossible to get from Madrid to Paris that quickly unless you could molecularly transport."

"What if it wasn't him," asked Brigit. "What if it was someone who just looked like him?"

"You mean someone who just so happened to closely resemble him, like identically resemble him?"

"Did he see you when you saw him?" asked Monique.

"Yes," said George.

"Then why didn't he say anything to you?" asked Monique. "Why didn't he at least say hello?"

"I don't know," said George. "And when I looked through the mirror, I could see a garden and there were other men out there. A lot of them looked really familiar to me, too."

"Okay, stop there," said Brigit. "Back up a little and tell me what happened from when you saw David."

"He came through a doorway that was marked stairwell," said George. "Then he looked down the hall, right at me, walked past a mirror, and then out a door. I walked down the hall and looked both ways at the end. No one was anywhere around so I looked at the mirror and I could see outside to a garden. David was out in the garden talking to other men."

"So someone could actually spy on these men in the garden?" asked Monique.

"Yes, they could."

"Was there a way out of the garden?" asked Brigit.

"I really didn't take the time to look, but I don't think so. I think they had to use the door."

Nicole came into the dining room. She had been spending most of her time with Jacques, ever since the attack. She sat down at the table.

"What's all this?" she asked.

"Food from the festival," said Raquel.

"Can I have some?"

"Of course, how about if I heat it up for you?" asked Raquel.

"No need," said Nicole. "I'm so hungry I'll eat it just like this."

"How's Jacques doing?" asked Brigit.

"He's coming along," said Nicole. "We talked to the doctor today and he wants to discuss skin grafting and plastic surgery with us. I told him, we would definitely discuss it, but I needed some sleep and a clear head to comprehend everything."

"George, plastic surgery," said Raquel.

"What about it?" asked George.

"How can you make someone look like another person?" asked Raquel.

"Plastic surgery," said George. "But why?"

"That's the question."

The news that Mahayin was no longer a problem was welcomed news on one hand, but on the other hand, it presented some problems. Since its inception, Craustof had been run by Mahayin. No one except him had ever given an order and to put someone new in there during this critical time was not feasible at all.

The *Chosen One* sat at his desk and made a list of everything that had to be done. He already knew that Mahayin had been running that facility at full capacity and had turned out enough devices to blow up five hundred cities. It was time to shut it down, pack up everything and put it into storage. When the time came where more devices had to be manufactured, a new facility could be opened anywhere.

There were some people there who had been with Mahayin even in Romania. Those were the ones he would have to trust to pack up everything and get the things moved. He would send Kannid and Raseem to collect men and material things that needed to be brought back to the camp.

This was going to hurt the timetable, but there wasn't anything that could be done. It just might serve them anyway. Not having an attack for a few days might make the world relax a bit and then that shock factor would be back when the next attack came.

The first thing he did was log into Mahayin's email. Thank goodness, as the administrator on the account, he was able to do so. He then wrote an email apprising everyone of what was going to take place. Some of the emails he personalized while those to the general workers, he kept as one collective email. After the last one was sent, he prepared the papers with instructions for Kannid and Raseem.

The first few times they watched the fireworks, they did so from the park. This time, they took the ferry to the other side and walked up the hill from the boat to watch them from across the Seven Seas Lagoon. Even though they couldn't hear the music, the boys enjoyed all the bursts of color. As soon as the fireworks were finished, they headed for the tram, ahead of the crowds.

Petru and Sorina took Lucian and Grigore's hands as soon as they got off. They walked into the parking lot.

"Do you remember where we parked?" asked Sorina.

Petru looked at the signs on the poles and then pointed in a direction.

"We're about six rows over that way, and then about halfway down," said Petru.

They looked both ways and started to cross the aisle. They walked between the cars to the next aisle and then looked both ways before starting to cross. A car came speeding down the aisle. Petru pulled Lucian along and flung him to the other side of the aisle. Sorina backed up with Grigore and crouched down between the cars. Gun shots rang out and Sorina reached back to make sure Grigore was behind her. She nudged him to move back and they moved ever so quietly and quickly back. As soon as she got to the space between cars, she moved Grigore in between them and motioned for him not to make a sound.

The car stopped, blocking the path Petru had taken. The passenger shined a light between the cars and caught a glimpse of Petru's shoe as he moved between cars. He pointed down the path. The two got out of the car. One went down the path Petru had taken, while the other went down the next one.

Petru tapped Lucian and put his fingers to his lips. Then he motioned to the area beneath the truck next to him. Lucian got down on his stomach and scooched under the truck. Petru motioned for him to go farther back until he was sure he couldn't be seen.

Petru heard the men's footsteps in the gravel. He held his breath. He knew they only had a few more steps and he could be seen. As he looked down the opening between the rows of the cars, he saw a form. Quickly it moved closer and then disappeared up a path. Petru's mind raced. All he wanted was his wife and kids to be safe. There wasn't much he could do except ...

Petru moved carefully forward towards the sound of the footsteps. He got to the end of the car and listened attentively to each step. When the man came to the end of the car to make the turn down the row, Petru stuck out his leg sweeping the other man's legs. The man fell on his face. Petru scrambled back. Another man came up the same path, grabbed the man by the legs and dragged him back up the path and back to the car.

The other man rounded the corner and aimed at Petru. Behind him a silhouetted figure raised an arm and struck the first man on the head. The gun discharged towards the ground as the man fell. The other man dragged him away.

Petru sat shaking. He could see Lucian under the truck. He listened and heard the car pull away. Petru crawled over to the truck.

"It's okay," he said. "Come on out of there."

Lucian slithered out from under the truck.

"That was fun!" said Lucian. "Can I do that again someday?"

"Someday," said Petru. "Let's go find your mother and Grigore."

Petru led Lucian through the narrow path between the cars and to the aisle. They looked both ways and crossed. There were people everywhere now and Petru felt a little safer.

"Sorina," he called. "It's okay. Where are you?"

"I'm here," she said standing up.

Sorina took Grigore by the hand and walked out to meet Petru.

"Grigore, I got to hide under a truck," said Lucian. "It was so much fun."

"Petru, what's going on?"

"I don't know, Sorina. I wish I knew."

Hanke downed another drink. It was the third one he had since he got the word they found Petru and his family. This was what he liked; what he was used to. Finally, he was working with competent people; people who could follow the directions he gave.

He had them trained to call before they began and again when it was finished. He looked at the clock. This was taking longer than he anticipated. How hard was it to kill a woman, two small children, and a man who spent the majority of his time sitting on a stool in a lab?

"Yes," said Hanke.

"I can't find them," said Coltan

"What do you mean you can't find them!"

"I mean they disappeared. There's no trace of them at all. We found Petru and his family and they went after them. I watched them go between the cars. I waited around where I could see them when they came out."

"Are you sure they didn't come out somewhere else?"

"Unless they came out when I had to move."

"You moved!" said Hanke. "Why?"

"A lot of people were leaving and I had to get out of the way," said Coltan, "but they should have called and I've heard nothing."

"What the hell is wrong with people?" said Hanke. "Doesn't anyone listen to what they're told to do? Idiots! I'm surrounded with idiots. What the fuck! Do I have to do everything myself?"

"Yes, sir. No, sir. I don't know, sir."

"You don't know! Well let me clear things up a bit. I want them found and found now, not later, now! Don't call me until you have them. But don't take too long or you may find that you're looking over your shoulder."

All the boys could talk about was hiding under the truck and between the cars. For them it was exciting. It was something they did in movies. They made the "pop pop" sounds of the guns being fired as they told their stories to each other. Neither Petru nor Sorina discouraged them from telling the stories. The last thing they wanted to do was scare the boys.

Sorina could tell the boys were too excited to go to sleep anytime soon, so she just left them to play in their room while she came out to talk to Petru.

"Petru," said Sorina. "What's going on?"

"I don't know," said Petru. "Josep must have known something, because he tried to warn me."

"And they killed him," said Sorina. "Whoever they are."

"Petru nodded.

"I don't know why he deleted the project files. It doesn't make sense."

"Maybe he didn't want anything to tie you to Craustof."

"Maybe, and that could be what the man who broke in was trying to find out. Maybe he wanted to see if I had anything about Craustof anywhere."

"So he didn't find anything and now he's dead," said Sorina. "Do you think they know you know?"

"I think that might be what they're afraid of. If I realize what I did, then I can connect Craustof to the attacks."

"So do you think tonight was a warning?"

"No, Sorina. I think they meant to kill all of us."

The boat went out into the Atlantic, far away from the shore and any other boats. The light of the quarter moon gave off just enough light for the men to see. This was not one of the facets of their job they liked to perform, but given the circumstances, it was the lesser of two evils.

Neither of the men who had gone after Petru and his family had regained consciousness. They had seen nothing except for the silhouettes of Petru as they chased to eliminate him. They tied their arms and legs together and then bound and weighted them. There would be no escape.

The three men picked up the first bound man and tossed him overboard. Then they did the same with the second. They watched as the bodies sank beneath the surface and then waited a few extra minutes to make sure they wouldn't float to the top.

"I hope this is the end."

"Don't hold your breath. There's got to be more."

Chapter Thirty-Two

Coltan did his best to find what happened to the other two agents. It was as though they vanished. They weren't his problem. What happened to Petru and his family was. He took the man's threat seriously.

There was no one lower in Coltan's estimation than a man who was armed and dangerous hiding behind his family. To him that man was the lowest of the low and needed to be taken out. He knew Petru thought he was safe bringing his family to Disney World. Who would attack a man in Disney World? Coltan knew he had to take his time and wait until he was off the property.

It didn't take long for the family to decide to do something else. Petru had promised the boys that as part of their vacation to America they would swim in the ocean they flew over in the airplane. Today, Petru and Sorina decided it would be a great day to relax at the beach. They purchased a small Styrofoam cooler and filled it with snacks and drinks to enjoy on the beach. The boys played with some of their dollar store beach toys during the ride in the car.

As soon as Coltan was apprised of the family's plans, he messaged other agents who might be able to assist in the directive from Hanke. Within the list of recipients was Agent Whitler. He knew, as Pearse did, that something was amiss in the agency. When Whitler received the message, he immediately notified Pearse of the circumstances.

Pearse knew it was going to take coordination to protect the family. Throughout his time in the CIA, he had made many friends outside the agency. These friends had done him favors over the years and they didn't hesitate to come to his assistance this time either. Pearse couldn't risk being seen with Petru and his family. As far as anyone in the agency was concerned, he was off limits. However, a complete scuba outfit would definitely enable him to be of aid without being detected.

Petru and the boys played in the sand making all sorts of shapes, though not necessarily sand castles. They would get dry, hot, and sandy and then return to the ocean to cool off. While they were in the water this time, Sorina started making a sand fort. She thought it would be fun to hide behind it and let them try to find her. She worked quickly. Some of the molds broke apart because the sand had become dry in some spots. She dug deeper to find the moister sand.

The beach and the waters around it had definitive lines as to where cars could drive and boats could sail. It was for the safety of the swimmers and sunbathers that the rules were made. Petru looked up from being splashed for the hundredth time by his boys and saw a boat out a distance getting bigger as it raced towards the beach. He scooped up Grigore and Lucian and moved towards the shore. His feet kept sinking in the oozy sand and it was hard to go very quickly. Others in the water did the same while some on the beach screamed at the boat to stop.

Sorina looked up and gasped. The boat was closing in on the beach. It had come inside the warning zone and didn't look like it was even trying to slow down. She ran towards Petru and grabbed Lucian from him. They kept running onto the beach.

People stood watching in horror as men raised weapons to fire.

"Get down," a man shouted. "Get down and stay down."

Sorina dropped to the ground and tucked Lucian close beside her. Petru put Grigore down first and then fell on the sand. Petru looked towards Sorina. As far as he could see, people were laying in the sand on the beach. Was this even a good idea, he wondered. Maybe a moving target would be far better than a still one.

The guns began to fire, and bullets skipped through the sand right next to Petru. He held his breath and prayed for it to stop. More shots were heard, but thankfully no screams.

Men in wet suits came up onto the boat from the stern. One man took a length of rope and tied a deck chair to the end. Two other men in wet suits ran towards the bow as the men were shooting towards the beach for the second time.

"I'll be damned if he's getting away this time," said Coltan. "Shoot 'em all. I want 'em all dead."

"That's not what the directive was," said Stankus. "We're to take out Wadimar and his family, no one else."

"Then you find him on that beach," said Coltan. "You find him and point him out to me."

Stankus stopped and looked across the beach.

"You can't, can you," said Coltan. "Hanke wants him dead, or we'll be dead."

"None of this rings right," said Stankus. "Nothing Hanke's doing is right."

"Do as you're told, or next thing, I'll be coming after you," said Coltan.

"Exactly," said a voice from behind.

Coltan reeled around to face Pearse.

"What the hell are you doing here?" said Coltan. "You weren't invited to this party."

"Just think of it as crashing," said Pearse.

He raised his hand and the rope tightened. Coltan's feet were pulled out from under him and the gun flew in the air. Coltan was dragged to the stern of the boat where Pearse and another man tossed him overboard. The other man went to the bow of the boat, started it, turned it and set a course for the open sea. He rigged the throttle so it would stay open and motioned to Stankus to join them. When they were out of clear sight of the beach, they dived off the boat and swam to an awaiting craft.

The noise from the boat was gone. People began stirring again. Police were on the scene. They had been called by one of the sunbathers when she first noticed the boat getting near the beach. It was something that had never happened before. No one had ever opened fire on a group at the beach.

The police went around trying to get some clue as to who the people might be. They wrote down accounts of what happened and from what it seemed, the men on the boat weren't after just one person in particular. These men were shooting at everyone. Petru ran his fingers through the sand and brought up several casings. He put one into the cooler and the rest he took over to the police.

Sorina sat on the beach with the boys. They were so excited about her sand fort. Even with the shooting, didn't squelch their spirits. The people on the beach returned to their activities as though nothing happened. They were back in the water and the laughter of the kids filled the air. Sorina and the boys took some buckets and toys to get some water to wet the sand. The whole time, Sorina kept saying prayers of thanks and she also asked for this to be over so they would be safe.

Petru sat down beside his family.

"What have we here?" he asked.

"Mama made a sand fort and we're going to make it bigger," said Grigore.

"Can we stay a little longer?" asked Lucian.

"If that's what you want," said Petru.

"Yes!" said the boys.

Just one simple message made Hanke smile for the first time.

The mission has been accomplished. We created a diversion at the beach by firing into the sand. While everyone was lying flat we grabbed the family from the far edge of the beach. They were executed and their bodies buried at sea. As far as anyone is concerned, they simply went missing and so will I be.

Coltan

Hanke smile.

"Ah, threats," said Hanke. "They work every time."

The trucks moved into the camp. The *Chosen One* came out onto the porch and watched as the men in back of the truck stepped off. He knew they would need an explanation as to why they were back at camp because no one ever returned once they were sent on a mission for the Divine One.

As they came off the truck, they stood in inspection formation as they had done many times before.

"My dear followers," said the *Chosen One*, "I know you're wondering why you have suddenly found yourself among us again. The Divine One does not always move in ways that are simple and straightforward. There are times when we do one thing and the Divine One, in His infinite wisdom, asks us to do something else. The Divine One has decided that it is imperative that we all be together in this camp and that everything we do for the missions are done here. So, from this point on, our missions will begin here. You, who have just returned, don't worry, you will still be the next ones to be chosen for the mission. I ask that you be patient while we get everything organized so that things will run as smoothly as they had before. At this time, my dear followers, you are dismissed. You will be shown to your new quarters."

Once the men left, he addressed Kannid and Raseem.

"I want all of that brought in here," he said.

"There's an awful lot of it," said Kannid.

"We'll find places for it."

"Yes, sir," said Kannid.

"I want it where I have control of it."

The first boxes contained all the notes, charts and maps that came from Mahayin's office. The *Chosen One* took everything out of the boxes carefully and then started putting things on the walls and putting other things in drawers and on bookcases. As he looked through the hundreds of pages of data that dealt with just one attack, he realized that he may have underestimated Mahayin's role in all of this. That didn't matter at all now. There was nothing that could be done to change the course of prior events.

Whenever anything that was strange or out of the ordinary made its way to the internet, Robert was one of the first to find it. He and his group of online monitors kept abreast of everything. Sometimes things would appear that announced events happening far in the future and they were able to watch with intent the period of preparation. Other times, things were kept secret until much closer to the time of the event. It didn't matter when something was announced, this group was able to find out everything about the event.

This time, when Robert entered the forum, one of the members brought to their attention a conference. The invitees were a hand-selected group of lawmakers from various countries. They would be the guests of Dr. Emilio D. Avidtaes, Head of the World Organization for Counteracting Economic and Global Terrorism. The place where the conference was being held was a secret. Dr. Avidtaes believed that because of the power the lawmakers possessed in being able to sway votes, world terror organizations might find them to be important targets.

Robert knew they would be able to find the location of the meeting. For some reason, location was one thing that couldn't remain totally secret. What he needed more was a list of lawmakers who had been invited. When he asked, the member told him he had a partial guest list and a list of the countries that were asked to participate.

As soon as Robert had the list and printed it out he returned to the dining room. He looked down the list as he walked. He got to one name and stopped. He slapped his hand with the papers and walked into the room.

"Stop whatever you're doing," he said.

"Wow!" said Monique, "What's gotten into you?"

"Listen," said Robert. "We have a lot of work to do."

"Honey," said Monique, "stop for a minute and start over."

"I'm sorry, I think my mind is racing faster than my mouth can speak."

"What do you have?" asked Pierre.

"According to my online group, there is a conference coming up that is being hosted by Dr. Emilio D. Avidtaes. Now, Dr. Avidtaes is supposedly the Head of the World Organization for Counteracting Economic and Global Terrorism. I say supposedly because with all the work we've already done, I have never read anything about this organization and I consider myself on top of things."

"When is this conference?" asked Gwen.

"We don't have a date, but we will," said Robert. "We'll find out."

"Okay, where is this meeting taking place?" asked Gina.

"The location is being kept secret because of the fact that the people who are being invited have the power to sway votes and he fears for their safety."

"What a crock," said Mark. "We have summit meetings with the world's most powerful leaders and everyone knows where they are. You don't think those meetings could be a terrorist target?"

"I'm only telling you what I was told," said Robert. "But what I found interesting was the guest list. Now bear in mind we only have a partial guest list, but guess who's on the guest list, George."

"David Renovet?"

"Exactly."

"Is Senator Richard Milner on the list?" asked Mark.

Robert looked over the list.

"Yes he is."

"Something's not right," said Gwen. "I feel like we missed something?"

"I don't think we missed anything," said Mark. "I just don't think we've put it together."

"Alright," said George. "I go to Spain and see David Renovet, but it can't be David Renovet because he's been here, in Paris, all the time. Then Nicole mentions plastic surgery and Raquel asks how you can make someone look like another person. Aside from makeup, it's plastic surgery. Now we have this and David's name on the invited list. Do I have everything right so far?"

"Let's see what we can come up with, people," said Gina walking over to the easel and grabbing a marker.

"Dr. Hempton is doing plastic surgery on common people turning them into lawmakers," said Paul.

"Dr. Avidtaes is hosting a conference inviting lawmakers," said Monique.

"The location is secret which means it's somewhere in the middle of nowhere," said Hal.

"But why?" asked Gwen.

"Because they're taking the plastic surgery duplicates to the location and hiding them there," said Tom. "Then when the real ones get there, they'll make them captives, and replace them with the fake ones when the conference is done."

"Why?" asked Mark.

"I don't know," said Tom, "so they can go back to their legislative meetings and blow the places to bits?"

Everyone sat looking at Tom with dropped jaws.

Zaid retuned in a tizzy. Never had he ever failed to complete an assignment until now. There was nothing he could do except tell Yamani what had happened.

"Good morning, Zaid. How are you this morning?"

"I am fine, sir."

"What did you find out?"

"Well, sir, I couldn't find out anything. When I got there, the whole place was empty. It had been moved somewhere, but I don't know where."

Yamani thought for a moment.

"I think with everything we were able to do, they may have had to do something," said Yamani. "Perhaps they thought the only way to be successful again was to move to another country."

"But where?" asked Zaid. "And how did they do it so quickly?"

"I have neither answer," said Yamani. "But we will find out. I am glad you are back Zaid. I do have some new information from our partners that we must begin to check out."

"Yes, sir," said Zaid. He was so glad that Yamani was not angry with him.

Some things could not be handled over the phone. Things of this nature had to be handled in person. With Tom's suggestion that duplicates had been "created" to take the place of lawmakers around the world, it caused a stir among all of those working to end the vicious attacks against the nations. No matter how farfetched it sounded, there was a possibility the scenario could turn out to be true.

Michael knew he needed to talk to four people concerning this, the first was Yamani. While meeting with him in person was not a viable option, chatting with a webcam was a close second. Michael valued his view on the situation because of Yamani's ability to see through the impossible to find the possible. It was both a gift and a curse. However, when Michael discussed the idea with him, Yamani immediately used the information concerning the maps with the titles "My Piece" that were found with the Intelligence Heads as definite proof that the idea did hold credence. He told Michael that he would do whatever he could and utilize his resources to substantiate the idea.

The second person was Senator Richard Milner. He and Michael had been friends since they were young. Richard had always wanted to be in politics and would run for class president or student government. He thrived on "campaigning," and never lost an election. The same was true when he got old enough to run for the Senate. It was what he always wanted to do aside from being President of the United States. Michael was still certain he intended to run some day and when that time came Michael knew he would be somehow involved in that campaign.

"Michael," said Senator Milner as he walked into the room. "It's so good to see you. How's Laura."

"She's fine," said Michael. "I was thinking about the time when Katie French's dog grabbed Billy Hemming's pant legs and ripped his pants while we were walking to school."

"That wasn't Katie's dog. It was Agnes' dog. You know the lady who always wanted us to walk on the other side of the street."

Michael laughed. Now that he was certain he was talking to the real Senator Milner he could continue.

"Richard, we have a problem," said Michael. "This can't go any further. I need to ask you some questions."

"Sure. Michael, you know you can tell me anything."

"Did you get an invitation for a conference from a Dr. Emilio D. Avidtaes?"

"Yes, I did. Why?"

"Do you have any idea who he is?"

"He's the Head of the World Organization for Counteracting Economic and Global Terrorism."

"Did you know that before you received the invitation, or is this the first you've ever heard of this organization?"

"You know, Michael, I don't think I ever heard of it before I got the invitation."

"I don't suppose you have the invitation."

"I do," said Richard picking up his briefcase and opening it. "Here you go."

Michael read through the invitation. Whoever wrote this knew how to make the recipient feel as though it was an honor to be invited to this gathering. While all the pleasantries were there and a list of the topics that would be discussed, there was no mention of the date nor the place. Those two things were conveniently left out. Instead the invitation promised another letter would be forthcoming with the pertinent details. Dr. Avidtaes would be taking care of all transportation and lodging reservations and costs. Indeed, it was an event that was too good to pass up.

"I noticed that you had to R.S.V.P. for this conference by last Friday, without even knowing the dates. Did you do so?"

"Yes, I did. I sent my reply that I would attend," said Richard. "Why all the interest in this conference?"

"I just know several people who were unsure about committing to go because of the lack of date," said Michael. "Perhaps they had other things coming up and weren't sure if there would be a conflict."

"Enough of business. Let's go get some lunch."

Taking all the bodies to Pittsburgh where the experts were seemed to be the logical solution. It wasn't that the people needed more work, but for some reason both Jeff Easterly and President Bartram felt that these bodies were somehow related to the attacks.

Roger Gimshaw's office seemed to have a revolving door. There was a constant flow of traffic. He saw more agents come through his door since the Heinz Field Bombing than he had in all the years he was in Pittsburgh.

He was sitting and enjoying a cup of coffee with Agent Hensen when Jeff Easterly knocked and walked in.

"How's it going today, gentlemen?" he asked.

"Well, just when I thought my workload was getting a bit more manageable, you show up with more," said Gimshaw. "What's this about?"

"Well, first of all, smart boy you have there, Ted. Calling you was the best thing he could have done."

"Thank you, sir," said Agent Hensen. "When Phil told me what they found, I told him I'd call you and for them not to tell anyone anything about it."

"We've found a lot of personal items and a lot of IDs," said Easterly. "Whoever was responsible for this never expected it to be found."

Easterly took out the IDs of two of the men and handed them to Gimshaw.

"See if you can find out anything about these two right now."

Roger Gimshaw put the names into a search and went through the pages of results matching them with what little he knew. Jeff had gone to get a cup of coffee and looked around at what else was going on before returning to the office.

"Got anything?" he asked.

"Dr. Louis Antwon is a world renowned geological engineer. He specializes in mountains, creating tunnels and man-made caverns. He is also quite an expert in technology and security. Irwin Selbring is one of Europe's most sought after interior designers."

"Now what the hell is that supposed to mean?" asked Easterly.

There weren't many places where Michael felt he could meet with President Bartram without causing attention. Not that it was a good thing about what happened in Pittsburgh, but President Bartram could always give the excuse that he wanted to touch base with the people working in Pittsburgh, especially now that Heinz Field was being reconstructed.

"Michael, good to see you again," said President Bartram.

"It's good to see you also, Mr. President," said Michael.

"What's going on?"

"We think we may have uncovered another layer to this. It's possible the attacks were planned to incapacitate cities, but also to mask a more sinister purpose."

"Sinister?" said President Bartram. "That's a strange word to use."

"I know."

"Why don't you tell me about this sinister purpose."

"When one of my partners went to pick up Mr. Allard from a clinic in Spain, he saw a French Senator there David Renovet. The next day, David Renovet was on television telling how he had been working for the past three day setting up a festival in Paris. That meant he couldn't have been in Madrid. George even went down to the festival and confronted him about it. The man's never been to Madrid."

"So maybe he was mistaken."

"No, he was sure it was him. Then Robert learned about a conference that was being hosted by Dr. Emilio D. Avidtaes, the Head of the World Organization for Counteracting Economic and Global Terrorism."

"I've never hear of that," said President Bartram, "and I've never heard of Dr. Avidtaes."

"Neither have we, and believe me, we know just about everyone who is anyone when it comes to terror or subjects on terror."

"Who's invited to this?"

"We have a partial guest list. There are people working to get the full list," said Michael and he handed a copy to President Bartram.

President Bartram looked over the list.

"I was able to see the invitation that was sent to Senator Milner. There was no date or place listed, but they had to respond by last Friday. Senator Milner said he would go."

"Now, Michael, what do you think this is all about?"

"We think they have created duplicates of these lawmakers. We're talking plastic surgery. We also think they're going to detain these lawmakers at this secret place while substituting the duplicates for them."

"For what reason?" asked President Bartram. "To get a bill passed?"

"No. To totally obliterate a government by calling a joint session of congress or parliament or whatever complete with the President, Prime

Minister, Vice President, whomever, and then detonate every last one of those duplicates."

President Bartram shook his head. It was about the most preposterous thing he had ever heard, yet most likely a real possibility especially considering what was uncovered in Appalachia.

"Look, I know this sounds ludicrous, but the Intel Heads we've found each had a folded map with the title "My Piece" on it. Each one so far has been promised a piece of the world. Blowing up a stadium, or a mall, or a performance venue, or even an airport or metro isn't going to get them their piece of the world. Only unseating the governing power will do it."

Michael stopped for a moment to let it settle with President Bartram.

"I know this is a lot to take in," said Michael. "We have a list of the countries where the invitees are coming from. Somehow we have to be able to talk to each of the leaders, like I'm talking to you right now. This is extremely important and I wouldn't be bothering you, if I didn't think the situation was critical."

"Well Michael, then here's some more. Yesterday, I was apprised of a secluded area, pretty far from the Appalachian Trail. Five hikers found a dumping ground for dead bodies. One of the hikers is the son of an FBI agent, so he called his father. I visited that site. I've never seen anything like it. Two of the men were killed rather recently. I would say just before the bombing in Pittsburgh. They found identification on them and I just talked to Jeff right before you came. The first one, Dr. Louis Antwon is a geological engineer specializing in mountains, mainly tunnels and man-made caverns. He's also a technology and security expert. The second one, Irwin Selbring, is one of Europe's most sought after interior designers. They haven't run the rest yet."

Michael shook his head.

Chapter Thirty-Three

Tom and Hal had been through all of the drama that had happened between Yamani and Laura and Michael. They knew first-hand what type of person he was and how he could command any of his followers to do anything. Now they were faced with a situation that, while it didn't have that personal essence, was every bit as evil and calculated as the one they faced with SecReSAC.

They separated all the information Yamani had sent regarding the Intel Chiefs and the promises made to them. Someone was promising to split up the world and give people pieces of it as payment for their part in the project. Margo had each one made into an overlay so they could put one piece over another to see how much of the world was promised. While each person would have felt he was given a major portion, in reality, it was only a small percentage of the world that had been promised. They knew that Hanke was also part of it and could only surmise that his part included the United States.

"I'm telling you, this is way bigger than just these attacks," said Tom. "Aside from death toll what did it really get them? Did they want to kill more people than nine eleven? Well, they did it, but they're still not stopping."

"I do agree with you, but we can't just ignore these and hope they stop, because they most likely aren't going to," said Margo. "I think they're a precursor. I think they're trying to see how accurate they can get."

"We have to find out who this Dr. Emilio D. Avidtaes is," said Robert. "I'm not saying that I know everything there is to know about terrorism, but I think if he's the head of a world organization, I would have run across his name before this."

George was seemingly lost in thought while the others were discussing various topics. He played back the conversation he had with Dr. Hempton. Some of the things didn't add up. He seemed more concerned with Helena than he did with his patient.

"How did he know about Helena?" said George, unaware that he had spoken aloud.

"How did who know about Helena?" asked Tom.

"Sorry," said George, "I didn't mean to interrupt."

"No, go on," said Margo.

"When I went to get Andre, Dr. Hempton seemed very curious about Helena and what happened to her. He first asked about whether there was someone with Andre and I told him that some people saw a woman hurrying from that direction to the terminal. He also wanted to know if I knew what happened to her and I told him I had been told she died when the airplane exploded. That wasn't good enough I guess because when he came back from getting the paperwork, he asked me how I knew Helena Rudarsnyan. I just said who?"

"Do you think he heard Andre talking in his sleep?" asked Robert.

"No," said George. "I don't even think Andre knows Helena's name. We tried to keep him in the dark as much as possible for his own safety."

"Now, listen," said Tom. "If Dr. Hempton was curious about Helena, it must have been because he was told about her. The only other way he would have heard or read her name was if the list of passengers aboard the flight was listed somewhere and he read it. Then, you have to ask why he would have chosen her name out of all the names that were listed. He knew about her. He was told about her. I'm certain of it."

"Who is this Dr. Hempton?" asked Gina. "He has to have some sort of track record if he's a real doctor. We have to be able to find something about him."

"Dr. Hempton is a board certified plastic surgeon," said Robert. "He earned his degree at Stanford. He has a long list of awards he received. This man has had a great career."

"Obviously someone must have offered him a great deal more than what he was getting to have him leave a prestigious career to do this," said Margo.

"What about a piece of the world?" asked Hal.

Every one of the invitees to the conference hosted by Dr. Emilio D. Avidtaes was sent an email concerning some of the details. Dr. Avidtaes wanted to make absolute certain that the invitees knew they would be treated in a style worthy of their station. He was intent upon giving them the royal treatment, for lack of a better term, and wanted to prove it to them before they actually arrived.

Contained in the email was a link to a website and a code to enter so the person could view the accommodations.

When Senator Richard Milner received the email he called Michael.

"Are you still here?" asked Senator Milner.

"Yes, I am," said Michael. "What's up?"

"I just received an email from Dr. Avidtaes with a video to watch. I was wondering if you wanted to see it."

"You know I do."

"I can be at your house in a few minutes."

Michael cleared the table of all the files he was going over.

"Done already?" asked Laura.

"I wish," said Michael. "Richard is coming over. He got an email from Dr. Avidtaes with a video and is coming so we can watch it."

"I'll put on the coffee and get some lunch ready."

"Good, I'm starved."

About five minutes after the call, Senator Milner arrived. He brought his computer with him and set it up on the table.

"Read the email first and then we can watch the video," said Richard.

"Did you watch it yet?" asked Michael.

"No, because I wanted you to see it if it was possible and I wasn't sure whether or not I could view it more than once."

Laura sat down in the third chair on the other side of Richard. He put in the code and the video began.

"Good day to you all!" began Dr. Avidtaes. *"I know there are many questions you are asking yourself and I would like to answer as many of them as I possibly can. The date, time, and location will be forthcoming. Everything in due time. What I would like to show you today is what we have prepared for your arrival and your comfort. Please follow along with me and I will graciously be your guide."*

The video continued as Dr. Avidtaes began the tour from after the entrance through the front door. The lobby had beautifully crafted wood and chandeliers hanging from the ceiling. There was a desk where the invitees would check in to get their room assignments and the itinerary of the conference events. From there, Dr. Avidtaes showed them the conference areas with the area where the keynote address would be given and then on to the rooms where small group topics would be discussed and debated. Next on the agenda were rooms where attendees could relax and enjoy the company of others and the dining areas where they would enjoy their meals. Last on the tour were the individual bedrooms. They were decorated beautifully and had a comfortable feel even on video.

"I hope that you enjoyed the tour. There will be other videos forthcoming concerning what to bring to make your stay more enjoyable as well as items needed for discussion. Until next time, I bid you well wishes."

"Now what do you think?" asked Richard.

"It's beautiful," said Laura, "but strange."

"Why strange?" asked Michael.

"There's not one window in the entire place," said Laura. There are wall treatments, mirrors, and beautiful paintings, but not one window."

"I can honestly say that I didn't notice that," said Richard. "I was too busy looking at all the beautiful rooms."

"He's certainly selling this conference," said Michael. "Can you try to get into it again?"

"I can try."

Richard tried to replay the video, but it wouldn't allow it. So he clicked the link again and entered the code. The video played again. This time both Michael and Richard watched the video looking for windows. And true to what Laura said, there were no windows.

"Who would build a conference center without windows?" asked Richard.

"Someone who has built it underground so it can't be found," said Laura.

Michael nodded his head. He was certain Laura was right. This wasn't meant to be a conference facility. It was a bunker, plain and simple. The video along with the information from President Bartram put a whole different light on things. If this was some underground facility, it was going to take quite a bit to find it and a whole lot more to devise a rescue plan and carry out that plan, if necessary.

"Not sure I like the thought of being underground," said Richard, "but it does look really nice."

"It does," said Laura.

"Do you happen to have the invitation with you?" asked Michael.

"I do," said Richard.

"Can I make a copy of it?"

"Sure."

Michael left the room and made a copy of the invitation. As soon as he was finished he handed the original back to Senator Milner.

"How long are the two of you going to be in the states?"

"For a little bit," said Michael. "I have some business to attend to."

"Richard, can you access this from another computer?" asked Laura.

"I assume so. I just don't think more than one person can access it at one time with the same code," he said. "Let me send you the link and code and you can try it. If it works, great. If not, then we know."

The palm trees waved gently in the breeze and the waves lapped the shore. The white sands seemed to go on forever and the children played making sand castles while others made mounds of sand balls they used to pelt others from behind their sand forts. Blankets were laid out randomly along the beach and families had coolers with all sorts of drinks and food to enjoy during their day.

Yamani held Maranissa's hand as they walked along the beach. It was good to feel the sun and sea spray on his face. For such a long time, he had been mostly in the house. He had forgotten how much he missed being outdoors.

For the most part, Yamani had been sending his men to do most of the searching and scouting, but this time, he insisted on doing it himself. After all he had been through at the hands of Hanke, he felt driven to find the man himself. Usually, he would never think of taking Maranissa on such a task, but he had no intention of confronting the man. He only wanted to find him, to find some trace of him.

During the time he was in exile, Hanke would taunt him whenever he could with talk about an island paradise he would frequent. He would talk about the white sands and the waves lapping against the beach and how he would walk with one of his beautiful women under the moonlight and stars. Hanke told Yamani about a house he bought on an island, a house purchased under an assumed name so that no one in the organization could ever find out. Yamani was certain Hanke told him these things because he never expected Yamani to be released from exile. He expected him to be killed during his time there. He hadn't counted on Yamani's cleverness and stubbornness. It wasn't for lack of trying on Hanke's part, that Yamani didn't die. One of Hanke's perverse pleasures was to give away Yamani's location as soon as Yamani seemed to be settled in.

Even back then, Yamani kept a notebook, a rather small one that could be easily hidden amongst some other mundane things. He developed a system of abbreviation that he committed to memory so he could review his notes at any time, yet if the notebook would fall into anyone else's hands, it would look like nothing more than notes for a children's book or poem. Even now, Yamani could go back and read his notes and understand every word and nuance. It was from that book that he deduced the name and location of the island.

Hanke was right. The island was beautiful and Yamani was enjoying the walk on the beach holding the hand of the woman he loved, the woman who loved him more than anything.

"Enjoying yourself?" asked Yamani.

"Very much," said Maranissa looking up at him. "It is very beautiful here. Thank you for bringing me."

"It is very beautiful indeed," said Yamani. "I had heard about it many years ago and have always wanted to visit. Now we can enjoy its beauty while I take care of business."

"Maybe some time in the future, we can come and spend a great deal of time," said Maranissa, "but until then, I will enjoy the time we have right now."

They walked along the beach a while and then headed back to the walkway that led into town. Yamani stopped when they got to the first street where the buildings had balconies that faced towards the ocean. He turned to the right and they began walking along the beach front street.

"It is the next one," said Yamani.

He looked up at the windows. They were exactly as Hanke had described them. He would have recognized the house anywhere. He led Maranissa along the stone path to the other side of the house. There was no sign that anyone was home, except that a bag of garbage had been left for pick up. Yamani put up a finger towards Maranissa and she nodded. He quietly and cautiously entered the house and softly closed the door. Yamani shook his head. It was exactly as he knew it would be. The notes in his book were absolutely accurate. It had, however, been many years since those notes had been made, and it could be that Hanke may have sold the property to someone else who kept everything exactly the same. Yamani checked the kitchen. There wasn't anything in the refrigerator that would indicate when the last time anyone had been there, but Yamani knew he would have gotten rid of anything perishable before leaving. There were things in the freezer and a great stock of items in the cabinets.

He cautiously walked up the stairs to the second floor. The bathroom was definitely that of a man, although there were also toiletries belonging to a woman. Yamani picked up a bottle of men's cologne and immediately recognized it as Hanke's scent. The door to the bedroom was open and he walked in and looked around. Hanke was right. He did have a lovely view. He looked at the mirror on the dresser and saw a picture of himself staring back at him. His face was circled and a red x was drawn across. Yamani hurriedly walked down the stairs and to the door. Beside the door was a small beautifully crafted console table where Hanke most likely put his keys and mail. Yamani looked on the table and picked up a piece of mail addressed to Mr. Joshua Nashton. Yamani made a mental note of the name, left, and locked the door behind him.

The list of the countries that had lawmakers who were invited to the conference was printed in large letters on several large sheets of paper and taped to the walls. Helena looked at the list and shook her head. Hal removed each one of the overlays and placed them down again. There were large sections of color missing, sections he thought would surely have been selected by someone. He would consider them prime real estate and prime cultures. It was obvious there were a great number of missing pieces.

Helena looked at the overlays as Hal put them down and removed them. She was trying to find any possible answer and was looking for any commonality there might be. Since this all began, she felt she was forever grasping at straws and even though she knew that no one knew where she was, she longed for this to be over so she could resume a life that was somewhat normal. As she moved from being lost in thought to a state of definite awareness, she looked again at the colored map pieces.

"Hal, would you mind reading the names of the countries that are in color on that map?" she asked.

"Sure."

As Hal read the names of the countries, Helena checked them off of Dr. Avidtaes list. Every country from the map appeared on the list of invited countries. When he was done reading, Hal listed the countries that he thought would have been taken. Those Helena notated in a different color. When Hal was finished with his thoughts, Helena looked at the list.

"Let's see," she said. "If the other countries you mentioned have actually been promised to other people, then I think we have something."

"What?" said Hal.

"Every one of the countries in color on the map is on this list as well as all the countries you mentioned. If this is right, then there has to be a connection. We have the rest of the list to a point where attacks are going to take place."

Helena took another color and marked off all the countries where attacks had happened, then using the same color, but a different symbol marked the countries that were still on the list of places to be attacked.

"Let's just say for argument's sake that the list of countries where the attacks have taken place and are going to take place is the same as the list of countries that are being promised to the Intel Leaders and other people who had important roles in this plan, and also that those two lists just happen to match up exactly with the list of countries who had lawmakers invited to this conference. If that is the case, as we have projected, then I think we now have the framework for the plan."

"I'm listening," said Hal. "and I think I see where you're going with this. Let me get some of the others and let's see what we can do."

Pierre put the call from Michael on speaker so everyone could hear. There was a lot of information to exchange. Michael wanted them to be sure to look over the copy of the invitation he sent. He also dictated the link for the website to Robert and the code. He wanted their thoughts on both. He told them he met with President Bartram and that in talking to him, he realized that the attacks on the countries weren't going to, in themselves, assure that the Intel Leaders would be able to take possession of their piece of the world. The only way that could happen was if the governments in power in all of those areas were somehow unseated. He also told them about the news President Bartram had told him.

Once Michael was finished, Hal and Helena explained what they had done and the premise that the list for all three aspects of the situation was indeed the same list. That coupled with what Michael put forth about unseating the governments in power sent chills up the spines of the group.

"I think you are really on to something," said Michael. "You need to take some time, think about it and flesh it out some more."

"Going back to what Tom said the other day about creating duplicates of the lawmakers and detonating them during a session," said Gina, 'that would unseat the governing power."

"Michael, Dr. Hempton is a board certified plastic surgeon," said Robert. "He studied at Stanford."

"Alright, I'll see what I can find out about his time at Stanford while I'm here." said Michael. "I think someone needs to pay a visit to Dr. Hempton, unannounced. Also, see what you can find out about this Dr. Avidtaes. Those who were invited are responding without even knowing where or when yet."

"I wonder what piece he was promised," said Hal.

"Good question," said Michael. "I also think someone needs to get to London to give some support to Jean and Angelique. I talked to him and he's exhausted. Laura and I will be here for a little while. We need to check on our friends and see how they're doing. We also have a few more meetings."

Pierre hung up the phone and Robert printed off a copy of the invitation and they watched the video.

"There aren't any windows in that place," said Raquel. "I couldn't stay there. I mean it's beautiful and all, but being underground is creepy."

"How do you know it's underground?" asked Monique.

"If you go through it again, look at the way the ceilings are beamed. They are holding up a lot of weigh. Also look at the vents in the rooms."

"Can we watch that again in a little bit?" asked Hal. "I want to talk about the lists and what Michael said."

"Sure," said Robert. "I think Michael's absolutely correct in his thinking."

"So do I," said Paul, while the rest of the group nodded in agreement.

"In the United States, there are times when someone will address a joint session of Congress," said Gwen. "Sometimes, the President, Vice-President and Justices of the Supreme Court are also there. I don't know if that happens elsewhere, but for us it would be the perfect time to unseat the governing powers."

"We can find that out," said Robert.

"We need to know where that session would be held, too," said Gina.

"Why?" asked Helena.

"Because that will tell us how many bombers it'll take to take them all out," said Gina. "That's why they chose Festhalle. I would bet money on it."

Clayton Pearse paced back and forth with the phone to his ear. He looked at the card again. Maybe he was crazy trying to call him again, but he was in dire need of help with this. That planted story was only going to go so far. Sooner or later Hanke was going to want to see proof, evidence that the task had been completed. How they had been able to find them, he was still trying to figure out, but they couldn't stay where they were.

"Hello," said Michael.

"Michael, this is Clayton. I need help."

"What's wrong?"

"Have you seen the news about the shooting on the beach?"

"No," said Michael pulling up news on the computer. "Give me a minute."

"The people who were supposedly taken are friends."

"Damn!" said Michael. "I thought they'd be safe."

"Yah, well, they were found," said Pearse. "I think I know how."

"Do you know where they are?"

"Yep."

"I'm sending my wife," said Michael. "Get them back on property, but not to their place. I'll have Laura call you."

"Where am I going?" asked Laura when Michael was finished.

"You have to go to Florida and get Petru and his family. They found them again."

Michael turned the computer screen around so Laura could see the news account of the shooting on the beach.

"My God," she said. "How did they find them? We changed everything over."

"I honestly don't know," said Michael, "although Clayton thinks he knows. The report says that a man, woman, and two small kids disappeared during the attack. Someone says he noticed them being dragged off. I don't think that's true. I think it's planted, because when I asked Clayton if he knew where they were he said he did. I told him to get them back on property, but not to their room."

"So now what?" asked Laura. "We obviously can't leave them down there."

"That's why I'd like you to go," said Michael. "I want you to bring them back."

"We can't fly," said Laura.

"I know, but you've driven those routes more times than I can count."

"Alright, book my flight."

Clayton took his time bringing Petru and his family home. He insisted that what they had brought with them to the beach, they left there. He told Petru it was important for everyone to think they were dragged off as eyewitnesses had recounted.

The boys bemoaned a bit about losing their gaming systems, but Petru promised they would soon have new ones. The boys were so worn out by the time on the beach and after they had stopped to eat dinner, they were soon asleep in the car.

"Now what, Mr. Pearse," asked Petru.

"Laura is on her way. She is going to take care of things," said Pearse. "I don't think you're going to be able to stay at Disney because they'll be able to find you again."

"I don't understand how," said Sorina. "We don't have anything the same as we did."

"Your fingerprint," said Pearse. "It took me a while to figure it out, but I know I'm right."

"A fingerprint?" asked Petru.

"You have to scan your magic band and your fingerprint to get into the park," said Pearse. "The fingerprints would be the same and so they would be able to find that you were now elsewhere under another name."

"So we don't dare go back to the room either," said Petru.

"No. If you do, they'll know you weren't dragged off. I've done a great deal to make it appear that you're gone. As far as the person is concerned who's trying to kill you, you're already dead. The eyewitnesses have confirmed your disappearance."

"Where are we going now?"

"We're off to do some shopping and then we'll meet Laura."

Clayton knew it would take Hanke some time to check out the story and the first person he would want to question was Coltan. He also knew that it would be impossible. Right about now some shark was most likely suffering indigestion from eating too much Coltan. Once he figured it was impossible to get in touch with him, Hanke would then search to see if Petru had entered any of the parks. By the time all of this transpired, Petru would be safe and hopefully all of this drama would be at an end.

Clayton parked the car and they entered Disney Springs. The boys were excited to see the dragon in the lagoon that was made out of Lego blocks. From one store to another, there were more and more things that the boys just couldn't do without. By the end of the evening, they had forgotten all about having to leave other things behind.

Clayton felt his phone vibrate and checked the screen before answering.

"Hi," he said.

"Where are you?" asked Laura.

"We're by the Lego store."

"See you in a minute."

Laura came down the path to the left of the Lego store and saw them standing by the Lego family with more bags than were humanly possible to hold.

"Did you buy everything in the store?" she asked the boys.

"No," said Grigore. "We left a few things."

"Not a whole lot," said Sorina.

"I need to stop in there," said Laura pointing a store. "I want to pick up some movies for the boys to watch."

"Can we pick them out?" asked Lucian handing his bags to his mother.

"Why not," said Laura. "You're the ones watching them."

It actually didn't take very long for them to make their choices and pay for them. They came bounding out of the store with more bags.

"Necessities," said Laura. "All necessities."

Chapter Thirty-Four

With time becoming short, things had to be done quickly. When Gina told them they were going to have to leave the house to solve this, she was absolutely correct. This time, things had to be checked out in person. Dr. Hempton's office was the only thing today on Gwen Braedon's list of things to do. She wanted to get a chance to talk to the good doctor or at least have the chance to get into his office to see what she could find.

Gwen had no trouble finding the clinic that was just past the Madrid Airport on the road going into town. Undoubtedly, it was built there to handle any sort of emergency that might occur this far away from the city. She walked through the front door and was amazed to see a bit of commotion in what she thought would be a quiet environment.

She walked up to the reception desk where people were dabbing their eyes.

"I'm sorry," said the receptionist, when she saw Gwen standing in front of her.

"It seems I may have come at a bad time," said Gwen.

"We just received word that they found Dr. Hempton's body and he had been murdered," said the receptionist.

"Oh no!" said Gwen. "It can't be. I just talked to him last week and he asked me to come help him. He said he needed me to work on a project."

"May I ask who you are?"

"I'm Sylvia Letterman. Dr. Sylvia Letterman. I was Dr. Hempton's partner before he took the job here."

"Do you know what Dr. Hempton wanted?"

"He told me that he was going to leave charts for several patients that he wanted a consult on," said Gwen. "He said he would leave them on his desk in his office because he may be on rounds."

"Let me take you back to his office," said the receptionist.

She and Gwen walked back to the office and she unlocked the door for her.

"I'm not sure who Dr. Hempton wanted the consult on. All the patients who were upstairs are gone. Perhaps it's one of the accident victims we have."

"Thank you," said Gwen.

"When you leave, please lock the door behind you."

Gwen waited until the woman left and then looked around the office. The screen saver on the computer looked like one of those old fashion ones that changed color and shape. She moved the mouse and took a look around the desktop. Shaking her head, she clicked on the folder marked "Conf Proj." In the folder were pictures of men from all angles. There were pages of notes along with letters and saved emails. She plugged in an external drive and copied the folder to it. She was careful not to save any of the files again. Then she returned the drive to the zipper part of her bag. She grabbed three patient folders off the desk and walked out of the office locking the door behind her.

What she knew about being a doctor could probably be best summed up in one word…television. She only knew what those scripted doctors did. She looked at the first folder and found her way into the room. She looked through the pages and figured out what the problem was. She asked a few questions to clarify some things and told the patient she was going to be back to discuss a course of treatment for him. She did the same thing with the other two. As she talked to them she literally scribbled notes in the chart much like Dr. Hempton had done. She knew it was always said that doctors had the worst handwriting and she was definitely making sure hers was atrocious.

When Gwen finished, she walked out to the nurses' station and put the folders on the desk. No one was around so she made her way back to the front of the clinic. This time, it was totally empty. She walked out the door and left the premises.

Edgar Reinholdt put down the phone and leaned back in his chair. He folded his hands and put his fingers to his lips. He shook his head. This situation had to end. Right now though, with the news he just received, he knew the opposition was just gearing up for more terror. He was walking a fine line. Certainly he had the power to stop this right now, or did he. If he told this company not to deliver the order of shielded wire, what would happen to that company? From what he could tell, those who were in charge of these attacks were ruthless. They would stop at nothing to get what they wanted. If he didn't let the order go through, chances are they would do one of two things; they would break in and rob the place when no one was there, or they would come calling during the workday, kill everyone and take what they wanted.

Was it preposterous for him to think that they could find out who picked up the package and then follow him wherever he went? Would it be even within the realm of possibility that this person could lead them to the man in charge? He didn't have any of the answers, but knew enough that at least with the second option, they might get one step closer.

He picked up the phone again.

Yamani typed in the name Joshua Nashton into the search engine. He wanted to make certain that he wasn't mistaken about Hanke and the island house. His search turned up empty. There was no such person to be found through his searches.

Yamani nodded his head and wrote the name in his notebook. Sooner or later he was certain that Hanke would use that name. Why he would do so, he wasn't sure, but he had already established that identity on the island.

Maranissa walked out of the bathroom with a beautiful long print dress on. She slipped on her sandals and then ran a brush through her hair. Yamani closed the computer and got up. They walked to a restaurant near Hanke's house.

Dinner was a wonderful treat of island specialties and their server was more of a tour guide than a server. He knew where the best places to explore were, those that weren't over packed with tourists. It was something that many of his repeat customers always appreciated. He had small laminated card he kept in his pocket. He took it out to double check on some of the areas. Yamani noticed there were letters in bright colors next to the places.

"If I might ask," said Yamani, "what do the letters next to the names mean?"

"The "H" means there is high tourist activity," said Sharid, "If you like a lot of people around, then those are places for you. The "M" means there is moderate tourist activity. So if you like some people, you would like these. The "L" means there is light tourist activity. Some of these places are a little out of the way, but are worth having to travel to see them. Do you know what you would like?"

Yamani looked at the card again.

"What does the "N" mean?" asked Yamani.

"Oh that means No. There is no tourist activity in those areas," said Sharid. "I only have one person who always asks about the "N." Mr. Nashton always wants to go there and when he's there he doesn't want anyone coming to bother him."

"So, is he there now?" asked Yamani.

"Oh, no, he had to leave a couple days ago. He had business to take care of. Lately he's been away a lot more than he's been here."

"I see. Can anyone besides him go to this place?"

"Yes, as long as he's not there and no one else is there."

"Well my love, would you like to take a walk there?"

"Yes."

They walked for more than half an hour before arriving at the "N" spot. It was far enough away from the city and the beaches that people didn't bother with it much. Yamani knew that if Hanke wanted to know about this place and frequented it when he was there, it was for a reason. He was not a man who just wanted to walk and meditate.

There were small little cave-like openings in the terrain, nothing large enough for any sort of animal to decide to use as a home. They walked about the area and then sat down on a seat made naturally from a few trees that had fallen during a strong windstorm.

"I do not know why he comes here," said Yamani. "There has to be a reason. There has to be something in it for him."

"Maybe he just comes here to relax," said Maranissa. Her kind, gentle soul couldn't bear to see the wickedness in anyone.

"Unfortunately, my love, he is a ruthless man who is always working to make someone's life more miserable than his own."

Maranissa kept looking around. Something caught her attention and she got up slowly keeping her eyes on it. She walked to the left, to one of the bigger recesses, bent down and ran her fingers along the side. It was deliberately carved. This wasn't something the wind or rain could possibly do.

"My darling," she said, "could you come here a moment?"

Yamani walked over to Maranissa.

"What is it?"

"Run your fingers along here," she said showing him the carvings.

Yamani ran his fingers over the carvings. He looked around and smiled at Maranissa. It was apparent that Hanke realized that with sand, wind, and water, the physical appearance of an area could change time and again. It he wanted to use this area to hide something, he needed to find a way to mark the spot; a way that would be almost undetectable. For Hanke, he would know exactly what to look for and others would merely pass it by.

Yamani knelt on the ground. He cautiously felt around the opening. There was nothing. He reached in a bit further straight along the floor and still felt nothing. He repositioned himself and reached to the right with his left hand. His hand hit something solid and he traced its form. He took his right hand and wedged his fingers between the object and the wall. Little by little he wiggled it free and brought it over to the opening. He pulled it out. It was a wooden box and from the looks of the water stains, it had been on the island for a long time. Hanke must have been quite positive that no one would find it because it had no lock. Yamani released the catches on all four sides. There were no indentations to get fingers into in order to take off the lid. He pulled up on two of the catches along the one side and the lid moved slightly. He went around the box pulling up on the catches and lifting the lid slightly. He could see that Hanke had taken the time and trouble to have the box constructed with a wax coating so the water couldn't penetrate and ruin what was inside.

Inside the box were pictures, papers, news clippings, and different objects. It was more like a child's box of mementoes. Yamani looked at a few objects and then realized that soon it would be getting dark. They needed to get back, but more importantly, they needed the contents of the box. Yamani placed the lid back on the box and latched it. Maranissa knelt down and opened the bag she always had with her. Carefully, Yamani placed the box with all of the pictures, papers, and news clippings in her bag. Maranissa zipped the bag shut and folded the flap over.

They stood up and Yamani walked in front of Maranissa. She followed his path exactly and as she did, the heaviness and movement of the fabric of her dress erased their footprints.

Everything had been readied at the bunker. This was a long time in coming. It had been worked on for years and was the effort of many men and women along with some of the world's most skilled engineers. The area was divided into two huge underground caverns that were connected by a long tunnel. The beauty of the configuration was that while they were connected, they were soundproof. It was one thing the man insisted on. He made sure it was tested and retested using all sorts of sounds. For this to work, the people in cavern one couldn't know the people in cavern two existed. Bus after bus pulled up to the entrance to cavern two and people got out and went inside. This was to be their home until the project was near its end.

The man had arranged that only those who were his most loyal followers would be chosen for this project. It was vitally important that nothing went wrong. It was necessary that all of the duplicates, as the man loved to call them, had time to settle in and practice whatever skills were still not perfect. This also gave them additional time to interact with one another as their new personage.

Once they had been shown to their rooms and given a tour of the facility, they met in the large room and took their seats in front of a screen. Dr. Avidtaes appeared on the screen, welcomed them, and told them what was expected of them during their time there. He told them how important their assignment was and that it was up to them to be as convincing as possible.

On the tables in front of them were papers that contained lists of what they needed to know for the individual they were becoming. He told them they had to be ready to slip right into their business, political, and personal lives and it was during these times they had to be the most convincing. It was imperative that they learn as much on those sheets as possible and they would be put through their paces to see who could master their person the best. And then he was gone.

"All I'm looking forward to is living the life this man lives," said one gesturing to his face.

"You really think we're going to get to live when this is over?" asked another.

"What are you saying?"

"I'm saying that when he's done with us, there won't be anything left of us. Boom!"

Robert had searched every way he knew trying to find Dr. Emilio D. Avidtaes and the World Organization for Counteracting Economic and Global Terrorism. There was nothing. There wasn't anything aside from what they had found before concerning the conference. For someone who is supposed to be the head of a world organization, there should have been something. There should have at least been a page on the internet dedicated to the organization.

Robert read over the invitation and watched the tour of the facility where the conference was going to be held. He had to agree with Laura in her assessment that it was being held underground. Now the problem was where.

"No one covers their tracks this well," said Robert, "no one."

Gwen walked into the house. It had been a very productive day as far as she was concerned.

"How is Dr. Hempton?" asked George.

"Dead," said Gwen. "They found his body. He'd been murdered."

"Wow," said George. "This guy is getting rid of everyone."

"He sure is," said Gwen. "Even though he wasn't there, I did get in his office and access to his computer. I copied a folder of files."

She handed the drive over to Robert.

"How did you get this?" he asked.

"He had no password, only one of those old fashioned screen savers."

Robert pulled up the files and started opening them. There were pictures with names. The pictures were taken from different newspapers, magazines, and videos. There were dozens of pictures of the same person all from different angles. Each group of pictures had a name, what the person's title was, and where they were from. Robert quickly went through all of them very quickly. He paused when he saw David Renovet's picture appear on the wall.

"There it is, George. You weren't crazy."

When he got to the last folder and opened it, there was a time table. It showed when the men first got there, when surgeries were done and on whom, and when they were ready to start their training. He kept going through page after page of notes that Dr. Hempton made concerning each person's progress.

"None of them are there anymore," said Gwen. "The receptionist told me that all the patients on the upper floors were already gone."

"So whoever killed him waited until he knew the good doctor was finished with everyone and they had been moved out," said George.

"It looks that way," said Gwen.

"Here it is," said Robert. "They left later the same day you got Andre."

"Does it say where they were going?" asked George.

Robert kept going through the pages, trying to skim the contents quickly.

"Well, all it says is that they left on a charter flight," said Robert. "I can leave this up if anyone wants to go through it. So far, I've run into a brick wall when it comes to Dr. Avidtaes and his organization. According to the internet, neither exists."

Maybe it was because she had driven it so many times, or maybe it was just because she had avoided rush hour in every city along the way, but Laura made excellent time getting back to Pittsburgh from Florida. Michael greeted them and showed them to their rooms. Even though they hadn't had much sleep, no one was in any mood to sleep. The boys were busy exploring the house and found the best play room in the world in Michael's game room. They dragged their bags of treasures down the steps and everyone knew they would be busy for hours.

"They've been so spoiled," said Petru. "We're going to have to ship some of this back when we leave."

"There's no way we can allow you to go back yet," said Michael. "We know they're trying to put an end to anyone who had anything to do with Craustof. They've tried multiple times with you."

"I know," said Petru. "I can't thank you enough for all that you've done for us."

"Right now, they think you and your family are dead," said Michael, "and we want to keep it that way."

"There are things around here to keep the children amused," said Laura, "and our parks don't attract worldwide attention. I think they'll enjoy some of the things here."

"The boys have found these incidents to be exciting," said Sorina. "I'm scared out of my wits, and they're watching with wide-eyed wonder."

"They have no idea what's going on," said Laura. "Thank goodness. I'm sure they think it's like something out of a superhero movie."

"Exactly," said Sorina nodding her head and smiling.

"We're making great strides in finding who's behind all this," said Michael, "but we're not there yet. There are just a lot of things going on and if there's only one person in charge, he's going to become distracted. You can't handle everything and do it well."

"How can I help?" asked Petru. "There has to be something."

"There's always something," said Michael.

To say that Jean was exhausted was an understatement. He had been at Angelique's side except to take a shower and get something to eat. Even then, he only left long enough to get it and come back.

Angelique opened her eyes when she heard the door. She smiled when she saw Margo and Pierre come in. Jean got up and gave Margo a hug.

"How are you?" she asked.

"Tired," said Jean.

"When's the last time you had sleep?" asked Margo.

"I doze off here," said Jean.

Margo shook her head and walked over to Angelique. She was not quite prepared to see Angelique so incapacitated. She was always the one who could run ahead of everyone else and was the most athletic of them all. To see her just lying there was a shock.

Pierre put his hand on Jean's shoulder. He knew his friend needed a long rest away from the hospital and something good to eat.

"Thank you for coming," said Angelique quietly. "I really appreciate it."

"I'm so sorry this happened to you," said Margo.

"It almost didn't," said Angelique. "We almost stopped it. It could have been so much worse."

"Angelique, I think I'm going to take this husband of yours out of here to get some proper rest," said Pierre.

"Please do," said Angelique. "He needs it."

Jean came over to Angelique and kissed her. Then he and Pierre left. Margo grabbed the chair and brought it closer to Angelique so she could sit facing her.

"A lot of lives were saved this time," said Angelique. "People were already running out when I came into the terminal. I looked around and saw them and called Jean immediately."

"It was a little girl who started warning everyone," said Margo. "Did you know that?"

"No. I only knew someone had started it. Good for her."

"I know. She deserves something for her bravery."

"I heard the first one go off when I was on the phone with Jean and they were going off one after another. I kept pleading for Edgar to shut it down. As they got closer, there was more dust and particles in the air and it made it harder to see. That's why I tripped over a bag someone left."

"I can't even imagine what it was like," said Margo.

"I was so grateful when the explosions stopped. I knew Edgar had stopped them. Then they were able to get the other ones. They took something and killed themselves."

"They did that in Tokyo, too."

"The only thing I could move was my neck so I raised my head and got security's attention. I was holding the instructions for diffusing the bombs, but I couldn't open my fingers. They had to pry them open to get the paper."

"O my God, Angelique."

"They kept apologizing and telling me they would get me out soon, but I told them I wanted to know that every last one of the bombers were diffused first. When they were done, they worked at getting me out and brought me to the hospital. When I was able to actually focus on what was going on, they showed me the x-rays, and I immediately thought of Humpty Dumpty."

"Oh, Angelique," said Margo smiling.

"Are we any closer to getting them?"

"Yes and no," said Margo. "It's a long story."

"Well, I don't think I'm going anywhere soon."

Chapter Thirty-Five

The box and its contents didn't leave their hiding place in Maranissa's bag until she and Yamani were safely inside their own house. Maranissa opened the bag and Yamani took out the box. He opened it and carefully began taking out the contents and stacking the pile again exactly as he found it. Then he took all the small items and placed them above the pile.

Yamani started going through the items one at a time. He read every word there was. He studied all the pictures and drawings. There were drawings of maps and diagrams of buildings and outdoor places. Every piece of paper was dated. This was everything Hanke was involved in. Everything he was doing. Was he stupid enough to trust that no one would ever find this? Could it be that everything was in this box?

Yamani began going through things a little quicker. He needed to see what all was contained. As he looked over each item he put it aside in a particular pile. Towards the bottom of the pile Yamani picked up a piece of paper and under it found a picture a much younger him. One after another he removed pictures from his past. From his days in exile and from his time at the right hand of the Ayatollah. He unfolded a piece of paper that revealed a map of Africa and on it were red circles where he knew he had once lived. Hanke had made him his special project. He followed him and leaked everything he knew about Yamani's whereabouts. These were the final pieces in the box and Yamani carefully stacked everything concerning himself in a separate pile.

Whatever this was all about, it began way back there with an obsession Hanke had with him. Knowing the basis, it was now time to study the papers and pictures and build on the basis to find just what he had in his hands. All those bits and pieces were important in their own right, even if they looked like nothing but junk. It was going to take much more concentration to do this and maybe, just maybe a few more pairs of eyes.

He came out to the kitchen to get something.

"How is it going?" asked Maranissa.

"There is something there," said Yamani, "but I do not know what yet. I know it has to do with me because I am part of what is in there."

"I made some lunch, more like something you could eat during the rest of the afternoon and even share," said Maranissa. "Would you like me to ask Qadir and Adarine to come to help? It would give me a chance to visit and see the children."

Yamani kissed his wife on the cheek.

"Yes."

Maranissa left and walked quickly through the streets of the small town. It was not a far walk at all only about five minutes, so when she told the men that Yamani needed them, they hurried to the house.

Yamani closed the door, picked up the platter and his drink and they went to where Yamani had things out on the table. He explained to them where he had found it and the importance of the find. They sat down and started reading every piece of paper. Anything that was questionable was discussed.

"Sir, he tells these men they have to enforce the wishes of the man. They have to keep everything quiet," said Qadir. "Who is the man?"

"We do not know that," said Yamani. "I was hoping there would be something here, because to stop this, we must find him."

Adarine picked up some pictures and waved them.

"None of these are the man," he said. "They are nothing more than enforcers."

"But it seems that the man only speaks through Hanke," said Qadir.

'All of these letters are asking Hanke to tell the man something or ask the man something," said Yamani. "All of those men, I believe, were recruited by Hanke. We must find him if we are going to find the man."

Yamani picked up a thin stack of papers stapled together. He flipped over the blank cover sheet. The heading said *Conference Project. Recruit someone to be Dr. Emilio D. Avidtaes. Can't be found anywhere even with face recognition. Head of a secret organization...the World Organization for Counteracting Economic and Global Terror. Create facility in the mountains. No one bothers these mountains. They're between here and nowhere. The do-gooders won't notice anything.* Yamani stopped reading and looked to find a date. It was dated on the last page. It was written almost eleven years ago. This wasn't something done on a whim. This was planned for over a decade. He continued reading every word. There were notes written in between the lines making it difficult at times to follow the train of thought. Everything that was happening now was going according to the timetable included. The written comments told him that Mayahin had been killed and the facility had to be broken apart. Things were being moved to places, but Hanke also used a sort of code so it wasn't easy to figure out what was where. Yamani followed the timetable and mentally thought about all that happened. He looked up at Qadir and Adarine.

"We have to alert the others," said Yamani. "This is going to happen very soon."

A large physical world map was spread out on the table. All of the other maps had countries and cities. This one was different. With the information from Yamani that the facility had been built in the mountains the race was on to find which mountains and then narrow it down from there.

"Do you have any idea how many mountain ranges there are in the world?" asked Gina. "I never thought about it before."

"I think there are places we can check off the list," said Helena. "Some have too much activity to make a good choice for this project."

"It has to be a range that's long enough to have those types of spots where nothing happens," said Hal. "Face it, no one skis the entire Rocky Mountain Range."

Helena took some strips of paper she had cut for use to mark things. She took a glue stick of Post-it glue and started covering up small mountain ranges and places that had too much activity. The world was becoming more manageable with every strip. When she was finished, there were still too many choices.

"Now, let's take out everywhere that's not on this list of countries," said Hal. "He's favoring these countries. He wants them to fall badly."

"That still gives us a lot," said Helen.

Mark was talking to Michael about what Yamani had found.

"It's the Appalachians," said Laura. "I know it."

"How are you sure?" asked Mark.

"Because he uses the words do-gooders. People are always going into Appalachia to help out. And they found all those bodies, the geological engineer, and interior decorator not far from the Appalachian Trail. I'm positive. There are some really desolate areas. The trail only touches a particular area."

"That's a big area, Laura," said Mark. "How are we going to find them?"

"Well, they flew out of Madrid on a charter," said Laura. "Find out where it went. Then they had to be transported somehow. He's not going to rent a ton of cars, so I'm inclined to think he used buses. Once we find out those particulars, we'll find out where they took them."

"How much time do we have?" asked Michael.

"Our contact said not much."

Tom kept looking at the speech given by the *Chosen One*. Then he looked at each of the pictures of the Intel leaders. Although he knew most were dead, he couldn't help thinking that there was no man; that one of these was the man. He stopped the speech when there was a good close-up of the *Chosen One* and zoomed in to see more detail. There were little things he could pick out. It looked like little bits of glue, but from a distance, no one would notice. The make-up wasn't bad either although there were a few places where you could see it caked a bit and streaked a bit. Again, from a distance, no one would notice.

Robert walked into Michael's office.

"Sorry," he said. "I didn't know you were working in here."

"Come in," said Tom. "I'm just really puzzled by something. I know you might think this is crazy, but I think I might have something."

"Crazy? That's a constant state around here. What do you have?"

"Look at this," said Tom pointing to some sections. "I think this is glue."

"May I?"

"Sure."

Robert magnified the image further and made it much clearer. Tom nodded.

"It is glue," said Tom. "Now look at the makeup. It's streaked here and caked here."

Tom pointed to those areas.

"Everything that Yamani sent us and told us, the fact that he was able to find and get to every one of the other Intel Leaders but not Hanke got me to thinking. What if Hanke isn't answering to anyone? What if Hanke is the man? What if he has disguised himself to look as much like Yamani as possible?"

"That's a lot of what ifs," said Robert as he pulled up another chair beside Tom. "Let's find a good picture of Hanke and see what we can do."

It was a long process, trying to duplicate everything exactly, but when they were finished, they looked at each other and smiled.

"As Laura would say, 'Can you print those for me?'" asked Tom.

Robert shook his head and laughed. As each one finished printing, he labeled them.

"Wait until Yamani sees these."

With photos in hand, Robert and Tom went to show them to the others. Tom put down the picture of Yamani and the picture from the speech.

"What's this?" asked Gina.

"This is a picture of Yamani and a picture of the man from the speech," said Tom.

"They're close, but you can see that the eyes are different," said Gwen.

Tom put down the picture that Robert had made on the computer. "What about this one?"

They looked back and forth from one picture to the other.

"Yamani is still different," said Gina and she removed his picture.

They kept looking at the two pictures and shaking their heads.

"I don't see any difference," said Gwen.

"Neither do I," said Gina.

"The eyes are identical," said Gwen. "What did you do just print two of the same picture to see what we would do?"

Robert looked at Tom.

"I think you're right," said Robert. "I don't think you're crazy at all."

"Okay, what's this about?" asked Gina.

"This is the picture from the speech," said Tom holding up the picture. "This is a picture Robert created using someone else's face."

"Whose face?" asked Mark picking up the picture and looking at it closely.

"Hanke's" said Tom holding up his picture. "Can we send those to Yamani and Michael? I want to see what they think."

They were still looking at the pictures when they had a reply from both Michael and Yamani. They were in agreement that the pictures were one and the same person. Yamani went so far as to show the pictures to Adarine and he picked out the person who now called himself the *Chosen One*. It was all the confirmation Tom needed.

"Someone needs to track him down," said Tom. "I think he's in Iraq. He has to be if he's trying to pass himself off as Yamani. He needs to have everything, setting and all to pull it off."

"So, someone needs to go to Iraq," said Gina.

"I think I should go," said Tom. "I've been there before, even if it was only briefly. I can get some information from Yamani and then become the most touristy tourist anyone has ever seen."

Michael didn't have time for long conversations about the weather or other pleasantries. They were racing the clock and a man who had access to anything the governments were doing. Shutting him off from all information was necessary. He had to act and react blindly. Michael also wanted him found before he could do any more devastation.

In order for some of the questions to be answered, Michael had to meet with General Anderson and Armand Fitch. Both men would have pertinent answers to questions he and his team couldn't spare the time to research for answers.

"Gentlemen, thank you for coming," said Michael leading them into the kitchen. "I hope you don't mind meeting in here. I thought we could have some lunch while we talk."

They filled their plates from the platters arranged on the counter and then sat down.

"First of all, I want you to know that President Bartram already knows about what we're going to discuss for the most part. The only thing he doesn't know is what I just found out."

"So why don't you lay it out for us," said General Anderson.

"Certain lawmakers from around the world have been invited to a conference hosted by Dr. Emilio D. Avidtaes, head of the World Organization for Counteracting Economic and Global Terrorism."

"Never heard of it," said General Anderson.

"Don't feel bad," said Michael. "You never heard of it because it doesn't exist. Both the man and organization were invented over a decade ago to help obliterate the governments of countries so others could walk in and take them over."

"You got this documented?" asked General Anderson.

"In the mastermind's own handwriting," said Michael handing the men a packet of papers. "Here's what we know. The ultimate end goal is to totally get rid of the governments of these countries. To do that, he had other men undergo plastic surgery to make them look like different lawmakers. He couldn't do that until he was sure who would be in office, but it gave him plenty of time nonetheless. Now, as I said, the real lawmakers have been invited to this conference. We know they're going to hold the real ones at a facility we think is in the Appalachian Mountains and then release the other lawmakers. There are plans to call emergency joint sessions together and we know that it's at that time they're going to detonate these lawmakers. We feel that everything they've been doing, all the attacks, are nothing more than ruses to distract anyone from finding out about this plan. What we need from you Mr. Fitch is how many men they would need, using the same equipment they've been using, to destroy these chambers. We need to make sure we have every single one of them."

Armand Fitch nodded and leafed through the papers.

"This may take me a couple hours to do."

"That's fine. Now General Anderson, the Appalachian Mountains is a pretty long range of mountains. We're working right now to find exactly where they are. Our problem is being able to get the duplicates away from there and someplace where they can do little to no damage. We also have to rescue the real lawmakers and keep them safe."

"You find where this is and I'll see to the rest. You said you had this in the mastermind's handwriting. Who's the mastermind?"

"Hanke."

Chapter Thirty-Six

Monique followed up on the lead that the lawmakers flew on a chartered flight. She called every company for those types of flights including the main commercial airlines. There were two possibilities. Both had flight plans bound for the United States. She next followed up with the airports where each flight was to have landed. Neither were big city airports, but each were able to accommodate a plane of this size. She contacted charter bus companies around those cities trying to find out if buses were chartered on the day the flight had arrived. The curious thing was that she found two companies, one in each city that had a number of buses rented that day. Each bus company told her that the buses were hired to go to a particular destination, but not one near to any city. Directions had been emailed to them to be printed and given to the drivers.

Monique asked for a copy of the directions from each of the companies. Once she had them, she printed out maps for the areas surrounding the two cities, and then sat at the table. Quietly she worked following the directions for the one city, marking the route in yellow highlighter. Then she did the same for the other route from the other city, this time marking it in pink highlighter. She looked at the two destinations. Aside from the approach, the destination was the same.

"There wasn't just one plane, there were two," said Monique when she finished. "They went to two different cities, rented buses from two different companies, and the destination was a list of directions. I know where they are."

D.A. Walters

Tom landed in Baghdad. He never thought he'd ever be back in this city. It wasn't one of those places he wanted to come back to visit when he had more time. As usual, at the airport, there were dozens of tour guides waiting to entice someone with the promise of seeing the city like no one had ever done before. He looked them over and approached a man with a small cardboard sign.

"Hey there. Do you take people anywhere?" asked Tom.

"Where do you want to go?"

"I want to go see that place where they had them hanging gardens. I've wanted to go there since I studied about them in sixth grade. May as well start my trip off right."

"Yes, sir, I can take you there. You need to get your bags first."

"Nah, this is all I have," said Tom patting his backpack. "I never check anything. Airlines tend to lose luggage."

"Yes, sir."

"Lead me to your wheels."

When they got to the car, Tom made himself at home in the front seat. He unzipped his backpack and took out his camera and binoculars before zipping it back up and stowing it on the floor behind his legs.

"You been doing this long?" asked Tom.

"Since I bought my first car right after I learned to drive.

"You do it every day?"

"Almost every day. Sometimes I take a day or two off after I have saved up some money to take my wife and kids somewhere. What about you? Are you married?"

"No, no, no, no, no," said Tom shaking his head. "I'm just on this quest to see everything I've always wanted to see. Plenty of time to get married. I don't want anyone telling me I can't go somewhere 'cause they think it's dumb. After I visit all these places, then I guess I'll start looking."

"If you had a wife and kids, you could have shared this with them."

Tom kept looking around as they traveled. He would take pictures and also used his binoculars. He looked for any trace that might be a camp Hanke set up. He knew Yamani's camp was somewhere this way. He remembered the missile exploding off in the distance.

"How do you know where to go? I mean there aren't many markings to go by."

"I've been driving and riding through this land all my life and I haven't gotten lost but maybe once. I found my way in a few minutes. You can't really make a wrong turn."

Tom kept talking the whole time they were driving. When they got to the area that was known as Babylon, the driver parked and they got out of the car. He took Tom for a tour of the area. Tom took a lot of pictures of everything including people and the driver. He had the driver take several pictures of him too. He told him he wanted it for his scrapbook.

Tom looked around the marketplace.

"Where can a couple fellows get lunch around here?"

With the location from Monique, General Anderson had his work ahead of him. This wasn't going to be an easy feat by any means. Doing it all without Hanke finding out was going to be difficult. That man seemed to have eyes and ears everywhere.

His first stop was to see Gimshaw and Pearse. They had been successful in diverting all information away from Hanke and he knew he was going to need their help if this was going to succeed.

"General Anderson, it's good to see you," said Gimshaw.

"You might not be so excited once you know the reason for my visit. Is Pearse around?"

Gimshaw put up a finger and walked out of the office. He came back with Pearse a few minutes later. As a force of habit, Gimshaw closed the door behind them.

"It seems someone has set up a conference and invited some of the most well-known lawmakers to it," said General Anderson.

"I've heard nothing about this," said Pearse.

"Neither have I," said Gimshaw.

"It doesn't surprise me," said General Anderson. "We wouldn't have had any idea had some strange circumstances not led us in this direction."

He opened his briefcase and took out papers, pictures, and maps. He went through everything with the two men. Then he opened the map and showed them the area where they were going to be holding the lawmakers.

"Did you confirm that this was indeed the location?" asked Gimshaw.

"Sent some drones in to do some scouting. We're really pleased with the results," said General Anderson.

"Well, this one is definitely under our jurisdiction," said Gimshaw. "How do you want to stop this?"

"Unfortunately we can't stop it before it begins. The real guys have to get there first before we can do anything. We have to plan this very carefully. Got a lot of important people to protect."

"Can I see that map again?" asked Gimshaw.

General Anderson put the map on the desk and Gimshaw got a map out of his drawer. He found markings on both that were the same and marked the location on his map.

"What are you looking for?" asked General Anderson.

"This is where the bodies were found," said Gimshaw pointing to a mark on the map. "The President and Jeff Easterly were sure they had something to do with the events that are happening. I think they thought it was Pittsburgh. Looking at the distance between these two places, I think those people worked on this."

On the way back from Babylon, Tom was looking out across the desert with his binoculars. There was something off in a distance.

"Hey do you know what's over there?" he asked.

"No, sir, I don't."

"Mind if we go that way a bit. I'd like to see what it is."

"Whatever you want."

The driver turned the car and headed in the direction Tom indicated. As they got closer, they were able to see buildings clustered together. There were trucks parked inside what looked like a play yard. The driver stopped and Tom got out. Other cars pulled alongside theirs and others got out and started taking pictures. Tom smiled to himself and joined all the other tourists.

"What are you doing?" asked the *Chosen One* from the porch of one of the buildings.

The people ignored him and continued taking pictures of everything.

"Hey, is this one of those there survival camp experiences?" asked Tom.

"Yes," said the *Chosen One*.

"I wish I would've seen this in the travel guide. I suppose you don't have any openings do you?"

"No openings, you have to make reservations," said the *Chosen One*.

"I just got to take one more picture, so I remember to make my reservation the next time I come to this country. This looks like a good one."

Tom turned and walked to the car and got in.

"Let's get back to the city."

Something bothered Laura about the plan to switch the lawmakers. The men chosen for these roles had similar bone structure and skin tone as the person they were duplicating. These men were not of Middle Eastern descent.

She went back through everything she knew from her time with Yamani. She knew the control he had over those men to make them willing to do whatever he asked, took time and conditioning. She knew Yamani was a master at that. Hanke, she was sure was trying and that was why he chose to pattern himself after Yamani and even try to pass himself off as him.

She thought about the description of the duplicate David Renovet. This was not the description of a man who had been conditioned. He couldn't risk conditioning the men. They were going to have to interact with others and convince them they were the real ones. That being the case, there was no way to secure these devices to the men. They were going to have to carry the bombs some other way. A way in which these men would have no idea they were carrying them.

Laura thought about it. She pictured in her mind the scene where the President walks in to address the joint session for the State of the Union. There are no briefcases. They are there to listen and show approval for the way the country is faring. She then looked at the individuals, all dressed in suits with ties and good shoes. She immediately eliminated underwear, socks, and shoes. Next she thought about the shirt and the pants. While the wires were extremely thin and pliable, the slightest pinch from one could lead to the discovery.

She walked into the bedroom and took out one of Michael's suit coats. She turned it inside out and looked it over. It was totally lined. Depending upon the cut of the jacket, the device could be hidden between the outer layer and the lining along any seam. With the stiffness of the interfacing in the collar, no one would notice anything lurking there.

She had no idea what story these men were told, but she was sure their death didn't enter into it. She knew they had to get the suit coats. The men, they could save.

The car pulled up in front of the hotel. Tom handed the driver what he owed him and a very generous tip.

"Thank you!" said the driver.

"If you could give me your information so I can hire you the next time I'm here, I'd appreciate it."

Tom handed him a piece of paper and a pen and the driver wrote down his contact information.

"Now you have a great evening with your family," said Tom as he got out of the car.

Tom walked slowly towards the hotel door, watching until the car was out of sight. He looked at the time, crossed the street in front of the bus going to the airport. He raised his hand for it to stop and then he got on.

Since Masun had been killed, nothing was taken out of Reinholdt International. Edgar was not about to let his guard down for any reason. Other policies were put in place in hopes that another incident of embezzlement of intellectual property would not take place. It was a different perspective to have to think how a criminal thought. There were all sorts of things that one would never consider when being a law-abiding citizen. However, if this was part of what it was going to take in order to keep his business safe and his employees as well then so be it.

Although his business was an absolute priority, right now, events happening in the world were also a priority and maybe more so. His discussion with Michael put him on edge. This had to stop happening. Edgar ran his fingers through his hair. How many more times was he going to have to sit in front of the computer?

Right now he was grateful for Albert making the suggestion that he go home to wait. Being stuck at the office was not something he relished. He had spent many a night there working on projects. This, however, was nerve wracking.

He sat in front of this computer for days when Laura was being held captive and her release was imminent. Now he was in front of it again. This time, all he had to do was stop something from happening instead of allowing something to happen.

He already had President Bartram's approval to take whatever action was necessary. Now he waited.

Chapter Thirty-Seven

"We got him!" said Tom coming through the door to Michael's house. "I know exactly where he is."

Tom put down his back pack, took out his camera and handed it over to Robert.

"Forget about all the other pictures, but I got some great ones of the camp and a couple close ups of him. He's cocky. He has no clue someone or anyone could find him or figure out who he is."

Robert didn't even bother putting the pictures up on the wall, he just clicked print. This was going to be interesting. If the man in these pictures that Tom took is the same as the ones they already had, then they had a match and conclusive proof.

Tom took out a piece of paper with the driver's contact information on it. He handed it to Gina.

"What's this?"

"The information for the driver I hired. If we catch this bastard, I want to make sure he gets a nice healthy compensation for helping me."

Robert put the pictures with the others and all who were there were in agreement that it was one and the same man.

"Yamani needs to see these pictures. I'm sure he can recognize things that we know nothing about," said Robert putting the email together.

"Clayton Pearse needs this information too," said Tom. "I think he's suspected this all along, but had no proof."

Robert nodded.

When Yamani received the email, he knew exactly where the camp was. After all, he first had built a camp there and then destroyed it and the traitors. He sat and smiled at the pictures. For the first time, he had the knowledge and power to put an end to this man's treachery.

It was evident that the Divine One was smiling upon him. He knew it was not the will of the Divine One to be malicious or vindictive, but Hanke had to be stopped. He said a prayer of thanksgiving for the information and a prayer for discernment on what should be done.

He felt certain he was to take part in the ending of Hanke's reign. No matter how small or large that task may be. Those Hanke had recruited, who were still in the camp, would need guidance and care. He was sure the Divine One meant for him to care for them.

After all that happened with Miss Darmer and Mr. Braedon, his ability to have complete mobility was greatly limited. He, once again, was thankful to have escaped capture and death at the hands of the bounty hunters, and while there were many others who came on the scene and who were greatly sought after, he was not stupid enough to think that there wasn't someone still trying to find him.

If he was going to take part in Hanke's capture, he was going to need help. He hoped the group could provide it.

All of the lawmakers had arrived and were welcomed by Dr. Avidtaes assistant. Dr. Avidtaes would arrive in the morning in time for the beginning of the conference. The lawmakers enjoyed a delicious dinner and had time to socialize with drinks and desserts afterwards. This was the time to meet with many people whom they would never be able to talk to under normal circumstances.

Senator Richard Milner made his rounds talking to representatives from other countries. He wanted to know what they knew about their host. No one really knew much of anything concerning the organization nor had anyone ever met or even heard of Dr. Avidtaes before receiving the invitation.

Could it be possible this was some sort of set up? Richard put his glass down and walked out into the hall. He took out his phone to make a call, but he had no service. He started down the long hallway that led to the entryway. When he got to the last turn, it was blocked by large locked metal doors. He turned around and headed back. The place was a maze of hallways and he looked down each one as he passed. Down most of them were a lot of doors leading to each representative's private quarters. Whoever was responsible for designing this, it was amazingly well thought out. He paused for a few minutes outside the door and composed an email.

Richard joined the rest of the group. Dr. Avidtaes' assistant came in.

"Dr. Avidtaes will be here early in the morning to get the conference started. It was his instruction that you retire early so that you will be rested for the day's events."

Anna Roudalco had nothing to keep her away from Clayton. She had no one to answer to since the man had moved the plant from Volgograd. She was just a bit sad about losing Farred. After all, they had been quite close for the past eleven years. He had never known it, but it was because of her relationship with Hanke that he was given the responsibility at Craustof. There was no way he had the experience for such a position, but she saw potential in him and was able to sell him to Hanke.

Now with that finished and Hanke or the man calling the shots, Anna was at loose ends. There was nothing for her to do. She took a flight to Pittsburgh and a limousine to Clayton's apartment.

"He should really change this lock. It's much too easy to get into his place," she said as she turned the knob and walked in.

She smiled when she looked around. He was exceedingly neat for a man. You could tell his mother trained him well and he always kept his apartment neat so he'd know if anyone had been there.

Anna made her way to the bedroom. She put her bag out of sight in the closet, undressed, and slipped into bed. She plumped the pillows and fanned her hair.

Clayton turned the key in the door, walked in, closed it, and locked it. He put his keys on the stand and walked towards the bedroom loosening his tie as he went. He walked through the doorway, saw Anna, and smiled.

"Well, hello, gorgeous!"

"I need a nap," said Anna patting the bed. "Jet lag, you know."

Clayton stood beside the bed. Anna had his trousers down to his ankles before he could say another word. It was, among other things, something she practiced and perfected. He stepped out of them and joined her.

Michael went through his emails, hoping for some sort of diversion. Instead he found an email from Richard Milner that just had gotten to him.

Can't place a call. Hoping this gets through We're at the conference. Something tells me that it may have been a mistake to say yes. It's 10:00 PM. The good Dr. arrives in the morning for the conference.

"Laura!" said Michael walking out of the study into the hallway. "They're at the conference."

He was already making a call to General Anderson when he saw her.

"I'm calling Anderson. Call Edgar."

Those two calls put Anderson's plan into motion and Edgar on alert.

"I have to talk to Fitch," said Laura.

"Why?"

"I need to know if what I'm thinking is plausible. I think they put the devices in the suit coats. I don't think the duplicates know they're going to be blown up."

Michael called the only person outside of Anderson who might be able to get him in touch with Fitch.

"Hal, Michael, I need to have Fitch call Laura."

"What's going on?"

"The lawmakers are at the conference. Laura thinks they've put the devices in the suit coats. She doesn't think the duplicates have any idea what their ultimate goal is."

"I'll get Fitch and have him call her asap."

Clayton Pearse's phone acted like it was going to vibrate itself right off the night stand. He reached over and grabbed it. He looked at the screen and saw a series of texts that were marked urgent. He shook his head. Well at least he knew it wasn't the agency getting him. They didn't know he had a personal phone.

He opened the texts and looked at the series of pictures. Clayton jumped out of bed.

"Get dressed," he said to Anna. "We have to leave."

"Why?"

He tossed her the phone and she caught it. She looked at the texts.

"That fucking little bastard!"

"Yah, exactly."

Helena looked at the charts that were taken from Volgograd. It had been too quiet for too long. She knew the conference was the most important event, but she couldn't help thinking that they weren't going to stop the attacks; not when they had been so successful. Knowing now that Hanke was in Baghdad, she looked over the list at the cities that hadn't been hit. Then she started looking on the internet to see if anything was going on at any of the venues listed for those cities.

There were concerts and festivals going on in several cities. It all came down to where she thought he could reach without taking too much concentration away from the conference. Today would be the day. This was the full day of the conference. Nothing was going to happen today. They were safe underground for the most part. Tomorrow would be the day Hanke would have to concern himself with the conference because the duplicates would be traveling and the real ones would be detained.

So it had to be today. She looked at the clock and then at the list. She took a pencil and wrote down the times next to the cities that were left. Then she put a line through all the cities that would not be possible. She touched every city and ran her finger from Baghdad to each one.

"Gwen, they're going to hit Paris tonight," said Helena.

"What?"

"Listen, it's been too quiet. He needs a diversion and it has to be tonight. He won't be able to control both an attack and everything that's going on with the conference tomorrow."

"What do we have," said Gina. "We need to be absolutely sure."

"I know," said Helena.

"What's this?" asked Paul pointing to the numbers and marks on the maps.

"The numbers are the time in each place as of a few minutes ago," said Helena. "It's too late in some of the cities for something to happen so I crossed them out."

"What's happening in Paris tonight that would draw a crowd?" asked Paul.

"A concert at Bercy Arena."

"Is it sold out?" asked Gina.

"Let me see if I can get tickets," said Paul going onto the website.

"Even if it's sold out, someone has to get down there to actually see if they're there," said Helena.

"Sold out," said Paul. "Doors open in an hour. Someone down there has to have tickets to sell."

"You're not serious about getting a ticket," said Gina.

"How else are we going to get inside to check?"

Hanke picked up a picture of Mahayin and stared at it for a moment.

"Well Farred, let me show you how it's done. No one but me could ever have pulled this off. I give you points for trying. It took brains to figure out which two cities would make good targets at the same time. I would have probably done cities that were closer in proximity, but I have to give it to you for being able to figure all that out. The problem I had with you Farred was your overrating of yourself. You thought you could replace me at the top. Ah Farred, you had so many more people to go through to get there. You were nowhere near the top. Oh and then there was Anna, lovely Anna. You thought she was yours didn't you? You thought she loved only you. What a laugh, my dear Farred. I'm not even sure she liked you. There were times I had to pay Anna to go to see you. And let me tell you, Farred, the cost was quite dear. You probably thought she only made love to you. Ha! Think again. I was the one she loved, Farred, not you. She would do anything for me, Farred, not you. I was the only one she truly made love to, Farred, not you."

Hanke walked around the room for several minutes and then sat in his chair. He moved Mahayin's picture so he could look it in the eyes.

"Well now, Farred. Now is the time for you to learn. I will show you what it was all about. The attacks, they were fantastic, don't you think? So much death and destruction. More than at any other time in history. Oh yes, I will have my place in history. Not since the time of the Roman Empire did one nation rise up and conquer people and nations in its path. Well, I am going to do it and tomorrow, I will be the emperor of the world. Not king, not president, but emperor."

He picked up a map and turned it towards the picture.

"All of this, Farred. All of this will be my empire. I will command it and I will become the emperor without having to walk my army through every single country fighting and taking over the capital. That would just take too long. No Farred, I'm doing it the smart way, the easy way, the no fail way. Yes, Farred, tonight I will make another attack. It's been too long since there's been one and while they're licking their wounds once again, I will take over every one of these countries. Be thankful Farred, you have the best seat in the house."

Dr. Avidtaes arrived early in the morning and began the conference promptly at 9:00 as promised. While he gave the appearance that he was indeed this successful man who had headed this world organization for more than ten years. He gave very little background concerning the organization at all. The presentation dragged on and on with very little substance actually being presented. There were charts and graphs that, while they looked professionally done, had nothing to do with the topic being presented.

When the group broke for lunch, Dr. Avidtaes and his aides hovered and moved around the group. No one dared say anything concerning the presentation although there were several raised eyebrows between the men.

The afternoon was not any better. Senator Milner raised his hand to be recognized.

"I'm sorry, but I cannot entertain any comments or questions," said Dr. Avidtaes. "There is much too much information to disseminate and I cannot afford to allow a single minute to be wasted."

Dr. Avidtaes continued his presentation until five o'clock when he allowed them to break to get ready for dinner.

"When you come back for dinner, you will be shown to your seat. We have assigned seats to give you a chance to get to know some other people."

Richard sat in his room hoping the email he tried to send got to Michael. Everything he would've warned someone about in an invitation like the one he got, he fell for. He was flattered by being one of the few selected. How many was a few? There were over a hundred men here. He didn't dare try to count them, especially after raising his hand today.

Dinner was relatively free of Dr. Avidtaes and his aides. The configuration was done in hopes that it would discourage conversation on anything that was too in depth.

"The conference is not exactly what I expected," said David Renovet quietly.

The others at his table nodded rather inconspicuously. Enrick Galstiv handed a basket of rolls to David. David took one and set the basket down.

"One would think it was a set-up of some kind," said Hisao Kagome moving his hand as though he needed the salt.

Richard Milner passed the salt to him.

"I'm beginning to think that way, too," said Savino Fattore pointing to the whipped butter in the bowl near Evgeny Pajari.

Evgeny passed the butter to Savino. Richard picked up the bottle of wine from the ice bucket. He stood up and made his way around the table pouring wine in everyone's glass. When he sat down everyone raised their glass.

"I think we're hostages," said Richard.

"Yes," said the others and they clinked their wine glasses.

Grigore and Lucian had made themselves at home in Michael's house. They knew their way around as though they had lived there all their lives. The game room downstairs was their favorite place to play. Sorina made sure that a movie was constantly playing so they wouldn't disturb Michael or Laura and all they were doing.

Michael's house in Pittsburgh looked nothing like the one in Paris. This one was devoid of all the items needed in working on this case. Now he wished he had just one presentation tablet. He felt the need to write big with thick markers. Instead he settled for a large map on the table and a stack of paper.

He had sent William to get Clayton Pearse. Roger Gimshaw was handling things with General Anderson. Because Clayton was connected with the CIA, and was given an assignment by Hanke that would keep him away from anything Hanke was involved in, he was careful not to be seen with Gimshaw or Anderson at this time. Michael knew things were about to get extremely difficult and hectic, but he kept the lines of communication between him and General Anderson open so he could get any pertinent information to the General. Right now, it was Clayton he needed to see.

"Helena is positive they're going to hit Bercy today," said Laura coming into the dining room. "She says it's been too quiet and that another attack is imminent. She also feels with all that's going on, this is the only day it could possibly happen before the incident with the conference."

"An attack on Bercy!" said Michael. "After what was discovered about the conference, I haven't given any thought to any other attack."

"The others were like that too. Helena said it kept gnawing at her. The event is sold out. Paul is going down to see if he can find a ticket."

"Why?"

"We need to know if they're really there."

Paul parked a distance away from Bercy Arena. The restaurants and cafes were all doing a great pre-event business and the crowds were getting denser as he made his way closer. It was amazing how people got all caught up in the spirit of these things. The make-up, face paint, and clothing all contributed to the atmosphere.

No matter when Paul would go to an event, there would always be people anxious to sell you a ticket to a sold out event at double or triple the face value of the ticket. It always amazed him that people would pay it and he always said he would never do such a thing. But here he was, searching to find that person who had just one ticket to sell.

With all the color he was seeing, certainly men dressed in tan would stick out like a sore thumb, yet he wasn't seeing any. Festhalle was sold out too, and by that time, every venue in the world had been alerted to what these men looked like. If a child could pick them out, how were they slipping by actual people who had to take tickets? He could understand the Metro or Heathrow. They didn't have to stand in front of any single person, but Festhalle, someone would have had to take their ticket. More than just a few of them would have had to go through one line. Why didn't anyone notice?

"Maybe they didn't go in with everyone else," said Paul aloud. "Maybe they're already in there."

Paul pulled out his cell phone and searched through his contacts.

"Blake, Paul Manuret."

"Paul, old man, what can I do for you?" asked Blake.

"I need to get into Bercy."

"It's sold out. I don't have any tickets I can give you."

"I just need to get in there before the doors open to check around."

"Why?" asked Blake. "Are you going to tell me you think someone's going to blow up Bercy?"

"I need to see if they're there."

"But the doors won't open for another hour."

"I know, but they got into Festhalle without going through the ticket lines or someone would have noticed them."

"I don't think they could get in here," said Blake.

"Are you willing to take that chance?"

"Come around to the service entrance. I'll get you in there."

Paul hurried through the crowd. This needed to be handled before the doors opened. If he could find them all without any of them detonating, he would consider this the greatest victory against Hanke thus far. Paul saw the service entrance and Blake standing with the door partially opened.

"Where do you think they'd be?" asked Blake.

"Somewhere they'd be totally unnoticed until they had to move and get in place right before everything begins."

"Let me grab the keys to all the rooms and let's go."

Paul followed Blake up to the main office. Blake unlocked his desk drawer and grabbed the keys. Then they made their way down to the first room.

"I don't hear anyone talking," said Blake.

"They don't talk. They just stare."

Blake looked at Paul and shook his head. He quietly turned the key in the lock and then opened the door just enough to peek in. He couldn't see anything, so he opened the door wider. The room was empty. They continued their search of the other rooms on the floor. Each one turned out to be vacant.

"What are we going to do when we find them?"

"I'm taking care of that."

Paul sent a text to Gina telling her he was inside and they were searching for them. They were going to need police and also the notes on disarming them once they did find them. Gina made the call to Edgar to get things going and to also let him know there was a chance he was going to have to take care of Paris.

"Are you sure they're here?" asked Blake.

"Absolutely. Everything we know points here and also points to today. There have to be other places to hide."

"There are store rooms and equipment rooms. That's about it."

"Well let's get going. We're running out of time."

The equipment rooms were down below the main level. Blake and Paul ran down the ramp leading to that level. It was what they liked to call the tomb. It was dimly lit but as you walked along, the lights grew brighter to light your way. Paul looked behind him and saw that as they went a certain distance the lights dimmed again. Blake stopped and looked straight ahead. The steel door at the end of the hallway was flip flopped so it wouldn't lock and someone could enter. That was definitely against safety procedures. He pointed to the door and Paul nodded.

There was a shuffling noise that came from the room to their left. Blake saw that the door was opened a crack and looking towards the bottom he could see that the doorstop had been put down to hold it in position. Paul looked through the crack, and because the room was equipped with sensor lights, he could see the men standing in rows with their hands crossed. He motioned for Blake and they walked down the hall towards the outside door.

"How can the police get to this door? All they have to do is take the ramp right past the service entrance."

Blake opened the door and looked up the ramp. The gate that was always locked at the top of the ramp was wide open.

"All we have to do is keep the people out and get them out of here," said Paul pointing to the room.

He looked down at his phone waiting for the second reply from Gina.

Police and the bomb squad are on the way. I passed on the info about the entrance. Mark said they will take something to kill themselves. Edgar is ready when you need him. Sending the instructions and Hal.

As soon as Paul finished reading the text, the door opened and the police came in with Hal and the camera crew bringing up the rear.

"Captain," said Blake. "This is Paul Manuret. He will give you all the information you need. Right now, I'm going to go upstairs and stall somehow. We will not open the doors on time. I will give you as much time as I can. Right now you have 30 minutes until they are supposed to open."

"Captain," said Paul. "They are in that room. Once they see you, they will put their hands to their faces and ingest something that will kill them. They won't fight you or even resist you. They are just trained to kill themselves so they can't be made to talk."

"Wow," said the Captain. "Then what?"

"Then they have to be diffused. We have the instructions."

An officer opened the door and the captain walked in.

"Gentlemen," he said, "you are under arrest."

Not one of the men moved to put anything in their mouths and not one of them reacted in any way to what the Captain said.

Officers walked up to the men and pulled their arms behind their backs and cuffed them. Hal handed the papers to Paul.

"If you want, I can read these. I think it will go faster," he said.

Hal and his crew began documenting everything that was happening. He knew it couldn't be put on the air right now, but it would make one hell of a story later.

After the first ones were diffused, one of the men looked at the officer. He had tears in his eyes.

"Thank you," said the man, "I never wanted to do this. They were going to kill my family."

Chapter Thirty-Eight

Clayton Pearse and Anna Roudalco arrived at Michael's.

"Michael, this is Anna Roudalco. She has been pretending to be Hanke's girlfriend for some time now in order to find information," said Pearse. "She's the one who has been supplying me with my information."

"Nice to meet you," said Michael.

"Nice to meet you, too," said Anna.

"I take it you got the texts and pictures from Robert."

"I did," said Pearse. "I toyed with the idea that he was the man behind this, but then he'd say things and do things that would make me think otherwise."

"What about you, Miss Roudalco. Did you suspect Hanke as being the head of this?"

"He never let on he was anything more than an errand boy. I always knew the idea for Craustof was his. He bragged about it constantly. He said he knew it would be used to make the powers bow to whoever wanted to pay him enough. Hank loves money. So I assumed someone had paid him an awful lot of money to use Craustof. How else was he able to afford the house on the island?"

"We have to get him to end this," said Pearse. "The problem is we don't know where he is."

"Yes we do," said Michael.

Every string that could possibly have been pulled was pulled. Pierre knew Angelique and Jean had to get back to Paris. This was crucial for her recovery. It was definitely going to be a long road. They needed their friends and family.

The attending doctor gave them a list of conditions that had to be met in order for Angelique to be transferred. Pierre and Jean worked through each one and checked them off. As the task got closer to being completed, he could see his friend begin to relax. There was actually a smile on his face at one point.

When they returned to the hospital to tell Angelique the news, all she could do was cry. More than anything, she wanted to be home.

Angelique rested comfortably in her hospital room in Paris. Jean quietly closed the door behind him.

"I can't thank you enough for doing all this," he said to Pierre and Margo.

"You would've done the same for us," said Pierre.

"I just couldn't think enough to do this."

"Jean, you were exhausted. How could you possibly think of anything," said Margo.

Angelique's mother and father walked down the hall. They had been in contact with Jean since he had arrived in London. Her mother gave Jean a hug.

"How are you?"

"Better now that we have her home," said Jean.

"Now, you get home and get some rest," she said. "I'm going to stay until late this evening and Dad is going to spend the night."

Jean looked at her and smiled.

"You're the best."

Michael and Laura finished washing the dishes and putting them away.

"I don't know how to do it, Laura. I can't be everywhere. I can't be here in the States, and in Paris, and Baghdad. I just can't do it all."

"No one is expecting you to do it all. That's why we have a team. Everyone has their part to do. You're here in the States. That's your focus. You have to see to things here. Everyone is in Paris and some of them are going to go to Baghdad."

Michael let out a big sigh.

"Listen Michael, you have to go with General Anderson. You have to talk to those lawmakers. General Anderson is a great guy, but he lacks diplomacy. If he goes in there, those guys are going to think he's going to kill them."

Michael shook his head and smiled. He knew exactly what Laura was talking about. General Anderson was quite gruff.

"I know the plan Anderson has is a good one. I don't know what we're going to do if something goes wrong. It took a long time for me to get the email from Richard. By that time, everyone could be dead."

Petru held up a finger and picked up his computer case. He unzipped pockets and pulled out some strange looking pieces.

"What's that?" asked Michael.

"This is the project I was working on for Craustof. It was the subject of the presentation I made that day. This will allow me to track you underground. It was meant to be used in mining, but underground is underground."

"Will they be able to detect it?" asked Michael.

"No, it's shielded so it can't inadvertently cause detonation of any device. I have the program here," he said pulling the drive out of his pocket. "All I have to do is install it and then set the rest up so I can do it. Okay?"

"Yes."

Petru installed the program. Then he got up and grabbed what looked like a handful of metal rods.

"I need to put these outside," he said and started towards the back door.

Michael walked out with him. He was curious to see what this all entailed.

"Can I put this anywhere?" asked Petru.

"Of course."

Petru looked around and found the place he wanted. He took the gadget and extended the rods. Then he shoved them into the ground. Some went in deeper than others, but with each one he nodded his head.

They went inside and Petru helped Michael put on the transmitter. He went to the computer and pulled up the program. He made adjustments until he was able to clearly read what the device was transmitting.

"We're good," said Petru. "This will let me know where you are, whether you are moving or not, whether there are others there, and if they are moving."

He turned the screen so Michael and Laura could see. It was amazing.

Petru handed him a small thing that looked like a miniature cell phone.

"This is a way for me to warn you or give you an ok. If something is wrong, you will feel a tiny vibration and then see a red light. If everything is good, you will still feel a tiny vibration, but the light will be green."

He signaled Michael for danger and then for an all clear to make sure it worked. Michael put the receiver in his pocket.

"Does this make you feel better?"

"Yes."

Chapter Thirty-Nine

The buses pulled up to the entrance of the facility. Dr. Avidtaes aide came out to talk to the drivers.

"Dr. Avidtaes wants to make sure you have your directives correct. These men are to go straight to the airport. They are flying out to their home countries. Each of them has their tickets and their carry on. Make certain they all take their carry on with them. We cannot have anyone leave it behind. Is that clear?"

"Yes," said the drivers.

The men boarded the buses carrying their garment bags. Each one was tagged with their name. They filed on taking their seats. The aide came on to each bus and addressed each set of men the same way.

"Your ticket and passport are in the zipper pocket of your garment bag. Please be careful not to get the bags confused or you will not have the documentation you need. Dr. Avidtaes knows that you will be proud to wear the suit with the emblem that makes you part of the World Organizations for Counteracting Economic and Global Terrorism. He wishes you well."

As soon as he was finished on all the buses, they left. This time all of the buses went the same way. The plan was to utilize the same airport and also the commercial airlines.

The buses drove until they were more than halfway to their destination. The drivers turned down another road and then made another turn into an open area. General Anderson stood with Armand Fitch, Roger Gimshaw, Jeff Easterly, and a number of soldiers. General Anderson boarded the first bus.

"Good day, Gentlemen. I apologize for having to stop you before you reached your destination, but there's been a change in plans. We cannot in good conscience allow you to continue with this ruse. Mr. Fitch, can you please check one of those garment bags?"

Fitch came onto the bus, and unzipped a bag. He took the pants off the hanger and felt down each of the seams. He folded the pants and handed them to the man sitting in front of him. Then he took the shirt off the hanger and again ran his hands down the seams. He folded the shirt and handed it to the same man. Then he took the tie. He checked it and nothing. Next was the suit coat. He carefully felt down the side seams. Then he checked the back seam. He stopped for a moment and then moved his hand carefully up the back seam towards the collar. He could feel the device inside the collar. He unwrapped his tools, turned the jacket inside out, pulled up the lining and slit it. He could see the wires running along the seam. There was a small space left without being tacked so that the device could be secured. He made the slit bigger on both sides so he could work. Two snips and he was done. He pulled out the device and the wires. He held them up for General Anderson to see.

"What did I tell you," said one of them. "Boom!"

John Hanke got to business. He sat at his desk, with the picture of Farred sitting squarely in front of him.

"See my dear Farred, every one of the emails has already been written and are scheduled to be delivered at a specific time. Much as I would've loved to have had every single one of the legislative chambers go up at the same time, I have to settle for a staggered event. So, it'll take me a little longer to become emperor of the world. Does that really matter? The fact is that I'm going to do it. I alone will be known as the smartest man on earth. Every single person will bow to me and pay me homage. Now, that is worth the wait."

Hanke got up and walked over to the window and looked out.

"What's that Farred? You want to know why I still have men in the camp? The men that are here will be used for enforcement purposes. I know I've thought of everything."

Kannid knocked on the door. Hanke put down Farred's picture and answered the door.

"I'm sorry to disturb you, sir, but you told me to let you know when we had returned."

"Yes, Kannid, how did everything go?"

"Sir, we were able to pick up more than fifty new recruits," said Kannid. "You were right about moving to another area. Even though it took a little longer, it was worth it."

"Very good, Kannid, very good. Did you see to it that they are settled in their new quarters?"

"Not yet, sir. I thought maybe you would want to welcome them the same way you have done every time we have brought recruits back."

"Indeed, Kannid. Let us go and welcome them."

Dr. Avidtaes' presentation made even less sense than it had the day before. He seemed to be very preoccupied about other things. He reached in his pocket and took out his handkerchief and wiped his brow. He finished the glass of water on the stand beside his podium and picked up the pitcher to pour another glass. His hands were shaking so terribly he couldn't even hold the pitcher steady enough to pour.

"I think it would be wise to take a short break. Perhaps we could all benefit from stretching our legs and getting something to drink and eat. I will return shortly."

With that, Dr. Avidtaes walked out of the room, two of his aides followed him. They closed the door behind them.

"I don't know how much longer I can do this," he said.

"What do you mean?" asked one of the aides. "You have to keep them occupied until dinner this evening. What were you doing all those years? You should've been preparing for this."

"Listen here, I was never given a date or a subject. I merely said I would host a conference. Host it, not be the speaker. That was not what I signed up for."

His aide grabbed him by the collar and got very close to his face.

"You listen. He expects you to follow his orders. These men are supposed to think that this is a very important conference and they are privileged to have been invited. The drivel you're spewing at them is making them wonder if this is even for real. Now, I suggest you pull yourself together and find something to talk about that has to do with economic and global terrorism, or you will, I'm sure, be on the receiving end of the man's wrath."

He let go of Dr. Avidtaes.

"How dare you speak to me that way? Do you have any idea who I am?"

"Yes, you're Herbie Jenstrohm and he pulled you out of a gutter in some small town in Germany and gave you a new identity. I know exactly who you are."

General Anderson found Laura's assessment of the situation to be exactly right. None of these men had any idea they were being used as human bombs. One by one they told their story of how they were recruited and what they were told was expected of them. Even though the reasoning behind why they were to become the exact look alike of the person was faulty, the money promised was more than enough to cloud even the smartest person's judgment.

Several of the men offered to help Fitch.

"I never signed up to be a human bomb," said one. "Show me what to do and I'll help."

They formed a line where several of them did each step up to the last crucial ones that Fitch took care of himself. With all the help, the process took a lot less time than expected. When they were finished it seemed as though there was a collective sigh exhaled.

"Now what are we to do?" asked another one.

"I know you all thought you were doing something that was so vitally important because you were sought out by your country's greatest intelligence agency," said General Anderson. "You will also understand why we cannot allow you to continue to look like these people. We can't permit you to rejoin the general populous yet."

"Does this mean more plastic surgery?" asked one man.

"Yes. Dr. Hempton's files contained detailed pictures of each of you before the surgery."

"Is Dr. Hempton going to be doing the surgery again?"

"Unfortunately, Dr. Hempton was murdered. We have facilities and doctors ready to perform the surgeries. I think you will be happy going back to just being yourselves."

They were racing against the clock. No one knew when the detonations would start. Paul counted the number of men who were standing there. He called Gina.

"Do we have any idea the number of men who are supposed to be at Bercy?"

"Let me see if we have those figures," said Gina.

"It should be on that chart. I forgot to look."

Gina started moving papers.

"Helena, do you know where the chart is that shows all the venues and the number of men?"

"I had it here when I was trying to decide which place it was. Here it is."

"What's the number for Bercy?"

"Seventy-three."

"Seventy-three," said Gina. "Why?"

"Shit! Some of them must be in place already."

"How many do you have?"

"Sixty-two."

"Hold on. Helena, how many marks are on the diagram of Bercy?"

Helena systematically counted the number of marks on the diagram of the performance and spectator areas of the arena as well as the entrances and hallways.

"There are sixty-two," said Helena.

"Helena counted sixty-two in all the areas where the public can get to. We don't have the diagrams of the rest of the facility."

"We're missing eleven. We have to find those eleven."

He ended the call with Gina and called Blake immediately.

"How's it going?"

"We're missing eleven of them. They're somewhere here. I have no idea where."

"What the hell! I'm coming."

Paul addressed the men in the room.

"Do any of you know where the other eleven are?"

"No, we were only shown where we needed to be and how to get there," said one of them.

Paul walked out the door with Hal and his crew.

"Any ideas?" asked Hal.

"Any place the public can't get to and it has to be accessible from here, and we know they're not on the top floor. Eleven, we have to find eleven."

Hanke returned to his office and made sure the door was locked. It was nearing the time when everything would come together. He was confident he had everything under control. He relied on no one. Although he promised many people their own piece of the world, the reality was they would be nothing more than regents in the area. The ultimate power rested with him.

Right now, he needed everyone on board. They all had to be in position to take control of each of their countries, once the government had been formally deposed. He pulled up the email and read it one more time to make sure it sounded like a true emergency and he was pleased with his work. He looked at the clock and knew he still had some time before he'd have to deal with Bercy. Soon his men would be moving into position.

He went through his contacts, all the way down to Wilson, Logan Wilson from Australia. He clicked on his name and it went immediately to voice mail. Then he tried Vargas, Remigio Vargas of Spain again it went to voice mail. He continued going through each one of his contacts and not one of them was available.

Hanke slammed his fists on his desks. What pissed him off more than anything was these men's arrogance, their disobedience. Perhaps they weren't the right people to be placed in the position of regent. How the hell was he going to do this now?

He paced his office and kicked whatever got in his way. The ding from the computer alerted him that all his emails had been sent. There was no turning back now. Everything was in motion.

He knew one thing for certain. He could always count on Anna. She was he staunchest ally. All things considered, he knew he could always put Anna in a territory to rule. She was strong and no one would dare oppose her.

He sat back down at his desk, and pulled up the list of numbers he had to call.

Dr. Avidtaes walked to the podium.

"Could everyone please take your seats? Just take your drink and whatever you have with you."

Once they were seated, he continued.

"When one thinks of terrorism, one naturally thinks of hostages. Regardless of the situation, regardless of the act, someone is being held hostage."

He ripped off all the preprinted pages and picked up a marker.

"Perhaps one of the best known hostage situations was the one in which Iranian students took over the U.S. Embassy. The standoff lasted for four hundred forty-four days. It had major implications. For the first time, Iran and its leader the Ayatollah Khomeini were taken seriously as an entity in their own right and not as a pawn for the world's super powers to control. This was an event that changed the political face of nations. It absolutely, beyond a doubt, cost Jimmy Carter his bid for a second term as President of the United States. Now, as you know, the hostages were released on the eve of the inauguration of Ronald Reagan. Now there are two schools of thought as to why the hostages were released when they were. One theory is that the hostage takers had succeeded in getting President Carter out of office. But if that was the reasoning, why not release the hostages in December after the Electoral College met and they were sure Carter had lost. The other theory is that they didn't want to have to deal with Reagan. Word had it that Reagan intended to use force to get the hostages back. They knew Carter believed everything could be solved with diplomacy. Reagan would have ordered strikes and told them they had enough time to talk."

"Even incidents, as small as hijacking a plane to Cuba, took passengers and crew as hostages. Nine eleven was a terrorist attack on American soil. Thousands of people were taken hostage and put into situations where they could not get out."

"The attacks now. Is escape possible? If you know what to look for, maybe. Are hostages taken? Absolutely, in every case. At Heinz Field, could they escape? Only some. West Edmonton Mall? Again, only some. Then we have Festhalle. Oh yes, Festhalle. No one escaped. They were hostages."

"Don't hostage situations have to have a motive? Absolutely! Is the motive always clearly stated? Not always. Obviously a plane hijacked to Cuba is pretty straight forward. Others, not so much."

He put down the marker and walked towards the attendees. He put his head down, pursed his lips, and then looked up.

"Let's pretend for the sake of discussion that you are all hostages. You have been lured here to this conference by an invitation appealing to your ego and need to be special. Now you know me as Dr. Emilio D. Avidtaes, the head of the World Organization for Counteracting Economic and Global Terrorism. Show of hands, how many searched for information on the organization?"

The attendees looked around and not one hand was raised.

"I see. Okay then, how many did a search for my name?"

Again not one hand was raised.

"So for all you know, I could be Herbie Jenstrohm and I could have been found in a gutter in a small town in Germany and given this new identity. For all you know, there is no World Organization for Counteracting Economic and Global Terrorism. For all you know, duplicates of you have been created, and while you're here, they're taking your place. Why? Hmmmm. Let me see."

Dr. Avidtaes put his head down again, walked for a moment, and then stopped.

"I got it. The duplicates are going to take your place at an emergency session, and because they're human bombs, they'll be detonated and the entire governments of your countries will be destroyed. Then whoever is the mastermind can take over the world."

There was silence.

"Making you think, isn't it? How many times have you looked at terrorists and wondered whatever would possess them to do such a thing. Well now I pose that question to you. Without checking my credentials or checking out the World Organization, whatever possessed you to accept this invitation?"

The event started. No matter what argument Paul gave to the contrary, Blake insisted the doors had to be opened. They were running out of time and Paul knew it. With people in the place, it was going to get harder to locate the remaining men. He knew from Festhalle that they wouldn't start detonating until the place was full.

It seemed they had searched everywhere and nothing new turned up.

"Gina, where the hell else could they be?" asked Paul. He called her because he was out of ideas and usually she could come up with something no one would think of.

"How many?"

"Four, only four."

"Closets, places where the breaker panels are, by the water heaters, under the stage, behind the curtains. I can't think."

"Call me if you think of more."

Being inconspicuous wasn't going to happen. Every door was opened and the inside area searched. Paul made his way back stage. He walked down a set of stairs that led below the stage floor. Taking out his phone, he shined the flashlight around the dark area. In the corner he spied a man sitting in the corner facing him with his hands folded. Paul motioned for police officers to escort him to the others. He knew enough that one would take care of the left side of the stage. One down, three to go. He climbed the stairs and went to the right side of the stage. There had to be someone on this side somewhere. He looked around for any sort of closet, or box someone might hide in.

Hal tapped him and motioned towards the dark red velvet curtains. They hung evenly on both sides. Paul looked back and forth from one side to the other until he saw what Hal had seen. Paul took hold of the far end of the curtain and felt until he could feel where it divided. Then he moved it and shined his flashlight. Again he motioned for the police to escort the man away.

Paul held up two fingers. So far two of the places Gina mentioned turned up missing men. Paul turned towards the main hall. He knew they had all of those men. He would have to go deeper towards the back.

They walked back well behind the stage area where the performers were relaxing and talking about last minute changes they wanted to make. A man knocked on the door.

"Come on. Are you going to stay in there all night? I have to go."

Paul walked up to him.

"How long have you been waiting?"

"A long time. Other people just took their chances and went out and used the public restrooms."

The door was like one he had at home. It had the hole so you could unlock it in case someone accidentally locked it. He took out his keys and used the tool he had put on there a long time ago. He opened the door and found number three.

"One more, just one more," said Paul.

A thorough search of the back area netted nothing more.

"What did we miss?" asked Hal. "We've been everywhere in this building."

"I don't know. I'm at a loss, but we can't give up."

Paul looked out at the audience. It was beginning to fill up, but was quite a-ways from being completely filled. He looked around the main area, figuring they may have missed one, but he couldn't see anyone. He walked back down to the room where they had initially found the bulk of the men. Maybe he miscounted.

He counted the men while one of the officers counted the devices. They both came up with the same number and one was missing.

"Are you sure about the number?" asked Blake.

"Absolutely sure. We've dealt with the numbers from the charts in other places and they've never been wrong," said Paul. "I'm going to get some air. See if you can think of any other place we missed."

Paul walked down the hall and out the door at the end. He was careful to leave it the way he found it so he could get in. He walked down the sort of alley way that ran along the back of the Arena. He walked a few more steps and stopped. There were docks for deliveries. All of the garage doors were locked down tight. Paul looked at them over again. He was sure this had to be it. Looking at the area, it was the only part they hadn't checked.

He hopped up on the dock and tried each of the doors. Nothing. He put his hands on his hips and looked around again. Off to the far side, there was a ramp that led to a door. It must have been put in so that trucks that couldn't use the docks, but had to make deliveries could still do so with ease. He ran up the ramp and tugged at the door. It opened with ease. He reached around the left side of the door frame, felt a switch and flipped it. Cowering between some boxes he saw a man all dressed in tan. He was shaking his head and rocking back and forth. Paul walked over to him and put his hand on his shoulder. The man looked up.

"It's going to be okay," said Paul.

Chapter Forty

Two of Dr. Avidtaes aides stood outside the doors to the facility smoking cigarettes.

"So help me, if he screws this up, I will choke him myself. All he has to do is read what's on the script and make it sound convincing. I could a better job than he's doing."

"How much longer do we have to keep this up?"

"Just until morning, then the buses will return for them."

"He's just letting them go?"

"Nah, they're just gonna disappear."

The two laughed and dropped to the ground like rocks. General Anderson stood over the men and shook his head. The doors to the facility were wide open.

"Nothing says 'here we are' like a lighted hallway in the mountains," he said.

He motioned for his men to move. Stealthily they moved down the hallway parting at the corridors. They checked each room as they passed. Each hall had other branches and the whole design was reminiscent of a maze. The command center had eight men in it. Each man was performing a particular task. Before they could do anything to alert anyone, General Anderson's men had cleanly picked them off.

Michael walked into the command center and looked around. He knew there had to be some sort of list of who was in the facility. Everything they came across pointed to the fact that Hanke was absolutely anal about names and numbers. He lifted one man's arm enough to slide a clip board from under him. He looked through the pages until he got to the staff pages. As he read it, he smiled. It not only showed how many men there were, but also where they were stationed in the facility. On the wall was a diagram that showed how the place was divided and yet connected by a long tunnel. They had gone through all of the rooms on this side. It had been the side that had housed the duplicates. Now they had to get through to the other side. Michael looked at the monitor showing the hallway on the other side. There was a post-it-note with the code for entrance.

"Let's go," said Michael.

He handed the General the clipboard with the post-it note and he motioned for his men to move forward. The tunnel was actually separated by two doors, one on each side, when the door on the one side opened it stayed opened until the door at the other end was opened. It was a safeguard so no one would get trapped in the tunnel. The general showed each man his target and they moved quietly though the hallways to complete their mission. Once they were all assembled again, they went through the beautiful rooms.

Michael marveled at the detail that was put into this. It was meant to make these men feel special, to give that feel of elegance. It was sad to think that anyone who had anything to do with the building of this structure was now dead. He knew that was true, because Hanke didn't let anyone live who could lead the authorities back to him.

They came to beautiful ornate double doors and beside the door slid into the gold holder was a placard that said World Organization for Counteracting Economic and Global Terrorism. Michael turned the knob and opened the door. Immediately, Dr. Avidtaes looked towards the noise. Armand Fitch walked into the room and stood off to the side. Michael strode into the room confidently and as though he was in command.

"Dr. Avidtaes, good day! I heard about your conference and thought I might be permitted to address the attendees," said Michael.

He walked onto the stage and over to Dr. Avidtaes.

"Please don't kill me," whispered Dr. Avidtaes. "I'm doing the best I can."

"I know you are Doctor and I haven't come to kill you. Why don't you just have a seat?"

He helped Dr. Avidtaes to a chair near the podium and then stepped up to the microphone.

"Good day. My name's Michael Braedon. Several of you know who I am because we've worked together on projects in the past. It was urgent for me to come and address you. This conference was nothing more than a ruse to get you away from your offices and to get you somewhere where it was virtually impossible for anyone to communicate with you or you with them. Senator Milner, I did get your email. It took some time, but I did get it. That's why I'm here. Let me tell you quickly what has and is supposed to be happening. Because of each of your media presence, a man decided to put together one of the most ruthless plans in history. For each one of you sitting here, a duplicate has been made. They were here on the other side when you got here. They were taken from here and were to take your place as a lawmaker in each of your countries. Today, and I'm using that term to mean the time of day wherever you are from, the man has called an emergency session to meet. This is a mandatory session including all lawmakers from your legislative branches, all members of the executive branches, and all members of the judicial branches. Each of the duplicates was outfitted with a special suit so the man could pick them out if the session was televised. Each of the suit coats contained a device exactly the same as the ones worn by the suicide bombers in the attacks on Heinz Field, West Edmonton, Festhalle, Heathrow, Tokyo Metro, and currently Bercy Arena. The purpose was to detonate those devices during the joint session killing every single member of the government."

There were gasps from the attendees.

"With the countries without a leader, this man was going to take over each of the countries. He even went so far as to promise those involved a piece of the world. Isn't that right, Dr. Avidtaes? Which piece were you to get?"

"The Scandinavian countries," said Dr. Avidtaes quietly.

"Earlier, we were able to detain the duplicates and diffuse the bombs. They have all been taken to a secure location and the governments are safe. The man has no idea any of this has taken place and hopefully we'll be able to apprehend him within the next couple days. We have to keep all of you safe until this is solved, but it can't be here. Unfortunately, Dr. Avidtaes, you'll also have to be detained. If he finds you, he'll kill you, the same as he has done to everyone who has had any part in this plan."

Many of you know General Anderson. He's here to aid and protect you. We have taken care of everyone else in the facility and we just need to get you out of here and to safety. I'm going to put you into General Anderson's capable hands."

Afmad Yamani appeared on the screen. Mark sat in front of the camera so they could talk face to face.

"I want to thank you for the pictures and the information," said Yamani. "This man needs to be stopped by whatever methods possible."

"We totally agree," said Mark. "He's not about to leave where he is and chance being caught. He's protected there."

"Yes, but since he's impersonating me, if I can get into his camp, I can order his men away. They won't question me."

"You want to risk your life to do this?"

"Mr. Braedon, I know this is the only way to put an end to all of this chaos. The Divine One has told me as much. Even though I put myself at risk, I take Him with me and trust He will protect me."

"Sir, there are others who will make this easier for you and also have a need to confront him. They have expressed desire to put an end to this also."

"I believe this job may need many participants. May I ask who these people are?"

"Clayton Pearse, an agent under Hanke who tried to warn the government about the attacks and Anna Roudalco."

"Ah, yes, I am well acquainted with Miss Roudalco. She and Hanke were at one time on opposite sides. I can somewhat understand her need."

"Tom Richards would also be accompanying you. He would like to see this to its end. Many good friends were killed in Pittsburgh."

"Mr. Richards would be most welcomed. I understand the need for documentation, and I understand that Mr. Milridge has been the person who has done such a thorough job. I have to insist that no pictures of those who are in this party be taken. What is planned is not within the confines of the law, but I also know Mr. Milridge's need to be there."

"I will tell Mr. Milridge and I know he will abide by your request. The only other ones are those from the group and I'm not sure who."

"We need to move quickly. I do not want him to have any time to breathe. The sooner we can do this the better."

"I agree. We will make arrangements to get to Baghdad."

"Tell Mr. Richards, I will contact him about the meeting place."

John Hanke knew everything that was to happen. He had absolute confidence in what he put together and that it would carry on without a hitch. He was so confident he didn't bother to check on the progress made. The first attack was thrilling, watching everything unfold for the first time. Now, there wasn't anything new about it.

Even the thought of the government chambers blowing up didn't get a rise out of him. There was plenty of time to bask in his success. The regents were the only glitch he had to figure out. As angry as he was with all those who were to rule a particular country or two, he couldn't bring himself to take that perk away from them; at least not yet. He needed time to make his presence known; time to make everyone either love him or fear him. He preferred the latter. Love was a fickle thing and when people loved you they sometimes tended to take advantage of you.

In forty-eight hours, in the midst of total anarchy, he would have to address the people of the world. This time, he would address them as their new leader. He took out a sheet of paper and began writing his speech.

When the guard at the control center didn't check in as he was supposed to, an alarm notified the commander stationed less than a mile away that something was amiss. Within seconds he had the troops mobilized and heading towards the facility.

They entered on the side where the duplicates were kept because the command center was located on that side. The troops marched through the hall opening doors and searching rooms. With the noise they were making, anyone on this side should have been alerted to their presence, but they saw no one.

Because the command center was located in the center of the maze in order to be protected, it took a while to get to it. The commander kept all his men together when they were going through the halls, rather than splitting them up. He felt they would be able to do a more thorough job this way and be prepared if they came under attack.

When they reached the command center, there wasn't one thing out of place, the only thing missing were the men who were supposed to be there. He checked each of the stations and everything was working perfectly. For a moment he felt a wave of relief, but it was fleeting, and he knew he had to find the men.

He led them to the tunnel, took a paper out of his pocket, and then keyed in the code to open the door. He walked to the next door, looked behind him and made sure that all the men were actually in the tunnel. Once they were, he keyed in the code.

They emerged from the tunnel and proceeded to the common areas. Still there was nothing and the only sound was that coming from the conference. General Anderson's keen ears picked up a foreign sound. He looked in the direction and then motioned his men to disperse into hallways and rooms.

Michael felt a small vibration and took out the receiver. It had a bright red light.

"They're going to kill us all," said Dr. Avidtaes. "They're going to kill us all."

Petru sat in front of the computer. He could see every movement Michael and those around him made. He always knew his project worked, but to see it working in a real life setting was really thrilling for him.

He watched as he left one group and joined another one. Michael seemed to be apart from the group for some reason. Although this was a great invention, it still couldn't identify what the person was actually doing. You had to surmise by studying their stature and gestures. Everything looked pretty status quo. From what he was seeing, he surmised that Michael had found the lawmakers and was addressing them.

His attention was suddenly drawn to another part of the screen. He saw another group come within range of the transmitter. The other group that had been there was dispersing. Petru could only assume they were the enemies. He pressed the button to send the warning to Michael. As he watched carefully, the transmitter picked up evidence of explosive devices.

"Oh my god! Oh my god!" yelled Petru.

"What is it?" asked Laura.

"They have explosives down there."

"Where?"

Petru showed Laura on the screen where the explosives were located. This time they weren't located on a person, they were planted throughout the facility. Laura grabbed her phone.

"Edgar," she said.

"Laura?"

"Yes, they have explosive devices in the facility in the mountain. What can we do?"

"I have to know where they are."

"Petru, do we know exactly where they are?"

Petru wrote the coordinates on a piece of paper and handed them to Laura. As she read them to Edgar he plotted them on the map.

"Laura, I can't do anything. It's one of the places in your country where there is actually a sort of shield. They can't send any sort of radio wave because it can't penetrate that zone. Cell phones won't work there. Whatever they're using has to be transmitted through a cable."

"Petru, they have to be connected through a cable."

Petru kept his eyes on the screen. He was watching a chess match in action. Sooner rather than later the forces were going to find each other and all hell was going to break loose.

His mind raced. He needed to somehow get the message to Michael about the explosives and all he had to work with were red and green lights.

One of Hanke's men caught a glimpse of a soldier and opened fire. The commander shot back a glare. Anderson's men returned fire.

"Get down!" shouted Michael.

The men hit the floor.

"What the hell is going on?" he asked aloud.

Being behind locked doors and not knowing what was happening on the other side took him back to his time as a guest in Yamani's camp. Those were some of the most frightening days of his life and it took him many months to just deal with it.

General Anderson motioned for his men to get into other positions. Where they were now put them on the defensive, a position Anderson hated more than anything. He was smart enough to have figured out that while the other side of the complex was in the shape of a maze, this side was set for esthetics and therefore was configured like five-star hotel. That gave him an instant advantage. He sent men to lock every door whether it went to a room or was at the end of a hall. His main focus was to keep some of his men in front of Hanke's men and get the rest of his men around and behind them. Locking the doors allowed him to seal off all their exits. He had no intention of turning tail and running and he was not about to allow the enemy to do so either.

From inside the room, the men could hear the shuffling of feet, banging and gun fire. Dr. Avidtaes didn't move from his seat near the podium. Michael felt a small vibration. He took out the receiver and looked at it. It continued to flash red and green, three reds, three greens, then three reds. There was a break and it happened again. Michael looked on the podium and took the pen. As the lights flashed, he wrote down letters. He was so engrossed in watching the lights that the sound of the gunfire faded into the background. Suddenly the lights stopped and flashed the initial signal of three reds, three greens, and three reds. Michael knew Petru was finished at least for now.

The gunfire sounded as if it was traveling back the way they had come. He could hear the return fire coming from a few feet past the end of the room. Soon a third source of gunfire was heard. This one farther down away near the end of the common areas, Michael figured. He smiled. It was true General Anderson fashion to encircle his opponent and crush them.

He looked at the letters he had written on the paper. Explosives planted places cable.

"Fitch, we have a problem," said Michael.

Fitch quickly came up to the podium. Michael showed him the words.

"They can't detonate by calling because of the mountain," said Fitch. "I wish we knew how many."

"I have no idea."

"Dr. Avidtaes, when is everyone supposed to leave?" asked Michael.

"In the morning, but we'll all be dead by then so it won't matter," said Dr. Avidtaes.

Fitch looked at Michael.

"How do you know that?" he asked.

"Because I have the button," said Dr. Avidtaes holding up a white plastic object about four inches long. "I already pressed it. All I have to do is let it go. You know, when I fall asleep, that's when it'll happen."

"What about your piece of the world?" asked Michael.

"He's never going to let me keep it. He's just going to take it away from me anyway."

"I have an idea," said Fitch. "I know how you can make sure your thumb stays on that button even when you sleep."

"How?"

Fitch unwrapped the tools and took a pair of cutters. He reached down and shut off the microphone and then clipped the wire. He peeled back the black plastic covering and pulled out the wire. Then he secured Dr. Avidtaes thumb and hand to the plastic object. He made sure his thumb could not be moved or slide off the button. Senator Milner and several other lawmakers quickly moved to the stage. Two of them went to watch Dr. Avidtaes so he didn't do anything foolish.

Fitch then followed the wire from Dr. Avidtaes. If it was going to detonate a number of other explosives, there had to be a way to disarm it further down from the trigger. The wire went through the floor of the stage through a hole. He felt the floor of the stage and found an area that looked like it had been removed and then replaced.

"I need to get this up, but carefully," said Fitch. "I don't know if the wires are stapled or taped to the underneath."

Senator Milner knelt down and put his fingers in the hole. He pulled up on that end of the board while holding the rest of the board down with his knee. It moved and he held it in position. Fitch knelt down hand wiggled his hand through the opening. He grabbed hold of the wire and followed it straight down as far as he could.

"Can you lift that piece?" asked Fitch. "The wire goes straight down."

David Renovet grabbed an end of the board. Richard Milner moved his knee off and the two me lifted the board, turning their heads as the nails slipped from gripping along the beams. They tossed the board aside and Michael shined the light from his phone into the hole. Down along the floor board, Fitch could see wires spreading out in all directions. He let out a sigh.

Their attention was diverted as someone tried to open the door.

"Barricade the door!" shouted Michael. "We need to keep them out!"

Several men used chairs to immobilize the knobs and then put whatever they could in front of the doors. The soldier on the other side shot at the door. Those near the door dropped to the floor and slithered away. Other shots were heard and the shots coming into the room ceased.

"We don't have time for this shit!" said Michael.

It wasn't a far drop through the hole, but Fitch had to be careful not to step on any wires. He moved as far from them as possible and eased himself down through the opening until he felt the floor then stooped to get under the floor of the stage. The light coming in from the room wasn't enough to light the area.

"Michael, I need your flashlight."

Fitch reached up and Michael handed him the phone. Fitch shined the light around the area. Directly ahead of him, up against the front of the stage was a bomb. He studied it for a moment and realized it was an isolated one. It branched off first. If they all did this, he was going to have to find every last one of them. Everything about what he was seeing was identical to what he had dealt with before. He was thankful for the simplicity in that respect.

"One down," he said yelling up through the opening. "Each wire needs to be followed to find the others."

"Is the floor of the stage clear?" asked Richard?

"Yes, no wires attached anywhere."

"Are there any more bombs under there?"

"None. There are wires leading in different directions and then through holes. The way these are wired, I have to find each one. Since Dr. Avidtaes already pressed the button, I have no choice."

While Hanke's troops had proven to be quite a formidable advisory for the General's soldiers, their lack of preparation was their undoing. It was now evident these troops were only meant to push back an uprising of the lawmakers. Since the lawmakers had no weapons, because none were permitted, the troops felt that whatever their guns were loaded with would be ample. General Anderson's men, on the other hand, came ready to do combat. With the opposing troops out of ammunition, they were subdued, arrested and readied for transport to the nearest military base.

While cell phone service wasn't the best, it was possible to make and receive calls once outside and a short distance away. General Anderson made a call to let the base know to be ready to accept these detainees and injured. Then he walked back in and tried to get into the conference room.

"Michael," said General Anderson. "Everything's under control. You can unblock the door."

The men moved tables and chairs away from the door, then unlocked it and opened it.

"You need to get all of these men out of here and far away," said Michael. "We have a situation."

"Alright," said General Anderson. "I trust you realize you cannot return to your rooms for anything at this time. Once the situation is stabilized, we'll get your belongings and deliver them to you."

The men filed out and onto buses.

General Anderson came back for one quick check before sending the buses on their way.

"Do I have everyone?"

"All but two," said Michael, "but they refuse to leave and they're old enough to make their own choices."

"Then I'll send them on their way to the city," said General Anderson.

"Did you say there is some phone service?"

"It's a bit tricky, and once you get it, you can't move around, but it'll do."

"Great," said Michael grabbing the clipboard off the podium and walking towards the door. "I'll be right back. Maybe I can get some answers."

Laura paced back and forth. She would look at the screen for a few moments and then get so nervous she couldn't stand to look anymore. Petru, on the other hand, didn't take his eyes off the screen. He watched everything unfold in a weird wavy pattern.

"They got them," he said. "It's over."

Both Laura and Sorina ran over to look. They watched figures walking and then disappearing.

"They disappear when they go outside," said Petru. "As long as Michael is inside and within proximity, we can see what's happening. It seems that he hasn't moved from the room he's been in."

"He's moving now," said Laura.

In a few minutes, Laura's phone rang.

"Michael, how are you?"

"I'm fine. Can Petru tell where the bombs are in here?"

"He wants to know if you can tell where the bombs are."

"Yes," said Petru. "I think I have them all, and one has been disarmed."

"Michael, did you disarm one?"

"Yes."

Laura handed the phone to Petru.

"Michael, I can tell you what rooms they're in, by how many doors to go down and which hall. I will use the room you were in as the reference."

"Perfect."

As Petru gave him directions, Michael repeated each one and a soldier wrote everything down on paper. The soldier meticulously wrote down each direction clearly, not leaving out anything. When they were finished, they went inside.

"Listen up, this is crucial," said Michael. "We have to find all of these bombs and you're going to have to be careful but quick. The man is expecting Dr. Avidtaes to detonate the bombs. As a failsafe, we know from every other time, the man will also attempt to detonate the bombs. Because of the fact that we are underground, it is most likely on a timer. I have no idea how much time we have, but we need to get all of these found and disarmed before then. We'll follow the directions and the two of you will be given the final direction for that room. Your job is to locate the bomb and carefully clear an area around it so that Fitch can get in and disarm it quickly. Are we clear?"

"Yes."

Michael read the directions and they counted doors and turns to get from one place to another. The directions took them all through the conference side of the facility. One soldier who was not assigned to a room looked down at the baseboards along the hallway. He tapped another soldier and pointed to wires running along the baseboards and into the tunnel.

"We need the code for the tunnel," said one of the soldiers.

Michael shouted out the code that the soldier keyed it in. They followed the wire through the tunnel to the other side. Whoever did the wiring wasn't as neat on this side and it was much easier to follow where it was going. At one point it crossed to the other side of the hallway and all they did was taped it to the floor so no one tripped over it. There was a hole drilled in the wall and the two men ran through the hall and turned down another one to get to the door for the room. It was the command center. One of the soldiers got down on the floor and looked under the desk unit. He could see the wire coming through the wall. He ran his hand along the wire, while moving others out of the way. Another hole was drilled into the desk so the wire could be brought through. He stuck his finger through the hole in the desk.

"Can you see where my finger is?"

The other soldier moved things to the side. He cleared away things on the desk until he could see it.

"I see it."

"Find where the wire goes."

He followed the wire to a digital clock that was counting down.

"We don't have a whole lot of time."

Inside the other rooms it wasn't that difficult for find where the bombs had been hidden. Once furniture was moved, the evidence of quickly completed plaster jobs and simply tacked wood pointed the way. Each group did as they were instructed and cleared as much wire as they could safely clear. Fitch went from one place to another working as quickly as possible.

One of the soldiers ran through the tunnel.

"General! General!"

General Anderson ran up one hallway and turned toward another that would eventually lead to the tunnel.

"What is it?" he asked.

"General, we have less than five minutes. Four forty-two to be exact. We found the countdown clock."

"Yell out at two thirty left," said the General.

General Anderson hustled down the hall towards Fitch. Fitch was on his way to the next place.

"We have less than four and a half before they detonate," said General Anderson. "Gotta step this up."

Fitch ran down the hallway looking for the next one.

"How many more?" he asked.

Michael looked at the board. He had checked each one off as they were done.

"Two after this."

Fitch quickly cut the wires, got up and moved on. He had worked under this kind of pressure before, but not inside a mountain. The chain reaction from something like this could be devastating and not just to the facility. The chances of it causing an earthquake were certainly good, there were fault lines through this part of the country too, although not as active as the western United States. With the amount of power and force that was packed inside this mountain, there was no telling, without adequate research and study, how much damage could be done.

The soldier yelled out the two thirty warning that General Anderson asked for. Fitch had gone into the last area and emerged mere seconds later. Then he ran to the soldier who led the way to the command center. Fitch looked at the clock counting down the last seconds. He turned it around, looked at it carefully and cut the wires. The numbers stopped and he finished disconnecting it.

He looked over at the two men.

"Let's go get Dr. Avidtaes."

Fitch snipped the wires leading from the detonator Dr. Avidtaes was holding. It was no longer an issue. Then he snipped the other wire that held the doctor's thumb in place. They helped Dr. Avidtaes to his feet and led him out of the room.

"Where are you sending Dr. Avidtaes?" asked Michael.

"He'll join the other detainees until charges are brought. Then he'll be tried and hopefully convicted."

Dr. Avidtaes stopped and looked around. Then he shook his head.

"We're all dead you know," said Dr. Avidtaes. "The man left nothing to chance."

A chill went up Michael's spine. He watched Dr. Avidtaes stretch his arms out and look up at the sky.

"Run!" screamed Michael.

Everyone ran except Dr. Avidtaes who just stood in that position. An explosion rang out and the force from it damaged everything in its path. Once the raining of dirt and rock ended, they slowly got up and looked around.

"This was worse than war," said one of the soldiers.

"Indeed, it was," said General Anderson.

He stood looking where Dr. Avidtaes once stood.

"Michael, they have to get him and they have to get him now," said General Anderson. "The world can't take much more of this idiot."

"I'm sure it's being taken care of," said Michael. "What about this place?"

"A lot of time and money was spent on this. It's a good design, well thought out. I see no reason why it can't be utilized. It'll be up to

Washington what they're going to want to do with it, but I can't see them destroying it. Let's get the personal items of the dignitaries collected and ready to go while we wait. I'm sure they want to get home."

Chapter Forty-One

The limousine pulled up to the camp. Sadik got out and opened the back door. Yamani emerged and looked around at the camp. It was almost exactly as it had been when he was there. The men were still in the building, so he made his way there. As he entered, the men stood up.

"Please be seated," he said. "We have urgent business to attend to. I apologize that you will not be able to take the time to gather anything. You must go immediately out the back door and onto the trucks that are waiting. It is no longer safe to be at this place."

"Yes, sir," the men said in unison.

"Where are we to take them?" asked Kannid.

"All of your directions and papers are in these envelopes," said Yamani. "You must leave quickly and quietly. I know you usually travel together, but it is much too dangerous. Each driver will take a different route."

"Yes, sir," said Kannid.

The men moved quickly and quietly through the back door to the trucks, boarded them, and within a few moments were gone.

Hanke sat on the edge of the bed. It was time to get up, but with all the stress and activity of recent times, he just didn't feel like moving today. He knew things were going on as they always had. His core of loyal followers was training more men and making sure everything was in order, just as he wanted it. Since this began, they never gave him any cause for concern.

The only bright spot was knowing that the majority of the world was now falling into anarchy. With the governments decimated and no one to rule the people, there would be lawlessness. He stopped and thought for a moment. Maybe it would be better to wait another day before bringing all the countries under his rule. Not only could he be the emperor, but he could also be the savior.

The doorknob turned and the door opened. Anna walked in and stood smiling at Hanke. She knew by the look on his face he was shocked to see her.

"Did you think you could hide from me forever?" asked Anna.

She walked over to him and touched his face.

"Who are you trying to be? She asked. "It doesn't matter really. I like it. It makes you look very sexy."

She bent down, kissed him, and pushed him back down on the bed. Hanke pulled his legs up onto the bed and moved over to give Anna room. She untied the scarf around her neck and slipped it off. She took his hand and wrapped the scarf around his wrist and then took the other wrist and wrapped it too.

"I see where this is going," said Hanke laughing.

"Do you now," said Anna pulling his arms above his head and tying them to the bedpost.

"Anna, what if someone comes in?"

"Then they can watch," said Anna blowing him a kiss.

She reached in her purse and took out another scarf. She ran her fingers up the inside of Hanke's leg and back down. Then she wrapped the scarf around his ankle and tied him to one of the bottom bedposts. She smiled at him and he lifted his head and ran his tongue over his lips. Anna flipped her hair, pulled another scarf from her bag, wrapped his other ankle, and tied the scarf to the bedpost.

"Comfy?" asked Anna.

"I will be," said Hanke.

"Ah, let's make this interesting," she said.

She reached in her bag and brought several coils of piano wire, a wire cutter and a crimping tool. She fastened the wire to the bed post, looped it around Hanke's ankle and then fastened it tautly to the other post.

"I know how much you loved using this when we were on opposite sides."

As she talked, Anna fastened the other ankle.

"I saw many a finished product."

"You're crazy, Anna!" said Hanke.

"Am I?" she asked.

She started working on his wrists.

Hanke started screaming

"Who are you yelling for?" asked Anna sliding the wire behind his neck and tossing it in the front.

"You're not going to get away with this," said Hanke.

"Who's going to stop me? Your men?"

She kissed her two fingers and touched his cheek.

"They all left," she said.

"Who told them to leave?" asked Hanke.

"The real man you're impersonating."

"Impossible! He's dead!"

"Actually, he's not," said Anna.

She pushed a coil of wire under Hanke's back. Then she brought it across his stomach. Anna took both coils and unrolled them as she walked to the window. She tossed both coils out the window and walked back to the bed. She picked up another coil of wire and pushed it under Hanke's back in the opposite direction. Then she brought it across his stomach. .

"I'll be right back," she said. "Don't go anywhere."

Anna walked out the door into the hall, unrolling the wire as she went and then tossed the rest of the coils out the window. She walked back into the room and put her hands on her hips.

"This is going to be so much fun. Did I miss anything? This is how you always did it. Right?"

"Why, Anna. Why?"

"Ah, my sweetheart, you promised everyone power and riches; and Anna, well Anna was supposed to be happy with you. Please! Anna has needs. And let's face it. You just weren't that good in bed."

Yamani strode into the room. One look at Hanke, tied to the bed somehow made all the suffering he had endured at that man's devices worthwhile. Hanke's mouth gaped.

"Ah, my dear Hanke," said Yamani, "we meet for one last time."

"But you're supposed to be dead," said Hanke, not quite believing what he was seeing.

"I assure you, that millions of people are also under that misconception, so do not blame yourself for the error in judgment."

"It doesn't matter what you do to me," said Hanke. "The others will carry on in my place. Nothing will change."

"I heard it said, that when one is dying, their life flashes before them," said Yamani. "Although you think you know everything concerning your master plan, we did not want you leaving here without truly knowing everything."

Clayton Pearse entered the room carrying a briefcase. He opened it and handed the contents to Yamani then stood with his arm around Anna. Hanke's eyes glared.

"What is this!" he said. "What's going on?"

"You mean Clayton?" asked Anna. "We've been together for years."

"But you were mine," said Hanke. "I courted you, I did everything to win you over."

"Yes, darling, I know you did," said Anna, "and for a brief few moments, I contemplated it. But once you revealed your plan, and my role in it, I realized the only reason you wanted me was to get me out of the way. Anna is not stupid, my darling. Anna knew exactly how to play you."

"Oh, and one more thing before we continue, we want this moment recorded for all to see," said Yamani. "Please come in, gentlemen."

Hal walked into the room followed by Jake, the camera man and Sam, the photographer. Tom was the last to enter and he brought with him several bottles, cotton swabs, cotton balls, and other items on a tray.

Hal looked at Yamani and he nodded.

"Perhaps you would like to tell us who you are," said Hal.

"Go to hell," said Hanke.

"What about who you're pretending to be."

"Fuck off!"

"You're pretending to be Afmad Yamani or more importantly the Chosen One, isn't that right?"

"Shut the fuck up!"

"It's the only way you could get all these men to do what you wanted. You pretended to be the Chosen One. You lured them here by telling them they were chosen by the Divine One. Isn't that so? And what did you do? You trained them to be completely obedient and follow every single order without asking any questions. Then you sent them to attack Heinz Field, West Edmonton Mall, Festhalle, Tokyo Metro, Heathrow, and Bercy Arena."

"You have no proof, you mother fucker."

"Ah, but that's where you're wrong. We do have proof. Lots of proof, and all written in your own handwriting."

Yamani handed over the box he had taken from the island.

"I see by the look on your face that you recognize this," said Hal. "You have to agree it's filled with all your notes and plans for all of this. And don't worry, we'll get to that in a few moments, but first we need to see who you really are."

Tom opened a bottle of solvent and wet a cotton swab. He used it on all the pieces that were glues to Hanke's face. Then he pulled them off one right after the other while Hanke screamed.

"What the hell do you think you're doing?" Hanke screamed.

"We're revealing who you really are," said Hal. "The reason every nation was left totally in the dark. Isn't that true, Mr. Hanke. For those of you who don't know who John Hanke is, he's the head of the United States Central Intelligence Agency. I'm sure that will change. In fact, I guarantee it. Oh, and John, sorry, but your plan to take over the world and become its emperor has failed miserably. Now relax, John, while we show you what we discovered."

Hal and Tom showed every piece of evidence found in the box. The more they showed, the further John Hanke sank into the pillow. The most difficult things for Hanke to hear was how his plan was thwarted over and over again. When he saw each one of the "My Piece of the World" followed by the name of the Intelligence Head and the word dead, he knew no one was going to come running to his rescue. Hal listed everyone Hanke had killed, whether by his own doing, or by the hands of someone else. It read like a never ending litany.

"You planned this alone. You set yourself apart, above everyone else, even those who actually thought they were your partners. You deserve to die alone," said Hal as he ended.

When Jake shut off the camera, Anna, Clayton, Yamani, Hal, Tom, Jake, and Sam walked out of the room and outside to the yard. Sadik and Gehran stood beside the trucks on either side of the building. Yamani strode to one. It was no doubt that this was something he felt he had to do. With everything Hanke put him through, this would be sweet revenge. Anna ran to the truck on the side closest to the window of Hanke's room.

"It won't be long now," she yelled to him. "This is for all those friends I lost because of you."

The rest made their way to the limousine and got in. The trucks started and Anna and Yamani kept going until they saw the wire drop to the ground behind them. They brought the trucks to a stop, turned them off, and got out. Then they got into the limousine and Sadik drove off.

Once they reached the main road, Sadik stopped. Pierre put his phone to his ear and waited.

"One last time, Edgar," said Pierre.

Sadik made the turn he had made that one day and drove into the desert where they were at a safe distance, but also had a clear view of the camp. Tom cowered when he heard the familiar whistle. They looked in the direction of the camp and saw the explosion as the missile hit. Sadik turned the car around and headed back towards the road.

D.A. Walters

Epilogue

Gina started boxing up every piece of paper. It was so reminiscent of the last time they had to do this. She knew every box had to be labeled with its contents so they could find something if they needed it. As they finished boxes, they were taken and put into storage. Little by little the house was beginning to look like a house instead of a building where an office supply store had exploded.

"Are you sure it was wise to put everything away?" asked Michael. "You know what happened last time."

"Those were different circumstances," said Gina. "I doubt anyone is going to want to look at any of this for quite some time."

"If you say so."

Laura was in the kitchen with Gwen and the two were putting together trays and checking on what was cooking. Henri was official taste tester, sampling a little of this and a little of that. When Laura cooked, he was a very happy man.

"Everything's ready," said Laura.

"They're here," said Michael coming into the kitchen. "It smells so good. Henri, do you think you can tear yourself away to join us?"

Henri lifted the lid again on a pot, took a small spoon and took a taste then put the spoon in the sink. Michael shook his head and smiled.

Everyone was talking and catching up. It had been a few weeks since everyone had gone back to their lives, except Petru's family and Helena. For them, there was nothing to go back to. Their jobs with Craustof were over and their homes were ransacked and destroyed.

Edgar immediately offered Petru a job in the lab. Edgar knew what he was capable of doing and the new project he had used to help Michael get the dignitaries rescued was something that could be perfected if he had a state of the art lab to work in. Petru wasted no time in accepting the job and Edgar's wife, Gabrielle, helped Sorina look for a place to live.

Working next to Helena for all that time showed the partners what an asset she would be at Global. A position was created, one that would showcase her skills and give her a chance to grow. Andre had become one of her constant companions and she looked the happiest when she was with him.

Hal and Tom walked into the house. They didn't bother knocking or ringing the doorbell. They greeted everyone with just a short hi and continued on into the dining room.

"I told you it would be put away," said Tom. "I told you Gina would have worked and cleared it away."

"Why? Why would she do that?" asked Hal walking back into the living room. "Gina, why did you put everything away?"

She looked over at Michael.

"Did you put him up to this?"

"No," said Michael.

"Is there something in particular you need?" asked Gina. "I can find it for you rather quickly. I logged everything."

"He needs it all," said Tom. "Really, we need it all."

"I want to make a documentary about everything," said Hal. "I already approached people about the funding and I have it. I think it could be good. I think it could be damn good. I think it could be so damn good it could be the first documentary nominated for best picture at the Academy Awards."

"We can get it out," said Henri, "but not until after we eat."

Made in the USA
Middletown, DE
03 April 2016